F◓REIGN AFFAIRS

Sun-drenched days...

Balmy nights...

The world's most eligible men!

Dreaming of a foreign affair? Then, look no further! We've brought together the best and sexiest men the world has to offer, the most exciting, exotic locations and the most powerful, passionate stories.

This month, in *Pacific Passions*, we bring back two best-selling novels by popular Modern Romance™ authors Anne Mather and Robyn Donald. It's passion by the Pacific – but both these heroines find themselves out of their depth with these dangerously sexy men. And from now on, every month in **Foreign Affairs** you can be swept away to a new location – and indulge in a little passion in the sun!

If you like strong rugged men, you'll love
WESTERN WEDDINGS
by Day Leclaire & Susan Fox
Out next month!

ANNE MATHER

Anne Mather began writing when she was a child, progressing through torrid teenage romances to the kind of adult romances she likes to read. She's married, with two children, and she lives in the north of England. After writing, she enjoys reading, driving, and travelling to different places to find settings for new novels. She considers herself very lucky to do something she not only enjoys but also gets paid for.

Don't miss Anne Mather's brand new story *The Spaniard's Seduction* on sale March 2002 in Modern Romance™!

ROBYN DONALD

Robyn Donald has always lived in Northland in New Zealand, initially on her father's stud dairy farm at Warkworth, then in the Bay of Islands, an area of great natural beauty, where she lives today with her husband and an ebullient and mostly Labrador dog. She resigned her teaching position when she found she enjoyed writing romances more and has now written over fifty of them. She spends any time not writing in reading, gardening, travelling and writing letters to keep up with her two adult children and her friends.

Look out for *Wolfe's Temptress* by Robyn Donald, available in April 2002 in Modern Romance™!

pacific
passions

ANNE MATHER & ROBYN DONALD

TEMPTATION IN PARADISE...

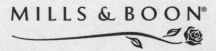

MILLS & BOON®

*All the characters in this book have no existence outside the imagination
of the author, and have no relation whatsoever to anyone bearing the
same name or names. They are not even distantly inspired by any
individual known or unknown to the author, and all the incidents are
pure invention.*

*Harlequin Mills & Boon Limited,
Eton House, 18-24 Paradise Road, Richmond, Surrey, TW9 1SR*

Pacific Passions © Harlequin Enterprises II B.V., 2002

Pacific Heat and *Surrender to Seduction*
were first published in Great Britain by
Harlequin Mills & Boon Limited in separate single volumes.

Pacific Heat © Anne Mather 1998
Surrender to Seduction © Robyn Donald 1998

ISBN 0 263 83184 1

126-0202

*Printed and bound in Spain
by Litografia Rosés S.A., Barcelona*

pacific passions

PACIFIC HEAT

SURRENDER TO SEDUCTION

PACIFIC HEAT

ANNE MATHER

CHAPTER ONE

'DIANE HARAN!'

Olivia was stunned. Never in her wildest dreams had she ever expected to be offered such an assignment. To be invited to write Diane Haran's extraordinary rags-to-riches story was amazing. Diane Haran: screen goddess; model; superstar—and the woman who five years ago had walked off with Olivia's husband.

'Yes, Diane Haran,' repeated Kay Goldsmith, rather impatiently. 'You have heard of her, I suppose? Well, of course you have. Everybody has. She's world-famous. What is amazing about this is that Diane Haran should have heard of *you*.'

Olivia took a deep breath and stared at her agent. 'What do you mean? Diane Haran's heard about me?'

'Well, it was her idea that you should be the first to be offered the opportunity to be her biographer. She'd read your book about Eileen Cusack, I believe, and she'd obviously been impressed with your approach.'

'Really?'

Olivia knew she sounded cynical, but she couldn't help it. The theory that Diane Haran might have come up with the idea of asking her to be her biographer based on Olivia's interpretation of the Irish poet's tragic existence was laughable. Eileen Cusack had been a heroine in the truest sense of the word, balancing the needs of her family against a crippling bone-wasting disease, and writing some of the most beautiful lyrical verse besides. She'd died just a few weeks after her biography was published, but Olivia knew she would never forget her bravery or her sweetness.

Diane Haran was neither brave nor sweet. She was selfish

5

and manipulative and greedy. She'd been introduced to
Richard Haig at a party his agency had given for the then
rising star they'd hoped to represent. And, even though
she'd known he was married—Olivia had been at the party,
too, for heaven's sake—she hadn't hesitated about seducing
him away from his wife.

'Liv?'

Kay's curious enquiry brought Olivia's attention back to
the present and she realised she had been staring into space
for quite some time. But the idea that Diane Haran should
have suggested that she might want to play any part in her
biography was ludicrous, and it was time she explained that
to Kay.

'I can't do it,' she said, and when Kay's dark eyes widened in disbelief she pushed back her chair and got up from
the desk, crossing the room to stare out of the window.
Below Kay's office window, high in a tower block near the
embankment, the city traffic created a constant hum of
sound. But it was reassuring to know that life was going
on regardless. For a moment, she'd felt an awful sense of
time suspended.

'What do you mean, you can't do it?' Kay was on her
feet now, coming round the desk to join her at the window,
her plump, diminutive form accentuating Olivia's height
and the extreme slenderness of her figure. 'Have you any
idea what's on offer here? A fantastic fee, a share in the
royalties, and the chance to spend a few months in the sun.'

Olivia looked down at her companion. 'A few months in
the sun?' she echoed, compelled into an involuntary reply.

'That's right.' Kay explained. 'She wants you to go out
to California and spend some time with her. She's almost
through making her current movie and her agent says she'll
have some free time before the next one is due to start
shooting in September.'

Olivia's mouth was dry. 'Her agent?' she said faintly.

'Yes. Phoebe Isaacs, of the Isaacs and Stone agency. I
don't suppose you've heard of them, but they're pretty big

in the film business. Phoebe Isaacs is quite a tough cookie, as they say on the other side of the water.'

Olivia blinked. 'You're saying that this Phoebe Isaacs was the person who contacted you?'

'That's right.' Kay sensed the younger woman was weakening and attempted to press her case. 'But make no mistake, it was Diane Haran herself who chose this agency, because she knew you were one of my clients.'

Olivia blew out a breath. 'I still can't do it,' she said, even though her mind was buzzing with what Kay had just said. As far as she'd known, Richard was Diane's agent. That was the carrot she'd dangled in front of him all those years ago. As if her own undisputed beauty hadn't been enough.

'Why not?'

Kay was irritated, and Olivia couldn't really blame her. After all, the deal she was being offered was considerably more generous than anything she'd been offered thus far in her career. But then, her association with Kay was only three years old. Kay didn't know why she and her ex-husband had separated. It wasn't something she talked about these days, and when Richard had left her she'd still been working for the women's magazine she'd joined when she first left college.

'I just can't,' she insisted now, and, feeling slightly intimidated by Kay's frustration, she went back to the desk. 'You don't understand,' she added, pressing her hot palms down onto the cool wood. 'I—I've met Diane Haran. Years ago. And I didn't like her.'

Kay groaned. 'You don't have to *like* her!' she exclaimed, returning to her own side of the desk. 'And it's obvious she doesn't remember you. Or if she does—and if she knew how you felt—she doesn't hold any grudges. She wants you to write the story of how she became successful against all the odds. She's not looking for a lifelong commitment. Just a few short weeks of your time.'

Olivia licked her lips. The idea of flying out to

California, of spending several weeks, or even months, with
Diane Haran, was anathema to her. It wasn't just that she
disliked the woman. She hated her; she despised her. She
blamed her totally for the break-up of her marriage. She
and Richard had been happy together. Everyone had said
they were the ideal couple. They'd known one another
since their college days, and when Richard asked her to
marry him she'd been in seventh heaven.

She hadn't been able to believe her luck, she remembered
now, recalling how envious all her friends had been.
Richard Haig had been the most attractive boy she'd ever
seen, and one of the few people in her year who was actually taller than she was. At five feet ten, she'd always
regarded her height as a drawback, but Richard had assured
her he loved willowy women. The fact that she wasn't
beautiful or outstandingly clever hadn't seemed to bother
him either. For some reason, he had fallen in love with her,
and she'd had no doubt that they'd live happily ever after...

'I can't do it,' she said again, aware that Kay was watching her closely. 'Kay, I'm flattered, but I'm sorry. This
assignment just isn't for me.'

'You still haven't given me a decent reason why not,'
retorted Kay, bumping down in her chair. 'Dammit, Liv,
this is a chance of a lifetime. I can't let you throw it away.'

Olivia hesitated, and then sank down in her chair again.
'All right,' she said. 'I suppose I do owe you an explanation. I can't work for Diane Haran because I—*know*—the
man she's married to—'

'Richard Haig?' Her ex-husband's name tripped carelessly off Kay's tongue, and Olivia made a concerted attempt not to show her surprise. 'Hey, you don't have to
worry about that. From what I hear their marriage is on the
rocks.'

Olivia swallowed. 'On the rocks?'

'So I hear.' Kay nodded. 'I gather they've been having
problems for some time. He drinks, you know. Or at least

that's the story. My guess is that some other man must have caught her eye.'

Olivia stared at her. 'I can't believe it.'

'Why not?' Kay was dismissive. 'You have to admit that this marriage has lasted longer than the other two she's had. Who was the first? Oh, yes, Gordon Rogers. She only lived with him for a couple of months.'

'I—I thought she'd only been married once—once before,' murmured Olivia faintly, but the woman opposite shook her head.

'No. Don't you remember that actor: Christian de Hanna? When she found out he was a needle-pusher, she threw him out.'

Olivia felt dazed. 'So—who is she seeing now?' she asked, trying to sound as if she was only casually interested, and Kay lay back in her chair with a rueful sigh.

'Search me,' she said. 'That's the million-dollar question. But you can be sure that he's got something your friend doesn't have.'

'My friend?'

For a moment, Olivia was confused, and Kay gave her a searching look.

'Richard Haig,' she said irritably. 'Our benefactor's current husband. If you want him, you can have him. Take my word for it.'

Olivia's lips parted. Was she so transparent? she wondered in dismay. With the little information she'd given Kay, had she exposed her feelings so clearly? 'I don't want him,' she declared hastily, but the words didn't sound convincing to her. The truth was, she did want him. She always had.

'Well, that's up to you,' said Kay briskly, evidently deciding she'd said enough. 'But I would seriously advise you not to turn this offer down. I don't think you realise the impact it could have, not just on the public but on your career. And goodness knows, you'd be in a position to pick up any number of other commissions at the same time.'

Olivia looked down at her hands, clasped together in her lap. She couldn't do this, she told herself fiercely, however attractive Kay was making it sound. She couldn't work with Diane Haran, not knowing what she'd done to Richard. And if Richard needed her he knew where to find her. It wasn't up to her to go looking for him.

But what if he was humiliated by what had happened? a small voice chided in her ear. What if he regretted the break-up of their marriage now, but was too ashamed of his own actions to approach her again? Richard had his pride, and their divorce had been rather acrimonious. He'd done his best to make her a scapegoat, and Olivia had been left feeling battered and bruised.

Which was another reason why she should refuse this commission, the same small voice reminded her sharply. Did she really want to lay herself open to that kind of emotional abuse again? And she wouldn't be working for Richard; she'd be working for Diane Haran. There was no guarantee that she'd even see him, if what Kay was saying was true. No matter how tempting it might be to imagine a reconciliation between them, she was thinking with her heart, not her head.

Realising Kay was waiting for her to say something, she asked the question that had first sprung into her mind. 'Why California?' she enquired. 'Doesn't she live in England any more?'

'I understand she has homes in both England and the United States,' said Kay immediately. 'Oh, and a villa in the South of France, as well. But as most of her films are made in America I suppose she finds it most convenient to live there.'

Olivia's mind boggled. She found it hard to conceive what it must be like to be so rich. Diane had probably found it hard, too, she acknowledged. At least, to begin with. A council flat in the East End of London was where she'd lived for the first fifteen years of her life.

'You'd have to do some research here,' Kay commented,

almost as if Olivia had agreed to her request. 'Her family have all moved away from Bermondsey, of course, thanks to Diane's generosity. But I expect there'll still be people there who remember her as a child. Schoolfriends, neighbours, and so on.'

Olivia regarded the other woman wryly. 'I do know how to go about researching a subject's background,' she remarked, wishing Kay would just let it go. But what she wished most of all was that Diane had never asked for her; had never ignited the spark of unwilling excitement that the thought of seeing Richard again could bring.

Kay had straightened in her chair now, and was watching her closely, and Olivia felt the heat from her thoughts invading the pale hollows of her throat. 'Does this mean you're thinking of accepting the commission?' Kay asked, leaning across her desk, and Olivia drew back from that avid stare.

'I—I have no desire to work with Diane Haran,' she insisted tensely, but they both knew that she hadn't actually said no.

Olivia got back to her flat in the late afternoon. Situated on the top floor of an old Victorian town house, the flat was her home and her refuge, the place where she'd sought sanctuary when Richard had got his divorce. Until the divorce, they'd been living in a pretty semi-detached house in Chiswick, but even without its unhappy memories Olivia couldn't afford to keep it on. Instead, she'd moved into this rather gloomy apartment in Kensington and over the years she'd transformed its narrow rooms and draughty hallways into a place of light and beauty.

Henry came to meet her as she opened the door. Rubbing himself against her legs, he showed her how much he had missed her, but Olivia wasn't deceived. He was hungry, and he was reminding her it was his dinner time, and for the first time since she'd left Kay's office Olivia's generous lips curved in a smile.

'It's all right. I haven't forgotten you,' she said, juggling the two bags she'd brought from the supermarket and shouldering the door closed behind her. 'How does salmon and shrimp appeal to you?' Henry purred his approval as Olivia started down the hall. 'I should have known,' she added ruefully. 'It's only cupboard love.'

The kitchen smelled reassuringly of the plants and herbs she cultivated so assiduously. Trailing fronds of greenery brushed her face as she deposited the bags on the counter. There were daffodils on the window-ledge, providing a vivid splash of colour, and although the skies were overcast outside the kitchen was bright and cosily immune from the cold March wind.

Once Henry had been dealt with, Olivia filled the kettle and set it to boil. She would eat later, but for now she thought she deserved a hot, sweet cup of tea. As she put the food she'd bought away, she tried not to think of Diane Haran and her commission. This was her home; she didn't want to sully it with thoughts of her ex-husband's lover. She'd felt safe here, secure, far from the misery that loving Richard had brought.

With the tea made, she had no excuse for lingering in the kitchen, and, taking a deep breath, she pushed open the door to the office she'd created for herself. With the walls lined with books—both for pleasure and for reference—and a modern computer and printer, it was comfortingly familiar, her desk still as cluttered with papers as it had been when she went out.

Taking a sip of her tea, she perched on the old leather diplomat chair she'd bought at a warehouse sale three years ago, and regarded the clutter resignedly. She'd been planning on spending some time catching up with her correspondence, but there were still notes and discarded pages of manuscript from her last book lying around. That was why she'd been to see Kay that afternoon: to hear her judgement on her latest profile of a woman sailor. Suzanne Howard had sailed single-handedly around the world at the age of seventy-three.

The fact that Kay had been delighted by the manuscript had been eclipsed by the conversation they'd had about Diane Haran. But Olivia was relieved to know that what she was producing was still on track. When her first book—a biography of Catherine Parr, the only one of his six wives to have survived Henry the Eighth—had been successful, she'd been afraid it was only a one-off, that her next book would bomb as many second books did. But the life of Eileen Cusack had proved a best-seller, and that had encouraged her to approach the Howard family last year.

She wondered if Richard knew what she was doing. When he'd walked out, she'd been working for *Milady* magazine, with no prospect of improving her career. Perhaps if he hadn't walked out she wouldn't have found the nerve to tackle a book, she thought consideringly. It was true that he'd always made fun of the gossipy pieces she'd been paid to produce for the magazine.

Which brought her back to the subject she'd been trying to avoid ever since she'd left Kay's office. Was she actually going to write Diane Haran's story—or at least as much of it as the public would be permitted to know?

The shrilling of the telephone was a welcome escape from her thoughts, and, pushing back a strand of dark, toffee-coloured hair, she reached for the receiver. It crossed her mind, as she brought it to her ear, that it could be Kay, but it was too late now. Besides, she was fairly sure that Kay was satisfied that she'd promised to think about the commission. She was unlikely to try and push her any further. Not today, anyway.

'Yes?'

'Liv. At last!' It was her father. 'I've been trying to reach you all afternoon.' He paused, and when she didn't instantly jump in with an explanation he continued, 'Are you all right? Not having a problem with the new book, are you?'

'No.' Olivia blew out a breath. 'No, Kay's very happy with it, as it happens.' She forced herself to sound positive.

Her father and stepmother had supported her all through her divorce from Richard, and they'd be most disturbed to hear what she was thinking of doing. 'I—er—I was just at the supermarket. I've just got in.'

'Ah.' Matthew Pyatt sounded relieved. 'Well, your mother and I were wondering if you'd like to come for supper.' He always referred to her stepmother as her mother. After all, she had acted as such since Olivia was barely five years old. 'We've got something we want to discuss with you, and as we haven't seen you for a couple of weeks we thought it would kill two birds with one stone. What do you think?'

'Oh, Dad—' Olivia wasn't enthusiastic. After the afternoon she'd had, she'd been looking forward to doing nothing more energetic than putting a frozen pizza in the microwave and curling up with a bottle of wine. Besides, she needed time to think before Kay came back to her. And she wasn't sure she could hide her anxieties from them. 'Could I take a rain check?'

'There is something wrong.' Her father had always been incredibly perceptive, which was one of the reasons why she'd hoped to put him off. 'What is it? What's happened? You might as well tell me.'

Olivia sighed. 'Nothing's happened,' she said, not very convincingly, she had to admit. 'I'm—tired, that's all. It's been a stressful few weeks, finishing the book and—'

'Why are you stressed?' Her father broke in before she could warm to her theme. 'You're not being harassed by some man, are you? You read about these things in the papers—young women who live alone being terrorised in their homes. I've never been entirely happy with the security at the flat. Anyone can get in downstairs.'

'No, they can't.' Olivia was impatient. 'You know visitors have to use the intercom to get in.'

'But when that door opens to admit a legitimate visitor anyone can push in with them,' retorted her father. 'I know.

When I used to install heating systems, you'd be surprised at how many robberies there were.'

Olivia had to smile. 'I'm sure you don't mean that the way it sounded.'

'No, I don't.' Her father snorted. 'And you're not going to avoid an answer by being smug.'

'Oh, all right.' Olivia gave in. 'I'll come for supper.' She suppressed her misgivings. 'Just give me time to take a shower and change. Is eight o'clock all right?'

The Pyatts lived in Chiswick, just a stone's throw from the station. It gave Olivia quite a pang getting off the train at Grove Park station. For the four years that she and Richard had been married, she'd got off there every evening on her way home from work. But at least her father's house lay in the opposite direction to the one she used to take. The Pyatts' house was detached, with double gates and a block-paved drive leading to the front door.

Her stepmother opened the door to her.

'Liv, my dear.' Alice Pyatt reached up to bestow a warm kiss on her stepdaughter's cheek. 'Your father's just gone down to the cellar to get some wine. He'll be annoyed he wasn't here to greet you himself. He's been watching for you for the past half-hour.'

'Am I late?' Olivia let her stepmother help her off with her coat before stepping into the living room. There was a fire glowing in the hearth, and she moved towards it gratefully. 'Mmm, this is cosy. I miss an open fire at the flat.'

Alice draped Olivia's overcoat over the banister and followed her stepdaughter into the room. 'You're not late,' she assured her. 'It's your father who's anxious. Now, what can I get you to drink? Sherry, perhaps, or a G and T?'

'Will I need one?' Olivia sank down into the armchair nearest the fire. 'You're looking well. Is that a new shade of lipstick you're wearing?'

'I am, and it is, but you're not going to get out of your father's questions that way,' responded Alice, with a smile.

'And I have to say you do look rather peaky. Something is wrong, isn't it? Your father's seldom mistaken.'

Olivia sighed. 'Nothing's wrong exactly,' she said, shaking her head at her stepmother's offer of the sherry she was pouring herself. 'I'll wait for the wine,' she added as Alice came to sit opposite her. And then, 'I don't look peaky, do I? I'm just feeling a bit—nervy, that's all.'

Alice shrugged and took a sip of her sherry, and, looking at the other woman, Olivia had to admit that she didn't look her age. As long as she could remember, Alice's hair had always been that particular shade of ash blonde, and although she knew it must be artificial now it still looked as soft and feminine as it had ever done.

'I'd say your father had some justification for his concern,' she declared now, crossing one silk-clad leg over the other.

Alice had good legs, too, and she'd never been afraid to display them to advantage. At fifty-five, she was ten years younger than her husband and looked at least twenty, and Olivia had always envied her plump, curvaceous figure.

'I've—I've been offered a new commission,' she said, deciding it might be easier to discuss it with her stepmother first. 'I'm just not sure whether I want to take it. It will mean living in the United States for a couple of months.'

'The United States!'

Alice sounded impressed, but before she could say anything more Matthew Pyatt strode into the room. 'The United States,' he echoed, bending to kiss his daughter. 'What about the United States? You're not going to live in New York, are you?'

'Of course not.' Olivia tried to breathe evenly, waiting until her father had lodged himself on the arm of his wife's chair before going on. 'It's just a—a commission I've been offered. In Los Angeles. I haven't decided whether I'm going to take it yet.'

'And that's what's on your mind, is it?' Matthew Pyatt stretched out his long legs towards the fire. His eyes narrowed. 'I must say, I'm not enthusiastic about you living out there either. A young woman, alone, in a volatile place like that.'

'I'm not a child, Dad.' Olivia wished she'd accepted a glass of sherry now. It would have given her something to do with her hands. As it was she clasped them between her legging-clad knees and pressed her legs together. 'It's not living in Los Angeles that's the problem.'

'Ah.' Her father nodded. 'You're concerned about us, is that it? Well—' he put an arm about his wife's shoulders '—that's what we wanted to talk to you about, actually. You know Alice has a sister living in New Zealand? As it happens, she's invited us to go out there for a couple of months, too. We were worried about leaving you alone, but if you're going to be away...'

Olivia swallowed. 'I see.'

'You don't mind, do you, Liv?' Alice leaned towards her anxiously, and Olivia knew she had to reassure them that that wasn't the case. But the truth was, she was a little apprehensive. It was as if all the circumstances were conspiring against her.

'I— Of course not,' she protested now, seeing the relief in her stepmother's face as she leaned back in her chair.

'That's good.' Alice smiled. 'It's nearly ten years since I saw Barbara.' She glanced up at her husband. 'That's one advantage of being retired. Matt won't be worrying about the business while we're gone.'

'So whose biography are you going to write now?' asked her father as his wife left the room to check on the supper, and Olivia knew she couldn't prevaricate any longer.

'Diane Haran's.' Her voice was flat. 'But I haven't decided yet whether I'm going to do it,' she added hastily as her father's face grew red. 'Don't look like that, Dad. It's a wonderful opportunity. And—and she and Richard are splitting up.'

'You're not serious!'

Matthew was on his feet now, and Olivia knew she had

been right to be apprehensive of seeking his advice. As far as her father was concerned, Richard Haig deserved a beating for the way he'd treated his daughter, and it was only because Olivia had pleaded with him not to get involved that they hadn't come to blows.

'Why not?' she asked, playing devil's advocate. 'According to Kay, I'll never be offered such a lucrative deal again.'

'You know why not,' grated her father. 'And that's why you're looking so worried, isn't it? I wondered why we hadn't seen you. I never suspected it was because of anything like this.'

'And it wasn't.' Olivia was indignant. 'Honestly, Dad, I just found out today. I've been doing the revisions on the other book. The one about Suzanne Howard. That's why I haven't seen you. Nothing else.'

Matthew Pyatt drew a steadying breath. 'But even so…'

'As I say, I haven't decided what I'm going to do yet,' said Olivia evenly, looping a strand of toffee-coloured hair behind her ear. Her hair was long, and she invariably wore it in a chignon when she was working, but this evening she'd created a rather precarious knot on top of her head.

Her father returned to the chair her stepmother had been occupying. 'But you are thinking of accepting it,' he pointed out. 'That's why you've mentioned it to me.'

'I've told you. I'm thinking about it.' Olivia half resented his interference. 'I'll let you know what I decide. It'll be before you leave for New Zealand, I expect.'

Her father scowled. 'I'm not sure I want to go to New Zealand now, knowing you're going to be seeing that swine again.' He sighed. 'Liv, there must be something else you can do. Can't you see, this woman's just using you to provide a convenient shoulder when she throws him out?'

That thought had occurred to Olivia, too, but she had no intention of admitting that to him. 'Let's leave it for now,' she begged. 'I'll let you know what I'm going to do.'

'And what about Henry?' Alice asked mischievously, after her husband had related Olivia's news to her, and Olivia thought how typical it was of her stepmother to try and lighten her husband's mood.

'Oh, my next-door neighbour will look after him,' said Olivia cheerfully. 'If I go, of course,' she added, with a nervous smile. 'But you're right, I can't forget the second most important man in my life.'

'And who's the first?' demanded her father grumpily.

'Why—you are, Daddy,' she assured him, meeting her stepmother's conspiratorial gaze.

CHAPTER TWO

DESPITE her decision, Olivia went through all the arguments why she shouldn't have accepted the commission on the flight from London to Los Angeles. At the very least, she knew her actions were open to all kinds of interpretation, and she preferred not to examine her motives too closely for fear of what she might find.

Her father wasn't pleased with her. And if he hadn't been going away himself she knew he'd have done everything in his power to persuade her not to do it. But, happily, Alice had been there to mediate for her, and they'd departed for Auckland on schedule just two weeks before her own flight was arranged.

And, on a purely objective level, she was quite excited at the prospect of spending several weeks in California. Although she'd been to New York before, she'd never travelled to the West Coast, and it was still sufficiently chilly in England to make the idea of a more temperate climate infinitely appealing.

The knowledge that she was probably going to see Richard again gave her mixed feelings. She couldn't deny that she was apprehensive, but she was also curious. She wanted to know what was happening in his life; whether the rumours about him and Diane were true. But most of all she wanted to know if she still cared about him. Whether her reasons for accepting this commission were as practical as she'd insisted.

She'd spent the month since she'd told Kay she would accept the commission researching Diane' s background in the East End of London, and she'd been surprised to learn how well thought of Diane still was amongst the people she'd grown up with. Contrary to the image Olivia had gained of a spoilt and selfish woman, the picture neighbours and classmates painted was of a generous, warm-hearted individual, who was not averse to helping out her friends in any way she could. Olivia was given dozens of anecdotes of the ways Diane had come through, from lending money when it was needed to offering her support when it was not.

According to the people Olivia had talked to, success had definitely not gone to Diane's head. She'd always been a little headstrong, they admitted, but she'd never forgotten her friends or her roots.

And her story was fascinating, Olivia had to admit. Fascinating, amazing, harrowing, at times, but always interesting. The eldest of a family of seven children—many of them with different fathers—her childhood had been blighted by poverty and abuse. Her mother, who had been described as both hard-working and ignorant, had had little time for any of her children, and Diane, as the eldest, had been expected to help care for her younger siblings.

From the beginning, Diane's outstanding physical beauty had caused problems and she'd become sexually aware at a very young age. But, ironically enough, it was because of an older man's attraction to the fifteen-year-old Diane that she'd become famous. A wealthy man, he'd taken her to dine at a swish London restaurant and she'd caught the eye of a fashion photographer who was looking for a face for the 'eighties'.

The rest was history, as they say, but Olivia guessed there was more to it than that. The years between could not have been easy, and although she was loath to admit it Olivia couldn't help seeing her subject in a different light.

Which was just as well for the job she had to do, she acknowledged. This biography had to be objective, and she was glad that the research she'd already done had enabled her to amend her opinion. Why Diane should have wanted her to write her story was something she had yet to find out. Perhaps she really had enjoyed Eileen Cusack's biography, Olivia reflected ruefully. After the things she'd learned, anything was possible.

But not probable, the small voice inside her argued as the big jet banked to make its approach to LAX. The sprawling mass that was Los Angeles was spread out below her, and there was no turning back. She was here; she was committed; and she had to stop worrying about Richard and concentrate on the job.

The oval-shaped airport buildings gleamed in the afternoon sunlight as the plane taxied along the runway. It was incredible to think that they'd left London at lunchtime and yet it was still only a quarter to four here. The miracle of international time zones, she thought as the aircraft approached its landing bay. She'd worry about the jet lag later.

The passengers were transferred from the plane to an air-conditioned walkway that conducted them to Passport Control. Because the expenses she was being allowed had enabled her to sit in the Club World section of the British Airways jet, Olivia found herself among the first to reach the Arrivals Hall, and like everyone else she spent the time waiting for her luggage by people-spotting.

She recognised a couple of famous faces who had apparently been travelling in the first-class compartment of the plane, and was surprised at the lack of interest shown towards them. It wasn't until she noticed the bodyguards, tucked discreetly behind a pillar, that she understood her mistake. But still, it was something to tell her parents when she got home.

She had been checking that her luggage tags were still safely attached to her boarding pass when she looked up to find a man watching her. The fact that his clothes looked expensive and he was wearing a Rolex watch should have reassured her, but it didn't. It just reminded her of how vulnerable she was as a stranger here.

Diane's secretary had faxed her that she would meet her at the airport, and she hoped she kept her word. Still, she could always take a taxi, she assured herself impatiently. She knew Diane's address and she wasn't a child.

Indeed, she thought ruefully, her height would be a deterrent for most men. And although she was slim she knew she was fairly strong. She wasn't a fitness freak, but she did enjoy swimming and cycling, and she knew from her experiences in New York that in the normal way she had nothing to be afraid of.

Unless her imaginary attacker looked like the man who had been watching her, she conceded, relieved to see that he had apparently lost interest. He was staring towards the carousel that would eventually spill out their luggage, and she found herself observing him with rather more interest than sense.

He was certainly big, she mused, and dark, with a lean, sinewy grace that was nothing like the muscle-bound heroes Hollywood seemed to spawn with such regularity. And although he was good to look at his appeal lay in the roughness of his features rather than their uniformity. Deep-set eyes beneath dark brows, and narrow cheekbones and a thin-lipped mouth; if there were lines on his face, they were lines of experience, and she realised he was probably ten years older than the twenty-five she'd originally judged him to be.

She wondered who he was. Not a film star, she decided, though there was another man hovering close by who could be a minder. If he needed one, she speculated doubtfully, realising she was being far too nosy. Whoever he was, he wasn't interested in her, and she was unlikely to see him again.

The carousel had begun to turn and suitcases appeared like magic from the chute above it. A black holdall appeared, and the man standing beside the man she had been watching went to rescue it. She noticed he also had a suit carrier looped across his shoulder, and after he'd plucked the holdall from the conveyor he and his companion turned towards the exit.

First class, Olivia informed herself silently, realising the two men must have travelled on the same flight from London. She grimaced. So what? It was nothing to do with her. It was time she started paying attention to her own luggage. She thought she could see one of her suitcases just starting along the metal belt.

'Would you happen to be Ms Pyatt?'

The unfamiliar voice was amazingly sexy. It conjured up images of hot sultry nights and bare brown limbs tangled in satin sheets. Olivia decided she was in danger of acting out her own fantasies, and, blaming the man who had fired her imagination, she turned to find that he hadn't left after all but was standing right behind her.

'I—' Swallowing to ease the dryness of her throat, she started over. 'Yes,' she said, a little reluctantly. 'I'm Olivia Pyatt.' She'd reverted to her own surname when she and Richard were divorced. Then, because it was the only thing she could think of, she asked, 'Did Miss Haran ask you to meet me?'

The man's lean mouth twitched. 'Not exactly,' he said, humour tugging at the corners of his lips. 'But Diane told me you were travelling on this flight.'

So he did know Diane. Olivia breathed a little more easily, although common sense told her it was the only explanation. 'Did you travel from London, too?' she asked, as if she didn't already know that he had. He was probably a Californian, which would explain his accent and his tan.

'Yeah.' He glanced towards his companion, who was waiting patiently for him to finish. 'B.J. and I make the trip fairly regularly.' He grimaced. 'It's not to be recommended.'

'Because of the jet lag?' guessed Olivia, aware that her suitcase was about to start going round again. 'Excuse me, I must get my luggage. I don't want to have to carry it any further than I have to.'

'I'll get it.'

Leaning past her, the man lifted the heavy bag off the carousel and set it down beside her. In jeans and a light cotton jacket, he moved much easier than she did in her corduroy suit. The suit had seemed reasonably lightweight, too, when she'd left London, but she was already sweating.

But that could be because of the present situation, she conceded. She wasn't used to being accosted by strange men.

'Is this all?' he asked, and for a moment she didn't know what he was talking about. 'Your luggage,' he prompted, and, glancing up at him, she noticed he had tawny eyes. Like a cat, she thought, realising she was behaving stupidly. For God's sake, he was being polite. Nothing else.

'Um—no, there's one more,' she said hurriedly, scanning the conveyor. 'It's always the way, isn't it? One comes, and then you've got to wait for ever for the other.' She glanced towards his companion, who was still standing with the holdall in his hand and the suit carrier draped over his shoulder. 'Please—don't let me keep you. I'm sure your friend must be getting impatient.'

'B.J.?' He, too, glanced the other man's way, and then turned back to give Olivia a lazy smile. 'No sweat,' he said as Olivia's toes curled inside her Doc Martens. 'It's cooler in here than outside.'

'Oh, but—' Olivia wanted to ask why he was waiting with her, but she couldn't. Loosening the tight cuffs of her jacket, she peeled them back over her wrists. 'Um—do you think Miss Haran's secretary will be waiting outside? She said she'd come to meet me herself.'

'Bonnie?'

He had the name right, and Olivia nodded. 'A Miss Lovelace,' she agreed, not used to using the woman's given name.

'I guess she'll be waiting in the Arrivals Hall,' he responded carelessly. 'I'll point her out to you when we go through.'

Olivia caught her lower lip between her teeth. 'I—gather you're a friend of Miss Haran's,' she said awkwardly, and he made a husky sound of disbelief.

'Hell, yes,' he said. 'I'm sorry; I didn't introduce myself, did I? I'm Joe Castellano. I—guess you could say I have an investment in Diane's career.'

He held out his hand, and Olivia had no choice but to shake it, hoping he wouldn't be too put off by her sweaty

palm. 'How do you do, Mr Castellano?' she said, wondering if he was a frequent visitor to Diane's Beverly Hills
mansion. It would be rather nice, she thought, if he was.

She barely had time to extract her hand before she saw
her other suitcase approaching. There were quite a lot of
people gathered round the carousel now, and she saw several of the women weighing up the man at her side. And
why not? she thought ruefully. He was attractive. Was he
married? she wondered, rather foolishly. He was wearing a
signet ring on his right hand but that was all.

When her suitcase was within reach, she lunged for it,
staggering as the unexpected weight of the bag pulled at
her arm. 'Let me,' he said shortly, and she felt his impatience. He set the suitcase down and summoned a porter
with a trolley. 'I guess we can get moving now?'

'Right.'

She had little choice but to follow the porter, and to her
relief they passed through the Customs channel without incident. It crossed her mind as they were walking past the
officials that he could be a drug smuggler using her as
cover. But she decided she was allowing her imagination
to get the better of her again. Just because he had an Italian
surname, that did not mean he was connected to the 'mob'.

Beyond the baggage collection area, a barrier separated
arriving passengers from those waiting to meet them, and
Olivia immediately saw her name on a board being held up
by a woman at the end of a line of similar boards.

'That must be Miss Lovelace,' she said to her companion, nodding towards the rather harassed-looking woman
with tinted blonde hair and immaculate make-up who was
scanning the new arrivals. Olivia guessed the woman was
in her forties but her skirt was shorter than anything she'd
have worn herself.

He nodded. 'Yeah, that's Bonnie. But don't call her Miss
Lovelace. She prefers the anonymous *Ms*.' He grinned at
Olivia, and once again she was struck by his magnetism.
'You're going to be dealing with some tender egos here.
Keep that in mind.'

The woman had seen them now but from her expression Olivia guessed she hadn't made any connection between them. Or perhaps she had and it was the wrong one, she reflected doubtfully. It was flattering to think Miss Lovelace—*Ms* Lovelace, she corrected herself firmly—had assumed she was travelling with him. But this was the moment when she had to come down to earth.

'Hey, Joe.' Bonnie Lovelace greeted him like a long-lost friend. Then her eyes moved suspiciously to Olivia. 'Diane said you'd be on this flight. She's missed you. Did you have a good trip?'

'The usual,' drawled Joe as the porter halted uncertainly beside them. He slipped a note into the man's hand and indicated Olivia. 'These ladies will show you where their transport is parked.'

Bonnie Lovelace's jaw dropped as she turned back to Olivia. 'You're Ms Pyatt?' she exclaimed, and Joe touched her shoulder with a mocking hand.

'Who else?' he asked. 'I just thought I'd do my good deed for the day and deliver her into your hands, Bonnie.' He arched a brow at Olivia. 'Take care. I'm sure I'll see you around.'

Olivia didn't know who was the most deflated as he strolled off with the man he'd called B.J. but she suspected it had to be her, judging by the way she felt. She swallowed her chagrin. So—he was a friend of Diane's. She'd been told as much so why did she feel so disappointed now?

'Ms Pyatt.' Bonnie seemed to come to her senses, too, and, holding out her hand, she took Olivia's in a limp grip. 'You must forgive me,' she said. 'I didn't realise it was you with Joe—er—with Mr Castellano.' She gestured to the porter to follow them and as they moved along she added, 'Did you travel out together? How did he know who you were?'

'He—helped me with my luggage so I suppose he read the labels,' said Olivia after a moment, curiously loath to discuss the details of how they'd met. It was nothing to do with this woman after all. She was just curious. Probably wondering why he'd even bothered to speak to her, she thought glumly, changing her tote bag from one shoulder to the other.

'Mmm.' Bonnie gave her another assessing look, and then excused herself to head first through the glass doors that gave onto the concourse outside. 'I left Manuel in the car,' she added, glancing about her as the porter halted beside them. 'Oh, there he is.' She waved her arm at a man seated behind the wheel of a huge Mercedes. 'It's so difficult to find a parking space. Do you have this problem back home?'

'Sometimes,' answered Olivia absently, her attention caught by the sleek black saloon that was just moving past them. Joe Castellano was at the wheel, and he raised one hand in a casual salute. 'Um—' She gathered her wits. 'I don't own a car, actually. It's not worth it in London, and if I want to go further I have an old Harley-Davidson in the garage.'

Bonnie stopped in the act of lifting the boot lid of the Mercedes to stare at her. 'You ride a motorcycle?' she exclaimed in horror. And then said, 'Well, I guess you are tall enough at that.'

'Yeah, right.' Olivia weathered the back-handed compliment with her usual forbearance, and as Manuel slid out from behind the wheel to open the rear door for her she slipped inside.

Soft leather, air-conditioning and the fragrance of expensive perfume were some consolation. Unbelievable, she thought, stretching her long legs luxuriously. Wait until she could tell her stepmother about this! Unlike her father, Alice had been able to see the advantages of what she was being offered, and there was no doubt that it was going to be an experience she wouldn't forget.

Which reminded her that she hadn't thought of her ex-husband for the past half hour. From the moment Joe Castellano had spoken to her, she'd completely forgotten that she'd soon be seeing Richard again. Oh, God, she thought as the realisation that she was actually here in

California penetrated the haze of anticipation she was feeling. She dreaded to think what his reaction was going to be.

Bonnie got in beside her at that moment, which prevented her from continuing along that stony track. And besides, she chided herself, she shouldn't care what Richard might think. It was Diane who had invited her. If he had any complaints he should take them up with her.

She expelled a deep breath and turned to look out of the window. She realised that for the first time since she'd been offered this commission she was actually feeling optimistic about the result. It was foolish, probably—*definitely*—but somehow meeting Joe Castellano had given a boost to her confidence. Richard wasn't the only man in the world. She'd been nursing her broken heart for far too long.

'There we are.' Bonnie seated herself beside her and cast the younger woman a relieved look. 'This place gets more and more like a bull ring. I swear to God I'll have a heart attack if I have to fight my way out of here one more time!'

'I'm sorry.' Olivia felt responsible. She watched Manuel get back behind the wheel and start the engine. 'Anyway, thank you for coming to meet me. I could have got a taxi, I suppose—'

'Diane wouldn't hear of it.' Bonnie interrupted her to make her point. 'So—you had a good flight, yeah? What was the movie? These days, the only time I get to see a decent movie is on a plane.'

'Oh, well, I'm afraid I didn't—' began Olivia, only to find her companion wasn't listening.

'Yeah, movies,' Bonnie went on reminiscently. 'You'd think living in a town like this I'd be up on all the latest blockbusters. But, you know what? I spend all my time watching television instead.'

'Really?' said Olivia. 'I like television, too.' Or she had since the break-up of her marriage. Somehow, she couldn't see herself as part of the singles scene again.

''Cause working for Diane takes up most of my day, so when I get home I'm exhausted,' Bonnie continued, almost

as if Olivia hadn't spoken. She flapped an expansive hand.
'I guess you'll get used to it. I swear to God, I sometimes
think Diane's too generous for her own good.'

Olivia nodded now, but she didn't make the mistake of
trying to join in again, and she saw Manuel watching her
with an amused expression on his olive-skinned face. He
winked at her in the rear-view mirror, and she hid a smile.
Obviously he was used to Ms Lovelace. Perhaps Olivia
should call her *Miss*. That might get her attention.

But she decided against it. It was too nice a day to spoil
it, and the last thing she wanted to do was make an enemy
here. She had yet to discover what Diane's attitude towards
her was going to be, and until she did it was safer to play
it cool.

Beyond the car's tinted windows, the streets of the City
of the Angels shimmered in the late afternoon sun. Olivia
was looking forward to the prospect of taking a shower and
changing into something cooler. She hoped she'd have time
to freshen up before she met her hostess. She wondered
where she was going to stay. Kay had merely said that
Diane's secretary had made the arrangements. Perhaps
she'd be expected to stay at the house. Again, according to
Kay, Diane's mansion was quite a showplace.

Their route from the airport was not immediately inspiring, however. They passed what seemed like dozens of car
dealerships and abandoned warehouses, with strip malls il-
luminated with garish neon signs. She saw houses with
flaking porches, and incongruously customised vehicles in
hot metallic shades. It made it easier for her to grasp the
fact that she was actually here. She'd read somewhere that
Los Angeles had taken over from Ellis Island as the most
heavily burdened immigration point in the United States.

They drove north through sprawling suburbs, passing
signs for well-known districts like Marina del Rey and
Santa Monica. Olivia seemed to remember there was a pier
at Santa Monica, and she guessed there was surfing, too.
She couldn't quite see herself standing up on a surfboard,

she mused, deliberately avoiding thoughts of her destination and what it would mean.

Santa Monica Boulevard drove through the heart of the wealthiest district of Los Angeles. Olivia recognised the names of some of the hotels they passed, and Bonnie pointed out the 'HOLLYWOOD' sign that towered over what had once been the movie capital of the world. Nowadays, the glitz had become rather tarnished, she told Olivia laconically. But there was still a thriving film community, supplemented by the successful soap stars from TV.

Beverly Hills lay to the west of Hollywood, but to Olivia's surprise they turned off before the road wound up into the quiet streets far away from the commercial district. A couple of turns and they were in Hunter Plaza, with the Moorish arches of the Beverly Plaza Hotel fronting its famous façade.

Olivia was still admiring the square-cut towers that rose behind its entrance when Manuel drove into the courtyard and stopped before the double glass doors. A major domo stepped forward instantly and opened the door of the limousine, and Bonnie said, 'Welcome to America,' before stepping out and gesturing to Olivia to do the same. 'I'm sure you're going to be very comfortable here.'

'Here' turned out to be a penthouse suite situated on the top floor of the twelve-storey hotel. While Manuel handed her bags over to one of the hotel's bellboys, Bonnie checked her in, and Olivia realised that it was only a formality by the speed with which Bonnie was given her key. Well, not a key, exactly, she learned, when Bonnie demonstrated how to use the laminated card. Apparently, the code was changed every time a new resident took possession of the room, the card being pressed into the slot to open the door of the suite. The card was obviously easier and lighter to carry around, too.

The suite itself was the most luxurious apartment Olivia could have imagined. Airy, high-ceilinged, furnished in delicate shades of green and blue, with expansive views of

Beverly Hills and the hazy downtown areas, it was apparently where she was going to stay. 'You're sort of in back of the Beverly Wiltshire,' explained Bonnie, mentioning the name of one of the landmark hotels. 'That's Rodeo Drive down there.'

Olivia guessed she was supposed to be impressed, but in fact she was feeling a bit let down. However reluctant she might have been to meet Diane—and possibly Richard— she'd been ready for it. Now she felt deflated, aware that at some future time she was going to have to face it again.

'You like it, don't you?' Bonnie was looking a little worried now and Olivia guessed that however indifferent the woman might be to her feelings she was anxious that Diane should have nothing to complain about. 'See.' She opened another door. 'This is the bedroom. And that's the bath— you've got a spa bath and a Jacuzzi—through there.'

'Very nice.'

Olivia tried to sound enthusiastic, but it wasn't easy. However luxurious it might be, it wasn't home. She half wished she'd insisted on making her own arrangements for accommodation. A small hotel would have suited her better than this.

'The hotel can supply you with a PC,' added Bonnie briskly. 'Diane didn't know what you'd need so she's left that up to me. I'll be checking in with you all the time, so that's not a problem, and Diane was sure that you'd work more easily here.'

And keep out of her hair.

The words were unspoken, but as the bellboy came in with her luggage and Bonnie went to tip him Olivia gazed around the suite with a cynical eye. Was this what Richard had really abandoned her for? she wondered. This wealthy lifestyle? What price now his accusations that she couldn't give him the children he wanted? As far as she knew, he and Diane hadn't had any children either. Though, of course, that could be her decision, not his.

'D'you need any help with your unpacking?'

The bellboy had departed now and Bonnie was regarding

her with a vaguely irritated air. Olivia guessed her reaction hadn't been the one she'd expected. She wondered if the secretary knew that Richard had once been married to her. Somehow, she doubted it.

'No,' she answered now, slipping off her corduroy jacket. It was quite a relief to feel the air-conditioned air cooling her bare arms. 'Um—thank you,' she added, almost as an afterthought. 'I can manage, really. You've been very kind.'

'Well, good.' Bonnie was mollified by her reply and with a tight smile she gave the apartment another thorough look. 'I suggest you rest up for a while, and then order yourself some dinner from Room Service. You'll have plenty of time to explore the hotel when your body's caught up with your mind.'

Olivia nodded. It was true: she was feeling a little dazed, and it wasn't just the shock of her arrival at the hotel. Perhaps Diane was right; perhaps she would be glad to have a place of her own to return to. Once she got used to it, that was. Right now, she was too exhausted to care.

CHAPTER THREE

IN FACT, Olivia left most of her unpacking until the next morning. After Bonnie left, she felt too exhausted to do much more than take out her nightshirt and the bag containing her toothbrush and soap. A shower, in a fluted glass cubicle, refreshed her sufficiently to order a light supper, but she fell asleep without finishing the shrimps and salad they'd brought her.

She was awake before it was light. Her watch said it was lunchtime, but the clock on the bedside cabinet told a different story. Four o'clock! she thought, in dismay. At least three hours until she could order an early breakfast. Goodness, how long would it take her body to adjust to an eight-hour time change? She'd be falling asleep when by Pacific time it would only be four p.m.

She was hungry now, so she rescued one of the bread rolls they'd supplied her with the night before and spread it with butter. The coffee was cold, but the water from the tap was a palatable alternative, and after enjoying her small feast she fell asleep again.

The next time she opened her eyes, a pale dawn was turning the sky to palest yellow, with fluffy white clouds shredding before the rising sun. Slipping off the huge bed, she went somewhat disbelievingly to the window. She was actually here, in California, she thought, running a hand through the tumbled weight of her hair. Incredible! Twenty-four hours ago she had just been leaving London.

She discovered, when she rang down for breakfast, that it was in fact a twenty-four-hour room service, which meant she could have ordered herself a snack at four a.m. Still, it was much more pleasant to eat cereal with fresh strawberries and scrambled eggs seated at the table in the window with the sunshine streaming over her. She felt much brighter this morning, and far more optimistic than she'd done the night before.

She'd unpacked her suitcases while she'd been waiting for her breakfast, and in consequence she was dressed and ready by eight o'clock. She'd taken another shower and decided on a simple short-skirted dress of lime-green cotton, and because her hair was too silky from the shampoo to behave neatly she'd used a scarf to hold it back instead.

The effect was quite dramatic for her, and she studied her reflection for some time before turning away. Was her skirt too short? Was her neckline too low? Should she have chosen something more businesslike? She realised she was starting to spook herself, and dismissed her misgivings. She'd need all the ammunition she possessed to face the interview ahead.

Assuming that no one was likely to contact her before nine o'clock, Olivia decided to go and take a look at the rest of the hotel. She knew that if she stayed in the suite she'd start worrying, and it would be much better if she kept her mind occupied with something other than the reason why she was here. Besides, she told herself fiercely, she was curious about her surroundings, and if she was staying here for any length of time she should know where everything was.

The lift transported her down to the foyer without incident, and she discovered that far from being the only person who was up and about the ground floor of the hotel was fairly buzzing with activity. She remembered now that when she'd stayed in New York she'd noticed this same phenomenon. Americans very often held business meetings at breakfast, and as if to prove this there were lots of immaculately suited men and women with briefcases passing in and out of the terrace restaurant.

They reminded her of Joe Castellano, and she wondered if he ever ate breakfast at this hotel. It was an unlikely scenario, she had to admit. Did she actually think he might come looking for her?

Brushing such a ridiculous thought aside, she saw the

glint of a swimming pool through the long windows that flanked a palm-shaded courtyard. The hotel appeared to be built around this inner courtyard, and she moved towards the automatic doors that gave access to the pool area. Striped umbrellas, cushioned loungers and a wealth of thick towels piled on an old-fashioned handcart invited investigation. The whole place had a 'twenties' feel about it, but the facilities were as luxurious as they come.

Still, it was good to know that she could take a swim whenever she felt like it. She could imagine how delightful that would be in the heat of the day. She smiled. She was in danger of enjoying this temporary exile. She had to remember exactly why she was here.

She'd had no problem remembering last night. Then, the strangeness of her surroundings, the fact that she hadn't met Diane, after all, and the news that she was to stay here and not at her subject's mansion, had left her feeling decidedly down. The only bright spot in her day had been her meeting with Joe Castellano at the airport, but she was intelligent enough to know that she was unlikely ever to run into him again.

But he had been kind, and because of him she hadn't done anything stupid. Like trying to ring Richard, or crying herself to sleep. And this morning she could safely say she was looking forward to starting work. That was the only reason she was here, she assured herself. She didn't care if she saw Richard or not.

She sighed. As she sauntered round the huge pool, she was forced to acknowledge that her last assertion wasn't precisely true. She did want to see Richard again—but only to reassure herself that he was all right, she told herself firmly. They had known one another for a long time, after all. It was natural that she should care what happened to him.

The fact that he hadn't particularly cared what happened to her when he walked out on her followed on from this assumption. But she wasn't like Richard, she reminded herself. She did care about people's feelings. She couldn't help it. But what she had to remember was that Richard had hurt her. She mustn't give him the chance to hurt her all over again.

The message light was flashing on the phone when she got back to her suite. Checking in with the receptionist, she learned that a car was coming to pick her up at ten o'clock. She was asked to be waiting in the foyer at that time, and she guessed that Bonnie Lovelace would be coming along to identify her to the driver.

Which left her just a short time to worry about her appearance. Having seen so much informal attire downstairs, she wondered if she ought to wear shorts. But no. Meeting Diane again, she wanted to look half decent. And a vest and shorts would put their association on far too familiar a level.

She was downstairs at five to ten, still wearing the lime-green cotton, with a tote bag containing her notebook and tape recorder slung over her shoulder. She'd managed to tame her hair into a French braid so it looked considerably tidier, and she'd added a pair of gold earloops for good measure.

'Liv?'

She'd been watching the antics of a toddler, who'd got away from his mother and was presently causing a lot of grief to one of the waiters who was trying to serve coffee from the foyer bar, when a hand touched her shoulder. She hadn't been aware of anyone's approach, and the unexpected British accent took her by surprise. She swung round, all thoughts of hiding her feelings going out of her head, and stared at the man behind her with her heart in her eyes.

'Richard!'

'Hello, Liv.'

His response was every bit as emotional as hers had been and before she knew what he was doing he'd bent his head and bestowed a lingering kiss on her mouth. His lips were warm and wet, as if he'd been licking them in anticipation, and although Olivia had expected to be gratified by the

warmth of his greeting she found she didn't care for his
assumption that she'd welcome it.

'I've missed you so much, Liv,' he added, and she was
dismayed to see that his eyes had filled with tears. Eyes
that were slightly red-rimmed, she noticed, with a telling
puffiness beneath each one.

Indeed, as she came to look at him properly, she saw
that his eyes weren't the only evidence of change about
him. He'd put on weight, for one thing. His limbs had
thickened, and his stomach swelled over the leather of his
belt. He'd bleached his hair, too, and although it accentuated his tan it looked artificial. In a polo shirt and shorts,
he looked little like the man she remembered.

'You look—terrific,' he went on, surveying her slim figure and bare legs with greedy eyes. 'Come on.' He gestured
towards the exit. 'I've got the car waiting.' His lips twisted.
'Is Diane going to get a shock when she sees you!'

'I doubt it.'

Olivia let him escort her towards the glass doors with
some reluctance. Although it was true that she had lost
weight since the divorce, otherwise she looked much the
same. Her hair was longer, of course. When she'd been
married to Richard and working in the city, it had been
easier to handle when it was shorter. But compared to
Diane Haran—or should she say Diane *Haig*?—she was
very ordinary indeed.

And no one knew that better than Richard himself.

Outside, the limousine in which she and Bonnie had travelled from the airport the previous afternoon was waiting,
with Manuel at the wheel. Actually, Olivia was quite relieved to see the chauffeur. For a moment, she'd wondered
if Richard had come alone. But, whether the unhappy rumours about his marriage were true or not, Diane had evidently decided they needed a chaperon. Or perhaps it was
the fact that, even at this early hour of the morning, Olivia
could smell the sour scent of alcohol on Richard's breath.

Once they were in the car, she took care to put a good
twelve inches of white leather between them, and Richard

turned to give her a wounded look. 'Don't you trust me, Liv?' he protested, making an abortive attempt to take her hand. 'God, you didn't used to look at me like that. What an unholy mess I've made of both our lives.'

Olivia caught her breath at this assertion. Although he was staring straight ahead, she prayed Manuel wasn't listening to Richard's maudlin complaints. Not only was he full of self-pity, but he was acting as if she shared his regrets.

And she didn't.

Well, not really, she amended, trying to be brutally honest with herself. She couldn't deny that she'd hoped it hadn't been all plain sailing for him. She was human, after all, and when Kay had said his marriage to Diane was in trouble she had felt a quiver of anticipation. But she'd never expected that Richard might really want to see her. Or that he might covet what he'd lost.

'So—how are you?' Richard asked now, evidently deciding he'd said enough about his feelings for the present.

'I'm fine,' she answered, with determined brightness. 'The jet lag's a bit of a problem. I was awake at four o'clock; can you believe that?' She grimaced. 'Thank goodness I managed to go back to sleep.'

Richard relaxed against the soft upholstery, one arm spread expansively along the back of the seat. 'It affects different people in different ways,' he said carelessly. 'Myself, it's no problem. But then, I'm used to travelling a lot.'

Olivia wound the strap of her bag round her fingers. 'With Diane?' she asked, and he gave her a jaded look.

'I used to,' he said. 'I used to think she wanted me with her. But these days I usually stay at home.'

Olivia pressed her lips together. 'Well, you certainly have a beautiful place to live in,' she murmured, gazing out of the car window. She didn't know what to say, what to think, and it was easier to talk about impersonal things. 'Is this Beverly Hills?' she asked as the limousine wound its way up quiet streets flanked by high hedges and stone walls. There was little to see of the estates that sprawled behind the wrought-iron security gates.

'You've been in Beverly Hills since you left the hotel,' replied Richard indifferently. 'This whole area is known as the City of Beverly Hills. What a laugh! It's really just the west side of Los Angeles. But people like my wife think it's paradise on earth.'

'Oh, I'm sure—'

'She does. I'm telling you. Diane's really into this West Coast lifestyle. My God, I don't think a scrap of meat has passed her lips in the last four years! It's all fruit and cereal and therapy and body massage. God, you don't know how sick of it all I am, Liv. That's why I'm so glad to have you here.'

'Richard—'

'It's not real, Liv. The people who live here don't live in the real world any more.' He cast a disparaging glance out of the window at the walled estates. 'Fortress America! Can you honestly say you know what all the excitement is about?'

Olivia's lower lip curled between her teeth and she bit on it, hard. It seemed obvious that whatever comment she made Richard was going to put it down. When had he got so cynical? she wondered unhappily. She didn't know what to say so she decided to hold her tongue.

'I suppose I should congratulate you on your success,' he remarked, after a moment, and once again she heard the bitterness in his voice. 'My Liv, an author! Who'd have thought it? I told you you were wasted at that rag you used to work for.'

He hadn't, actually. Quite the reverse, but she didn't contradict him. She had no desire to arrive at Diane's estate while he was in this mood. If she wasn't careful he'd be crying on her shoulder. God knew what Diane would say if she found out.

She wished he'd pull himself together and stop treating her like an accomplice. As if the only reason she'd come here was to be with him. She drew an uneven breath. She was beginning to wonder what she'd ever seen in him. Had he always blamed other people when things went wrong?

The memory of what he'd said when they'd been trying to have a family returned to haunt her. Although they'd both had tests and there'd seemed no reason why they shouldn't have a baby, she knew he'd blamed her. And perhaps it was her fault, she reflected. They'd probably never know. And at that time she'd been far more willing to blame herself.

'I meant what I said, you know, Liv,' he muttered, attracting her attention. 'I have missed you more than you'll ever know. Leaving you was the biggest mistake I've ever made in my life. I wanted to tell you that right from the start.'

'Then you shouldn't have!' exclaimed Olivia hotly, convinced that Manuel could hear what he was saying. He had no right to involve her in his marital problems, whatever excuse he thought he had. She chewed her lip. She suspected his confession was a deliberate attempt to gain her sympathy, and also make her a party to his resentment whether she liked it or not.

'I can't help myself,' he told her now, and once again she had to suffer his efforts to touch her. His arm along the back of the seat descended onto her shoulders and she felt his fingers stroking her neck. 'I know I hurt you, Liv, but I'm hoping you'll find it in your heart to forgive me. The love we shared—I can't believe we let it go.'

'*You* let it go, Richard,' said Olivia flatly, removing his arm from her shoulder and shifting onto the opposite seat. She glanced about her. 'Is it much further?'

Richard heaved a heavy sigh. 'No,' he said, and although his tone was sulky Olivia was relieved. Sulky was acceptable; tearful wasn't. She gave a slight shake of her head. She couldn't believe this was happening to her.

The limousine began to slow a few minutes later, and as Olivia glanced round to see where they were Manuel turned between wrought-iron gates that had opened at their approach. A long curving drive confronted them, hedged with laurel and acacia, and she felt her nerves tighten as they drove up to the house.

A pillared façade of cream sandstone confronted them. Within its shadows, a shaded loggia stretched along the front of the house. Built on two floors, its many windows protected by terracotta-painted shutters, it was large and impressive, with a wealth of flowering shrubs and trees surrounding its manicured lawns.

'Well, this is it,' said Richard sardonically as Manuel got out of his seat to open the rear doors. 'The Villa Mariposa. Are you ready to meet your employer?'

'She's not my employer,' said Olivia, rather too vehemently, and was annoyed when Richard's lips curved in a knowing smile.

'No, she's not,' he applauded, 'and don't you let her forget it.' He clutched her arm, and she was forced to follow him out of the car. 'Go for it, Liv,' he added softly. 'I knew you weren't as indifferent to me as you pretended.'

Olivia dragged her arm away as soon as she was able, aware that once again Manuel was watching their exchange with curious eyes. And who could blame him? she thought, regarding Richard with some frustration. This was hard enough without Richard making it worse.

The doors at the top of the shallow flight of steps had opened, and Olivia glanced somewhat apprehensively in that direction. But she saw to her relief that it was just a maid who stood there, dressed in a navy uniform and a white apron.

She gestured for Olivia to come up the steps and offered a polite smile as they entered a cool marble-floored reception hall with an arched ceiling stretching up two floors. At its peak, a circular stained-glass window cast a rainbow shaft of sunlight down into the hall, while the gentle hum of air-conditioning prevented any surge of heat.

'Mees Haran is waiting by the pool, Mees Pyatt,' she said, inviting Olivia to follow her. And her announcement solved Olivia's other problem of what to call Richard's wife.

'Thank you.'

Olivia shouldered her tote bag, and, not caring whether Richard was following them or not, she accompanied the maid across the hall. An arched doorway exposed several steps down into a sunlit garden room, where a pair of glass doors stood wide to a flagged terrace. Rattan tables and chairs stood in the shade of the upstairs balcony, and a pair of inquisitive sparrows picked crumbs from between the stones.

There were flowers everywhere, Olivia noticed. In pots and planters in the garden room, in tubs and hanging baskets on the terrace, and climbing over the columns that supported the balcony above. The scent was glorious, but perhaps a little overpowering, and she was glad when they descended more steps and she glimpsed the aquamarine waters of the pool glinting below them.

She saw Diane at once.

The woman she had never expected to meet again was propped on a cushioned lounge chair, with a huge yellow umbrella protecting her from the direct rays of the sun. Although she must have known that Olivia had arrived, she didn't look in her direction. Her attention was focussed on a child who was splashing about at the edge of the pool beside her.

Her child?

Olivia caught her breath. If it was, it had been a well-kept secret. She couldn't believe she wouldn't have heard about Diane's having a child if it had appeared in the press. Richard's child, too? she wondered, aware of a not unnatural sense of envy. Not for the fact that it was Richard's child, she assured herself, but because she would have so much liked a child of her own.

Diane had evidently heard the sound of her feet on the tiled apron, and with another quick word to her companion she got smoothly to her feet. In a one-piece bathing suit with exotic orchids adorning its navy background, she looked magnificent. No sign of excess flesh here, thought

Olivia ruefully. Diane was every bit as beautiful as she recalled.

'Hi,' Diane said, by way of a greeting, coming to meet her. Her bare feet left damp patches on the tiles, revealing that she had been in the water, too. It made her seem more human, somehow, Olivia thought, aware of how tense she was feeling. No statue, this, but a living, breathing woman.

'Hello.'

The word stuck in Olivia's throat, making any further speech impossible at that moment, and she glanced behind her, half hoping that Richard was there. But if she'd expected his support she was disappointed. She and Diane were alone together, apart from the child.

'I'm so glad you agreed to come.' Diane pushed a hand through the sun-streaked cap of blonde hair that curved confidingly in at her chin. The action was unstudied, but so elegant that Olivia could only admire her composure. 'Ms Pyatt—or may I call you Olivia?—you probably won't believe this, but I'm hoping we can be friends.'

Olivia felt the hot colour invading her cheeks and despised herself for it. It was Diane who should be feeling uncomfortable here, not her. But Diane was probably used to handling difficult interviews, and she wasn't. Indeed, the other woman's casual approach took her breath away.

'I don't think that's possible, Ms Haran,' she declared now, swinging her tote bag off her shoulder and allowing it to hang from its straps in front of her knees like a shield.

'Well—we'll see,' said Diane, with an enigmatic little smile. She indicated the chair beside hers. 'Why don't you sit down and we'll talk about it? Oh, and call me Diane. Ms Haran is far too formal.'

Olivia drew a breath. In fact, what she really wanted to do was turn around and go back to the hotel. Her anticipation of this meeting had not prepared her for Diane's familiarity, and she wondered now what she had expected from Richard's wife.

But the sun was hot, and she knew she shouldn't take unnecessary risks by standing in its glare. Besides, however surreal this seemed, she had come here to do a job. Unless she was prepared to be sued for breach of contract, she had to do as Diane said and accept the status quo.

Nevertheless, she seated herself on the next but one chair to Diane's, grateful for the shade offered by its striped canopy and the distance it put between them. With her face in shadow, her colour subsided, and she opened her tote bag and extracted her notebook and tape recorder.

Meanwhile, Diane had approached the child again, who was still hanging onto the tiles at the side of the pool. He was a little boy, Olivia saw as Diane lifted him out. Dark-haired and dark-skinned, with a mischievous smile that exposed several missing teeth.

'Go and find your mother,' Diane advised him, after wrapping a fluffy towel about his shoulders. 'My maid,' she added, by way of an explanation as the boy ran off. 'She and Manuel have three grown-up sons. Antonio is their baby.'

'Ah.'

Olivia nodded, making a play of checking that there were batteries in the recorder. But Diane's careless clarification had answered her question. Not Richard's son, but Manuel's.

'Would you like a drink?'

Diane had seated herself again and was regarding her with enquiring eyes and Olivia wondered what she was really thinking. Was this any easier for her than it was for Olivia? Was she really as indifferent to her feelings as she'd like to appear?

'Oh, I don't think—'

'Oh, yes, let's have some coffee.' Without waiting for her guest to finish, Diane got up again and pressed a button that Olivia now saw was set into the wall beside a row of changing cabanas. She came back and sat down again. 'I think we should get to know one another before we start work.'

Olivia rolled her lips inward. And then, putting the recorder aside, she clasped her hands together in her lap.

'You mean, you're going to tell me why you really wanted me to write your biography?' she asked tightly, amazed at her own audacity. She'd never expected to have the courage to challenge her like this.

Diane shrugged. 'You know why I wanted you. I told your agent: I like your work.'

'Have you read my work?'

'Some of it.' Diane nodded. 'I read your biography of Eileen Cusack.' She shook her head. 'I'd never heard of her, you know, but after reading your story of her life I have so much admiration for her.'

Olivia drew a breath. 'You read it?'

'Yes.' Diane looked puzzled. 'Didn't Mrs Goldsmith tell you?'

'Well, yes.' Olivia made a little gesture of dismissal, but that didn't stop the heat from re-entering her cheeks. 'But— people—say things they think you want to hear.'

'People?' Diane gave her an arch look. 'You mean me?'

'Does it matter?' Olivia wished she'd never questioned Diane's statement. 'I—I'm glad you enjoyed the book.' She tried to speak objectively. 'Eileen was a brave woman.'

'Yes, she was.' Diane was thoughtful, but happily the maid arrived at that moment to divert her. 'Coffee and fresh orange juice, please, María,' she ordered pleasantly.

The maid said, 'Yes, Mees Haran,' and departed again.

The heat around the pool was excessive, and Olivia could feel herself perspiring in spite of the thinness of her dress. The cluster of cyprus trees across the pool created a kind of suntrap, and she wondered if the canopy above her was equal to its task.

'Perhaps you think I only invited you here because of Ricky,' Diane remarked after a moment, and Olivia thought how odd the abbreviation of Richard's name sounded to her ears. Indeed, for a moment she wondered if Diane was talking about the same person. 'I didn't—though you've probably realised he's delighted to have you here.'

'Is he?' Rummaging in her bag for a paper tissue to wipe her hot face, Olivia couldn't think of anything else to say.

'You know he is,' said Diane flatly. 'Don't insult my intelligence by pretending he hasn't told you. He's probably already hinted that we're having problems. I know what he's like.'

'It's nothing to do with me,' said Olivia uncomfortably, half wishing Richard had joined them. She wasn't at all sure she wanted to handle this conversation on her own. When she'd contemplated meeting Diane again, she hadn't anticipated that Diane would be so friendly. She was hostile, and she'd expected Diane to be hostile, too.

'If you say so.' Evidently Diane had decided not to pursue it. At least for the present anyway. 'So—' She stretched her legs on the cushioned lounge chair, looking years younger than the thirty-five Olivia knew her to be. 'Tell me how you came to write.'

Olivia shook her head. 'Well, I've always written—' she was beginning awkwardly, when a disturbance on the terrace interrupted them. Another visitor had just arrived: a man, who was exchanging a few teasing words with María. She must have just let him in and she was laughing at something he'd said. Then, as both Diane and Olivia turned their heads, he came casually down the steps towards them.

He was wearing a black collarless shirt under a cream linen jacket and trousers this morning, but Olivia had no difficulty in recognising who he was. She didn't need the other woman's delighted use of his name to remind her, or appreciate the view of Diane as she flew across the pool deck into his arms. As her pulse raced—and her spirits sank almost in counterpoint—she realised that Joe Castellano was apparently a closer friend of Diane's than she'd thought.

CHAPTER FOUR

OLIVIA tore her gaze away from the embracing couple and tried to simulate some interest in the notebook on her knees. Questions, she thought, uncapping her pen; she should make a list of the questions she wanted to ask Diane. Not historical details like what her father did or where she'd been born, but questions about her persuasions: about what she thought of the increase in crime, perhaps, or the proliferation of dangerous drugs.

But apart from jotting down the words 'Guns' and 'Heroin' she couldn't think of anything else to write. Her mind was like a movie screen that was filled with the image of Diane's swimsuited figure melded to Joe Castellano's muscled frame. His legs were parted, and she could see one of Diane's feet stroking his calf, and one brown masculine hand was spread against the creamy skin of her spine.

Suddenly, she was reminded of what Kay had said: that she had heard some other man must have caught her eye. Oh, God! Was that who Joe Castellano was: Diane Haran's lover? When he'd said he was a friend of Diane's, she'd taken him at his word.

If she'd felt hot before, she was fairly burning up now, and it wasn't just the temperature around the pool. She wished desperately that she wasn't there, or that Joe Castellano had chosen some other occasion to announce his return. After the crazy thoughts she'd had about him, she didn't want to meet him again. Not now. If only one of the area's famous earthquakes would swallow her up.

She could hear voices now, and realised that they had separated and were coming towards her. Somehow, she had to get through the next few minutes without betraying how she felt. Should she stand up? Would her legs support her? She couldn't be certain of anything, she thought despairingly. And she probably looked like a sun-dried tomato to boot.

'Joe tells me the two of you have already met,' said Diane without hesitation, and, judging by the openness of her smile, there was no animosity either. And why should there be? thought Olivia, aware of her own imperfections. Compared to Diane, there could be no contest, after all.

'Oh—yes,' she said now, closing her notebook and running sticky fingers over its laminated back. She looked up into his lean dark face and felt her body tingle. 'Um—how do you do, Mr Castellano? How—how nice to see you again.'

He grinned down at her. 'You made it, then?'

'What? Oh, yes.' She licked her dry lips. 'Miss—Ms—Lovelace was very kind.'

'Who, Bonnie?' Joe Castellano laughed, and then to her dismay dropped down onto the footrest of her own lounge chair. 'Hey, if she heard you call her that, she'd blow her top.'

Diane came to stand beside him, running a possessive hand over his shoulder as she spoke. 'Stop teasing Ms Pyatt,' she chided him, evidently not wanting him to be familiar with Olivia's name. Then, as if realising how her actions could be construed, she sank into the adjoining chair. Drawing one leg up to her chest, she rested her chin upon her knee, but her eyes never left him. 'You will join us for coffee, won't you?'

'Coffee?' His dark brows ascended mockingly. 'Something long and cold sounds more like it.'

'A beer, then.' Diane was obviously eager for him to stay.

'A beer.' His mouth compressed. 'It's too early in the day for me.'

Olivia wondered if that was a dig at Richard, but although he could easily have made some comment about the other man he didn't. She wondered if he knew of her relationship with Richard. Had Diane told him that she'd asked her husband's ex-wife to write her story?

'Do you think you're going to like it here?' he asked, turning to Olivia, and she managed not to stumble over her reply.

'It's different,' she said, realising her response was non-committal. 'Do you live in Los Angeles, Mr Castellano?'

'He has a house at Malibu but he lives in San Francisco.' Diane answered for him. Then, as if impatient at the interruption, she attracted his attention again. 'Are you staying for a few days this time?' she asked impulsively. 'I've got so much I want to discuss with you before I leave for the East Coast.'

Joe Castellano shrugged. 'I'd have said you've got your hands full here,' he remarked, his tawny eyes flickering over Olivia's averted head as she struggled to make herself invisible. 'Aren't you pretty tied up with this biography you've decided to have written?'

'I've always got time for you,' Diane retorted, her voice soft and sensual. 'Are you staying at the beach house tonight?'

'Maybe,' he responded carelessly. 'But I want to check in at the hotel. I've got some business meetings scheduled for tomorrow and the beginning of next week, so it may be easier to stay in town. I might spend the weekend in Malibu, though. Why? Do you and Richard fancy joining me for drinks on Saturday night?'

'I—why—' Diane seemed uncertain at first and then, catching Olivia's eye, she seemed to come to a decision. 'Why not?' she agreed lightly. 'So long as Ms Pyatt can come, too.' And as Olivia's lips parted in consternation she added, 'I'm sure she'd love to see the Pacific at sunset. I can get Ricky to play tour guide. What do you think?'

'I'm sure Mr Castellano didn't expect you to ask me—' started Olivia hurriedly, uneasily aware that there was something going on here that she didn't like. What was Diane trying to do? Get her to take Richard—*Ricky*—off her hands?

'Mr Castellano would be delighted if you'd join us,' he interposed easily, and once again Olivia glimpsed the sat-

isfaction in Diane's face. 'But call me Joe, for God's sake!
We don't stand on ceremony here.'

'Well…'

'Joe's right,' put in Diane quickly, apparently prepared
to be generous if she was getting her own way. 'It's a great
idea, Olivia. Joe's house is quite a showplace at the beach.
Perhaps you should bring your swimsuit. We could have a
moonlight swim.'

Olivia shook her head. She knew she was being manoeuvred into an impossible position and she didn't like it. But
she wasn't really surprised. She'd suspected Diane's motives before she left England.

'Trust me—Olivia, right? You'll enjoy it.'

Joe Castellano, at least, seemed to have sensed her am-
bivalence and Olivia wondered if he knew exactly what
Diane was doing. He had to, she decided, her nails digging
into her notebook. Why else had he come here the day after
he got back?

'I—thought I might do some sightseeing this weekend,'
she said stiffly, determined not to be railroaded into acting
as Richard's nanny, and Diane gave her an impatient look.

'You'll have plenty of time for sightseeing!' she exclaimed. 'Surely you're not going to turn down the invitation? I thought you'd have jumped at the chance to—
to—'

'Spend time with my ex-husband?' demanded Olivia,
realising Diane wasn't the only one who could speak her
mind. She heard Joe Castellano's sudden intake of breath
but she didn't falter. 'I'm sorry, Ms Haran,' she added,
getting to her feet, 'but that's not why I came.'

'I was going to say, I thought you would have jumped
at the chance to—to speak to people who know me,' retorted Diane coldly. 'You don't imagine we'd have been
Joe's only guests, do you? We—he—has lots of friends.
You might even have found it interesting to talk to his
brother. He's an actor, like me.'

Olivia's face was burning. 'Well, I'm sorry,' she mumbled uncomfortably, 'but I—I don't usually mix business

with pleasure.' She licked her lips. 'And—and as Mr Castellano obviously wants to speak to you, perhaps you'd prefer it if I came back at some more convenient time—'

'Oh, for God's sake—' began Diane irritably, only to break off when Joe Castellano got to his feet.

'Cool it,' he said, and Olivia wasn't sure which of them he was talking to. 'I've got an appointment anyway. I won't hold you up any longer.'

'You're not holding us up.' Diane sprang up now, grasping his arm, forcing him to look at her and no one else. 'Don't go,' she cried. 'María's fetching coffee and juice. You can stay for a little while, surely.'

'And be accused of preventing—Ms Pyatt—from doing her job?' he asked, and Olivia didn't know if he was being sarcastic or not. 'I'll ring you later, okay? Give Ricky my regards, won't you?'

'But, Joe—'

Diane's tone was desperate, but he was already walking away. With a casual salute that included both of them, he disappeared into the house, and presently they heard the muffled roar of a car's exhaust.

Silence descended—an uneasy silence that wasn't much improved when Diane turned away and sought the chair she had occupied earlier. Olivia wished she had her own transport, too; that she had the means to get out of there herself. It would be the next thing she'd do, she thought vehemently. Providing she was still employed, of course.

'Oh, sit down, for heaven's sake!'

Diane's impatient command almost had her hurrying to do her bidding, but somehow she stiffened her spine and managed to stay where she was. 'Do you still want to do this?' she asked, half hoping Diane would say no. But she should have known that the other woman wouldn't give up that easily.

'Do I still want to do it?' she echoed, looking up at Olivia with a frustrated stare. 'Of course I want to do it, as you so succinctly put it. That's what I've brought you out here for. If you choose to ruin any chance of a social life you might have while you're here, that's up to you.'

Olivia swallowed, and, hearing the unmistakable sound of footsteps behind her, she sank down weakly onto the chair. She knew it must be María, and she had no desire to arouse her curiosity as well. But she couldn't help wishing that Diane would suggest continuing their interview indoors. It might just be that little altercation with Joe Castellano, but she felt as if her temperature was sky-high.

'Coffee and fruit juice, madam,' said María cheerfully, setting the tray on the low table beside her mistress. 'Would you like me to pour?'

'No, thanks,' answered Diane, dismissing her somewhat ungraciously, and Olivia was aware of the maid's confusion as she hurried back to the house.

Meanwhile, Diane had picked up the pot of coffee. 'How do you like it?' she asked. 'Or do you prefer orange juice?'

'Yes.' Olivia's lips felt parched. 'That is—I would prefer orange juice,' she murmured awkwardly. There were ice cubes floating on the top of the jug and they were a mouth-watering sight.

Diane shrugged, set down the coffee pot again and took charge of the jug. She filled a tall glass and handed it to Olivia. 'You look as though you need this,' she commented drily. 'It may help you to cool down.'

Olivia doubted it, but rather than make any retort she took a generous gulp of the juice. 'It's very hot out here,' she said at last, determined not to let Diane think she could intimidate her. 'If I'd known we were going to work outside, I'd have come more prepared.'

Diane finished pouring herself a cup of coffee, which Olivia noticed she drank without either cream or sugar. 'You'd prefer to work indoors?' she asked, viewing her companion critically. 'I suppose your skin is sensitive. You're like Ricky. You're used to cooler climes.'

Olivia wanted to say that she wasn't like Richard at all, but as she had no desire to bring Richard's name into their conversation again she kept her mouth shut. Besides, she sensed that Diane was only baiting her, and it didn't really matter what she said as long as Olivia didn't respond.

'Tell me how you met Joe at the airport,' Diane invited, changing tack when it became apparent that the other woman wasn't going to rise to her previous lure. She frowned. 'He must have recognised you from your picture on the book about Eileen Cusack.'

Olivia nodded. She had wondered about that, too. She could hardly tell Diane she had been staring at him across the concourse. Had he really recognised her, or had he seen the label on her bag?

'He's quite a dish, isn't he?' Diane went on encouragingly. 'I bet you wondered who he was. I assume he must have approached you. You don't look the type to initiate a pass.'

Olivia put down her glass. 'You're right, of course,' she said flatly. 'Unlike you, I don't covet every man I see. Um—Mr Castellano was very kind, very thoughtful. He could see I was a stranger and he helped me out.'

Diane's lips twisted. 'Believe it or not, but I don't 'covet every man I see' either,' she retorted shortly. 'All right. I know you're still peeved about what happened between you and Ricky, but that wasn't all my fault. It takes two to tango, as they say in Rio. Ricky was ripe for a bit of seduction. I hate to tell you this, Olivia, but *he* came on to *me*.'

'I don't believe you!'

The words were out before she could stop them and Olivia suspected that she'd said exactly what Diane had hoped she'd say.

'Well, that's up to you,' she said now, sipping her coffee and watching Olivia with cool, assessing eyes. 'It doesn't matter, anyway. We've all had plenty of time to ponder our mistakes.'

Olivia pressed her lips together and forced herself to breathe evenly. She would not allow Diane to manipulate her, she thought fiercely, no matter how much she'd looked forward to seeing Richard again. In fact, it was hard to remember now how she'd felt before she left England. Had she really welcomed the news that he and Diane were having problems? Somehow it was difficult to imagine those errant emotions now.

'The relationship you've had—or are having—with your husband is of no interest to me,' she declared, trying to concentrate on what she'd written on her pad. 'Shall we get on with the interview? I'd like to confirm a few preliminary details this morning. Then we can concentrate on the form you want the biography to take.'

Diane's lips twisted. 'I don't believe you, you know.'

Olivia took a deep breath. 'What don't you believe?' she asked, reaching for her glass again with a slightly unsteady hand.

'That you don't care about me and Richard; that you only came here to do a job.' Diane put down her cup with a measured grace. 'You're not that unfeeling, Olivia. I should know.'

Olivia closed her eyes for a moment, praying for strength, and then opened them again before she spoke. 'You don't know anything about me,' she stated firmly. 'It's five years since—since we had any contact with one another, and that's a long time. I've changed; you've changed; we're all five years older. I'm not a junior reporter any more, Ms Haran. I've got an independent career of my own.'

'I know that.' Diane was impatient. 'And I respect the success you've had. That's why you're here, for God's sake!' She broke off and then continued more calmly, 'But don't pretend that you don't still care about Ricky. I don't flatter myself that it was my invitation that brought you here.'

'Well, it was,' said Olivia swiftly, though not very truthfully. It was the chance that she might see Richard again that had overcome her reluctance to work with Diane. But she had no intention of giving Diane that satisfaction, and in any case meeting Richard again had somehow soured that enthusiasm, too.

That—and the startling realisation that she'd been attracted to another man...

'You're lying,' persisted Diane now, leaning forward to pour herself another cup of coffee. But there was no animosity in the words. And before Olivia could attempt to defend herself she went on evenly, 'But perhaps this isn't the time to go into that.' She paused. 'It's Friday tomorrow. I suggest we both take the weekend to think things over, and we'll meet here again on Monday morning.'

Olivia caught her breath. 'You mean—you want me to go?'

Diane shrugged. 'I think it's a good idea, don't you?' She looked at the other woman over the rim of her coffee cup. 'I've got to go into the studios this afternoon anyway, and you'd probably welcome the chance to get your bearings. I suppose I should have realised you can't be expected to work on your first day.'

Manuel drove Olivia back to her hotel, and she was grateful to find that Richard wasn't with him. She needed some time to collect her thoughts before she saw her ex-husband again, and she couldn't help wondering if he knew what his wife was thinking. It seemed obvious to Olivia that Diane's motives weren't as straightforward as she'd have her believe.

She was tired when she reached her room, despite the fact that it was only midday. But her body clock was telling her that it was evening and although she hadn't actually done any work yet her encounter with Diane had taken its toll.

Perhaps she'd done her a favour by suggesting that she take the weekend off, thought Olivia unwillingly, but she doubted Diane had her best interests at heart. No, there was another agenda that only Diane knew about, and while she had been remarkably civil to her Olivia sensed that there was something going on.

An image of Joe Castellano insinuated itself into her mind as she sat down on the side of her bed and kicked off her shoes. Was he really just a friend, as he'd said, or were he and Diane lovers, as she suspected? It was ironic, she thought bitterly, that she and the other woman should be attracted to the same men. But she wasn't foolish enough to think there was any competition between them.

Flopping back on the mattress, she spread her arms out to either side and stretched wearily. The quilt was cool beneath her bare arms and it was so nice just to relax. For the present it wasn't important that Diane was paying for her accommodation. She was too exhausted to care about anything else.

The telephone awakened her. Its shrill distinctive peal penetrated the many layers of sleep and brought her upright with a start. For a moment she was disorientated, not understanding how it could be light outside and she still had her clothes on. She didn't usually need a nap in the middle of the day.

Then, as the phone continued to ring, she remembered where she was and what she was doing. A quick glance at the slim watch on her wrist advised her that it was after half-past four. She'd slept for nearly five hours. She must have been tired. No wonder she felt hungry. She hadn't eaten a thing since early that morning.

Rubbing an impatient hand across her eyes, she reached for the receiver. 'Hello,' she said huskily, but she knew as soon as she spoke who was on the line.

'Liv? Hell, you are there. I was beginning to think you'd passed out in the bath or something. The receptionist insisted you were in your room, but I've been trying this number for hours!'

'For hours?' Olivia blinked. 'Richard, I—'

'Well, for the last half hour, anyway,' he amended quickly, evidently realising it wasn't wise to exaggerate that much. 'If you hadn't answered this time, I was going to come over. I've been worried about you, Liv. Why'd you leave like that without even letting me know?'

Olivia shook her head. She could do without this, she thought wearily, sensing the beginnings of a headache nudging at her temples. It was the fault of being woken up so suddenly that was making her feel so groggy. That, and the emptiness she was feeling inside.

'Didn't Diane tell you why I left?' she asked now, realising he was unlikely to be put off by anything less than an explanation. 'We—talked, and then she suggested I used the next couple of days to familiarise myself with my surroundings. I'm seeing her again on Monday morning. But I'm sure you must know this for yourself.'

'I know what she said,' declared Richard harshly, 'but that doesn't mean that I believed it. I know my wife. She looks as if butter wouldn't melt in her mouth, but I know better.'

'Oh, Richard—'

'I know, I know. That's not your problem.' His tone was bitter. 'But at least give me the credit for caring what happens to you.'

Which implied that she didn't care what happened to him, and that simply couldn't be true. For heaven's sake, before she'd left England she'd believed she was still in love with him, and it wasn't wholly his fault that she'd changed her mind. You couldn't be married to someone for four years without their feelings meaning something to you, she admitted ruefully. Their marriage might be over but the memory lingered on.

'I was asleep,' she said now, hoping to avoid any further discussion of Diane. 'It's the jet lag, I think. I was exhausted when I got back.'

'But—you're all right?' he asked anxiously. 'Um—Diane didn't say anything to upset you?'

'No.'

Olivia was abrupt, but she couldn't help it. She wondered what exactly he thought she was. She found she resented the fact that he believed Diane could still hurt her. Had she given him the impression that she'd spent the last four years pining for him?

'Oh—good.' He sounded relieved, but she wondered if

he believed her. 'When I found you'd left like that, I was worried in case she'd said something—bad.'

Or incriminating, reflected Olivia, her lips tightening involuntarily. She was suddenly reminded of what Diane had said about him. Was that the real reason for the phone call? she wondered incredulously. Or was she being unnecessarily paranoid? Was he afraid that Diane might have betrayed the fact that he'd destroyed his marriage and not her?

But, no. She blew out a breath. She was overreacting. Richard had rung her, as he said, because he'd been concerned about why she'd left without saying goodbye. It crossed her mind that it had taken him the best part of five hours to express his regrets, but she didn't dwell on it. In the circumstances, it wasn't her concern.

'Diane was—charming,' she said now, although the description barely fitted the facts. But Richard wasn't to know that. He could only take her word for it. And there was a certain amount of illicit satisfaction in assuring him that they had got on so well.

'Was she?' His response was tight. 'Well—don't let that—bewitching façade fool you. Diane's an actress, in every sense of the word. She doesn't know how to be sincere.'

'Richard—'

'I know. I'm doing it again, aren't I? I'm sorry.' His apology sounded genuine, and Olivia sighed. 'In any case, I didn't ring for you to get embroiled in my personal problems. I wanted to ask you if you'd have dinner with me.' He paused. 'I'd really like for us to talk, Liv.'

Olivia stifled a groan. 'Oh—well, not tonight, Richard,' she protested. 'I was thinking of having an early night.'

'Tomorrow, then. Just the two of us. Diane's spending the weekend at the beach. We could have the place to ourselves.'

Olivia didn't know which was worse: the fact that Diane was apparently going to spend the weekend at Joe Castellano's beach house, or that Richard should expect her to dine with him at Diane's. Both alternatives were distasteful to her, but she suspected the former had the edge.

Nevertheless, she would not play into anyone's hands by dining at Diane's house, and she told him so in no uncertain terms.

'I'm—I'm surprised that you would ask me to do such a thing,' she added stiffly. 'I may have to work there, but I don't have to like it.'

'But you said—'

'That Diane was pleasant?' she interrupted him swiftly. 'Yes, she was. But I don't intend to make a friend of her, Richard. Our association is a matter of business, that's all.'

'I understand.' But she doubted he did. 'And I realise it was insensitive of me to suggest that we dined here. It's just a little difficult to make arrangements at such short notice.' He paused. 'I suppose we could always dine at the hotel.'

Olivia's shoulders sagged. 'You mean in the restaurant, don't you?' There was no way she was going to invite him to her suite.

'Unless you can suggest an alternative,' he answered huskily, the insinuation clear in his voice.

'I can't,' she replied, realising that in her haste to avoid a tête-à-tête she had virtually agreed to his suggestion. 'Um—perhaps you ought to ring me again tomorrow. We can finalise the details then.'

Or not!

'There's no need for that.' Evidently he had detected her uncertainty and was not prepared to give her an escape route. 'Look, let's arrange to meet—downstairs in the Orchid Bar at seven o'clock tomorrow evening. If you can't make it, you can always give me a ring.'

CHAPTER FIVE

IT WASN'T until the following morning that Olivia realised she didn't have Richard's number. There'd been no reason for Kay to have Diane's phone number, and she hadn't thought of asking for it herself. She supposed she could contact Diane's agent, but she was loath to publicise the event. And sooner or later she and Richard would have to talk. There was no point in pretending she could ignore what was going on.

Meanwhile, she had the day to herself, and despite the fact that she'd awakened early again she felt much more optimistic this morning. Her first anxious interview was over, and she was determined not to be daunted by anything Diane might say. Instead of using room service, she decided to have breakfast in the terrace restaurant, and after spending several minutes assessing her wardrobe she eventually elected to wear cream shorts and a peach-coloured linen jacket. A thin silk vest, also in peach, completed her ensemble and she secured her hair at her nape with a tortoise-shell barrette.

She thought she looked smart without being too formal, and she assumed she'd struck the right note when the waiter who escorted her to her table gave her an admiring look. 'Just for one?' he asked, his accent faintly Spanish, and she felt her cheeks colour slightly as she nodded.

'I'm afraid so,' she told him half defensively, and was disarmed by his smile.

'No problem, madam,' he told her easily, and led her to a table for two in the sunlit conservatory.

Yet, despite the waiter's reassurance, Olivia was aware that her table drew a lot of curious stares. Perhaps they thought she was someone of importance, she thought, hiding behind the enormous menu. What must it be like to be a celebrity, constantly in the public eye?

Not very nice, she decided, after the waiter had taken her order, and she took refuge in the complimentary newspaper lying beside her plate. Perhaps she should have had room service, after all. Then she wouldn't be feeling such an oddity now.

Still, the food was good, and, ignoring her fellow diners, Olivia succeeded in clearing her plate. She'd not had blueberry pancakes and maple syrup since her visit to New York a couple of years ago, and she refused to count the calories today.

She was finishing her second cup of coffee when a shadow fell across her table, and, glancing up, she found a tall black woman of middle years looking down at her. The woman's hair had been tinted with henna and Olivia was sure she must weigh at least two hundred and fifty pounds. She was stylishly dressed in a navy power suit, with huge padded shoulders and a tightly buttoned jacket.

'Ms Pyatt?' she asked, and Olivia was so taken aback she could just nod. 'Phoebe Isaacs,' the woman added. 'Can I join you?' And, without waiting for an answer, she pulled out a chair and sat down.

Olivia put down her cup. 'How—how did you know who I was?'

'Well, I was gonna ask the waiter,' said Phoebe laconically, 'but as it happens it wasn't necessary. That gentleman over there pointed you out.'

Olivia blinked. 'What gentleman—?' she was beginning, when she saw the man who was seated across the room. He wasn't looking her way at the moment, but his profile was unmistakable. 'You mean—Mr Castellano?' she asked, in a high-pitched voice.

'Yeah. Joe Castellano,' said Phoebe carelessly. 'I gather you've already met him. He often has breakfast meetings here when he's in town.'

Olivia was stunned, as much by the fact that she was seated just a few yards away from the man who had been occupying far too many of her thoughts as by the casual way that Phoebe Isaacs had introduced herself. 'Um—it's very nice to meet you,' she said, forcing herself not to look in Joe Castellano's direction. 'You're Ms Haran's agent, aren't you? Did—did she ask you to come and see me?'

Thoughts that Diane might be thinking of dismissing her were flooding her head, but Phoebe just said, 'Hell, no,' and grinned broadly. She snapped her fingers for the waiter and ordered some fresh coffee. 'I just wanted to meet you for myself. I'm a big fan, Ms Pyatt.'

'Well—thank you.' Olivia would have been flattered if she hadn't felt so flustered, but her awareness of Diane's lover superseded all else. 'I—er—I believe it was you who contacted my agent, Kay—Kay Goldsmith.'

'Sure did.'

The waiter brought a fresh pot of coffee and another cup and Phoebe helped herself before going on. It gave Olivia a moment to register that her accent was different from the ones she'd heard locally. There was a definite southern twang to what she said.

'Anyway, I'm glad you were able to come on out here,' Phoebe continued, after tasting her coffee. 'There's just no way Diane could have packed up and gone to London at this time. What with fittings for the new film, interviews and personal appearances, her schedule is pretty busy. Besides, I dare say you'll be looking forward to a few weeks in the sun.'

'Yes.' Olivia hoped she sounded more enthusiastic than she felt. 'Well—' she swallowed '—it was kind of Ms Haran to invite me. I suppose I could have done most of the research at home.'

'Hey, there's nothing like hearing it from the horse's mouth,' Phoebe assured her lightly. 'And Diane's a generous person, but I guess you know that already.' She paused. 'I understand you've spent the last couple of weeks talking to people who knew her before she was famous. Guess you never found anyone with a bad word for her, isn't that right?'

'Oh—yes.'

Olivia didn't know what else to say, and to a certain extent it was true. But it seemed obvious that Phoebe knew nothing about her previous marriage to Richard. Had Joe Castellano known before she blurted it out? She cast a surreptitious look in his direction. From his gasp he had seemed to be shocked but she suspected he must have known. He was the kind of man who'd want to know everything about the woman he loved.

If he loved her...

Right now, his mind was obviously on other matters. There were three other men at his table and they seemed to be deep in discussion. One of the men was holding forth, waving the bagel he was eating to emphasise his point. Meanwhile, Joe was lounging in the chair beside him, apparently concentrating on what was being said.

Olivia made herself look away. It wasn't as if he had any interest in her, she told herself severely. He'd been polite, that was all, and if he'd noticed her in the restaurant when she hadn't noticed him that was hardly surprising. She was on her own. The waiter had seated her in a prominent position by the window. And she'd attracted a lot of attention, most of it unwanted, she had to admit.

'So—what are you planning to do today?' Phoebe asked now, and Olivia hoped her thoughts weren't obvious to anyone else. The older woman rested her elbows on the table and propped her chin in her hands. Impossibly long nails, painted scarlet, framed her features. 'Diane wondered if you'd like to go shopping. You can get anything you want on Rodeo Drive.'

Olivia took a deep breath. Was that why Phoebe was here? she wondered. Had Diane sent her to look after her, or to ensure she knew exactly where Olivia was? Perhaps she knew Richard had been in touch with her and she was hoping to catch them out.

'Well, I—haven't made any arrangements,' Olivia murmured now. 'I—had thought of sunbathing by the pool.'

'Sunbathing!' Phoebe grimaced. 'Well—I guess if that's

what you want to do. But, you know, I'd be happy to show you around.'

'Thank you.'

Olivia didn't know what else to say, but happily Phoebe had no such problem. 'And is this your first trip to the States?' she persisted, with interest. 'I know your books have been published here, but…'

Phoebe shrugged, inviting Olivia to respond, and, deciding there was no harm in discussing her work, she replied, 'No. It isn't my first trip across the Atlantic. I visited New York about two years ago, to publicise *Silent Song*.'

'*Silent Song*.' Phoebe nodded. 'That was a wonderful book. Diane and I were both touched by the sensitivity you showed in dealing with such a heart-breaking subject.' She smoothed the rim of her eye with one scarlet-tipped finger, as if wiping away a tear. 'I'm sure the Cusack family were real happy with the way you handled their mother's story.'

Olivia pressed her lips together. She wasn't used to such overt flattery, and it was difficult not to show her embarrassment. 'It was a touching story,' she murmured at last, but Phoebe wasn't finished.

'You're too modest,' she said. 'Believe me, I know what I'm talking about. In my job, I represent all sorts of people, and I get to read novels, biographies, scripts, all kinds of stuff. And, girl, let me tell you, you'd be amazed at some of the stuff that gets into print; you know what I'm saying? Stories that are sick. *Sick!* Not inspiring stuff like yours.'

'Oh, well—'

'It's true.' Those scarlet-tipped fingers descended on Olivia's arm. 'Hey, they'll make movies about anything these days; anything that the producer or the director thinks is going to make a stack of bucks.' She gave a disgusted snort. 'Some of them wouldn't know a class piece of writing if it jumped up and bit them on the neck.'

Olivia shook her head. 'I'm afraid I don't know anything about the film industry,' she protested, wondering if Phoebe was aware that her nails were digging into her arm. 'I'm just a writer—'

'*Just* a writer!' exclaimed Phoebe incredulously, her nails digging deeper, and Olivia had to steel herself to stop from crying out. 'Don't put yourself down, girl. You're a fine writer, a fine biographer, a fine human being, I'm sure. Diane wouldn't have wanted you to write her story if that wasn't true.'

Wouldn't she? Olivia wondered, but she didn't voice her doubts about that particular opinion. She was too busy being relieved that Phoebe had withdrawn her hand.

But the reason she'd done' so wasn't out of kindness. Olivia was surreptitiously rubbing her arm, trying to get the blood circulating around the slash of whitened flesh where the marks of Phoebe's nails still showed, when she became aware that someone else was standing beside the table. She disliked the fact, but she didn't need the evidence of lean hips and powerfully muscled legs beneath the narrow trousers of his navy three-piece suit to guess who it was. She knew his identity immediately, and although she was forced to acknowledge him the look she cast towards his lazily enquiring face was almost insultingly brief.

Happily, Phoebe had no such reservations. 'Hey, Joe!' she exclaimed, even though Olivia sensed she wasn't altogether pleased at the interruption. 'I thought you were locked in high-level negotiations. Diane said that was why you couldn't have breakfast with her.'

'Does Diane tell you everything, Phoebs?' he asked, and although he used what was obviously Diane's name for her there was a certain trace of censure in his voice. Olivia knew he was looking down at her, but she couldn't bring herself to face him. Which was ridiculous, she thought, when she ought to have been grateful that Diane and Richard were probably splitting up because of him.

'Most things,' Phoebe answered now, unconsciously giving Olivia a few more minutes' grace. 'I know she was disappointed,' she added. 'With you just getting back and all. Still, I guess you've got the weekend, don't you? Plenty of time to catch up.'

'It's good to know you've got my weekend mapped out

for me,' he remarked silkily, but Olivia knew she wasn't
mistaken this time: he resented Phoebe's remarks. The
amazing thing was that Phoebe wasn't aware of it. Or, if
she was, she chose to ignore it in favour of Diane.

'Hey, that's what agents are for,' she said now. 'It's my
job to keep Diane happy. You can't argue with that.'

'I wouldn't want to,' he assured her drily. Then, as Olivia
had known he would, he spoke to her. 'It seems you've got
the weekend off, Ms Pyatt.'

Olivia nodded, and then, because it would have looked
odd not to do so, she slanted a gaze up at him. 'That's
right,' she said. 'Um—Ms Isaacs has just offered to take
me shopping on Rodeo Drive.'

'Has she?' His tawny gaze moved to Phoebe again, to
her relief. 'Well, you couldn't be in safer hands,' he remarked mockingly. 'Apart from looking after her clients,
there's nothing Phoebe enjoys more than shopping.' His
hard face tightened for a moment. 'It was—kind of Diane
to make sure you weren't—lonely. I guess this can be a
strange and frightening place.'

Olivia clasped her hands together in her lap. Once again,
she had the distinct impression that what was being said
wasn't the same as what was meant. But she wasn't in a
position to query his comments. It was hard enough to think
of a response.

'I'm sure I'm going to enjoy my stay,' she declared at
last, stung into defending her ability to look after herself.
For all she was obliged to acknowledge his concern, she
wasn't a child, and she resented being made to feel like
one.

'Of course you will,' put in Phoebe before she could
continue. 'Diane and I are going to see to that. Don't you
worry about Olivia, Joe. We'll see she doesn't come to any
harm.'

Joe smiled then, a lazy, knowing smile which, even
though Olivia could see had an element of cynicism in it,
still had the power to curl her toes. 'I'm sure you will,' he
agreed, checking his tie with one brown, long-fingered

hand. 'Well, as they say here, be happy!' And, with a nod to both of them, he walked away.

Olivia made the mistake of expelling the breath she had hardly been aware she was holding, and then wished she hadn't when Phoebe's sharp eyes registered her relief. 'Does he make you nervous?' she asked, watching her closely. 'He's a sexy hunk, isn't he? One of a kind.'

'Oh, really, I—'

'You don't have to be afraid to admit it.' Phoebe shrugged her padded shoulders. 'He affects me, too. I guess that's why Diane's crazy about him.' Her eyes narrowed. 'I'm sure you've realised that she and Ricky are all washed up.'

'No, I—that is—' Olivia took a moment to compose herself. 'Are they?' she asked, in a strangled voice.

'Afraid so,' said Phoebe ruefully. 'Which is a pity. Ricky's a nice guy. He just doesn't have what it takes to hold Diane.'

Olivia was tempted to say, Does anyone? But, remembering the way Diane had reacted to Joe Castellano, she held her tongue. 'Um—maybe they'll work things out,' she said instead, trying not to look towards the exit where Joe and his party were just leaving. She dragged her eyes away. 'She—must have loved him when she married him.'

But once again Phoebe had noticed what Olivia was looking at, and after glancing over her shoulder she impaled the other woman with a sardonic look. 'Yeah,' she said, 'but that was a long time ago, you hear? She's older now and—well, wouldn't you choose Joe instead of Ricky—if you had the chance?'

Olivia flushed and concentrated her attention on the table. 'I really wouldn't know,' she denied, wishing Phoebe would go, too. Then, forcing a smile, she summoned the waiter. 'Please,' she said, 'would you put Ms Isaacs' coffee on my bill?'

If she'd thought her action would shut Phoebe up, she was mistaken. 'Why not?' she drawled. 'Let's make Diane pay for my coffee, too.' Then, as if sensing she'd gone too far, she opened her purse, took out a card, and pushed it across the table. 'There, that's my home number as well as the number of my office. If you need anything—anything at all—just give me a call.'

'Thank you.'

Olivia took the card reluctantly, noting almost absently that Phoebe lived in the Westwood area of the city. She knew from the guidebooks she'd read that that was where most of the new Hollywood films were first shown. She wondered if that was why Phoebe had chosen to be an agent, or whether she'd really wanted to star in films herself.

It wasn't important, and Olivia was relieved when the woman pushed back her chair and got to her feet. For a few anxious moments, before Phoebe had given her her card, she'd been afraid she'd been appointed her watchdog. But no. It seemed that now Joe Castellano had gone Phoebe was perfectly happy to leave her to her own devices.

'Have a nice day,' she said, tucking her purse under her arm in a businesslike manner. 'And if you do decide to leave the hotel, grab a cab.'

Olivia breathed a sigh of relief when the woman left the restaurant, and after giving her time to clear the lobby she followed her out of the door. But the idea of sunbathing seemed to have lost its attraction, and she knew it was the knowledge that she was no longer her own mistress that was spoiling her day.

Still, there was nothing she could do about it now, short of packing up and going back to London, and it was silly to let anything Phoebe had said distress her. For heaven's sake, the woman was Diane's agent. She was bound to be partisan. And she'd known Diane and Richard were having problems before she'd left England.

Feeling more relaxed, she glanced around her. The early morning crowds were dispersing, and the boutiques that lined the corridor to the pool and leisure area were beginning to show signs of life. They wouldn't open until later, but that didn't stop her from window-shopping, admiring

the silk scarves and exquisite items of jewellery that filled
several of the displays.

'You'll have more choice on Rodeo Drive,' remarked a
voice that was becoming embarrassingly familiar to her.
'Where's Phoebs? Has she gone to summon Diane's limousine?'

Olivia swung round. 'Ms Isaacs has left,' she declared
politely. 'I thought you would have, too, Mr Castellano. I
saw—that is, Ms Isaacs mentioned that you were leaving
about fifteen minutes ago.'

'And you didn't notice?'

'I didn't say that.' Olivia held up her head. 'Of course I
did,' she admitted, half afraid he'd seen her watching him.
'But—I understood you had some business meetings to at-
tend to.'

'*One* business meeting,' he corrected her drily. 'And
you'll have noticed that it's over.' He paused. 'So you
thought I'd left the building. Or was that what you were
told? You know, I guess that's what Phoebs thought, too.'

Olivia stiffened at the implication. 'If you think—'

When she broke off, he regarded her enquiringly. 'Yes?
If I think what, Ms Pyatt? Finish what you were going to
say.'

'It doesn't matter,' muttered Olivia unhappily, aware that
she had been in danger of being indiscreet. 'If—if you'll
excuse me, I'm going up to my room. I—er—I've got some
work to do.'

'Today?' He sounded disbelieving, and she wondered
why he was bothering to ask. It wasn't as if it mattered to
him what she did.

'Yes, today,' she said firmly, and saw the cynicism that
crossed his lean face at her words.

'And, of course, you don't mix business with pleasure,'
he taunted lazily, pushing his hands into his trouser pockets.
He rocked back on his heels. 'So there's no point in me
offering to take you out.'

'To take me out?' Olivia stared at him, aghast. 'Why
would you want to do that?'

'Why do you think?' He shrugged. 'Perhaps you interest me.' His brows lifted mockingly. 'Perhaps I find your candour refreshingly—new.'

'Don't you mean *gauche*?' she demanded, convinced now that he was only baiting her. 'If I accepted your invitation, you'd run a mile.'

'Well, I do that, too,' he admitted modestly. 'Exercise is good for the body.'

Olivia sighed. 'Where I come from, people say what they mean.'

'But I am saying what I mean,' he protested. 'You intrigue me. You do. I don't think I've ever met anyone quite so intriguing before.'

'You don't mean that.'

He feigned hurt. 'Why don't you believe me?' He paused. 'Can't we put the past behind us and start again?'

'Start what again?' Olivia shook her head. 'This is just a game to you, isn't it? Do you flirt with every woman who happens to cross your path? If you do, I can understand why Diane sent that Isaacs woman to keep an eye on you. She probably doesn't trust you at all.'

'No?' His attractive mouth twisted. 'And why should you say that unless you think I really am interested in you?'

'I don't—' Olivia was embarrassed now, and she was sure she showed it. She glanced enviously towards the lifts. 'Look, I've got to go.'

'If you insist…' He seemed to accept her ultimatum and she pressed her lips together nervously as she started across the foyer. 'Oh, Olivia,' he called, just before she pressed the button to summon the lift, and she turned apprehensively towards him. 'Don't believe everything you hear.'

CHAPTER SIX

THE rest of the day was an anticlimax.

Despite her determination not to think about Joe Castellano, Olivia couldn't seem to put him out of her mind. Wherever she went in the hotel, she half expected him to be there, waiting for her, and when he wasn't she knew a sense of flatness she'd never experienced before.

It was stupid, she knew, particularly as their conversation had been so antagonistic, but she'd seemed to come alive when she was talking to him. It was his experience, of course, his ability to make any woman feel as if he was interested in her, but she couldn't remember the last time she'd enjoyed talking to a man so much.

Which was pathetic as well as stupid, she thought later that morning as she lounged somewhat restlessly beside the pool. She was letting a man she knew to be involved with someone else interfere with the reasons she was here. Worse than that, he was the man who was involved with the woman she'd come to study. If she'd taken him seriously, she could have been in danger of blowing her commission as well.

In the event, she decided not to leave the hotel that day, and by the time the evening came and she had to start thinking about getting ready to meet Richard she was almost relieved to have something to do. She could have worked, she supposed, as she'd told Joe she intended to do, but she seemed incapable of concentrating on anything—except images of Joe and Diane in each other's arms...

She decided to wear an ankle-length skirt and wraparound top for the evening. The skirt was patterned in blues and greens and the crêpe top was a matching shade of jade. It fitted tightly to her arms and displayed a modest cleavage, as well as leaving a narrow band of exposed flesh at her midriff.

She'd washed her hair after her swim as it was inclined to be unruly. It wasn't much more than shoulder-length, but she thought twisting it into a French braid was probably the safest means of keeping it tame. Red lights glinted in its dark gold strands as she secured the braid at her nape, and she was reasonably pleased with her appearance as she checked her reflection in the mirror.

Not that she could hope to compete with Diane's beauty, she admitted as the thing she had been trying to avoid needled back into her thoughts. She couldn't help wondering if Joe would approve of her appearance, and what he'd really meant by accosting her today. Why had he waited? she wondered. What could he possibly hope to gain by playing such a game? Perhaps he enjoyed living life dangerously. She couldn't believe he'd meant what he'd said.

The phone rang as she was stepping into low-heeled strappy shoes that added a couple of inches to her height, and her heart accelerated in her chest. It couldn't be him, she assured herself. Just because she'd been thinking about him it didn't mean she had some kind of extra perception. But her voice was breathy as she said, 'Hello.'

'Liv!'

Her pulse slowed. 'Richard.'

'Who else?' He sounded more cheerful this evening. 'Shall I come up?'

'No.' Her response was unflatteringly swift. 'No, don't bother,' she added quickly. 'I'll come down.'

Richard was evidently disappointed, but he managed to stifle his frustration and only said stiffly, 'Don't be long.'

'I won't be.'

Olivia replaced the receiver, wondering if this had been the wisest move, after all. Wasn't she just playing into Diane's hands whichever way you looked at it? Whether they ate here or at Diane's house, they were still together.

A glance at her watch told her it was still just a quarter to seven. Richard was early, which accounted for the fact that she hadn't been waiting for him in the bar downstairs. Perhaps he'd planned it that way. Perhaps he'd hoped she'd relent, and invite him for a drink in her suite. It must have been quite a blow when she'd said she'd come down.

Whatever, there was no point in keeping him waiting now. There was always the danger that he might take a chance and come up anyway, and it would be difficult to get rid of him if he was at the door.

A final glance in the mirror assured her that if she wasn't exactly glamorous she had nothing to be ashamed of, and after collecting her purse she left the room. But she couldn't get rid of the feeling that she was making a mistake, and she wished she wasn't such a pushover where Richard was concerned.

He was waiting in the lobby, his blond hair glinting brilliantly in the light. She suspected he'd had a root job since she'd seen him the day before, and in a formal shirt and white tuxedo he looked more like the man she remembered.

'Liv!' Once again, he came eagerly to meet her, but this time she was prepared for him and turned her face aside from his seeking lips. 'Oh, Liv,' he muttered huskily, drawing back to survey her, 'you look bloody marvellous! I can't believe I was such a fool to let you go.'

Olivia managed a smile, but she extricated herself from his clinging hands and glanced around. 'Is that the bar?' she asked unnecessarily as the preponderance of orchids should have given her an answer, and he was obliged to nod and accompany her across the foyer.

'I can't believe you're here,' he said, after they were seated on tall stools at the bar. He would have guided her to a secluded booth in the corner, but Olivia had climbed onto a stool before he could do anything to prevent her. 'White wine, right? You see, I even remember what you used to drink.'

Was she so predictable? Olivia considered the point, conceding to herself that her choice of drink hadn't changed in more than ten years. 'Um—I'd prefer a G and T,' she said, even though she rarely drank spirits, and Richard gave her a startled glance before making the order.

'So,' he said, after their drinks were served—Olivia noticing that he'd ordered a double Jack Daniels for himself. He took a swallow from his glass, evidently savouring the stimulation. 'Here we are again. It's just as if we'd never been apart.'

'Not quite like that,' murmured Olivia drily, wondering if Richard had always deluded himself in this way. When they were married, she'd usually deferred to him, so perhaps he was accustomed to her agreeing with everything he said. But he had to realise that she had changed.

'Okay, okay.' He took another generous gulp of his Scotch. 'I know a lot of water's flowed under the bridge since the old days and we've both had time to regret our mistakes. But we're here now and that's important. It shows that something has survived our separation. We might not be able to forget the past, but we can forgive—'

'Richard—'

'I know what you're going to say.' He held up one hand, as if in conciliation, while raising his glass again with the other. Draining it, he handed the empty glass to the bartender, and Olivia realised the gesture he'd made had not been to her. 'Same again, pal,' he ordered, after a desultory check that her glass was still full. 'But believe me, Liv, I've learned my lesson.' He grimaced. 'But good!'

'Richard, I—'

'You're doing it again.'

She frowned. 'Doing what again exactly?'

'Judging me, before you've heard what I have to say.' The waiter brought his second drink, and he took another mouthful before continuing, 'You're not sure if you can trust me. We've just met again, and you're naturally a little nervous. But I swear to God I mean what I say.'

Olivia decided to say nothing. Sipping her drink, she wondered rather cynically if there was anything significant in the fact that Richard had used the same expression as Bonnie Lovelace had done in the car. Well, whatever, she thought ruefully, it really wasn't important any more. If she felt anything for Richard, it was pity, not love.

He was staring at her now, evidently expecting her to make some comment, and she searched her brain for something uncontroversial to say. 'Er—do you come here often?' she asked, licking a pearl of moisture from her lip. 'I must say, it's a beautiful hotel.'

Richard glowered. There was no other word for it. Then he took another huge swig of his drink before going on.

'It's okay, I guess,' he said indifferently. 'It lacks character, but most things do over here. Give me a beamed ceiling and an open fire any time.'

Olivia rolled her lips inwards. 'A beamed ceiling and an open fire,' she echoed disbelievingly. 'This from the man who wouldn't stay in a thatched cottage in case the roof leaked!'

Richard's expression lightened. 'You see, you do remember!' he exclaimed eagerly. 'Our first anniversary, wasn't it? You wanted to see *Romeo and Juliet* at Stratford, and I said *Cats* was more my thing.'

'Yes.' Olivia sighed. 'I guess we were incompatible even then.'

'No—'

'Yes.' She was firm. 'I suppose I just didn't want to see it. Richard, I'll never forget those years we had together, but I don't want them back.'

Richard's expression darkened again. 'Oh, I see,' he said coldly. 'You're going to punish me. It's not enough that I've spilled my guts to you, you're still determined to have your pound of flesh!'

'Oh, don't be silly.' Olivia was impatient. 'I'm sorry if things haven't worked out for you and Diane, but that's not my fault.'

'Did I say it was?' He had already finished his second drink and was summoning the bartender again. 'Fill it up,' he ordered rudely. Then, to Olivia, 'I've ordered dinner for eight.'

'Eight?'

Olivia repeated the words barely audibly, mentally calculating how many Scotches Richard could consume before then. More than she wanted to think about, she acknowledged, imagining the scene that was likely to ensue. She had no desire for him to make an exhibition of himself here.

'Yes, eight.' Clearly, his hearing hadn't been impaired, and when his third drink arrived he reached eagerly for the glass. He nodded towards her G and T. 'You're not drinking much tonight. Are you sure you wouldn't prefer a glass of wine?'

'No, I—' What she would have preferred was for him to go and sober up. She was firmly convinced now that he'd been drinking before he arrived. 'Um—why don't we go for a walk? I'd enjoy the exercise. I haven't been out of the hotel all day.'

'Are you kidding?' Richard looked at her as if she were mad. 'You can't go walking around the streets at night.'

'It's hardly night—'

'All right. People don't walk here. Except maybe on Rodeo Drive. This isn't Westwood Village, you know.'

'Westwood?' The name struck a chord. 'Oh, yes. That's where Phoebe Isaacs lives.'

'Phoebe? Yeah, it might be.' He frowned. 'How would you know that?'

'She came here. This morning.' Olivia could feel her cheeks filling with colour, but it wasn't because of Phoebe Isaacs. 'Um—she joined me. At breakfast. In the restaurant.'

Richard scowled. 'She joined you for breakfast?' He regarded her with suspicious eyes. 'So, you had time for her but not for me.'

Olivia's lips parted. 'Richard, that was last night—'

'What's the difference?'

'A lot. I was jet-lagged last night.'

'Well, how the hell did she know who you were?'

'My—my picture.' Olivia moistened her lips. 'It's on the back of all my books.' And then, because she was angry at herself for hedging, she added, 'And—and Mr Castellano was there.'

'Joe Castellano?' Richard stared at her through narrowed lids. 'You know Joe Castellano?'

'I've met him,' said Olivia uncomfortably, half wishing she hadn't been so honest after all. 'He—er—he was at Diane's yesterday morning.' She hesitated. 'I believe he has some—some investment in her career.'

'Oh, yeah.' Richard was bitter. 'He has an investment all right.'

Olivia took a deep breath. 'How about that walk?' she asked brightly, not wanting to get into a discussion about Joe Castellano with him. 'If—if you think it's unwise to go outside the hotel, we could always go and look at the shops.'

Richard's jaw clenched. 'So, how well do you know this guy?' he demanded. 'Are you saying he had breakfast with you, too?'

'No—'

''Cos I have to tell you, Di won't like that. Hey, did she know Castellano was going to be there? If she did, that's probably why she sent Isaacs along.'

'He wasn't there,' retorted Olivia hotly, but she disliked the thought that Richard should have had the same thought as she'd had herself. 'He—just pointed me out to Ms Isaacs, that's all.' She slid abruptly off her stool. 'Now, are you coming for a walk or not? I do not intend to sit at this bar for another hour.'

'Another half-hour,' protested Richard, but he must have realised she meant what she said. 'Oh, all right.' He finished his drink and got down from his stool, taking a moment to sign the tab the barman slid across to him. 'We'll go and look around the foyer. You can tell me what you think of macho man!'

Olivia's lips tightened. She refused to be drawn into a discussion about Joe Castellano, and she found she resented the fact that Richard should speak so disparagingly of him. And yet, she acknowledged ruefully, perhaps she shouldn't blame Richard. It couldn't be easy for him competing with a man who seemed to be everything he was not.

The shops in the foyer were still open. Their signs indicated that they would be so until ten o'clock. A long day, thought Olivia, recognising one of the sales assistants she'd seen earlier. But the girl was still as immaculately made up as she'd been that morning.

'He's sleeping with her, you know,' Richard persisted, when Olivia stopped to look in a jeweller's window. 'Castellano, I mean. Theirs isn't just a business arrangement.'

'It's nothing to do with me,' said Olivia tightly. 'Um— that ring's beautiful, isn't it? My God, it's fifty thousand dollars! I thought it was five thousand at first.'

'Chicken feed,' said Richard carelessly, scarcely paying any attention to the ring she was admiring. 'Diane spends more than that on her personal trainer, and all he does is supervise what exercise she's taking in the gym.' He grimaced. 'His name's Lorenzo; can you believe it? Lorenzo MacNamara! Isn't that a hoot?'

Olivia blew out a breath. 'If you're going to talk about Diane all evening—'

'I'm not.' Once again, he seemed to realise he was going too far. 'But you can't blame me if I get aggrieved sometimes. And it's so good to have someone —sympathetic— to talk to.'

Sympathetic? Olivia frowned. Was she? She was frustrated, perhaps, and a little resentful that Richard should think she'd be willing to take up where they'd left off, but sympathetic? She didn't know if she was that.

'Anyway,' he continued, tucking his hand through her arm, 'I promise not to talk about Diane and her—well, Castellano, any more. How's that?'

Olivia forced a smile. 'Good,' she said, wishing she could put them out of her thoughts so easily. Instead of which, she spent the remainder of the evening half wishing Richard would tell her what their connection was. Did Joe intend to marry Diane when she was free? Was that an option? From what she knew of Castellano, she couldn't see him as anyone's pawn.

By Sunday evening, Olivia had done some preliminary work on the computer the hotel had supplied for her. She'd precis-ed her initial impressions of Los Angeles, and typed out the notes she'd made before she left England. She had several tapes of interviews, but she'd left them back in London. She hadn't wanted to take the risk that they might get lost during her trip.

She'd bought some magazines in the drug store downstairs and spent Sunday afternoon checking for pictures of Diane. She thought it would be interesting to read another person's point of view of her subject, but in the event she'd found nothing of any note. Except an edition of *Forbes* that featured the brilliant tycoon, Joseph Castellano. Although she'd despised herself for doing so, she'd bought the magazine and read every word of the article about him.

Which had told her a lot more than Richard had confided. Although he'd broken his promise not to talk about his wife several times during the dinner they'd had together on Friday night, his comments concerning her relationship with the other man had been judgmental at best. He didn't like Castellano—which was reasonable in the circumstances. But not every word he'd said about him was true.

For instance, he'd said that Joe was sleeping with Diane, but there'd been no mention of their association in the article Olivia had read. On the contrary, the woman who most often featured in the article was someone called Anna Fellini. They were partners in a winery that was situated in the Napa Valley.

There'd been lots more, of course: about his investments in the film industry and banking, and the fact that he owned a string of luxury hotels. She'd been disturbed to find that he owned the Beverly Plaza. It was just one of several along the coastal strip.

That kind of success was overwhelming, and she'd been glad she hadn't read the article before they'd met. She would never have dared to say what she'd said to him on Friday morning, she thought, with a shiver of remorse. It was just as well he'd gone away for the weekend.

The last two days had passed reasonably quickly, she acknowledged as she closed down the computer. On Saturday morning, she'd taken a cab to Century City, and spent a couple of hours wandering in what was really an extensive shopping mall. Then, on Sunday morning, she'd visited Rodeo Drive, buying herself some expensive perfume she didn't really need.

She'd taken most of her meals in her room, preferring not to run the gauntlet of open curiosity. Except at breakfast, when she felt less conspicuous, and the waiter, whose name she now knew was Carlos, made sure she always had a table in the window.

She'd missed Henry, of course. When she was working, he often came to sit on the window-ledge beside her, hissing his disapproval when he saw a dog go by in the street. She missed the Harley, too. At weekends, she often took the old machine for a spin.

But, for the most part, she'd been too busy to feel homesick, although she had to admit she was not looking forward to the following day. Having been made an unwilling party to the problems Richard and Diane were having, she couldn't help being influenced by them, and her own association with the man who was causing their unhappiness didn't help.

It was ironic, she thought. She had come here more than ready to take advantage of the situation. Indeed, it had been the knowledge that Richard's marriage was in difficulties that had persuaded her to take the commission. Until then, she'd been adamant that nothing Kay said could change her mind, but the tantalising prospect of comforting the man she'd believed she still loved had swung the balance.

Yet now, after only a few days, she knew that the image she'd kept of Richard over the years wasn't real. Had never been real, she suspected. She'd just made it so. The destruction of her marriage had been so painful, so unexpected, she'd convinced herself that everything Richard had done had been manipulated by Diane. Now, she had to admit to being doubtful. She couldn't believe that Richard had changed that much.

And Diane...

Getting up from the table where she had been working, Olivia stretched her arms above her head and gave a sigh. She didn't like her, she thought, but she could admire her. And perhaps Kay was right. Perhaps this *would* be good for her writing career.

CHAPTER SEVEN

OLIVIA had dreaded going back to Diane's on Monday morning, but in the event her fears proved groundless. A call from Diane's secretary, Bonnie Lovelace, first thing Monday morning confirmed that Manuel would pick her up at nine-thirty sharp, and when she arrived at the Beverly Hills mansion Diane was waiting for her in a sunlit sitting room off the entrance hall.

The sitting room was small compared to the arching atrium, but Olivia guessed her own sitting room would fit into it several times over. It was furnished in limed oak, with chairs and sofas upholstered in flowery pastels, and once again there were flowers everywhere, scenting the cool, conditioned air.

Diane herself was fully dressed this morning, but the businesslike suit of dark blue linen only accentuated her blonde good looks. Nevertheless, she was apparently prepared to treat the interview with all seriousness, and although she greeted Olivia courteously her mind was obviously on other things.

'Please, sit down,' she said, indicating the chair opposite her at a marble-topped table by the flower-filled hearth. 'Did you have a good weekend?'

'I—yes.' Olivia was taken aback by her change of attitude. Gone was any attempt at familiarity, and in its place was a cool politeness that Olivia decided she preferred. 'I went shopping,' she added, sure Diane wasn't really interested. She would have liked to ask, Did you? but she wasn't sure she wanted to hear the reply.

'Good.' But Diane's response was absent. 'Then, if you're ready, I suggest we get down to work.' She paused, and for a moment Olivia caught a glimpse of the woman she'd met before. 'That is,' she appended, 'if you're still interested in the commission. I realise I haven't given you an opportunity to say what you think.'

Olivia hesitated. *Tell her you can't do it*, a small voice urged her, and she knew this was her last chance to back away. But, although she had the feeling she would live to regret it, some perverse impulse was egging her on.

'I'm still interested,' she said, but her hand shook a little as she removed her tape recorder from her bag and put it on the table. But fortunately Diane didn't appear to notice. Her expression mirrored a satisfaction all its own. Who was she thinking about? Olivia wondered. Richard or Joe Castellano? And once again that small voice mocked her for even having to ask.

Yet, for all that, the next two weeks were productive ones for Olivia. Diane had arranged things so that most of her mornings were free of other commitments, and, although there were occasions when Bonnie Lovelace rang to cancel an appointment, on the whole Olivia's visits were treated with respect.

Olivia soon discovered that, like many women in her sphere of entertainment, Diane enjoyed talking about her childhood. Although it had been far from happy—she pulled no punches when she talked about the stepfather who had abused her—she seemed to regard those years as character-forming. They were past now, so therefore they couldn't hurt her, and if she chose to embellish any of the details there was no one likely to contradict her now.

Her own mother and father were dead, she explained without emotion. Her parents had never been married and Diane had hardly known the Scandinavian seaman who her mother had maintained had sired her. She had died fairly recently, Diane continued with rather more feeling. She'd always neglected herself when her children were young, and although things had been easier for her since Diane became successful she hadn't discovered she had a terminal form of cancer until it was too late.

Diane's brothers and sisters were scattered around the globe, with one of them settled a comparatively short distance away in Nevada. They all kept in touch, she said with some pride, but it wasn't always easy because they had family commitments. She regretted not having any children, she added, but her career came first and she considered she still had plenty of time.

Olivia had wanted to ask her then if Richard had had a part in her decision. Remembering his cruel denunciation of her for not giving him a child, she couldn't believe he'd accepted it without complaint. But perhaps it was enough to be married to an icon. She could hardly compare Diane's situation to hers.

And she reminded herself that she wasn't here to question Diane's lifestyle. It might just be that she didn't consider Richard a suitable father for her child. Of course, Olivia had no doubt about whom Diane would consider a suitable candidate for fatherhood. Although she hadn't encountered Joe Castellano again, she had no doubt that he and Diane continued to see one another on a regular basis.

In any case, she'd found it safer not to dwell on their relationship. Imagining what they did together would have caused her far too many sleepless nights. As it was, it was too easy to let thoughts of him dominate her consciousness, so she did her best not to think about him at all.

She'd seen little of Richard either, which was equally a bonus. According to Diane, he was a keen golfer these days, and his absence from the estate was due to the fact that he'd flown to Las Vegas to take part in a tournament there. In a rare moment of confidence, Diane had hinted that he usually spent more time in the clubhouse than on the golf course, but Olivia had chosen not to comment. She was just relieved that he wasn't around to complicate the situation.

Despite her working schedule, Olivia also found time to do some sightseeing. Her afternoons were usually free, and she'd found she could work just as easily in the evenings. In consequence, she joined several of the organised tours around the area, visiting Disneyland and Universal Studios, as well as the breathtaking beauty of the Orange coast.

She was beginning to feel at home in the hotel, too. Now that she'd become accustomed to its noise and bustle—and she'd stopped being afraid she was going to meet the hotel's owner round every corner—she often booked a table in one of the restaurants, and spent some time people-watching from behind her menu before going up to her room to do some more work.

The hotel certainly attracted a lot of famous people. The main restaurant—the Pineapple Room—was renowned for its excellent cuisine, and Olivia appreciated how lucky she was to be able to dine there every night if she wished. Sometimes, she chose the Bistro, which concentrated on Italian food. And real Italian food, she acknowledged. Not the fast-food variety she was used to eating back home.

It was just as well she didn't have to worry about putting on weight, she thought one evening about three weeks after her arrival. She was sitting in the Bistro, enjoying a luscious pizza with all the trimmings, while the anorexic woman at the next table was picking at a Caesar salad, and sending envious looks in her direction. Olivia thought how awful it must be to be always counting the calories. Did Diane do that? Was that how she stayed so slim?

Her thoughts broke off at that moment. Swallowing rapidly, she put down her knife and fork and stared disbelievingly across the room. Either she was hallucinating, or that was Joe Castellano sitting at a table half-hidden by the trailing greenery. He was alone, she saw; or perhaps his companion had left the table for a few minutes. Either way, he wasn't paying much attention to what he was eating. He appeared to be reading papers from a file that was propped beside his plate.

He hadn't seen her. Or if he had he'd chosen to ignore her. And who could blame him? she mused, remembering how she'd responded the last time he'd spoken to her. She'd been little short of rude and that wasn't like her.

But how was she supposed to behave when a man like him came on to her? It had amused him to make fun of her, that was all, and if she'd fallen for it she'd have been a fool. Of course, he might just have wanted to be friendly and she'd overreacted because of what she knew of him. Surely she wasn't considering Diane's feelings? She would really be a fool to do that.

She looked down at her plate consideringly. If Diane found out he was seeing someone else, what would she do? She didn't appear to care about Anna Fellini, but she was just his business partner. If there was someone else, would her marriage to Richard stand a chance?

She blew out a breath. Not that she owed Richard any favours, but who'd be glad to get him off her back. Joe Castellano's feelings were not her problem. If he was having an affair with a married woman, he deserved everything he got.

She looked up again. Joe hadn't moved. He was still sitting there, scanning the papers he'd taken from the file and sipping his wine. A desolate sigh escaped her. Could she do it? With Diane as a rival, she didn't really stand a chance.

Was he alone? It seemed he was. Stretching her neck in his direction, she could see no evidence that anyone else was dining at his table. The woman at the next table was staring openly at her now and Olivia forced a rueful smile. Did she have the nerve to speak to him? she wondered. And if she did, what did she expect him to say in return?

She took a deep breath. It was ludicrous. For heaven's sake, Richard had left her for Diane and Joe Castellano was infatuated with her, too. What possible chance did she have of attracting his attention? She was tilting at windmills if she imagined she could change his mind.

But... She sighed. She'd never know unless she did something about it. Yet did she really want to get involved in something like this? She frowned. It could be fun, she supposed, but it could also be dangerous. Not just for her peace of mind but because of her career.

Yet she wasn't planning on making a serious commitment, she reminded herself. And it might just save Richard's marriage, after all. And revenge? her conscience chided, bringing a wave of heat to moisten her hairline. She wouldn't have been human if she hadn't thought about that. She sighed. The truth was, her motives were complicated. She wasn't sure what she hoped to achieve.

And she wouldn't achieve anything if she continued sitting here, staring at her congealing pizza, she acknowledged. She glanced down at what she was wearing, wishing she'd dressed with more care, as she did when she dined in the Pineapple Room. Not that her black trousers and cropped black vest were unattractive. But a slinky dress might have helped her to feel more like a *femme fatale*.

'Don't I know you?' As Olivia was trying to summon up the courage to make her move, the woman at the next table, who had been staring at her, spoke to her. 'You're Elizabeth Jennings, aren't you? Oh, this is so exciting! I love the role you play in *Cat's Crusade*.'

Olivia's jaw dropped. 'Oh, no,' she said, hardly able to believe that anyone could have mistaken her for a television personality. 'I'm sorry. You're mistaken. I'm not Elizabeth Jennings, I'm afraid.'

'Are you sure?' The woman had got up from the table she had been sharing with a male companion and approached Olivia's table. 'You're so like her—and you've got an English accent, too.'

'Well, I'm sorry,' said Olivia again, unhappily aware that they were attracting an audience. 'Um—it's very kind of you to say so, but I can assure you I'm not an actress at all.' She pushed back her chair and got to her feet just as Joe Castellano did the same at the other side of the restaurant, and when he turned his head to see what was going on across the room their eyes met.

It was not the way she'd wanted to do it. She'd planned on sauntering by his table and pretending surprise when she noticed who it was. Now, she was caught in the middle of what was rapidly becoming an embarrassing situation. Despite her denials, the woman seemed unwilling to accept the truth.

However, Joe Castellano seemed to sum up the situation

in an instant. Whether he'd heard what the other woman had said, she didn't know, but he didn't walk away. His eyes narrowed for a moment and then, picking up the file he'd been reading, he walked casually towards them. In navy trousers and a matching button-down shirt he looked absurdly familiar—and Olivia had never been so glad to see anyone in her life.

'Olivia,' he said, by way of an acknowledgement, and the woman who had mistaken her for a celebrity produced a frown.

'You're really not Elizabeth Jennings!' she exclaimed as her companion came to join her. 'But you must be an actress. I'm sure I know your face.'

'Perhaps you've seen it on the jacket of one of her books,' remarked Joe smoothly, and the woman's lips parted in a triumphant smile.

'Of course,' she cried. 'You're a writer. Oh, may I have your autograph? I'm an avid reader, you know. I must have read one of your books.'

Joe's brows arched in silent humour as the woman bent to search her purse for a pen and paper, and, meeting his gaze, Olivia felt a surge of excitement herself. It was as if they were sharing more than just this moment, and she decided the woman's intervention hadn't been such a bad thing, after all.

With Olivia's signature on the back of an envelope, the woman was persuaded back to her table, and Joe pulled a wry face as he watched her retreat. 'Sorry about that,' he said. 'We try to ensure that our guests aren't troubled by autograph hunters.' He smiled, and Olivia felt warm all over. 'Though I must admit you do look rather familiar to me, too.'

'Well, I'm sure *she* doesn't know me from Adam,' she murmured modestly. 'I doubt if she's even seen—let alone read—any of my books.'

'Don't underestimate yourself.' His tawny eyes glinted humorously. 'And no one could mistake you for Adam in that outfit.'

'Why, thank you.' Olivia's breath seemed to be caught in the back of her throat. 'That was a nice thing to say.'

'But true,' he declared easily. 'With that tan, you look as if you should be famous, and that's what counts here.'

Olivia bent to pick up her bag. She wasn't embarrassed exactly, but no one had paid her such a compliment before. And then, because she knew she'd never have such an opportunity again, she turned to him. 'If you've got time, perhaps you'd let me buy you a drink.' She hesitated. 'To make up for the way I behaved the last time we met.'

They walked towards the exit together. As he hadn't answered her yet, she didn't know if he wanted her company or not. But once they were outside in the foyer he turned to face her, and she endeavoured to look more confident than she felt.

'You want to buy me a drink?' he queried disbelievingly, and she nodded. 'Hey—what happened just now wasn't your fault.'

'I know that. But that's not the point.' Olivia gripped her bag with nervous fingers. 'Actually, I'd be glad of your company. I don't like going into a bar on my own.'

Joe regarded her intently. 'Do you mean that?'

'Of course.' Olivia licked her dry lips before continuing, 'You can tell me all about this woman, Elizabeth Jennings.' She forced a laugh. 'Being mistaken for her—is it a compliment or not?'

If he was puzzled by her change of attitude, he chose not to show it. 'Okay,' he said. 'You've got a deal, if you'll let me buy you a drink instead.'

'Why not?' She felt a little dizzy with her success. 'Whoever said we had to stop at one?'

The foyer was reasonably quiet at this hour of the evening, and no one took any notice of them as they strolled across to the Orchid Bar. Olivia knew a moment's panic at the thought that Richard might be propping up the bar, but then she calmed herself. So what if he was? she chided. She wasn't doing anything wrong.

Except flirting with the boyfriend of the woman whose

biography she was researching, her conscience reminded her. This wasn't the way she usually behaved. That was the truth. But what did she have to lose? she argued impatiently. If Diane chose to sever her contract, so what?

So, she'd go back to England, she acknowledged flatly. But at least she'd have the satisfaction of knowing she'd done what she could. To destroy Diane's relationship, or to save Richard's marriage? she wondered ruefully. She wasn't absolutely sure, she admitted honestly. And what about her own self-esteem?

'D'you want to sit at the bar?' asked Joe as they entered the subdued lighting of the cocktail lounge, but, glancing about her, Olivia noticed an empty booth against the wall.

'How about there?' She pointed, squashing the memory of how she'd responded to Richard when he'd made the same suggestion. And when Joe nodded his agreement she started across the room.

The booths were cushioned in dark blue velvet and they had scarcely seated themselves before the waiter was there to serve them. 'Good evening, Mr Castellano,' he said, and Olivia wondered if he was surprised at whom his employer was escorting this evening. 'What can I get you, sir—' his smile included Olivia '—and madam?'

Joe arched a brow at Olivia, and she said, 'A martini, please,' as if she never drank anything else.

'A club soda for me,' said Joe, when the waiter turned to him, and Olivia couldn't suppress a little gasp. 'I've got work to do later,' he explained, when the waiter had walked away.

'Work?' Although she'd been taken aback by his decision, Olivia refused to let it daunt her. After all, she didn't want him to have the excuse that he'd been drunk. She cupped her chin in her hands and looked at him. 'Isn't it a little late to be making that excuse?' She moistened her lips with the tip of her tongue. 'If you didn't want to have a drink with me, you should have said so.'

Joe's eyes narrowed sardonically. 'As I recall, the deal was that you should have a drink with me, providing I dished the dirt on Mrs T—Mrs Torrance, that is. Catherine Torrance. She's the sexy private eye from *Cat's Crusade*.'

Sexy?

Olivia swallowed the protest that rose automatically to her lips. 'You mean this Catherine Torrance is the Cat in the title?'

'And the role that Elizabeth Jennings plays.'

Olivia shook her head. 'And—you've seen it?'

'A couple of times,' he acknowledged. 'It's not bad.'

'And—do you think I look anything like this Elizabeth Jennings?' Olivia asked curiously, and then coloured at the look that crossed his face.

'Maybe,' he said, studying her unnervingly. 'I'd have to know you better before I decide.'

'I meant—in appearance,' muttered Olivia, with some embarrassment, before realising he was only teasing her again.

As luck would have it, the waiter returned with their drinks at that moment, and Olivia took an impulsive gulp of hers to give herself some Dutch courage. Unfortunately the gin in the martini was stronger than she'd expected, and the sharpness of it caught the back of her throat. She had to swallow several times to stop herself from coughing. Some seductress, she thought. Did she really think he'd be deceived by her attempts to appear experienced with men?

'So, how are you and Diane getting on?' he asked, after a moment, and she guessed he was only being polite. He must know perfectly well how she and Diane were faring. Unlike Richard, he hadn't been in Las Vegas for the past ten days.

'Pretty good,' she replied casually, relieved to hear her voice sounded normal. She'd been half afraid she'd scraped her vocal chords raw. But she didn't want to talk about Diane. That wasn't her objective. 'Um—I haven't seen you around the hotel for—for a couple of weeks.'

His lips twitched. 'Since that morning you accused me of flirting with every woman I came into contact with?' he asked softly. 'Well, no. I went home to San Francisco when my business meetings were done.'

'San Francisco!' Olivia heard her voice rising and quickly controlled it. 'Oh, yes. Didn't—didn't Diane say that that was where you lived?'

'When I can,' he conceded, swallowing a mouthful of his soda. The ice clinked in his glass, and she thought what a pleasant sound it was. But his voice was better. 'In my business, I spend a lot of time travelling. But I'm learning to delegate if I want some time to myself.'

'And do you?' she asked, feeling on safer ground. She picked up her glass and cooled her palms around it. Then she tipped her head and looked up at him through her lashes. 'Want some time to yourself, I mean?'

'Doesn't everyone?' he asked, and although she was feeling more confident his words disturbed her. She had the feeling he knew exactly what she had in mind.

'That depends,' she said, tasting her drink with rather more caution. 'Not everyone knows exactly what they want.'

'Do you?' he asked, relaxing back against the velvet upholstery, and when he stretched his legs she was made aware of how close his thigh was to hers.

What would he do if she touched him? she wondered. If she put her hand on his knee, would he stop looking at her in that teasing way? But what would she do if he covered her hand with his, and moved closer to her? How far was she prepared to go to prove her point?

A finger stroking lightly down her bare arm startled her. 'I guess you don't,' he said huskily, and for a moment she didn't have any idea what he meant. She'd been so intent on her thoughts, so bemused by the notion of getting close to him, that she'd lost the initiative. 'Can I get you another of those?' He indicated her drink. 'I'm going to have another soda myself.'

'Oh—' Olivia was about to say no, and then changed her mind. 'Why not?' she murmured, burying her face in her glass. She needed more time for this to work, she told herself firmly. If she let him go now, she didn't know when she'd see him again.

'Diane said you and Ricky were still married when she met him,' Joe remarked after the waiter had served them, and Olivia stared at him in surprise.

'Yes, we were,' she said, although she would have preferred not to talk about her ex-husband either. 'Um—have you known Diane long?'

'About two years,' he conceded, propping his elbows on the table. He stirred the ice in his glass with one finger and then licked its tip. He was watching her all the time, and she thought how incredibly sexy his action had been. 'How long has Ricky been drinking? Do you know?'

'No.' Now Olivia was defensive. 'He didn't drink when he was married to me. Well—only socially,' she added, forced to be honest. 'You should ask Diane that question. She should know.'

Joe drew the corner of his lower lip between his teeth. He had nice teeth, she noticed, very white with just a trace of crookedness in the middle. 'Do I take it you don't like Diane?' he queried.

'I—neither like nor dislike her,' protested Olivia, and she suddenly knew that was true. She sighed. 'I admit I was doubtful about accepting this commission. But, in the event, I think we get on together fairly well.'

'And Ricky?'

'Richard,' Olivia corrected him. And then, taking another gulp of her martini, she pulled a wry face. 'I think Richard thinks I'm still in love with him. That's why he believes I agreed to come out here. '

'And is it?'

'No.' Olivia was feeling increasingly reckless. 'I'm not in love with anyone right now.'

'There's no special man in England?' Joe asked, meeting her eyes across the rim of his glass. 'You know, I find that very hard to believe.'

'No special man,' Olivia insisted, without hesitation. 'I'd like there to be, but all the men I'm attracted to are either married or involved with someone else.' She licked her lips. 'Like you,' she ventured, wondering if she was drunk or just stupid. 'I think I was wrong about you. You're nice.'

Joe regarded her from between his lashes. 'You'll regret saying that tomorrow,' he murmured, stroking the back of her hand, which was lying on the table beside her glass. 'And I'm not nice, Olivia,' he added softly. 'I'm quite nasty. For instance, I'm tempted to prove you don't mean what you say.'

Olivia blinked. 'How do you know I don't mean it?' she demanded. She looked down at his hand caressing hers and felt the blood surging hotly though her veins. 'And how could you prove it? I'm not an innocent, you know. I have been married.'

'To Ricky,' said Joe mockingly, and she pursed her lips.

'Yes, to Richard,' she agreed, wishing he wouldn't keep talking about him. She blew out a breath to cool her cheeks. 'He's a man, isn't he?'

'Yes.' Joe's fingers touched her knuckles. 'Do you know a lot about men?'

'Not a lot.' Olivia's wasn't drunk enough to lie about something like that. 'Um—enough.'

'From Ricky?'

'From Richard,' she conceded again. Then, because he seemed to be playing with her, she added, 'I suppose it's too much to expect you to show him some respect.'

'Did I say I didn't respect him?'

'You didn't have to.'

'Really?' He frowned. 'Well, as a matter of fact, I don't know him well enough to judge. He tends to act the heavy when I'm around.'

'Do you blame him?'

Olivia was defensive now, and Joe's mouth took on a sardonic slant. 'Well, evidently you don't,' he remarked, withdrawing his hand and breathing deeply. 'Are you sure you're not still in love with him?'

'No.' Olivia wished she hadn't spoken so impulsively. 'I—I feel sorry for him, that's all.'

'Oh.' Joe pulled a face. 'Sorry for him. The death-knell of any relationship.' He gave a humorous smile. 'I hope you never feel sorry for me.'

'As if I would!' Olivia was impatient.

Joe's smile was a little ironic now. 'Why? You don't think I can be hurt?'

'I didn't say that.' Olivia sighed and pressed her lips together for a moment. 'I only meant that you don't really care what I think.'

'Don't I?'

'I don't think so.'

'And you're an expert, are you?'

'No.' Olivia drew her lower lip between her teeth. 'But perhaps I'd like to have the chance to find out.' She caught her breath, shocked at her own audacity. 'If you cared what I think we wouldn't be sitting here arguing about it, would we?'

Joe regarded her impassively. 'What would we be doing?' he asked, but she knew he didn't really expect her to tell him. He was far too sophisticated to respond to her amateur psychology, but, looking at his lean, hard mouth, Olivia knew exactly what she wanted to do.

'I'll show you,' she said, leaning closer, and, cupping her hand against his cheek, she kissed his mouth.

CHAPTER EIGHT

His withdrawal was not flattering. But then, she could hardly blame him for not responding to her advances in a public place. This was his hotel, for heaven's sake. He was probably cringing at the thought that one of his staff might have seen them. How could she have been so stupid? She'd probably destroyed any chance of retaining his friendship, let alone anything else.

'I'm sorry.'

The words spilled automatically from her lips, her head clearing and allowing her to see exactly how foolishly she'd behaved. She desperately wanted to leave, to avoid any further humiliation, but when she would have slid along the banquette to make her escape his hand descended on her knee.

It was funny, she thought, trying to quell her panic. When she'd tried to imagine how he would react if she put her hand on his knee she'd never expected that their positions might be reversed. And his fingers were strong and masculine. She just knew that if she tried to pull away he'd cause a scene.

'Stay where you are,' he said, and the harshness of his tone brooked no argument. 'It's my own fault. I shouldn't have baited you. Though, in my own defence, I have to say I didn't think you'd take me seriously.'

The words 'I didn't!' trembled on Olivia's tongue but she swallowed them back. She would have liked to say something flip and belittling in return, but she couldn't think of anything. And in any case he'd have known it for what it was: a pitiful attempt to redeem her self-respect. So, instead, she told the truth. 'You were right,' she said, with a careless shrug. 'I don't know enough about men.'

Joe's voice was gentler. 'I wouldn't say that.'

'Wouldn't you?' Olivia still couldn't look at him. She looked down at his hand instead, still gripping her knee, and as if he'd just realised what he was doing Joe pulled his hand away. 'I suppose that's because you're too polite.'

'I'm not polite!' he retorted savagely, and then, expelling a weary breath, added, 'For God's sake, Olivia, stop beating up on yourself, will you? It was a kiss, right? Maybe I'm not used to beautiful women making passes at me.'

Beautiful women?

Olivia wanted to laugh, but there was no humour in it. She wasn't beautiful and he knew that. It was just his way of getting out of a difficult situation.

'Please,' she said, and now she turned her head because she wanted to see his lying face, 'don't treat me like a fool!'

'I'm not.' His nostrils flared with sudden impatience, and his strange cat's eyes darkened until they looked almost black. 'Come on.' He took her arm. 'Let's get out of here.'

And do what? she wondered, but she had no intention of staying around to find out. She went with him because she had no choice with his hard fingers circling the flesh of her upper arm, but once they were outside the bar she broke free of him.

'Thanks for the drink,' she said politely, as if there were nothing more between them than a casual acquaintance. 'Goodnight.'

'Wait!'

He caught up with her before she reached the lifts, and she turned to him with what she hoped appeared to be cool composure. 'Yes?'

'Tomorrow,' he said grimly. 'What are you doing tomorrow?'

Olivia's eyes widened. She couldn't help it. 'I—I'm working,' she faltered unevenly, and then despised herself for sounding so weak.

'All day?' he demanded, and she struggled to recover her self-control.

'Why?' she asked stiffly, and, aware that they were attracting a lot of unwelcome attention, he stifled an oath.

'You just work in the mornings, don't you?' he asked, in a low, angry voice, and because she didn't want to embarrass herself any more than she'd done already Olivia nodded. 'Okay.' He took a breath. 'Let me—make amends for this evening's fiasco by taking you to the beach. What do you say?'

Olivia's breath seemed constricted to the back of her throat. 'I—I don't know what to say—'

'Then don't say anything,' he advised shortly. 'I'll meet you here, by the elevators, at two o'clock.'

Olivia licked lips that were suddenly dry with anticipation. 'I—all right.'

God knew why she'd accepted, she chided herself as she went up in the lift to the penthouse floor. But she had and she was going to have to live with it. Or regret it, as the case may be...

When Manuel came to pick her up the next morning, Richard was with him.

She hadn't spoken to her ex-husband for more than two weeks, and she'd come to enjoy the short journey between the hotel and Diane's house. Manuel didn't talk a lot, but he was friendly, and they'd established an easy rapport that was both comfortable and undemanding. Finding Richard lounging in the back of the limousine was not welcome, and she was afraid that her expression showed it.

'Some surprise, eh?' remarked Richard, with obvious resentment at her reaction. 'Foolishly, I thought you might be glad to see me.'

Olivia sighed. 'I am, of course,' she said, without much conviction. 'Did you have a good trip?'

'Oh, you noticed?'

'Noticed what?'

'That I'd been away,' retorted Richard shortly. And then he said to Manuel, 'Get this heap moving, can't you?'

Olivia sucked in a breath and exchanged a helpless look with the chauffeur. She felt embarrassed for Manuel and herself, and she wondered why Richard had chosen to announce his return in this way.

'I knew you'd gone to Las Vegas,' she said now as Manuel drove onto Santa Monica Boulevard. 'Ms Haran mentioned something about a golf tournament.'

'Ms Haran!' Richard was scornful. 'You're not still calling her Ms Haran, are you? For God's sake, Liv, her name's Diane. You didn't call her Ms Haran when you first met her.'

'No.'

But Olivia refused to be drawn into a discussion about how they'd met. And, in all honesty, she always thought of her as Diane. But she now never addressed her as anything other than 'Ms Haran'.

'Anyway, I understand you're still working on the biography,' Richard went on disparagingly. 'I'm surprised you haven't been at one another's throats before now.'

'Because of you?'

Olivia's tone was more incredulous than she'd have liked and it inspired exactly the reaction she'd hoped to avoid. 'Why not?' he snarled. 'You haven't convinced me, you know. You didn't come out here just to write a book. You had something else in mind.'

Olivia sighed. 'You can think what you like,' she said, looking out of the window and wishing she'd stuck to her original intention to get herself a rental car. But she'd fallen into the habit of letting Manuel drive her, deciding that it was probably safer as she didn't really know her way around.

'Oh, Liv—' His next words were spoken in an entirely different tone and she prayed he wasn't going to try and rekindle their relationship again. 'I know you despise me for letting myself get into this situation, but have a little pity, will you? I need your support.'

Olivia shook her head. 'I don't despise you,' she protested, but she wondered if that was really true. She blew out a breath. 'I'd like to think we could remain friends.'

'Friends!' His voice rose again. 'Like Diane and Joe Castellano are friends, you mean?'

Olivia hesitated 'I—I don't know what—what Diane and Mr Castellano are,' she murmured unhappily. 'I just meant—'

'Well, I'd like us to be friends that way, too!' exclaimed Richard harshly. 'That way, we'd be together, every chance we got.'

'I don't think—'

Olivia started to say that she didn't think Diane and Joe were together every chance they got and then broke off. She had no desire to have to explain how she felt equipped to make that kind of claim, but Richard wouldn't leave it alone.

'You don't think what?' he demanded, half turning towards her. 'That Castellano and my wife aren't having an affair? Give me a break, Liv. I've got proof.'

Olivia swallowed. 'Proof?' she said faintly, unwilling to admit why she was humouring him in this way.

'Yeah, proof,' said Richard smugly. 'And she knows it.'

Olivia glanced towards the back of Manuel's head. 'Well, I—'

'Does it make a difference?'

Richard's question was urgent, but Olivia felt uncharacteristically blank. 'A difference?' she said, blinking. 'A difference to what?'

'To you and me, of course. To us!' Richard captured one of her hands before she could stop him and brought it to his lips. 'I love you, Liv.'

'Don't say that!' She cast another horrified look in Manuel's direction as she snatched her hand away. 'Richard, please, there is no us! And you know it.'

'I can't accept that,' he declared bitterly. 'I've just not given you enough time, that's all.'

'Time?' Olivia shook her head. 'Time for what?'

'To forgive me,' said Richard doggedly. 'I know you want to.'

Olivia stifled a groan. 'I have forgiven you, Richard, but

that doesn't mean I want you back.' She saw the gates of Diane's mansion up ahead and moved forward in her seat. 'I'm sorry.'

'You will be,' muttered Richard, flinging open his door as soon as the limousine stopped, and without waiting for her to alight he lurched up the steps and into the house, almost knocking María off her feet.

'Meester Haig is one angry *hombre*,' remarked Manuel wryly as he helped Olivia out of the car, and she was glad of his cheerful grin to restore her composure.

'Isn't he though?' she agreed ruefully, looping the strap of her bag over her shoulder. 'I'm sorry you had to be a party to that, Manuel.'

'Hey, no sweat,' Manuel assured her as his wife came down the steps to greet them. 'You're okay, aren't you, *chiquita*?' And at his wife's nod he said, 'I see you later, Mees Pyatt, okay?'

'Okay.'

Olivia gave María an apologetic smile but her mind was already leaping towards the afternoon ahead. She had the feeling she was a fool to get any deeper involved in Diane's affairs than she already was.

As usual, Diane was waiting for her in her sitting room, but this morning her slim figure was wrapped in the peacock blue kimono she'd apparently donned after taking her bath. Her hair was still damp and tousled, and the remains of the continental breakfast she had been picking at were still in front of her on a tray. As Olivia entered the room, she flung the script she had been flicking through onto the floor, her expression warning the younger woman that she was not in an amicable mood.

'You're late,' she greeted Olivia irritably, though it was still barely ten minutes to ten. Often, Olivia had to wait until ten o'clock for Diane to join her. 'I suppose Ricky was telling you about his trip. I must say, I was surprised he cleared off to Las Vegas just a few days after you arrived.'

Olivia's fingers tightened around the strap of her bag.

'What Richard chooses to do doesn't concern me, Ms Haran,' she replied, hoping Diane would let it go at that. 'Um—I'm sorry if I've kept you waiting. The traffic was quite heavy this morning.'

Diane pursed her lips. 'But Ricky did go with Manuel to pick you up, didn't he? At least, that's what he told me he was going to do.'

'Well, yes.' Olivia suppressed her frustration. 'Er, shall we make a start? I've got a few queries about what we were discussing yesterday.'

Diane regarded her dourly. 'You're so efficient, aren't you, Olivia? You never let anything get you down. Not an unfaithful husband, or a dead-end job, or the fact that you're living here at my beck and call. How do you do it? I'd like to know.'

'It's my career,' said Olivia tightly, determined not to be provoked.

'And you consider yourself better than me, don't you?' Diane fixed her with a baleful stare. 'Just because you've had a better education. You think women like me are only good enough to sell our bodies to get a decent living.'

'That's not true.'

Olivia had to defend herself, but in all honesty she didn't think of Diane in that way. Not any more. She doubted she would ever like her, but she did admire her. With the background she'd been describing, Olivia considered Diane's success was little short of a miracle.

'But you do despise me.'

'No, I don't.'

'Ricky says you do.'

Richard!

Olivia wanted to scream. 'He's mistaken,' she said firmly. 'Ms Haran, I don't think you're in the mood for working this morning. Would you rather I went back to the hotel?'

'And come back this afternoon, you mean?'

Diane seemed to be considering this, and Olivia wondered what she'd do if she said yes. But perhaps it would be for the best, she thought, remembering her misgivings. She was risking more than her self-respect by playing this game.

'I—I could—' she began, but Diane overruled her.

'No. Joe might come by this afternoon, and I don't want you here if he does.' She frowned. 'I thought he might have come last night, but I guess he heard that Ricky was back from Vegas.' She grimaced. 'I want to ask him about that woman he's been seeing behind my back.'

Olivia felt as if all the colour had drained out of her face. Keeping her head lowered, she sank down weakly onto the sofa opposite Diane. Oh, God, she thought unsteadily, someone must have seen her with Joe last night.

'Cow,' went on Diane expressively, and Olivia stiffened her spine and lifted her head. She wasn't a coward, she told herself fiercely, so she should stop behaving like one. Have it out with Diane now, if that was what this little charade was all about.

But Diane wasn't looking at her; she was thumbing through the pages of a magazine she had at her side. Olivia thought she recognised the magazine. It was the edition of *Forbes* she herself had bought at the hotel.

'What does he see in her?' Diane demanded suddenly, finding the page she'd apparently been looking for and thrusting it across the table at Olivia. 'Have you seen her? Anna Fellini. The woman Joe's mother expects him to marry?'

Olivia stared at the picture of Joe and his business partner with new interest. So their relationship wasn't a platonic one, after all. Her lips tightened. And Diane already had a rival, did she? And one far more adequate to fight for what she wanted than her.

'Well?'

Diane was waiting for her reaction, and Olivia wet her lips as she tried to think of something relevant to say. 'Um—she's very elegant,' she said, not quite knowing what was expected of her. She could hardly denigrate someone who was clearly one of the most attractive women she'd seen.

'Elegant!' scoffed Diane contemptuously. Then, as if revising her opinion, she snatched the magazine out of Olivia's hands. 'Well, yeah,' she said grudgingly. 'I suppose she is sophisticated, if you like that kind of thing. But she's not hot. She's not sexy. She doesn't turn on every man she meets.'

'No, I suppose not.' Olivia had to admit that Anna Fellini's looks were not sensual. Hers was a more classical appeal. Straight blunt-cut hair that shaped her scalp, and a Roman nose to die for. She guessed that, like Joe's, her predecessors had been Italian. Which was probably why his mother would approve of the match.

'I wonder if she's come to LA with him?' Diane brooded. 'He was due back from San Francisco yesterday afternoon.' She scowled, and looked at Olivia. 'I guess you think I'm crazy, don't you? As if he'd prefer a tight-assed bitch like her to me.'

Olivia didn't know what to say to that. 'Maybe he was busy,' she offered, apropos of nothing at all. Then, in an effort to change the subject, she asked, 'Did you find those photographs of when you were a teenager that you were going to show me?'

Diane tossed the magazine aside, her shoulders slumping gloomily. 'No,' she said impatiently. 'I forgot all about them, if you want to know. Ask Ricky where they are. I don't see why he shouldn't make himself useful. I'm going to take another shower and get dressed, just in case Castellano decides to show.'

Olivia made no attempt to find Richard after Diane had gone up to get changed. The idea of asking her ex-husband for anything, after the conversation they had had earlier, was abhorrent to her, and she had enough to worry about as it was. Not least the arrangement she had made to meet Joe that afternoon. When she'd agreed to his request, she'd never considered how he might spend his morning. The thought that he could turn up here at any moment caused a feeling of sick apprehension in her stomach.

Oh, she was no good at intrigue, she told herself crossly. Last night—well, last night she had had too much to drink, as witness the aspirin she'd had to take to ease her headache this morning, and what had happened seemed like some crazy dream. She couldn't believe that she'd behaved so outrageously. Did she really need this kind of hassle? Wouldn't it be simpler if she finished the book at home?

Of course it would, but for all that she knew she wasn't eager to do it. Well, not yet, she amended, reluctant to think it through. For all her fears—her anxieties about Diane's reaction—it was a long time, if ever, since she'd felt such excitement. She was tempting fate, maybe, but she'd never know until she tried.

Diane came back about forty-five minutes later with Bonnie Lovelace in tow. Olivia hadn't been aware of the other woman's arrival, but she'd learned from experience that Bonnie was often at the house. 'I've decided you two can work together this morning,' Diane announced, to Olivia's dismay. She checked her hair in the mirror and admired the shapely curves of her figure. In a cream silk dress piped with red that flared from the hips and swirled some inches above her knees, she looked delightfully cool and svelte. 'I'm going to try and find a date for lunch at Spago's,' she declared confidentially. 'Tell Ricky not to bother to wait up.'

'I will.'

Bonnie simpered; but then Bonnie always simpered when she was around Diane, thought Olivia irritably. But she couldn't help a twinge of envy that Diane could just take off without even an apology. She grimaced. She should have known it was going to be one of those days when she'd found Richard waiting in the car.

CHAPTER NINE

It was nearly half-past one by the time Olivia got back to the hotel.

She felt tired and frustrated, aware that most of the morning had been a waste of time. As usual, Bonnie had taken her responsibilities seriously, and although she'd paid little attention to anything Olivia had said she'd managed to talk continuously for almost two hours.

Diane had apparently suggested that she should show Olivia the photographs she'd been asking about earlier, and to Olivia's dismay she had produced a box which must have contained every photograph Diane had ever had taken. And, ignoring Olivia's protests, she'd insisted on staying with her, poring over her shoulder, and discussing them at length.

Olivia's head had been aching when Bonnie seemed to realise the time, and she'd turned down Bonnie's offer to have lunch at the house. Not that she expected Joe to turn up after Diane's rather obvious announcement. But she'd desperately wanted to get away from the other woman's nasal tones.

It was deliciously cool in her suite, and someone had placed a bowl of cream roses on an end table by the sofa. Their delicate fragrance eased her tension immediately, and, noticing the card that was attached to them, she turned it over.

'To an English rose,' she read disbelievingly, and the handwriting was not Richard's.

Her heartbeat quickened. There was only one other person she could think of who might send her roses, and she glanced hurriedly at her watch. A quarter to two, she thought, feeling a twinge of panic. If the flowers weren't a form of compensation, then she'd never be ready in time.

Dropping her bag onto the Chinese rug, she took a can of Diet Coke from the freezer and popped the tab. He wasn't coming, she assured herself, drinking thirstily. There was no reason for her to worry about the time.

But what if he did?

The thought was irresistible, and without giving herself the opportunity to have second thoughts she scooted into her room. A quick shower, a change of shirt, and some fresh lipstick, she decided firmly. Even if he didn't turn up, she had to eat.

She was downstairs again at a minute past two. In a bronze short-sleeved shirt and the black Bermudas she'd worn earlier, she looked cooler than she felt. The hair at her temples was damp and it wasn't because of the hasty shower. She was sweating with nerves and wishing she'd had time to eat something to settle her stomach.

He wasn't there.

Well, she hadn't expected him to be, she told herself grimly. Diane hadn't gone out that morning, dressed to kill, in order to have lunch with her accountant. No; Olivia had known exactly where she was going. Castellano might be playing hard to get, but Diane had his number—in more ways than one.

All the same, Olivia couldn't help a feeling of disappointment. Even though she'd virtually convinced herself that he wouldn't be here before she came down, somewhere deep inside her she'd sustained the fragile hope that she might be wrong. But she wasn't. It was nearly ten minutes past two and there was no sign of him. She was wasting her time hanging about here. She should just forget all about Joe Castellano and go and get herself some lunch.

'Ms Pyatt?'

The voice was male, but unfamiliar, and the brief spurt of anticipation she'd felt upon hearing it died. She swung round to find a tall man who looked strangely familiar staring at her. But she didn't know anyone in Los Angeles, she thought crossly. It was possible that with that muscular build he was a celebrity she'd seen on television. But if so, how had he known her name?

'Yes,' she said at last, reluctantly, trying desperately to remember where she'd seen him before. She supposed he could work in the hotel. Was he a bodyguard, perhaps?

'Sorry I'm late,' he went on easily. But when she still looked blank he explained. 'I'm Benedict Jeremiah Freemantle, Mr Castellano's personal assistant.'

B.J.

Olivia's lips parted in sudden comprehension. Of course, that was where she'd seen him before. He'd been with Joe at the airport. She'd seen him on the day she arrived.

But what was he doing here? she wondered. Had Joe sent him to make his apologies or what? She didn't like the idea that Castellano should have someone else to do his dirty work for him. Why couldn't he have just picked up the phone?

'Mr Castellano had to fly to San Francisco this morning,' he continued, his gesture inviting her to accompany him towards the exit. 'But he'll be back by the time we get to the house. If you'll come with me, Ms Pyatt, I'll take you to him. He was very sorry he couldn't come to meet you himself.'

'Wait!' Olivia realised she had obediently fallen into step beside him, but now she came to an abrupt halt in the middle of the foyer. 'The house?' she echoed, not understanding him. Her pulse quickened. 'You mean Ms Haran's house in Beverly Hills?'

B.J.'s stocky features shared an equal lack of comprehension now. 'Ms Haran's house?' he echoed, as she had done. 'No. I'm to take you to Mr Castellano's house in Malibu.'

'Oh!'

Olivia's lips formed a complete circle, and B.J. gave her a slightly wary look. 'You were planning on spending the afternoon with Mr Castellano?' he queried. 'I was told you knew all about it.'

'Oh, yes.' Olivia hurried into speech. 'Yes, I did.'

But Joe's house in Malibu! she thought, her pulse accelerating. She'd certainly never expected he'd take her there. He'd invited her to the beach and she'd foolishly taken him at his word.

'Good.'

B.J. was looking considerably relieved now, but she wondered how he'd react if she said she'd changed her mind. She wasn't entirely convinced of the sense in behaving so recklessly. Yet, after last night, what did she have to fear?

The car waiting outside was nothing like the limousine that took her to and from Diane's. It was a dark green sports saloon with low sleek lines and broad tyres. A thoroughbred, she thought, in every sense of the word.

B.J. made sure she was comfortably seated before walking round the car to get in beside her, and Olivia was intensely conscious of her bare knees below the cuffs of her shorts. She should have worn a skirt or trousers, she thought, trying to limit the exposure. But B.J. barely glanced at her before starting the engine of the powerful car.

The car drew a certain amount of attention, but Olivia guessed the man beside her drew some as well. B.J. was thirty-something, blond-haired, and undeniably good-looking. A Californian beach boy, she mused, but it was hardly an original thought.

'So how are you enjoying your stay in Los Angeles?' he asked, after they'd negotiated the ramp onto the freeway, and Olivia forced herself to consider what he'd said. So long as she didn't think too much, she thought she'd avoid any pitfalls. It was thinking about Joe that caused her so much stress.

'Um—very much,' she answered after a moment, covering her knees with her hands. 'I've never been to the West Coast before so I've done a lot of sightseeing.' She stopped, realising she was sounding like a tourist. 'When I wasn't working, of course.'

B.J. cast her an amused glance. 'Of course.' He swung

the wheel to overtake a vehicle on the nearside and Olivia's fingers tightened automatically. She still wasn't used to this style of driving, but the manoeuvre was accomplished without incident and she relaxed. 'Have you met anyone interesting yet?'

'Interesting?' Olivia's shoulders lifted. 'Do you mean someone famous or just—well, anyone?'

'Aren't the two descriptions mutually exclusive?' asked B.J. drily and then laughed when she gave him a worried look. 'Just joking,' he added, but she wasn't sure he was. Like his employer, he seemed to enjoy mocking the establishment.

To her relief, Olivia found the scenery a more than adequate substitute for her thoughts. Beyond the hills north of Los Angeles, the tumbling surf of the Pacific had a wild, untrammelled beauty. Inland, the twisting canyons where the rich had their homes only gave way to the chaparral-covered slopes of the state parks, while along the shoreline the miles of inviting beaches were practically deserted.

'Have you ever been surfing?' B.J. asked as the sun glinted on the gleaming shoulders of two men, lying out in the bay, waiting for the big wave to ride their boards into the beach, and Olivia shook her head.

'No,' she admitted. 'I'm not even a particularly strong swimmer. But I expect you are.' She paused, and then added nervously, 'Does—er—does Mr Castellano go surfing, too?'

'Only on the Internet,' replied B.J. ruefully. 'He's usually too busy to waste time having fun.' He glanced her way. 'Except on special occasions,' he said, grinning at her. 'You'll have to teach him to relax.'

Olivia stiffened. 'I don't think I could teach Mr Castellano anything,' she said, alert to any insinuation. 'I don't know Mr Castellano very well as it happens. But I expect you know that. You were there when we met.'

'Yeah.' B.J. gave her another studied look, and then nodded his head. 'Yeah, I was,' he repeated, with a curious

inflection to his voice. 'I guess you don't know Mr
Castellano at all.'

Olivia barely had time to consider what he might mean
by that before B.J. took an exit ramp for the Pacific coast
highway that curved down towards the gleaming waters of
Santa Monica Bay. The road curved around a headland
where flowering broom and cyprus trees screened the
ocean, and then the iron gates of a private estate appeared
on their left.

An octagonal-shaped gatehouse that B.J. carelessly announced had once been a mission chapel stood beside the
entrance, but no deferential retainer hurried out to open the
gates. Instead, B.J. inserted a plastic card into a slot beside
the mailbox, and the gates opened automatically to allow
them through.

Despite the fact that Diane had called it a beach house,
Joe's sprawling residence bore little resemblance to the
kind of place Olivia had expected. An image of a clapboard
house, with a wrap-around porch, and deckchairs under the
awning, suddenly seemed so inadequate. At least she didn't
have to worry about their isolation, she thought ruefully. It
must take an army of staff to run an estate like this.

Yet, for all her misgivings—and the still lurking belief
that she shouldn't have accepted his invitation—Olivia was
enchanted by her first sight of the house. Nestling on a bluff
of land, overlooking its own private stretch of beach, it was,
quite simply, breathtaking.

Like the gatehouse, the first impression she got was of
an octagonal building, with an uninterrupted view of the
ocean. But as they drew closer she realised that it was a
kind of conservatory she could see, and that the single-
storey dwelling itself was reassuringly rectangular in shape.

But there were windows everywhere, each with its own
set of shutters. Square windows, round windows, and oriel
windows in the glass-walled conservatory. The shutters
were painted black and were a stark contrast to the white-
painted walls, while the double doors that stood wide
looked solidly substantial.

Another car stood on the crushed-shell drive: an open-topped convertible that was clearly built for speed. 'You can relax, he's back,' said B.J. cheerfully, but Olivia wasn't so sure. As her pulse quickened and her knees turned to jelly, she wondered if she'd ever relax again.

It wasn't until she was getting out of the car that another worrying thought struck her. What would she do if Diane was here? She'd said she was going to find Joe, so why not come out to the house? It was possible, she thought apprehensively. Anything was possible in this totally unreal environment, and she licked her lips rather anxiously as B.J. sauntered round the bonnet of the car.

'Go right ahead,' he said, indicating the open doors, and as they crossed the forecourt she was intensely conscious of the noise their feet were making. It seemed inordinately intrusive, and she wondered if it was a good or bad sign when Joe didn't come to meet them.

The entrance hall briefly distracted her attention. The high ceiling was inset with a row of skylights that cast bars of sunlight down across the veined marble floor. Urns, overflowing with flowering plants and shrubs, provided oases of colour and delicate sculptures in ebony and bronze were set against the walls.

There were paintings on the walls too, mostly modern pieces, she thought, that blended well with their surroundings. It would have been impossible for the place to look cluttered. It was far too spacious for that, the walls a neutral shade of oyster beige, with earth-toned rugs to give the room depth.

'He's probably in the den,' said B.J., dismissing the maid who came to meet them and crossing the hall with the familiarity of long use. He started down a long gallery, whose windows were screened against the sun, bidding her to follow him, and despite the screening the whole place had an open feel to it, with tall archways on either side inviting further exploration.

Olivia heard Joe's voice before they reached the den, and the withdrawal she felt at knowing they weren't going to be alone was tempered by her reaction to his voice. It was so familiar to her, and she knew she ought not to be so aware of him. She was doing this for Richard, she told herself fiercely, but the words had a hollow ring.

The den was at the back of the house and, in spite of her nerves, Olivia's first impression was of light and space. Once again, the room was dominated by the windows that overlooked the ocean, the book-lined walls and leather-topped desk barely registering when compared to the view.

But it was the man seated behind the desk, his booted heels propped indifferently on a corner of the polished wood, who instantly drew her eyes. In a cream silk shirt and the dark trousers of a suit, the jacket of which was thrown carelessly across the desk, his only concession to informality was in the fact that he'd removed his tie and loosened his collar. Yet, for all that, he looked just as attractive as ever, particularly so when she realised he was alone and merely talking on the phone.

His dark brows arched ruefully when she and B.J appeared in the doorway, and, swinging his feet to the floor, he got abruptly to his feet. 'Yeah,' he said, to whoever he was talking to. 'I'm sorry about that, too. No. No, I'm afraid that won't be possible. Um—well, maybe, later in the week.'

It was obvious he was trying to get off the phone, but when B.J. mimed that they would go away again he shook his head. 'Stay,' he mouthed. And then, into the receiver, he said, 'Oh, of course. I am, too. I'll speak to you soon. Yeah. Right.'

He hung up with obvious relief, his face lightening as he turned to his guests. 'Sorry about that,' he said, raking back his hair with a weary hand. 'I've not even had time to change.'

'Well, I'll get back to L.A.' said B.J., saluting his employer good-naturedly, and Joe nodded gratefully as the other man turned to go.

'Thanks,' he said, and Olivia felt a little shiver slide down her spine. So they were to be alone, then, she thought uneasily. She'd half hoped that B.J. would be around to drive her back to the hotel.

B.J. sauntered off, his deck shoes making little squeaking noises on the marbled floor. Olivia hadn't noticed the sound when they were coming here, but then her heart had been thundering in her ears. Now, the silence was oppressive, and she wondered if Joe was wishing she hadn't come.

He sighed suddenly, his breath escaping from his lungs in a rush, and Olivia couldn't help flinching at the sound. 'So,' he said, as if aware of her state of tension, 'will you excuse me while I go and take a shower?'

'Of course.'

Olivia was only too pleased at the prospect of having a few moments to herself. She needed the time to get used to the luxury of her surroundings; to come to terms with the unwilling emotions that seeing him again had aroused.

'Good. Good.' Joe looked at her a little too intently for a minute. 'You're okay with this, aren't you?' he asked, his eyes narrowing. 'As you turned me down before, I suppose it was slightly autocratic bringing you here to the house.'

'It's okay.' Olivia knew she had to handle this, and behaving like a shrinking violet was not going to do any of them any good. 'It's fine,' she added, when he still continued to stare at her. 'Do you mind if I go outside?' A safer option? 'I'd like to look around.'

'No problem.' Joe came round the desk, and although her instincts were to retreat she stayed where she was. 'I'll show you the way,' he said, halting beside her. 'Perhaps you'd like to take a swim. There's a pool in back that gets sadly underused.'

'I'll—er—I'll just look around for now,' Olivia murmured tensely, her skin warming at his closeness, prickling with the awareness of his powerful frame. She forced herself to look up at him. 'Perhaps we could both swim later. I don't like swimming alone.'

'Don't you?' There was a wealth of experience behind those two words, and she was sure he knew exactly what

she was trying to do. The strange thing was, he was letting
her get away with it, and she pondered his motives for
doing so. 'Well, we'll see,' he conceded now, and to her
relief he moved towards the door. 'D'you want to look
around the house first?'

Olivia's jaw dropped. 'The house?' she echoed faintly.
'But—I thought you were going to take a shower.'

'I am.' His mouth twisted. 'I'm not suggesting you join
me. I just thought you might like to find your way around,
that's all.'

Olivia swallowed. 'All right.'

'Right.' His eyes slid thoughtfully over her determinedly
smiling face, and then he shook his head. 'Right,' he said
again. 'Follow me.' And Olivia squared her shoulders as
she trailed him out into the gallery.

They turned away from the entrance hall this time, passing through what appeared to be another reception room
before entering an enormous room on their right. Here a
cathedral-like ceiling with more of the signature skylights
spread light over what seemed like acres of polished wood,
with curving armchairs and hide sofas in cream and beige
and brown.

Like the entrance hall she had seen earlier, the colour in
the room came from plants and flowers, with an enormous
Chinese carpet occupying the centre of the floor. There
were glass-topped tables and tall lamps with bronze shades,
and a stately baby grand against the far wall.

But it was the light streaming in through wide sliding
doors that drew Olivia into the room, and without waiting
for Joe to accompany her she stepped outside. Only not
outside, she saw at once. Instead, she was in the octagonal
solarium she'd seen as they'd driven up to the house, with
the blue sweep of the bay all around her.

'D'you like it?'

Apparently prepared to delay his shower indefinitely, Joe
lingered in the doorway, his arms crossed over his chest.
His cuffs were turned back and the hands he had been running through his hair had left it ruffled and standing on end

in places. Yet for all that he was still the most disturbing man she'd ever seen.

'It's—incredible,' she said, speaking impulsively at last. 'I don't know what I— Well, I never expected anything like this.'

'I like it,' he declared simply, propping one shoulder against the frame of the door and crossing one ankle over the other. 'It used to belong to an old movie actress, believe it or not, but that was many moons ago. She'd dead now, sadly, but they say she used to love this place. When it came on the market, I made an offer.'

'That they couldn't refuse, I'll bet,' said Olivia without thinking, and Joe's mouth compressed into a rueful smile.

'You could say that,' he conceded. 'Do you blame me? When you want something, you don't hang around.'

Olivia moved towards the long windows. 'Is that your credo in life, Mr Castellano?' she asked lightly. 'If you want something, go for it, no matter who gets hurt?'

'The woman was dead—'

'I know.'

'But you're not talking about Lilli Thurman, are you, Olivia?' His voice roughened. 'If you're talking about yourself, that's a whole different ballgame.'

CHAPTER TEN

'MYSELF!' Olivia had bent one knee on the cushioned window seat that circled the solarium to enable her to look down at the beach, but now she lowered her foot rather jerkily to the floor. 'I don't know quite what you mean,' she said, and meant it. She wasn't in any danger of hurting anyone—least of all him.

'If you say so,' he said, cupping the back of his neck now with both hands and stretching the muscles of his spine. His eyes turned towards her. 'Why did you come?'

Olivia's throat felt tight. 'Why did you invite me?'

'Good question.' His arms fell to his sides and he straightened away from the door. He regarded her from beneath his thick straight lashes. 'Perhaps I was curious to see how far you intended to go.'

Olivia stiffened. 'Perhaps that's why I came, too,' she declared coolly, refusing to let him see that he'd disconcerted her. She paused. 'Do you want me to go?'

'No.' But his response was harsh, and although his gaze moved down over the betraying contours of her breasts to the slim bare legs below her shorts the brooding darkness of his expression made her think he was having some trouble with his feelings as well. He took a deep breath. 'I guess this is where I go take that shower.'

'If you must,' she said recklessly, and although he had turned away her words brought him to an ominous halt.

'What's that supposed to mean?' he demanded, looking back at her over his shoulder.

'It doesn't mean anything.' But Olivia was suddenly aware of how easy it was to heighten the tension here, and the knowledge excited her. She ran a provocative tongue over her upper lip. 'Unless you want it to, of course.'

'Don't,' he said abruptly, turning fully to face her. 'Don't even think about it.'

'Think about what?' she asked innocently. 'I haven't done anything.'

'Not yet,' he retorted harshly, one hand balling into a fist at his side. His mouth twisted. 'It doesn't suit you, Olivia.'

It was a deliberate insult, but she chose not to let it upset her. She sensed that Joe had only said it to try and take charge of a situation that was running beyond his control, and although he could have meant what he said she'd never have a better chance to put her own sexuality to the test.

'Doesn't it?' she countered now, turning sideways so that the sun profiled the upward tilt of her breasts and lifting the moist hair from her nape. 'So what does suit me, Mr Castellano? Saying nothing? Doing as I'm told? Letting other people walk all over me?'

'No one's walking over you!' exclaimed Joe tightly, and when she arched a mocking eyebrow he demanded, 'Well, who is it? Not me, that's for sure.'

'Aren't you?' She didn't know what was driving her to say these things; she only knew she felt compelled to go on. 'You feel sorry for me, don't you, Mr Castellano? Go on. Admit it.'

'I don't feel sorry for you,' he grated between his teeth. 'For myself, maybe.' He raked back his hair with a hand that wasn't entirely steady. 'Why are you doing this, Olivia? You're not really interested in me.'

Her breath caught in the back of her throat. 'Aren't I?' she asked faintly, and then took a gulp of air when he uttered an oath and came towards her.

He halted directly in front of her, the scent of his male sweat mingling with the warmth in the room to create a potent mixture. 'Stop this!' he ordered angrily. 'It's gone on long enough, do you hear me? I don't know what the hell you think you're playing at, but I think you've forgotten I'm no green youth and you're definitely no *femme fatale*!'

Olivia winced. He certainly didn't pull his punches, and what had been an exciting game suddenly became an embarrassing confrontation. He wasn't amused, that was obvious, and she had to steel herself not to flinch when he thrust his face towards her.

She was breathing shallowly, nonetheless, and in spite of her efforts to appear unmoved by his deliberately cruel words she was forced to take a step backwards, her hand raised in an involuntary gesture of defence. No one, not even Richard, had ever made her feel so small, but she refused to let him see what he'd done.

'Do you always attack things you can't deal with?' she demanded tensely, hoping he couldn't hear the tremor in her voice. 'If I didn't know better, I'd say you were afraid to show your emotions—or afraid *of* them, perhaps.'

Joe glared at her. He was breathing rapidly, and the movement of his chest caused a curl of dark hair to appear in the opened neckline of his shirt. She could see more of his chest hair, outlined beneath the fine cloth of his shirt, and she concentrated on this to avoid looking into his grim face.

'You don't know what you're talking about,' he said savagely, and she felt a ripple of anticipation feather her skin. She was right, she thought incredulously. She had upset his cool self-control. Whatever reason he'd had for inviting her here, she'd confounded him, and she felt a little burst of power at the thought.

'Don't I?' she said now, holding her ground with difficulty nevertheless. The urge to move away from the aggressive inclination of his body was tempting, but she wouldn't give him that satisfaction. 'How do you know?'

'For God's sake, Olivia—'

With an angry exclamation, he raised his hand to push her away from him. Or, at least, that was what she thought he'd planned to do, judging from the fury in his face. But although his fingers connected with her body just below her shoulder they curled into the soft fabric of her shirt, bunching it into a ball, and using the leverage to jerk her towards him.

Her breasts thudded against his chest, but although she clutched at him for support he made no attempt to put his arms around her. What was happening here was no gentle flirtation but a primitive demonstration of sexual domination.

'Take my word for it,' he said in a low voice, his hot breath filling her nostrils, 'this is not a good idea!'

She believed him.

Trapped against him as she was, she had a whole different slant on the situation, and while there was something infinitely appealing about the muscled strength of his body crushing her breasts she doubted she would sustain any credibility if he attempted to call her bluff.

'All right,' she said, lifting her hands from his waist and pressing them against his chest. 'All right, I believe you.' But when she tilted back her head to look into his face she saw not anger there but raw frustration.

'Dammit,' he said harshly, his fingers releasing their hold on her shirt only to slide over her shoulder. They tightened over the narrow bones, probing and kneading her taut flesh. 'Dammit, Olivia, you shouldn't have started this!' And his other hand came up to cup the back of her neck.

There was a moment when she had the crazy thought that he was about to strangle her, but his touch was possessive now, not violent. His fingers slid inside the neckline of her shirt, cool against her hot skin. His breathing was still rapid, but its heat was no longer threatening, and she was mesmerised by the narrowed tawny eyes that seemed to be searching every inch of her upturned face.

Then he lowered his head and kissed her.

His lips brushed hers, once, twice, coaxing her lips to part, and then took possession, his tongue slipping between her teeth. Olivia swayed against him, and any thought of resistance was forgotten beneath the all-consuming pressure of his mouth. His mouth was incredibly soft, incredibly hot, and incredibly sensual, robbing her of any opposition and turning her quivering limbs to water.

The impact of his kiss flowed down into her stomach, leaving her breasts tingling and flooding her loins with heat. Her knees felt weak, uncertain, and between her legs a pulse throbbed with an insistent need. She couldn't ever remember feeling so sexually aroused, or so powerless to hide the way she felt.

His hand slid down between them, popping the buttons on her shirt and exposing the lacy stitching of her bra. His fingers insinuated themselves into the bra, finding the swollen nub of her breast. He rolled the hard bud between his thumb and forefinger, and she arched against him urgently, helpless to hide her desire.

And as she did so she became conscious of his shaft, hard against her stomach. Thrusting against the taut line of his zip, it was a blatant advertisement of his own arousal. As if she needed any proof, she thought dizzily as the hand that had been massaging her nape slipped down her back and cupped her bottom.

His hand didn't feel cool now; it felt hot, the heat burning through the thin cotton of her shorts. She knew the craziest urge to release the button at her waist and send the shorts tumbling down to her ankles. She wanted his hands on her flesh, she realised madly. She wanted to feel his hot skin against hers…

When he abruptly let her go, she was totally unprepared for it. One moment her palms had been flat against his shirt, her thumbs probing between the taut buttons, her nails scraping his hair-covered chest, and the next he was propelling her away from him at top speed. Rough hands captured the two sides of her shirt and dragged them together, and as he struggled to fasten the buttons again Olivia realised it had come free of her shorts and she was displaying a bare midriff as well.

She tilted back on her heels, grateful for the window-seat that supported the backs of her knees as she endeavoured to regain her balance. But although she brushed his hands away and fastened the shirt herself she couldn't look at him. She was too afraid of what she'd see if she looked into his face.

The silence was ripe with recriminations. Although neither of them spoke at first, Olivia was overwhelmingly aware of the emotions they were both trying to control. Dismay, on her part, and an aching sense of shame at her own stupidity, and bitterness, she thought, on his, and disgust at what she'd made him do.

'I'm sorry,' she got out, at last, as he was turning away from her, and he swung round almost violently, piercing her with a savage look.

'Don't,' he said, somewhat ambiguously, and she wasn't sure whether he meant that she shouldn't apologise or simply not speak at all. He heaved a breath. 'Like I said before, I need a shower. Can you—entertain yourself while I go and get out of this suit?'

Olivia nodded, not trusting herself to speak, and without another word he left the solarium. She heard him cross the vaulted living room and then the sound of his footsteps died away along the gallery beyond. Only then did she sink somewhat weakly down onto the cushions behind her and give way to a shuddering sigh.

What had she done?

As the possible consequences of her behaviour swept over her, she propped her elbows on her knees and pushed her fingers up into her hair. She hadn't had time to braid it before she left the hotel, so she had secured it at the back of her head with a leather barrette. Now, though, the moist hair was escaping, partly because of her own actions and partly because Joe had dislodged the barrette. The strands that curled down around her fingers made her suddenly aware of how she must look. With her shirt loose and her mouth bare of any lipstick, she suspected no one could have any doubts as to what had been going on.

'Are you all right, madam? Can I get you anything?'

As if her humiliation wasn't yet complete, Olivia lifted her head to find the maid she and B.J. had seen on their arrival hovering by the sliding glass doors. Had Joe sent her to check on her, she wondered, or was the woman acting purely on her own initiative? She was obviously curious about what had been going on, and Olivia could have done without those intent dark eyes assessing her appearance.

'I—' The impulse to ask the maid to call her a cab, to leave before Joe returned from taking his shower, was tempting, but she suppressed it. She wasn't a coward, she told herself severely. And she had nothing to be ashamed about. Well, not much, she conceded grudgingly. 'Um—' She swallowed. 'Do you think I could have some tea?'

'Tea?' That had clearly not been high on the maid's list of expectations. Vodka, perhaps; or something stronger. But tea? However, she managed to contain her reaction, and added politely, 'Of course. Would that be with milk or lemon, madam?'

Olivia sighed again. 'Milk, please,' she said, refusing to be intimidated. But she was relieved when the woman departed, even if she wished she'd asked her where the bathroom was as soon as she'd gone.

Getting up, she glanced ruefully about her. It was just as well that the beach was private, she reflected, making an attempt to tuck her shirt back into her shorts. She hadn't chosen the most appropriate place to conduct her big seduction scene. She grimaced. Some scene; some seduction! After the way he'd behaved when she'd tried to kiss him the night before, she should have known better than to try again.

And yet he had sent her the roses...

The roses!

Olivia groaned. She'd been so disconcerted by her own reactions at seeing Joe again that she'd forgotten all about the roses. Dear Lord, he probably thought she was pig ignorant as well as everything else. All the same, she couldn't help wondering why he had sent them when he obviously had no interest in her.

Well, not of a sexual nature anyway, she amended, pacing rather agitatedly about the room. Unless sending roses was to him just a formality. He'd probably asked his secretary to send them. The wording might even have been her idea as well.

She didn't know what to think, and that was a fact. For a man who had two women in his life already, he showed an extraordinary lack of loyalty to either. He was having an affair with Diane at the same time that Diane was telling her his mother expected him to marry Anna Fellini. And although she didn't kid herself that he'd been in any danger of succumbing to her charms there had been moments when he was kissing her that she'd sensed he was close to the edge.

She lifted both hands and smoothed them over her hair. She definitely needed a bathroom, she fretted, before he came back and found her like this. She wanted to renew her make-up and comb her hair and try and restore some semblance of composure.

Picking up the purse that she had dropped earlier, she ventured somewhat tentatively into the living room. Looking about her, she was once again charmed by the uncluttered beauty of her surroundings, and although the temptation was to linger she forced herself to go on.

Cool marble floors stretched in either direction when she stepped out into the gallery. Mentally tossing a coin, she turned to her left, pausing at every open doorway, hoping to find what she was looking for.

The size of the house was staggering. She glimpsed a dining room and several sitting rooms before gazing aghast at an indoor pool. Several archways opened into the pool room, and she saw it had a sliding roof that could be opened to the sun. And, like all the other rooms, the view from the long windows was extensive, this time looking out on a palm-fringed patio, with sloping lawns and terraces leading down to the shore.

But the pool room seemed to mark the end of the gallery, and, retracing her steps, she felt a twinge of panic quickening her feet. Joe had said she could look around but she still had the feeling she was intruding. But, dammit, where were the bathrooms in this place?

The truth was she'd hoped to tidy herself before the maid returned with the tea. What kind of guest allowed herself to get into such a state without even knowing the layout of the house? The woman was curious enough about her as it was.

Deciding that perhaps one of the sitting rooms might have a mirror at least, she entered the first room on her right. Like the rest of the house, it was exquisitely—though in this case austerely—furnished, with dark mahogany furniture and a pair of sofas upholstered in dark orange suede.

But there were no mirrors here. The walls were hung with more of the modern paintings she had seen in the entrance hall. But open double-panelled doors indicated that there was another room beyond this, and, squaring her shoulders, Olivia crossed the bronze patterned rug that was set squarely in the middle of the polished floor.

She paused in the doorway of a large bedroom, which, like the sitting room before it, had a decidedly masculine air about it. The walls were a dark gold in colour, and the huge carpet was essentially a shade of burnt umber, with a huge colonial bed whose solid head- and baseboards enclosed a king-sized mattress spread with a dark gold quilt.

Olivia's lips parted in some confusion. There were clothes draped over the end of the bed, and now she became aware of it she could hear water running some place close at hand. In the adjoining bathroom, she realised belatedly, though the knowledge didn't answer her needs. Dear Lord, she thought, this must be Joe's bedroom. The water she could hear running was from the shower.

Panic paralysed her. Of all the bedrooms in the house she had had to choose his. If he discovered her here, he was bound to think she'd come looking for him. Would he believe her if she said that simply wasn't the case?

Her brain kicked into action. There was absolutely no reason why he should find her there, she reminded herself impatiently. He didn't even know she'd left the solarium, after all. All she had to do was scoot back along the gallery to the living room. She could even take a chance and investigate one of the other sitting rooms. There were bound to be suites of rooms that were not occupied.

She would have turned away then had not a photograph on a bedside table caught her eye. The picture was of a woman; she could see that from the doorway. But the woman's identity was hidden. The frame was turned slightly too far towards the bed.

The water was still running, and although she knew it was nothing to do with her Olivia couldn't resist finding out whose picture he kept beside his bed. Was it Anna Fellini's, or Diane's? She couldn't believe it was the latter, when he'd invited Richard as well as Diane to the house.

It was neither. Inching the picture round with the tip of her finger, Olivia saw that the woman in the photograph was much older than she'd thought. Elegant, still, with long, slender limbs and a coil of night-dark hair secured to the back of her head, her resemblance to Joe was unmistakable. She guessed this was his mother. How discriminating of him to keep her picture beside his bed.

'Ah, you are here, madam.'

Once again, the maid's supercilious voice startled her into action. Olivia swung round hurriedly, desperate to stop the woman from saying anything more—and knocked the photograph off the table.

It tumbled noisily to the floor. Olivia snatched it up at once, miming for the maid to go away. 'I'm coming,' she mouthed, grateful to see that the glass in the frame wasn't broken, but even as she set it back on the table Joe himself opened the bathroom door.

The maid had disappeared now, any idea of pretending not to understand Olivia's silent pleas quickly suppressed. She knew when to make an exit, thought Olivia, wishing she had known the same. As it was, she was left to stare at her host, his shoulders streaming with water, his hips swathed in a hastily wrapped towel, his frowning countenance a mirror of his discontent.

'Olivia!' he said, not without some frustration. 'What the hell's going on?'

CHAPTER ELEVEN

'WHERE did you disappear to yesterday afternoon?'

Diane posed the question the next morning as Olivia was enjoying an unexpected cup of coffee prior to starting work. Usually, Diane wanted to get straight down to business as soon as Olivia arrived, but this morning she'd chosen to offer the younger woman some refreshment first.

Was it a coincidence? Olivia wondered, praying her pink-tinted cheeks wouldn't give her away. But it was odd for Diane to show any interest in what she'd been doing, when she normally preferred talking about herself.

Olivia expelled a breath as the memory of the previous afternoon came back to her. Had she really visited the house at Malibu? Had she really talked herself into Joe Castellano's arms? Had she really stood in his bedroom and stared open-mouthed at his towel-clad figure? God, she'd wanted to die when he'd emerged from the bathroom and found her poking about in his room.

But of course she hadn't, even though the memory still caused a quivering in her stomach. People didn't die, not from mortification anyway. That would have been much too easy a solution to being caught.

'I was looking for a bathroom,' she'd said, aware that her explanation wasn't convincing him. 'And—and then I saw that picture and—and—'

'Wanted to see who it was?'

'Well, yes.' Olivia had chewed her lip. 'I suppose you think I was being nosy. It's—it's your mother, isn't it? She looks a lot like you.'

Joe's expression had grown sardonic. 'I'm not sure if she'll regard that as a compliment or not.'

Olivia had coloured at his sarcasm, and sought desperately for an alternative. 'And—well, I forgot to thank you for the roses, too.'

'The roses?'

She'd known as soon as he said the words that he knew nothing about them, and she'd hurried into speech to rescue her gaffe. 'I mean—the hotel, of course,' she'd muttered, though she couldn't believe they would have put such a message on them. 'Um—I'm sorry for the intrusion.' She'd backed away towards the door. 'I'll see you later on.'

Thankfully, he hadn't pursued it, and she'd been left with the uneasy suspicion that Richard must have sent them, after all. It was the kind of thing he might do, and she'd been foolish to give Joe Castellano the credit. Just because she hadn't recognised the handwriting... How stupid that seemed now.

But then, she reflected, she seldom thought sensibly when he was around. And even now, sitting in Diane's sitting room, the image of his lean, muscled torso, with its triangle of coarse dark hair arrowing down to his navel, was still disturbingly vivid. The towel, knotted carelessly about his hips, had exposed the bones of his pelvis, but she'd been hotly aware of what it had concealed. After all, only minutes before, he'd been moulding her body to his thrusting maleness, and the sensuality of what had happened between them was too acute to be denied.

She couldn't ever remember feeling that way with Richard. The sex they'd shared had been satisfactory enough, she supposed, but there'd been none of the excitement that being with Joe had aroused. Excitement, and a wholly sexual awareness, she acknowledged tremulously. She'd been aware of herself as well as him, and of the loss his withdrawal had made her feel.

But, obviously, he hadn't felt the same. Despite the fact that there'd been moments when she was sure he had lost control of his emotions, common sense had prevailed. But, whatever loyalties he had, he was only human, and when she'd thrown herself at his head he'd been tempted.

But not for long...

Olivia had found a bathroom without the maid's assistance. She'd decided it would be too humiliating to ask the woman something which would prove she'd had no right to enter Joe's suite of rooms. It had been easy enough, as it happened. The door further along the gallery had opened into another bedroom suite. With every possible amenity in the bathroom, she'd noticed tensely, including cut-glass jars of creams and crystals, and exclusive bottles of perfume for a guest's use.

But what guest? she'd wondered ruefully as she'd viewed her own dishevelled appearance in the mirror. Not someone like her, who looked and behaved as if she'd never seen a naked man before. Dear Lord, what must he have thought of her stumbling around in his bedroom like a schoolgirl on her first date? She'd been married and divorced, for God's sake. What was there about this man that made her act in such a way?

Yet, although she'd been quite prepared for him to come back and say he'd called a cab to take her back to the hotel, he hadn't. Even though, when he'd returned to the solarium to find her wolfing down the plate of muffins the maid had provided with the tray of tea, he must have felt like it. Instead, he'd gone to stand by the windows, giving her some privacy to empty her mouth. And then, when he'd thought it was appropriate, he'd suggested that she might like to join him for a walk on the beach.

Olivia had finished the muffin before replying, deciding that to explain that she hadn't had any lunch would imply an eagerness to get here she didn't want to convey. 'That sounds inviting,' she said, trying to sound casual as she licked a crumb of chocolate from her lips. She gulped the remainder of her tea and glanced behind her. 'I'm ready if you are.'

'Are you sure?'

There was a trace of humour in his expression as he turned away from the windows, and she was instantly aware that his tawny gaze missed nothing. But it was too late now to make an explanation, and she dabbed her mouth with a napkin, and got to her feet. 'I'm sure.'

'Okay.' He gestured towards the sliding doors. 'Let's go.'

She was intensely conscious of his presence as they walked back along the gallery. In denim cut-offs and a cotton polo shirt, he seemed more approachable than before. His bare feet were slipped casually into a pair of worn deck shoes, and no one meeting him for the first time would have imagined the commercial power he possessed.

Commercial power?

She chose not to examine that thought too closely, and when she passed the door to his suite of rooms again she deliberately looked away. She was glad of the sight of the pool room to give her something to talk about, and Joe explained they had cool days even in southern California.

In the event, they went out through the pool room onto the patio at the side of the house. From here, it was possible to see that the land shelved down to the shoreline in a series of terraces, with tree-covered slopes and tumbling waterfalls breaking up the view.

'Oh, it's so beautiful!' said Olivia impulsively, turning her face up to the sun. 'I can't believe you call this a beach house. If I lived here, I'd never want to leave.'

'Is that so?' His tone was sardonic, and she realised she had spoken childishly again. 'Well, it is a house, and it's at the beach,' he murmured mildly. 'I like it, too, but I also like my house in San Francisco. It's cooler there, so I guess I have the best of both worlds.'

Olivia nodded, managing a tight smile, but she was warning herself not to make any more mistakes. He was humouring her; she knew it; she was almost sure now he didn't want her here. He would have preferred to send her packing, only he'd decided to disarm her first.

They walked down through the gardens, Joe pausing every now and then to point out some rare flower or to draw her attention to the view. And, although she had determined to be on her guard with him, his manner was persuasive. It was so easy to believe he was having fun.

The air was magic, a combination of exotic plants, a Pacific breeze, and warmth. In normal circumstances, Olivia wouldn't have been able to wait to dive into the ocean. The anticipation of how that cool water would feel against her hot skin was almost irresistible.

A long wooden dock jutted out from the shore, and Joe explained that he had a boat moored at Marina del Rey. Although he was reticent about its size, Olivia guessed it would be elegant. If there was one thing she had learned about him from his house, it was that he had exquisite taste.

They spent some time on the dock, watching the waves curling under the boardwalk, and then strolled companionably along the shoreline, their shoes making a trail in the wet sand. And although Olivia had promised herself that she wouldn't get swept away again by his charm and influence she found she was talking about her work without restraint.

She'd realised later that he was probably skilled at gaining people's confidence, at introducing certain topics and drawing them out. But at the time she wasn't thinking; she was just flattered by his interest, and this was one area, at least, where she felt at ease.

'So what made you decide to write Diane's story?' he asked at last, after expressing his sympathy at the tragic death of Eileen Cusack. 'I mean—' For once, he was diffident. 'I'd have thought she was unlikely to accept your motives. You were her husband's ex-wife, after all. It could have been a recipe for disaster.'

'Why?' Olivia frowned, glancing up into his lean, intelligent face with curious eyes. Then, because she found it difficult to sustain his gaze, she looked away. 'In any case, it was Diane who asked me.'

'You're kidding!'

'No, I'm not.' Olivia felt vaguely indignant now. 'I admit, I was surprised at first, but it's been okay.'

'But she couldn't be sure your motives were genuine.

When you accepted the commission, I mean,' he added swiftly. 'How did she know you hadn't changed your mind?'

'Changed my mind?' Olivia was confused. She shook her head and several wisps of hair that had escaped from the braid she'd fastened so hurriedly earlier floated about her face. 'Changed my mind about what?'

His mouth tightened and she sensed her reply hadn't pleased him, but his voice was mild when he spoke. 'I'm sure you know,' he said. 'You told me yourself that Ricky believed you were still in love with him. You might have wanted him back. That was always a possibility, but I guess Diane cared more about your reputation as a biographer then the inherent dangers to her marriage.'

'Now wait a minute…' Olivia halted now, her reluctance to get involved in any more controversy muted by a very real need to understand. She brushed back her hair with an impatient hand. 'Diane has nothing to fear from me.' She blew out a breath. 'Whatever she's told you, Richard means nothing to me.'

'Do you mean that?'

Olivia felt the heat invading her neck. 'Of course I mean it.'

'But you don't deny you're not still with the man you left Ricky for?'

'The man I left him for?' Olivia was indignant. 'I didn't leave Richard for a man!'

She thought he paled slightly at that, but before she could elaborate he spoke again. 'The—woman, then,' he said harshly, a line of white appearing around his mouth. 'The—the person you said you'd fallen in love with.'

Olivia gasped. 'Are you implying that—?'

'You said there was no special man in England,' Joe reminded her doggedly, and she stared at him as if she couldn't believe her eyes.

'And that made you think—' She broke off, and then continued, unsteadily, 'There is no special man, but there's no special *woman* either. I didn't leave Richard for anyone. He left me!'

'But Di—that is, I thought—'

'Yes? What did you think?' Olivia found she was shaking with anger now. 'I'm sorry to disappoint you, but I wasn't the guilty party. Unless the fact that Richard thought I was *dull*, and I couldn't produce any children, constitutes a breach of the marriage contract in your eyes!'

Joe's jaw dropped. 'Then—what—?'

'Oh, ask Diane,' muttered Olivia disgustedly, striding back along the beach. Her eyes were smarting with unshed tears, but at least she now knew what Diane was telling everyone. No wonder she'd had no objections to Olivia's coming here. She'd probably told her friends that Richard had invited her.

Joe caught up with her before she reached the place where the dock acted as a breakwater to the incoming tide. He looked frustrated, and although she was hot and angry she realised she could hardly put the blame on him. 'I'm sorry,' he said, his lean frame blocking her path to the terrace. 'I realise this must be painful for you. I'd no idea that Ricky wanted a divorce.'

Olivia took a deep breath. 'It's all right—'

'It's not all right.' He regarded her with doubtful eyes. 'Look, it's probably my fault. I've—misunderstood the situation. I guess your coming out here— Well, you must admit it is unusual. But if Diane asked you—'

'She did.'

'Then I apologise.'

Olivia shrugged. 'It doesn't matter.'

'It does matter.' He sighed. 'Look, this must be bloody painful for you.'

'No.' The last thing she wanted was for him to feel sorry for her. 'It isn't painful at all. I admit I thought it might be. But it's not.'

Joe frowned. 'So you're not still harbouring some great passion for him?'

'For Richard?' If she hadn't felt so emotional, she might

have laughed. 'No.' Then, because she was afraid that if he continued looking at her like that she'd make a fool of herself again, she glanced at her watch. 'Gosh, is that the time? I really ought to be getting back.'

She thought he looked as if he would have liked to object, but it was probably just wishful thinking on her part. And, when he moved aside, she started up the path. She forced herself to walk slowly, even though her nerves were urging her to rush madly back to the house and call a cab. She hoped he wouldn't offer to drive her back to the hotel. She badly needed some time alone.

She saw the Harley when she was crossing the grassy slope that led up to the patio. She hadn't noticed it when they left the house because she'd been too busy admiring her surroundings, but it was propped on its stand, a few feet from the windows of the pool room.

She halted in surprise and Joe walked on a couple of steps before realising she wasn't with him. 'That's—that's a Sportster, isn't it?' she exclaimed, gazing at the motorcycle with undisguised admiration. And although she'd been desperate to leave before its gleaming frame reminded her nostalgically of home.

Joe's brows arched. 'You're a fan?' he asked, in surprise, and she found herself smiling into his enquiring face.

'I'm an owner,' she corrected him. 'I've got an old 750 back home.'

'No sweat!' The tension that had been between them as they'd walked up from the beach was suddenly lifted, and Joe led the way over to the powerful road machine with evident pride. 'Yeah,' he said, 'this is a fairly contemporary model. But I've got one of the old Ironheads back in Frisco.'

'An Ironhead!' Olivia was impressed. 'Oh, mine's just a fairly beaten-up Panhead with telescopic front forks. Big deal!'

'Hey, those old Glides, as we called them, were pretty impressive,' he declared energetically. 'Have you had it long? When did you get interested in bikes?'

'In Harleys,' Olivia corrected him lightly, running an admiring hand over the motorcycle's gleaming paintwork. 'Oh—well, I guess I've always been interested, but I bought my machine when I got the royalties from my first book.'

Joe grinned, their earlier contretemps forgotten. 'D'you want to ride it?' he asked. 'I can see the yearning in your eyes.' He swung the bike off its stand, and tested its balance. 'There you go. If you follow that path through the trees, it'll bring you down to the beach.'

'Oh, no.' Olivia stepped back, shaking her head, one hand moving negatively from side to side. 'Really, I couldn't,' she added ruefully. 'Besides—the sand will get into the engine. It's kind of you to offer, but—'

'These bikes race on the beach at Daytona,' said Joe drily. 'But, if you're nervous of having a skid, hop on the back.' He patted the seat, and although Olivia knew it was reckless she found herself doing as he suggested, and a moment later he had started the powerful machine and pulled away.

'Hold on,' he yelled as they started down a tree-lined track that was narrow and undoubtedly dangerous for an unskilled rider, although Olivia felt no fear with Joe in charge. With a feeling of excitement, she slipped her arms about his waist and hung on tightly, revelling equally in the thrill of the ride and the nearness of his taut frame.

Once they reached the beach, he opened it up, and they sped along the damp sand so fast that the barrette came out of Olivia's hair and blew away. But it was so exhilarating to feel the wind tearing at her scalp that she hardly noticed. She'd never ridden without a helmet before.

He turned at speed, the rear wheel sliding madly across the sand, and then he brought the powerful engine to a halt. 'Your turn,' he said, getting off the bike, and this time she didn't object.

She didn't drive as fast as Joe. She wasn't used to having a pillion rider, for one thing, and for another she was intensely conscious of Joe's hands at her waist. He didn't cling to her, but he did grasp a handful of her hair and wrap it round his fingers. 'It's blinding me,' he said, into her ear, and the bike wobbled as Olivia felt his hand against her neck.

She stopped again before the path started up to the house. 'You take over now,' she said, her cheeks scarlet from the wind.

'Okay.' He slid across the seat, and grasped the handle-bars. 'You did good,' he added admiringly, and Olivia scrambled onto the back to hide her foolish pride.

They reached the patio all too soon, and when Joe parked the bike in its previous position Olivia was ready to swing her leg to the ground. 'Wait.' His hand gripped her bare leg just above her knee, successfully stopping her. He turned and looked at her over his shoulder, his eyes warmly sensual as they rested on her flushed face. 'I just wanted you to know I'm—sorry about what happened before—'

'It doesn't matter—'

'It does.' His fingers splayed over her knee. 'It wasn't your fault, it was mine.'

Olivia's knee quivered beneath his fingers, and to distract him from that stark betrayal she uttered a forced laugh. 'You can tell I've spent too long at a desk. I'm out of condition,' she said, hoping he'd believe her. But all he did was slide his hand up her thigh, his fingers invading the hem of her shorts.

'I can tell when you're lying,' he said softly, and damp-ness pooled between her legs. God, could he smell the ef-fect his words were having on her? Every pore in her body was oozing sexual need.

'I've got to go,' she said desperately, and abruptly he released her.

'Yeah, I know,' he muttered harshly as she fairly vaulted off the bike. 'But I want you to know I'm glad you came here. And I hope you'll want to see me again…'

Olivia dragged her thoughts back to the present. He'd not meant it, she assured herself. He was just being polite, letting her off the hook for taking advantage of the situation earlier on. He hadn't wanted to send her back to the hotel thinking that what had happened had disturbed him. He'd probably been trying to ensure that she didn't spill the beans to Diane.

As if she would!

Olivia sighed. She would say nothing to Diane. Apart from anything else, telling tales would require her to admit that she'd been at the Malibu house, and that was something she'd rather keep to herself. Stupid as it was, she preferred to keep the memory private. It had been an afternoon out of time, a few hours when she'd had him all to herself.

All the same, Diane's question demanded an answer, and she'd spent far too long staring into space. 'Yesterday afternoon?' she repeated lightly, as if it were difficult to remember. 'Why? Were you trying to reach me?' She manufactured an enquiring look. 'I—went shopping.'

'Did you?' Diane's response was ominous, but Olivia assured herself she couldn't possibly know what she'd really done. Unless someone had seen B.J. when he'd come to collect her. Despite Joe's protests, she'd insisted on coming back in a cab. 'I was trying to reach you,' Diane added coolly, crossing one silk-clad leg over the other. 'Joe was too busy to see me, and I wanted to talk about the book.'

'Really?'

Olivia bent her head and set her coffee cup carefully back on its saucer. She had the uneasy feeling that nothing about this morning was usual at all. First the coffee, and now this interrogation. Diane had never shown an interest in what she'd done before.

'Yes, really,' said Diane now, leaning towards her. Her blue eyes were steely sharp in her delicate face. 'I think you'll agree that we've covered most of the personal details. It occurred to me that you'd probably rather not discuss your husband's attraction to me. Like the details about my other two marriages, I'm sure Phoebe can give you what you need. And, of course, you'll want to visit the studios. She can arrange that, too.'

Olivia cleared her throat. 'I see,' she said, and caught her lower lip between her teeth. 'Then you don't want me coming here again—on a regular basis, that is?'

Diane seemed to hesitate, and Olivia steeled herself for some outburst, but then the other woman merely shook her head. 'No,' she said, picking a thread of cotton from her short linen tunic. 'It's too—boring. I've got things to do, people to see, appointments to keep. Spending every morning closeted with you is much too demanding. I'm neglecting my—friends, and—Joe's complaining because I'm never free.'

Olivia stiffened. Had that been deliberate? She was almost sure it had. 'I'm sorry you find talking about yourself boring,' she said tightly, and then cursed herself for letting her feelings show.

'I didn't say that,' retorted Diane. 'I said spending every morning with you was boring. God, I don't know what Ricky sees in you. What he ever saw, if it comes to that.'

Olivia got to her feet. 'In that case—' she began, feeling an intense sense of relief that it was all over, but before she could move away Diane uttered a remorseful sound.

'Oh, please,' she said, getting up now and offering her famous smile in conciliation. 'I'm so sorry, Olivia. That was unforgivable. But Ricky gets me so on edge at times I don't know what I'm doing. Really, that wasn't what I intended to say at all.'

But it was what she was thinking, thought Diane uneasily, not at all convinced that her ex-husband was the only reason for this scene. 'I think we both know that my coming here was a mistake,' she declared swiftly. 'I'm sorry if Richard's making life difficult for you, but—'

'No. Please.' Diane's smile had thinned now, and Olivia knew it wasn't only her imagination that made her think that it didn't reach her eyes. 'Sit down, Olivia. Let me explain.'

'There's nothing to explain—'

'There is.' Diane's tone was still polite, but Olivia had the feeling she was only keeping her temper with an effort.

'I suppose the truth is I didn't realise it would—upset Ricky so much. Having you here, I mean.'

'Ms Haran—'

'No, let me finish.' Diane sank down onto the sofa again, and rather than continue standing over her Olivia felt compelled to resume her seat. 'I—told Ricky I wouldn't say anything; that I'd pretend this was my idea and not his. But, you're obviously far too intelligent to be put off with half-truths, when you probably know how he feels for yourself.'

Olivia sighed. 'I don't think—'

'Hear me out, please.' Diane put out an imploring hand. 'I've spoken to Phoebe, and she agrees with me. You can get anything you need from her. You can stay on at the hotel, of course—until the end of the week, at least. Then send me the first draft of the manuscript when it's completed. I can fax any amendments I think are necessary.'

'But I thought—'

The words were out before she could prevent them, and Olivia knew a feeling of frustration when Diane lifted one expertly plucked brow. 'You thought?' she said, evidently prepared to listen in this instance. Had she guessed what Olivia had been thinking? 'Go on. What were you about to say?'

'It was nothing,' said Olivia firmly, annoyed with herself for saying anything. She had no intention of admitting that she'd been looking forward to writing the first draft of the book in Los Angeles. 'I—if you're still sure you want me to write your biography—'

'I do.'

'Then—okay. I can do that.'

'Good.' Diane nodded. 'Good.' She paused. 'I'll tell Ricky you're leaving.'

'Oh, please—' Now it was Olivia's turn to make an imploring gesture. 'I'd rather you didn't say anything.' She felt the annoying heat of her embarrassment entering her cheeks. She wanted no more roses arriving at the hotel. 'I—I think it's best, don't you?'

'If you say so.' But Diane's face had a strangely feral look to it now, and Olivia wondered if she had been entirely wise to show her feelings. 'But now I suggest you finish your coffee, and then we'll try and tie up any loose ends you feel are still outstanding.'

CHAPTER TWELVE

OLIVIA sighed, sinking lower into the foaming water and allowing the powerful jets to ease her cares away. This was a luxury she wouldn't have when she got back to England, and although it was something she could live without it was just another reminder that this time tomorrow night she'd be on the plane to London.

She sighed again, putting up her hand to check that her hair was still secured in the knot she'd pinned earlier. Wet strands clung to her cheeks, but she was relieved to find the knot was holding. She didn't have time to wash her hair tonight. Not if she wanted to get down to the restaurant at a reasonable hour.

Of course, she was late because Max Audrey, Diane's producer, had kept her waiting so long at the studios. Like a few of the people she'd contacted in the past few days, he considered his job far more important than hers. She wasn't rich, therefore she was expendable. In his world only money oiled the wheels of success.

And when she'd finally got to talk to him he'd been less than courteous. His phone had kept ringing throughout the interview, and he hadn't asked her to excuse him every time he'd reached for the receiver. She had the feeling she could have learned as much about his opinion of Diane if she'd spoken to his secretary. Just as Manuel and María knew their employer better than anyone else.

Still, she had learned a lot more about her subject's standing in the film community. Phoebe had arranged for her to visit the studios where Diane's last film had been made, and Olivia had spoken to cameramen and technicians, make-up artists, and her director, all of whom had been generous in the anecdotes they'd conveyed. Apparently, Diane was well liked by the people who'd

142

worked with her, but Olivia couldn't help the suspicion that they'd have said anything to keep their jobs.

It had been a strenuous week, made more so by the fact that she'd been constantly in Phoebe's presence. Diane's agent had insisted that it would be easier for her if she came along. Once again, Olivia suspected that her motives weren't all altruistic. She had the feeling Diane had sent her to ensure she didn't spend her time with anyone else.

As if...

Olivia's lips tightened a little at the realisation that it was almost a week since she'd spent that afternoon with Joe. She hadn't really expected him to get in touch with her again, but she couldn't help feeling disappointed that she hadn't even seen him about the hotel. He'd probably gone back to San Francisco and thought nothing more about her, she reflected ruefully. Except, perhaps, a sense of relief that he'd avoided a more disastrous scene.

The realisation that the phone was ringing jarred her out of her introspection. Diane, she thought wearily. She often rang at this time. To check up on her? Olivia was cynical. If she only knew, she had nothing to check up on her for. But if she didn't answer the phone Diane would be suspicious, and the last thing she wanted was for her to come to the hotel.

Switching off the jets, she sat up and reached for the extension. Like all the best establishments, there was a phone in the bathroom as well. It had been a novelty when she'd first got here, but pretty soon the novelty had worn off. It meant there was no place where Diane couldn't reach her, which was one advantage she would have when she went home.

Her hand slipped on the receiver and she almost dropped it into the bath so that there was a lilt of laughter in her voice when she said, 'Hello.' And why not? she thought determinedly. She should be looking forward to seeing her flat again. And Henry! She pulled a wry face. She hoped he hadn't forgotten all about her.

'Liv?'

Her heart sank. 'Hello, Richard,' she said, wishing she hadn't answered after all.

'Liv, I want to see you. Diane says that you're leaving, and I must talk to you before you go. I know it's late, and you're probably exhausted, but I can't let you go without making you understand how I feel.'

'No, Richard.'

'What do you mean, no?'

'I mean I don't want to see you,' said Olivia flatly. 'I'm sorry, but that's the way it is. I—I'm sure you and Diane can iron your problems out if you just put your minds to it.' She paused. 'Have you thought of having a baby? If I remember correctly that was one of the reasons why you wanted a divorce.'

'Oh, yes.' Richard sneered. 'You had to bring that up, didn't you? You know as well as I do that I can't father a child.'

'I didn't know that,' protested Olivia, dry-mouthed, as the injustice of his accusations assailed her. She swallowed. 'But thank you for telling me.' She shook her head. 'Better late than never.'

Richard swore. 'Are you trying to tell me you didn't have any suspicions that I was to blame?'

'No, I didn't.' Olivia caught her breath. 'How could I? You swore it wasn't you.'

'I swore a lot of things,' muttered Richard bitterly. 'But you didn't hear them all. I can't believe you didn't check up on me. After I'd left, at least.'

'And they'd have told me?' Olivia was impatient. 'Get real, Richard. A person's medical history is private. Besides—' she drew a trembling breath '—I had no reason to believe you were lying.'

'No.' He sounded frustrated now. 'I guess I have been a complete bastard!' He sighed. 'That's why I want you to forgive me. You've no idea how much your—understanding would mean to me.'

Olivia bit her lip. 'All right,' she said. 'All right, I forgive you. Now—I've got to go. I'm—busy, and I want to get on.'

'Still working?' Richard was sardonic. 'My, what a conscientious little girl you are.' And then, as if sensing her indignation, he added, 'Sorry. That was uncalled for.' He paused. 'Maybe I'll speak to you again before you leave.'

Not if I have anything to do with it, thought Olivia fiercely as she replaced the receiver. She could only hope Diane hadn't told him exactly when she was leaving. But, as she'd told him everything else, what chance did she have of that?

The phone rang again, almost before she'd had time to settle down again. The final few moments she'd been promising herself were obviously not meant to be. 'Yes?' she said ungraciously, wondering what else Richard could have thought of, and then almost lost her voice when Joe Castellano's husky tenor caressed her ear.

'Olivia? Hi.' He paused. 'I was wondering. Have you had dinner?'

Olivia collapsed against the side of the bath. 'Joe,' she said, when she could speak again. Her voice was strangely hoarse. 'What a surprise.'

'But a pleasant one, I hope,' he said, though there was an unexpected edge to his voice. 'I—don't want to intrude on your privacy, but I'd like to see you. If you haven't had dinner, perhaps we could eat together.'

Olivia expelled a trembling breath. 'I haven't had dinner,' she said, realising she didn't sound very enthusiastic, but too overwhelmed by his sudden phone call to select her words.

'Well, good.' He waited a beat. 'Does that mean you do want to see me? Or was that merely an observation, and you'd rather eat alone?'

'No, I—' Olivia struggled to pull herself together. 'You don't understand. Um—Richard was on the phone just now, and I thought it was him calling back.' She moistened her lips, and then forced herself to continue. 'I—suppose I thought you'd be dining with Diane.'

'Well, I'm not.' He didn't elaborate, so she didn't know whether that was her decision or his. 'Look, if you've made some arrangement to meet Richard, forget it. I should have given you some warning, but I just got back from Frisco this evening.'

So he had been away again.

Olivia hurried into speech. 'No, I'm not seeing Richard. And—and I'd love to have dinner with you. If—if you'll give me a few minutes, I'll be ready.'

'May I come up?'

Olivia's breathing was suspended. 'Come up?'

'Yeah, as in you offering me a drink before dinner,' he responded lightly. 'But if you'd rather not—'

'No.' Olivia gulped for air, and dismissed the thought that it wasn't a good idea. 'Please—' Her voice cracked, and she cleared her throat to hide her embarrassment. 'Yes. Come on up. I'll leave the door unlocked.'

Which meant wedging the 'Do Not Disturb' notice between the door and the lock, she discovered moments later, after flinging on one of the towelling bathrobes the hotel supplied and scurrying through the bedroom and across the sitting room in her bare feet. But if she'd told Joe she was still in the bath he might have suspected her of making excuses, and this might be her last chance of saying goodbye.

She had barely made it into the bath again before she heard someone enter the suite. She prayed it wasn't a prowler, and listened attentively to him closing the door. Then, 'Olivia?' she heard him call, and her breath escaped her in a relieved sigh.

'I'm here,' she called back lightly, and reached for the soap.

She was lathering her arms with one of the expensively perfumed cushions that appeared in various parts of the bathroom every morning and disappeared as soon as she had used them, when he opened the bathroom door. If he was surprised to find her in the bath he didn't show it.

Instead, he propped his shoulder against the frame of the door and regarded her as if he had every right to be there.

'Hi.'

Olivia was too shocked to speak, so she didn't say anything. She was too busy reviewing her Victorian morals, and finding them wanting. She was a modern woman, she chided herself, and it wasn't as if she wasn't attracted to him. But she'd never dreamt he might walk into the bathroom.

Her initial impulse was to slide down so that her body was hidden beneath the water. Her breasts were responding to his appraisal and their rosy peaks were already button-hard and tight. But he'd seen her breasts, she reminded herself, so surely they were no novelty to him, and he was not to know there was a pulse beating between her legs.

And he looked so good, she thought avidly, feeding on his dark attractive face. In a dark grey lounge suit and matching shirt, the jacket parted by the hand he'd pushed into his trouser pocket, he made her acutely aware of what she was missing by not having a man in her life.

She wouldn't have been human if she hadn't reacted, but instead of acting like a shrinking violet she continued soaping her arms as if having a man standing watching her were an everyday occurrence. She wasn't aware of being deliberately provocative, even when her hands strayed to her breasts, but his sudden instinctive intake of breath brought a half-challenging look to her eyes.

'D'you want some help?' he asked huskily, and now she was forced to look away. But she wondered what he was doing here when a week ago he'd made his feelings blatantly obvious.

'I don't think so,' she said, finding her voice at last. 'If—if you'll help yourself to a drink, I'll be with you as soon as I can.'

'I don't want a drink,' he countered, and, straightening away from the door, he approached the huge corner bath. His eyes darkened as they looked down at her. 'Is there room for another one in there?'

Olivia's jaw sagged. 'I—why—no—'

'Why not?' He squatted down on his haunches beside her. 'My architect informed me that these tubs are big enough to hold a party.'

'Well, they're not.' Olivia was swift to disabuse him, the idea of provoking him again losing its appeal. 'Besides—' she forced herself to meet his sensual gaze '—I thought you weren't interested in me.'

His eyes narrowed. 'What gave you that idea?'

'What gave me that idea?' echoed Olivia disbelievingly. 'I should have thought you'd know that better than me.'

'Well, I don't,' he said annoyingly, dipping his hand into the water and allowing its contents to spill over her shoulder and down her breast. 'In any case, I thought this was what you wanted. If not, you did a damn good job of convincing me that it was.'

Olivia swallowed, his nearness overwhelming the urge to send him away. And though she doubted her motives had anything do to with Richard what he was suggesting was temptation in its finest form.

But she couldn't do this, she thought unsteadily. He'd said she was no *femme fatale* and he was right. And in her prescribed world people didn't act so recklessly. She trembled at the thought of him getting into the bath with her. God, she could imagine her father's reaction if he could see her now.

Taking a deep breath, she turned to look at him. 'What do you really want?' she asked, uncaring if he thought her naïve.

Instead of answering her, however, he picked up the soap and lathered his hands with it. 'Isn't it obvious?' he asked, and stroked his hand down her cheek.

'Not to me,' she lied, even though her heart was thumping. Dear God, did he really mean precisely what he said? 'You're wetting your sleeve,' she added, hoping to distract him. His cuff had trailed in the water and was dripping on her arm.

'So what?' he asked now, but he rinsed his hands and

shed his jacket onto the floor. 'That better?' he suggested, his gaze moving deliberately over her body, and she pressed her thighs together almost in defence.

'Mr Castellano—'

He was pulling off his tie and loosening his collar as she said this, and he rested his forearms on the bath and gave her a knowing look. 'Don't call me that, for God's sake,' he said drily. 'This isn't the 1890s. I don't make love to women who call me Mr Castellano.'

'Then perhaps that's what I should call you, Mr Castellano,' responded Olivia breathily, aware that it was his teasing that was making her feel brave.

'Could be,' he agreed smoothly, disconcerting her. He slipped off his shirt and unbuttoned the waistband of his trousers. 'I can always make an exception in your case.'

Olivia's eyes widened. 'Joe—' she gasped in protest. 'You can't do this.'

But he'd pushed himself to his feet and was already tackling his zip. 'You can help me,' he said, kicking off his loafers and stepping out of his trousers. And as she looked up at him in mute confusion he added, pointing at his silk boxers, 'You can tell me if you want me to keep these on for modesty's sake.'

Olivia couldn't answer him. She'd never been in a situation like this before and he took her tightened lips as her assent. Before she could move aside, he had stepped down into the deep water, his legs brushing hers as he sat down opposite.

Although she knew she should look elsewhere, she found herself staring at him. Was this some crazy dream, or was Joe Castellano actually sharing her bath? She moved her foot and her toes brushed a hair-roughened calf and ankle. It was really him, and she flinched at the contact.

'Isn't this cosy?' he said, spreading his arms along the sides of the bath and relaxing completely. He took a breath. 'Don't tell me you've never done anything like this before.'

'I haven't,' said Olivia tersely, wishing she was more

experienced. Her eyes felt riveted to the dark hair beneath his arms.

And not just beneath his arms, she noticed. She could now see the hair that arrowed down below his waist. Richard's skin had been smooth, she remembered, and it had always been a source of annoyance to him. But Olivia had always told him she didn't like hairy men.

And she didn't, she insisted fiercely, wishing she could just ignore him. But she couldn't make a move without encountering his outstretched feet. And just when she thought he couldn't do anything more to upset her he drew up his knees and moved so that her feet were between his legs.

'What do you—?' she began unsteadily, and then broke off when he grasped her ankles. 'What do you think you're doing?' she finished breathlessly as his hands slid over her slim calves.

'I thought you might like a massage,' he responded, without looking at her. He was looking down at his hands, at what they were doing to her legs. 'I'm good at this sort of thing,' he added huskily, moving closer until her toes were brushing his groin.

Olivia's stomach quivered. She could feel the swollen heat of him against her feet, and although she knew it was crazy she wished he wasn't wearing the boxers after all. There was something intensely intimate about touching him in this way.

'Like it?' he asked, looking up at her through his straight lashes, and Olivia, who had been scarcely aware of his kneading fingers, could only nod her head. 'I told you I was good,' he appended softly. 'Come closer and I'll loosen up your thighs.'

Olivia's breath escaped in a sound that was half-gulp, half-sob, and she wondered if he could hear the hysteria in her voice. If he only knew, she thought, suppressing the urge to tell him. If he loosened her up any more she'd fall apart.

Yet she didn't stop him when he moved even closer, and

she was obliged to draw her knees up to her chest. 'Open your legs,' he directed roughly, and she heard the raw emotion underlying the request. His thumb brushed over her lower lip. 'Open your mouth.'

Olivia's legs slid down, under his, and he parted his knees and moved closer still. They were face to face and limb to limb, his chest hair tickling her breasts, their lower bodies barely inches apart.

'You're the sexiest woman I've ever known, do you know that?' he muttered, his tongue stroking her lips. He gripped her waist and brought her closer, his thumbs caressing the underside of her breasts.

Sexy? Her?

Olivia felt dizzy, as much from what he was saying as from the tantalising touch of his mouth. But between her legs his arousal was hard against her softness, pushing with urgent need against his shorts.

'You don't mean that,' she said unsteadily, when he released her mouth to nuzzle the hollow of her neck.

'Don't I?' He bit her deliberately, sucking the soft flesh into his mouth 'I'm not—Richard,' he added, when he was able to speak again. 'I don't say things I don't mean.'

Olivia expelled a tremulous breath. 'I don't want to talk about Richard right now.'

'And nor do I,' he conceded, his hands moving up to encircle her breasts. His thumbs pressed almost cruelly on her taut nipples. 'But I want you to know I'm not him.'

'I—I'm not likely to forget,' she got out jerkily, her own hands coming up to grip his waist. And although she wondered later how she'd found the courage to do it her fingers slid inside the waistband of his shorts.

'God...'

His involuntary recoil was instantaneous as her slim fingers explored his buttocks, and for one awful moment she thought he was going to vault out of the bath. She closed her eyes for a moment, not sure she could bear it if he did so, but when she opened them again he was peeling the boxers off his legs. He tossed them aside without taking his eyes from her, and she felt her limbs melting beneath his sensual gaze. 'Come here,' he muttered huskily, reclaiming his position, and this time she felt his muscled heat between her legs.

There was no barrier between them now, no film of silk to prevent an intimacy she'd never known before. When his hand slipped down between them to find the aching nub that craved his attention, she arched helplessly against his fingers, unable to hold back.

Wave upon wave of feeling swept over her, and she sought his mouth eagerly, thrusting her tongue between his teeth. Her hands were gripping his neck, holding him even closer, and he groaned deep in his throat at this evidence of how sweetly responsive she really was.

'Easy, now,' he said unsteadily as she covered his face with kisses, but he turned his mouth against hers with increasing need. His fingers were in her now, stroking her slick honeycomb, making her feel as if she was drowning in sensual pleasure.

But she was instantly aware of the moment when his male sex replaced his fingers. His muscled hardness spread the petals that enfolded him, thick and heavy, thrusting into her core. But her body deepened, expanded, stretched to meet his need, until they were closer than ever before.

'Am I hurting you?' he asked harshly as he heard her sudden intake of breath, but she shook her head and wound her arms around his neck.

'It feels—perfect,' she said huskily, curling her legs about him. She caressed his ear with her tongue. 'Is it good for you?'

Joe gave a groan. 'It's good,' he assured her thickly, closing his eyes. 'But God knows how long I can stand this. I have the feeling that if you move I'll spill my guts.'

'Not your guts, surely,' murmured Olivia breathlessly, never having shared her feelings with anyone else. Richard had been adequate, but not romantic; not adventurous at all. She rocked against Joe deliberately. 'D'you mean like that?'

He swore then, but it wasn't an angry sound, though she glimpsed the undisguised anguish in his face. 'If you want this to be over, just go on the way you are,' he told her, suppressing a moan. 'Oh, God, I don't think I want to wait any longer.'

It took only a moment. Pressing her against the bath, he withdrew only a couple of times before his thrusting body shuddered in her arms. And she found to her amazement that her own climax followed his, the tremors of his ejaculation and the spilling warmth of his seed driving her over the brink...

CHAPTER THIRTEEN

HE TOOK her again later, on the carelessly tumbled covers of her bed. Somehow, he found the strength to lift her out of the water and carry her into her bedroom, and, uncaring that they were wet, he sought a second release.

Then he rolled groaning onto his back, gathering her against him with lazy arms. 'You are beautiful,' he told her urgently, his hand cupping her breast. 'Richard must have been crazy to let you go.'

Olivia propped herself up on one elbow. 'I've told you,' she said tensely. 'I don't want to talk about Richard.' But when she looked at Joe she found he'd closed his eyes.

'Okay, okay,' he conceded drowsily. 'God, but I'm exhausted! Can we leave it till I've had some sleep?'

'Leave what?' she persisted, wanting him to commit himself, but Joe's breathing warned her he wasn't listening to her. He was breathing deeply, his dark lashes spread against his tanned face giving him a curious vulnerability, his impressive manhood dormant now in its moist nest of curling dark hair.

'Damn,' she muttered, barely audibly, taking a deep breath and sliding off the bed. He offered an involuntary movement of protest, but he was too far gone to waken, and she took the quilt and flung it over his sleeping form.

In the living room, the undrawn curtains displayed an unreal vista of downtown Los Angeles. As she tied the belt of her robe about her, she saw the ribbons of incandescence marking every street and highway, a multicoloured panorama of fairy lights. Every now and then, the solid bulk of a tall building added its own illumination to the scene. So many lights, she thought; so many people. Were any of them feeling as confused and anxious as she was tonight?

What to do?

154

She glanced back at the bedroom. Joe was obviously exhausted. He would probably sleep for several hours. But she had a distinct feeling of hollowness inside. She told herself it was hunger; that she'd feel better if she had some dinner. But she suspected its origins were far more complicated than that.

What was she going to do? What would he—Joe—expect her to do? He hadn't mentioned anything about her leaving the following day, but that didn't mean he didn't know she was going. If he was as intimate with Diane as Richard would have her believe, surely she'd have mentioned the change of plan to him?

Diane!

Olivia shivered. She'd almost forgotten Diane's part in this during the last couple of hours. But she'd certainly had her revenge, if that was what she'd been looking for, so why did she feel as if it was herself that she'd betrayed?

She shook her head. The answer was too painful to consider right now. She didn't want to think about the possibility that Joe might eventually marry Diane. How ignorant she'd been to imagine that what she'd felt for Richard was all there was to feel.

A feeling of nausea rose into the back of her throat but she fought it down. She was hungry, she told herself again. Once she'd got some food inside her, she'd stop feeling as if the bottom had dropped out of her world. She didn't love Joe Castellano. She couldn't. She was letting the sexual pleasure he'd given her blind her to his faults.

And he'd never said he cared about her. Not once. He'd told her that she was sexy, and beautiful—both attributes unwarranted, she was sure. But he'd never said he loved her, or that he wanted to spend the rest of his life with her. Heaven knew, he hadn't even mentioned that he wanted to see her again.

She shivered again. She should have told him she was leaving. Before she'd invited him up to the suite, she should have made it known that it was for a farewell drink. That way, he wouldn't have got the wrong impression—that she had intended that he should find her in the bath. As it was, he'd assumed her actions were a form of provocation. That when she'd unlocked the door, and answered his greeting, she'd been deliberately inciting his response.

Even so, she sighed, she couldn't have anticipated what would happen. Even in her wildest dreams, she'd never have imagined that he might join her in the bath. Dear God, in all the time she'd been married to Richard, he'd never done anything so outrageous. Or exciting, she admitted incredulously. Every nerve in her body quivered with expectancy when she remembered how desirable he'd made her feel.

She strayed to the open bedroom door again, but Joe was still sleeping. He'd rolled onto his stomach in her absence and his face was buried in the pillow where her head had been. She badly wanted to go in there and wake him and ask him what he intended. But what stopped her was the thought that he might tell her.

She felt the hollowness again, and this time her stomach rumbled. Perhaps it would be a good idea to go and get something to eat. She thought of calling Room Service, but in that case she'd feel obliged to order for two. And the last thing she wanted on her bill was proof that she'd been sharing her suite with someone else.

But what if Joe woke up and found she wasn't there? she fretted. If she left him a note, he could always come and join her downstairs. She sighed. Wouldn't a note be rather presumptuous? she argued worriedly. He might not want to join her for dinner now. The situation had changed.

For the better?

She wasn't certain. Richard had said he had proof that Diane and Joe were having an affair, so what was this all about? Was she perhaps just a brief diversion? If he knew she was leaving tomorrow, he must know there was no future in it.

With a feeling of despair, she went back into the bathroom and took a shower. Then, as he still hadn't stirred, she donned a silk bra and panties, and a sleeveless dress that fell to her ankles. Her hair was still damp, so she plaited it into a thick braid and secured it with a ribbon. Then, without even looking back, she left the room.

Downstairs, the hotel was busy. She didn't try to get a reservation for dinner in the Pineapple Room this evening, choosing the Bistro instead, for reasons best known to herself. She refused to acknowledge she'd chosen the Italian restaurant because of Joe's background, but she couldn't forget that he'd been eating in here the night she'd decided to play the vamp.

And, although she ordered her favourite pasta dish, she found she couldn't eat it. She was pushing it desultorily round her plate, when someone came to cast a shadow across the meal. She looked up in sudden relief, convinced it must be Joe come to find her. But it was a woman, and her heart sagged with disappointment.

'Hello, Miss Pyatt. Remember me?'

She was vaguely familiar, and Olivia was racking her brains, trying to think where she'd seen her before, when she saw the copy of Eileen Cusack's biography tucked under her arm. 'Oh, yes,' she said, somewhat flatly. 'You're the woman who thought I was Elizabeth Jennings.'

'Sherie Madsen,' supplied the woman eagerly. 'Yes, that's right.' She paused, as if she needed time to formulate what she was about to say. 'Um—did you get the roses?'

Olivia blinked. 'You sent the roses?'

'Well, it was my husband, actually,' Sherie admitted ruefully. 'After the patience you showed over my mistake, he said it was the least we could do.'

'Well, thank you.' Olivia was stunned. She'd never have suspected these people. 'And—and yes. They were beautiful. Thank you very much.'

'It's our pleasure.'

A man spoke, and Olivia saw Sherie's husband behind her now. He was smiling, too, and despite her disappointment Olivia couldn't help feeling flattered.

'Anyway, I just—well, I wondered if you'd mind signing your book now,' Sherie continued, proffering the biography. 'I haven't read it yet, but I'm taking it home to Wisconsin and I assure you I will.'

Olivia smiled. 'Not at all.' She held out her hand for the book and Sherie's husband quickly handed her a pen. She made the dedication and signed her name, and then gave it back to her admirer. 'I hope you enjoy it,' she added as they bid her goodnight.

The unexpected experience had lifted her spirits somewhat, so that by the time she went back up to her suite she was feeling slightly more optimistic than before. She closed the door with some care, and hurried to the door of the bedroom. But, although she'd been away less than an hour, Joe was gone.

The flight to Heathrow left at six o'clock and Olivia, who had been hanging around the airport since just after four, knew a curious kind of relief when the plane lifted off the ground. The decision was made, she thought. She was leaving. Whatever misgivings she might have had that morning were all behind her now. She'd checked out of the hotel, and she was on her way to London. The sooner she reached home and resumed a normal existence, the sooner she'd be able to put all thoughts of Joe Castellano out of her mind.

Well, that was what she'd told herself, she reflected ruefully as the big jet banked over the sprawling city below. She'd come here reluctantly, and she was going home in like mind. The only difference was the reasons. She'd exchanged one unhappy association for another.

But, despite her reluctance to leave Los Angeles, she was glad the past twenty-four hours were over. Making love—or, more accurately, having sex, she amended bitterly—with Joe had been exciting, she had to admit, but it was what had come after that had destroyed what little faith she'd had in herself. How could he do it? she wondered. How could he make love to her and then leave her, without even bothering to say farewell? When she'd got back to the suite and found he'd gone, it had been one of the worst moments of her life.

Yet, even then, she hadn't quite believed it. She'd been quite prepared to accept that Joe had woken up in her absence and gone to look for her. In consequence she'd gone back down to the lobby, only to have no success in any of the restaurants or bars. He wasn't even enjoying an espresso in the coffee shop, despite the fact that neither of them had had anything to eat.

She'd gone back to the suite, half hoping he might have turned up there; but he hadn't, and although she'd contemplated contacting Reception she hadn't been convinced he'd appreciate her doing that. The trouble was, she hadn't known what her position was as far as he was concerned, and the last thing she wanted to do was embarrass him— or herself, which was much more likely.

Realising she'd never sleep unless she had something to eat, she'd ordered a sandwich from Room Service, and forced herself to eat it when it arrived. Then, because she had to do something, she'd rung the phone company and asked if they could give her the number of the house at Malibu.

Of course, they couldn't. It was what they called an 'unpublished' number, and once again she'd come up against a brick wall. Short of alerting all his staff she was looking for him, she'd been helpless, and, deciding she would think of something else in the morning, she'd gone to bed.

She hadn't slept very well. Although she was physically tired, her brain refused to rest, and by six o'clock she'd been sitting at the window again. Why had he left? she'd asked herself, for what must have been the umpteenth time. If there'd been some sort of emergency, surely he'd have let her know.

When the phone had rung at eight o'clock, she'd been sure it must be him, ringing to offer his apologies, but it was Bonnie Lovelace instead. She'd been ringing to remind her that the usual checkout time was noon. 'But Diane's had me extend that to four o'clock,' she'd added grandly. 'She also said to tell you that she'd have invited you to the house, but she's away right now.'

'Is she?'

Olivia hadn't been particularly interested in what Diane was doing, but Bonnie had adopted her usual self-important style. 'Yes, she left last night for Malibu,' she'd continued, as if she was bestowing a confidence. 'She's staying with Mr Castellano. She said to tell you goodbye.'

That was the moment when Olivia's world had fallen apart. How could he do it? she thought. How could he have gone from her bed to Diane's? Or invite her to *his* bed, she amended, suppressing a moan of anguish. Were all men such bastards, or did she just attract that kind?

The rest of the day had been an anticlimax. Although she'd gone down to the lobby to buy some last-minute presents, her heart hadn't been in it, and she couldn't wait for four o'clock to come. As it was, she'd left for the airport with almost an hour to spare, and spent the rest of her time in Los Angeles in the departure lounge.

Even then, even after all that had happened, she'd still nurtured the hope that she might be wrong. He would know what time she was leaving. He'd said himself he was a frequent traveller. But, although she'd listened intently to every announcement from the public-address system, there was never one for her.

So, it was over, she told herself painfully. She hadn't come here with the best of intentions, so perhaps it served her right. She'd wanted to hurt Diane, but all she'd ended up doing was hurting herself. Which was probably nothing more than she deserved.

The plane had levelled off now, and the warning sign about fastening your seat belt had been switched off. The pilot had introduced himself by way of the microphones above her head, and he was presently telling his passengers what kind of flight they might expect. The forecast, he said, was good, and with a tail wind they should make good time. He expected to land the plane in London at twelve o'clock the following afternoon.

'Is this seat taken?'

Olivia, who had been grateful that the seat beside her

was unoccupied, looked up in surprise. To her dismay, she found Richard easing himself down beside her, his expression a mixture of satisfaction and smug relief.

Her jaw dropped. 'What are you doing here?' she exclaimed, rather too loudly, and then, at his gesture of protest, she lowered her tone. 'I mean...' She glanced with some embarrassment at the stewardess who was watching them. 'Why are you on this flight?'

Richard leaned back in his seat. 'Why do you think?' he asked impatiently, waving at the stewardess. 'Scotch,' he said, when the woman approached him, then, glancing down at what Olivia was drinking, an amused smile crossed his face. 'White wine,' he remarked triumphantly. 'D'you want another one of those?'

'No, thank you.' Olivia controlled her temper with difficulty. This was not a good time for Richard to try and rekindle their relationship. 'I asked you what you were doing on this flight.'

'And I told you,' retorted Richard comfortably, settling more comfortably in his chair as the stewardess went to get his drink.

'No. You said, why did *I* think you were travelling,' Olivia corrected him tersely. 'And I really don't have an answer for that.'

Richard's mouth turned down. 'If you say so.'

'I do say so.' Olivia closed her eyes for a moment in an effort to keep her emotions in check. Then she opened them again and looked at him coldly. 'Where's your wife? Or is that a leading question?'

'You know where she is,' muttered Richard sulkily. 'Bonnie told you.' And then, when Olivia frowned, he gave a defensive shrug. 'I was there. When she made the call,' he explained offhandedly. 'She told me you were travelling on this flight. And—' He thought for a moment, and then appended firmly, 'I decided to keep you company.'

'To keep me company?' Olivia was appalled. The last thing she wanted was Richard doing anything for her.

'Well, I have relatives in London, too,' he declared indignantly. 'It must be nine months since I saw my old man.'

'Really?' As Richard had seldom visited his father when he lived in England, that was hardly relevant. And she didn't believe that was his excuse for travelling now.

'Yes, really.' The stewardess brought his Scotch, and he took a moment to thank her before continuing. 'But I admit I took the chance to see you again. We couldn't talk before, what with Manuel listening in and so on. And that night in the bar you didn't give me a chance.'

'Oh, Richard…' Olivia spoke wearily now, wondering if she'd ever convince him she wasn't interested in him any more. 'We've said all we had to say. Whatever was between us is over. You're married to Diane, and I think you should give your marriage a second chance.'

'A second chance!' Richard sipped his Scotch derisively. 'Liv, I've told you Diane and I are washed up. Ever since Joe Castellano came on the scene, she's been running circles round herself trying to please him. I know he's invested a lot of money in her last two films, but that's not why she's been beating a path to his door.'

Olivia told herself she didn't want to hear this, but there was a strange kind of satisfaction in proving to herself that he'd been fooling her all along. 'You said—you said they were having an affair,' she murmured, trying to sound offhand, 'but how do you know that?' She moistened her lips. 'I read in a magazine that he was—seeing someone else.'

'Anna Fellini,' said Richard at once, evidently knowing all the details. 'Yeah, that's the woman his mother would have liked to welcome into the family.' He paused. 'It's the usual story: Giovanni Castellano—Joe's father—and Paolo Fellini were partners. Giovanni's dead now, but if Joe married Anna, her father would make his share of the vineyards over to him.'

Olivia expelled a low breath. 'I see.'

'But it's not going to happen,' continued Richard positively. 'Much as Castellano likes money, my guess is he likes Diane more.'

Olivia nodded. 'And—you've got proof?'

'Sure have.' Richard was smug. 'I've got a picture of them, together, in San Diego. And when I say together I mean *together*, if you get my drift.'

Olivia felt sick. 'You mean—?'

'Yeah. You got it. Naked, in bed; the whole nine yards.' His lips twisted. 'And Diane knows that picture is going to cost her. If she wants a divorce, she's got to make me happy first.'

Olivia stared at him. 'You wouldn't—'

'Wouldn't I?' Richard sneered. 'Don't you believe it. It was their mistake using that sleazy motel in the first place.' He chuckled, but it wasn't a pleasant sound. 'I heard her making the arrangements. That's how I was able to fix the pictures. I swear to God, you can get anything in L.A. if the price is right. She thought I was out, but I was listening on the extension in—in another room.'

He faltered over those last few words, and Olivia wondered what he had been about to say that he'd thought better of. Maybe the extension he'd been listening in on had been in someone else's room, she reflected sagely. Like Bonnie Lovelace's, for instance. Olivia knew she had rooms at the Beverly Hills mansion. And Richard had used that 'I swear to God' phrase again that Olivia had heard Bonnie use so many times before.

But this possible proof of Richard's duplicity didn't mean anything to her. It was what he'd said about Joe and Diane that made her feel sick at heart. She'd never have believed that Joe would leave himself open to any kind of extortion. And why use a motel in San Diego, when he owned a house in Malibu?

'I've shocked you, haven't I?' Richard said now, finishing his Scotch and ringing for the stewardess to order another. 'Well, don't worry. If there's any scandal, it won't reflect badly on me.'

'But have you told him?' asked Olivia, unable to prevent the automatic question. 'I mean, this is blackmail, isn't it? Isn't that a criminal offence?'

'I guess.' Richard was indifferent. 'But Diane's not going to let it get that far. It's her butt that's recognisable, not his.'

Olivia sucked in a breath. 'Are you saying it might not be—Joe Castellano, then?' she ventured faintly.

'Hell, no.' Richard was adamant. 'It's him all right. He used his own name when they checked in; can you believe it?' He snorted. 'Mr and *Mrs* Castellano! And Diane thinks I'm a dope.'

Olivia hesitated. 'Well—what if it's someone else using that name?' she suggested, and Richard's expression darkened as she spoke.

'Oh, yeah,' he said accusingly. 'You'd like to believe that. Don't think I don't know you had the hots for him yourself.'

Olivia gasped. 'I beg your pardon—?'

'Don't pretend you don't know what I'm talking about.' Richard's lips twisted. 'I saw you myself that afternoon at Malibu.' He smiled at her confusion, but there was no humour in it. 'Oh, yeah, I saw you tearing along the beach on the back of his Harley.'

Olivia was horrified. 'But—how—?'

'I was in the lobby of the hotel when that goon of his came to fetch you,' explained Richard carelessly. 'After the way you cut me up that morning, I knew there had to be a reason. So I staked out your hotel and bingo!—there he was.'

Olivia swallowed. 'I can't believe you'd do a thing like that!' she exclaimed, even as her mind was racing. She supposed she should be grateful he hadn't seen them at the house. She remembered thinking that the solarium was too exposed for lovemaking.

'Desperate needs take desperate measures,' he misquoted smugly. 'Diane was extremely interested to hear where you'd been.'

Olivia blinked. 'You told Diane?'

'Oh, yeah.' Richard picked up the glass the stewardess had just set beside him and viewed her over the rim.

'Why'd you think she changed her mind about you staying on at the hotel? If there's one thing Diane can't stand it's competition.'

Olivia couldn't believe it. 'You told Diane,' she said again. 'For God's sake, why?'

'Because I knew we weren't going to get it together in Lala-land,' he responded. 'And Castellano was a complication I couldn't afford.'

Olivia was stunned. 'I still can't believe you'd do this. Jeopardise your marriage and my career because you can't accept a simple truth. Richard, I told you, I don't love you, I don't care if I never see you again. You had no right to interfere in my life. No right at all.'

Richard's mouth took on a sullen slant. 'You're just saying that because you're angry with Diane. Once you've had time to think about it, I know you'll see I'm right. We were meant for one another, Liv, only I was too blind to see it before. And with the settlement Diane's promised me—'

'Richard, read my lips,' said Olivia grimly, staring at him. 'When we land in London, I never want to see you again. I'm sorry if you're not happy with Diane, but that's not my problem. Now, I suggest you go back to your own seat.'

Richard scowled. 'You don't mean that.'

'I do mean it.'

'You're wasting your time if you think Castellano will come after you,' Richard blurted suddenly. 'I told him you and I had decided to get back together, and that I was accompanying you home.'

'When?' Olivia gulped. 'When did you talk to Joe about our relationship?'

'Last night, of course,' said Richard sulkily. 'Where were you, by the way? When I phoned the suite the second time lover-boy answered the phone.'

CHAPTER FOURTEEN

JOE'S house was in Marin county, north of San Francisco. The houses here had magnificent views of the water, with the green hills surrounding the Berkeley campus visible across the bay. On a clear day, that was, the taxi driver had told Olivia cheerfully. The bay area could be foggy, especially in the height of summer. But it was always beautiful, he'd added proudly. Like all the locals she'd met so far, he never wanted to live anywhere else.

Which was probably why Joe lived here, too, she reflected tensely. That, and the fact that the vineyard he owned was in the Napa Valley, which wasn't far away.

Not that she wanted to think about the vineyard. To do so meant thinking about Anna Fellini, too, and she was one obstacle she was not yet prepared to face. For the present, it was enough to know that Joe wasn't with Diane. That her departure for Malibu had had nothing to do with him.

But that didn't mean she wasn't a fool for coming here, Olivia acknowledged. In fact, if she'd stopped to think what she was doing, she'd never have found the courage to book her flight. And, after all, she had no proof that Joe would want to see her. Only an instinct that was getting weaker by the minute.

Yet, when Richard had dropped his bombshell, she'd been determined to do something. Even if it was only speaking to Joe on the phone, and telling him what a liar her ex-husband was. It had seemed important that she should explain to him that it was not because of Richard that she was leaving. That she'd assumed he knew all about Diane's decision before he came to the hotel.

Getting rid of Richard at the airport hadn't been a problem. After she'd told him what she really thought of him, he'd barely spoken to her for the rest of the trip. He hadn't moved back to his own seat but she knew that was because he was too embarrassed to do so. He'd evidently told the stewardess they were old friends.

Friends!

Olivia had wanted to kill him. She'd told herself she should have suspected something was wrong when she got back to the suite and found Joe was gone. But the truth was, she'd had so little confidence in her own sexuality that, even though she'd tried to reach him by phone, she hadn't really believed he'd want to see her again.

Back at her flat, with Henry purring his welcome, she'd wondered what she could do. No one, least of all Diane and her cohorts, was going to give her Joe's number. She'd already faced that problem in L.A.

But that was when she'd thought of B.J. Benedict Jeremiah Freemantle. She was unlikely to forget his name. How many Benedict Jeremiah Freemantles were there likely to be in California? Although Joe's number had been unlisted, she couldn't believe B.J.'s would be as well.

And it wasn't. As she'd suspected, although his employer divided his time between Los Angeles and San Francisco, B.J.'s apartment was in L.A. He probably had a room at each of Joe's houses, too, just as Bonnie did at Diane's. But his own home was in Westwood, just like Phoebe's.

She'd rung B.J. later that same evening. But it was lunchtime in L.A. and all she'd got was his answering service. However, she'd been able to leave a message, asking him to call her, and she'd spent the next twenty-four hours praying that he would.

B.J. had eventually returned her call two days later. He'd been out of the city, he said, and he'd only just got back. He'd obviously been reluctant to tell her anything about his employer, but when Olivia had explained that it was a personal matter he'd seemed more suspicious than anything else.

It wasn't until Olivia had virtually revealed her feelings for Joe that he'd shown a little more interest. Joe wasn't still in L.A., he'd told her. He'd returned to San Francisco four nights ago. The same night he'd spoken to Richard, Olivia had realised numbly, wondering if she was a fool to pursue him like this.

But something had been driving her on, and somehow she'd succeeded in convincing B.J. that she had to speak to his employer again. But although he'd been prepared to give her Joe's address in San Francisco so she could write to him he had drawn the line at giving her his phone number.

And it was as she was putting down the phone that she had had this brainwave. The brainwave that had caused her to book herself a flight for the following day. She'd never been to San Francisco, she'd consoled herself as she'd paid her fare. If Joe refused to see her, she could always use the trip as research.

Not that that was a very convincing argument, she conceded now. She had the feeling that if Joe refused to speak to her she'd want to take the first flight home. She'd always preferred to lick her wounds in private, and her little flat had never seemed more appealing than it did right now.

'You sure this is the place you want?'

The taxi driver was looking at her reflection in the rear-view mirror, and Olivia guessed that with her cream cotton shirt, mud-brown skirt and bare legs she didn't look as if she'd be at home in these sprawling estates. Or perhaps he'd taken his cue from the small hotel where she was staying. She remembered now that he'd looked rather shocked when she'd given him the address.

'I'm sure,' she said, though her voice was constricted. Her nerves were tight enough without him voicing her own fears. Dear God, she must have been crazy coming here on the strength of a brief—if passionate—association. Would he even care that Richard hadn't been telling the truth?

A few minutes earlier, they'd left Highway 101 and the taxi was now descending a steep curve towards the water. Below them, she could see the roofs and main street of a small town. In the guidebook she'd bought at the airport, she'd read about Sausalito and Tiburon, and the ferry that plied across San Francisco Bay.

'Okay. Well, this is it,' the driver told her suddenly, and Olivia dragged her eyes from the hillside that fell away sharply on their left to the solid wooden gates that faced the road.

The roof of a house could be glimpsed between the trees that grew so thickly beyond the gates. Olivia could see turrets rising above the trees, and a cream-painted façade laced with wooden slats. It looked dignified and imposing, and nothing like the house at Malibu. Yet they each shared the quality of being unique in their own particular way.

And impressive, thought Olivia ruefully, avoiding the driver's eyes as she got out of the car. And how was she supposed to get inside? she wondered. As far as she could see, there was no bell or intercom in sight.

'D'you want me to hang around, in case no one's home?' The man took the dollars she'd offered him but he didn't immediately pull away.

'I— Oh, no.' Despite the distance she was from the nearest town, Olivia was loath to keep him hanging about. Besides, she thought, she could do without an audience if she was forced to abandon her trip.

'Okay.'

With some reluctance, the man put the vehicle into 'drive' and moved off down the road. He was probably hoping to pick up a fare down by the harbour, she decided, wondering if she'd made a huge mistake.

The sound of a car's horn almost scared the life out of her. While she had been fretting about the wisdom of letting the taxi go, a huge estate car had been bearing down on her, its flashing light indicating that it wanted to turn in at the gate. She was in its path, she realised immediately, but as she stepped aside another thought occurred to her. Who was driving the estate car? she wondered tensely. This was Joe's house. Could it be him?

It wasn't. It was a woman at the wheel, but despite her apprehension Olivia knew instantly who it was. *Mrs*

Castellano, she acknowledged incredulously. She'd only seen her picture once, but her resemblance to Joe—or, rather, his to her—made the identification unmistakable.

Olivia was trying to think of some way to introduce herself, when the woman stopped the car beside her and rolled down the window. 'Yes?' she said tersely. 'Can I help you?'

Olivia licked her lips. Having the initiative taken out of her hands had startled her somewhat, and she struggled to find something suitable to say. 'Um—is—is Mr Castellano here?' she asked lamely. 'Mr *Joe* Castellano? I'd like to see him if he is.'

'Joseph?'

Olivia groaned. Of course, his mother would call him Joseph. 'Yes—Joseph,' she agreed, rather weakly. 'Do you think you could tell him I'm here?'

Mrs Castellano frowned. 'Could I tell him *who's* here?' she asked pointedly, her eyes—darker eyes than Joe's, Olivia noticed—taking a brief inventory of Olivia's appearance.

'Oh—Olivia,' she said hurriedly. 'Olivia Pyatt. I—I met your son when I was working in—'

'You're—Olivia?'

The woman was staring at her disbelievingly now, and Olivia guessed that if she had heard of her she was thinking that she was not the type of woman her son would normally be attracted to. 'Yes,' she answered, feeling her colour deepening. 'Is he here? Joe, I mean. I really would like to speak to him.'

'Would you?' Mrs Castellano shook her head, and Olivia was convinced she was going to refuse her request. 'Well—' she shrugged her shoulders '—you'd better get in. I'll take you up to the house.'

Olivia stared at her. 'You will?'

'It's what you want, isn't it?' The woman arched an imperious brow that was so like her son's that Olivia caught her breath.

'Well—yes,' she muttered, and when the woman pushed

open the door she hurried round the car. 'Thank you. Thank you very much.'

'Don't thank me.' The woman sounded the horn again, and this time an elderly man appeared to open the gates. She nodded at him as they passed, and then gave Olivia another appraising look. 'I hope you're not going to tell Joseph any more lies,' she added coolly. 'He may be the head of the family, but to me he's just my eldest son.'

Olivia stared at her now. 'Lies?' she echoed defensively. 'I haven't told him any lies.'

'No?' Mrs Castellano looked sceptical. 'Then why did I get the impression that you had?'

Olivia blinked. 'What exactly did Joe tell you, Mrs Castellano?'

'I don't think that's any concern of yours.' Joe's mother spoke impulsively, and then seemed to think better of it. 'Oh—he hasn't talked to me, but I know my son.'

Olivia shook her head. 'I'm sorry.' A thought occurred to her. 'But perhaps it's not me who's upset him.' She hesitated. 'I expect you know of his— his friendship with Diane Haran?'

'The actress?' Mrs Castellano was scathing. 'Oh, she'd like to think Joseph was interested in her. But I'm afraid she'll have to be content with Mark instead.'

Olivia blinked. 'Mark?'

'My younger son,' prompted Joe's mother impatiently, and Olivia remembered the first morning she had spent at the Beverly Hills mansion, and Diane saying that Joe's brother was an actor, too. 'I don't approve of him getting involved with a married woman,' she went on irritably. 'Particularly as I'm fairly sure she only used the connection to get to Joseph.'

Olivia tried to absorb what she was hearing. Was this woman saying that Diane had been having an affair with Joe's brother, not with him?

'In Los Angeles, people will do anything for money,' Mrs Castellano continued, unaware of her guest's confusion. 'They're always looking for finance for their films, you know.'

Olivia didn't know what to say. She was trembling, as much with disbelief at what she had heard as with apprehension at seeing Joe again. 'But—Joe—Joseph is here, isn't he?' she ventured nervously.

'Yes, he's here,' declared his mother, somewhat unwillingly. 'I don't suppose you'd like to tell me why you've come?'

'I—need to see him,' said Olivia awkwardly. And then, remembering something else, she asked, 'Could you tell me how you knew my name?'

The older woman's lips twisted. 'I'm not a psychic, Miss Pyatt. Joseph has spoken to me about you. Though not this week, I must admit.' Her brows arched. 'But don't ask me to tell you in what context you were mentioned. Like you, I prefer to keep my feelings to myself.'

As they'd been speaking, Mrs Castellano had been driving along the twisting track up to the house, but it was only as they each fell silent that Olivia was able to take any notice of her surroundings. Tall pines, dwarf poplars and cyprus hedged the path with their branches, and the smell of resin drifted in through the estate car's windows.

Up close, the house was less intimidating. Olivia could now see that what she had thought was a parapet was really a widow's walk. But there were turrets, and a kind of round tower marked one corner of the building. And it was much older than the house at Malibu, with a fascinating aura of the past.

'It used to belong to a seafaring family,' remarked Mrs Castellano, noticing Olivia's interest in the house. 'In the days when the big clippers sailed to China. My husband bought the place in 1922.'

Olivia was getting out of the car. 'You live here?' she asked, unaware of the apprehension in her voice.

'Not since Giovanni died,' returned her hostess, with a wry expression. 'I live in the city. But I don't deny I worry about Joseph living here alone.'

Was that why she wanted Joe to marry Anna Fellini? Olivia wondered tensely, half afraid to dismiss the threat Diane had presented from her thoughts. But she was beginning to see that Richard had been mistaken about so many things; or perhaps he'd just chosen to interpret them that way.

Like that photograph, for example. What if it was of Mark Castellano and Diane? It would possibly explain why they'd chosen to go to San Diego. Mr and Mrs Castellano. Was she clutching at straws to think that Joe was too fastidious to do something like that?

'I expect Joseph's in the library,' his mother went on briskly, and Olivia realised how much she cared about her son. 'I won't ask Victor to announce you—not unless you want me to, of course?' She raised a questioning brow, nodding at Olivia's quick denial. 'I thought not.'

They entered the house by way of a charming entrance hall with a dark-stained staircase leading up on the right. The floor was polished wood with a hand-woven rug in the centre, and there were several seascapes and a magnificent barometer hanging on the panelled walls.

Through open, double-panelled doors on her left, Olivia could see a high-ceilinged living room, with long, square-cut windows, giving a delightful view of the bay. Tall cabinets, antique tables, and plenty of easy chairs and sofas strewn with cushions, gave the room a homely ambience, and it was this as much as anything that distinguished it from the house at Malibu.

This was where Joe *lived*, thought Olivia, with an involuntary shiver. This was his home in the truest sense of the word. She would have liked to spend a few moments absorbing that fact and holding it to her. But an older man had appeared through a door set beneath the stairs, his lined face breaking into a smile when he saw who one of his visitors was.

'Good morning, ma'am.' He greeted Joe's mother warmly. And, although he must have been curious as to her identity, he was too polite to ask who Olivia was. 'I didn't

know you were expected,' he added. 'Would you like me
to tell your son that you're here?'

'That won't be necessary, Victor,' said Mrs Castellano
firmly. 'Joseph isn't expecting me, but I think we'd like to
give him a surprise. This is Miss Pyatt, by the way. She's
a—friend of Joseph's. Tell me, is he in the library or holed
up in his den?'

'I believe he's in the library, Mrs Castellano,' said Victor
politely. Then, turning to Olivia, he said, 'Welcome to
Dragon's Rest, Miss Pyatt. Can I get you anything? A cup
of coffee or—?'

'*I'll* have an espresso, Victor,' broke in Joe's mother,
with another glance in Olivia's direction. 'I think Miss
Pyatt would prefer to see Joseph. Isn't that right?'

Olivia nodded her head a little energetically, and then,
realising it wasn't very polite, she managed a faint, 'Yes.'
But in all honesty she would have preferred to sit down
with Joe's mother and delay the moment when she would
have to face him. She was suddenly assaulted with the conviction that she shouldn't have come.

'Would you like me to—?' began Victor, but once again
Mrs Castellano interrupted him.

'I'll make sure Miss Pyatt finds the library,' she in-
structed him crisply. 'If you'll bring my coffee to the living
room, I'd be very grateful.'

'Yes, ma'am.'

Victor departed, not without some misgivings, Olivia
suspected, but he knew better than to offend his employer's
mother. 'Now,' she said, turning to the younger woman, 'I
trust you won't betray my confidence in you. If you go up
to the second floor, it's the first door on your right.'

In fact, Olivia reflected as she climbed the stairs on
slightly unsteady legs, she meant the first floor. Americans
called the ground floor the first floor, and therefore the next
floor up was the second. It made sense, she decided, aware
that she was trying to divert her fears. But she was so afraid
she'd made a terrible mistake.

She emerged onto a galleried landing, with a long corridor leading in the opposite direction that was panelled with richly polished oak like the hall below. The walls here were hung with miniatures of sailing ships, and a brass lantern set on a semicircular table reminded her of Victorian lamps she'd seen in England.

The door Mrs Castellano had indicated was leather-studded and imposing. Like the panelling and the pictures, it reminded her of how old the house was. But beautifully maintained, she conceded, once again delaying her entrance. Everything about this place spelled old money and affluence.

She realised that if she waited any longer Joe's mother might come out of the living room and see her hovering on the landing. Or Joe himself could have heard his mother's arrival and surely then he'd feel obliged to greet his guest. With a jerky movement, she grazed her knuckles on the leather, before summoning all her courage and giving an audible tap.

'Come in.'

It was his voice, albeit it didn't sound very welcoming, and Olivia turned the handle of the door and stepped inside the room before she could change her mind. But even the effort of opening the door had exhausted her, and she held onto the handle for support.

'I heard the car,' said Joe's voice impatiently, but although Olivia scanned the book-lined room she couldn't see where he was. 'You don't have to keep coming here, Mom. I don't need company. I'll be perfectly all right if you'll give me a little space.'

Olivia blinked, and carefully closed the door behind her. Where was he? she wondered, leaning back against the panels, as if she was afraid to move away. He wasn't sitting at the desk or examining any of the leather-bound volumes on the shelves that gave the room its distinctive odour, and she was frowning in confusion when a high-backed chair that had been facing the windows swung about.

His expression when he saw her wasn't encouraging. It was obvious he'd been expecting to see his mother, and he stared at Olivia with narrow-lidded eyes. He didn't even get to his feet; he just sat there gazing as if at an apparition. Then, shaking his head, he raked back his hair with an unsteady hand.

Olivia swallowed. Although she could see his face, his eyes were in shadow, and, realising it was up to her to say something, she murmured, 'Hello, Joe.' And then, when he still didn't speak, she forced a smile to her lips. 'I—I guess you're surprised to see me, aren't you?'

'You could say that.' His voice was harsh and unfriendly. His hands closed on the chair arms. 'Where's Rick— Richard? Does he know you're here?'

'Of course not.' Olivia was defensive. She was not sufficiently sure of herself to dissemble in any way. 'I—as far as I know, he's still in England. What he chooses to do doesn't have anything to do with me.'

'Don't lie.' Joe moved now, pushing himself to his feet and stepping away from the chair. 'What happened? Didn't it work out as you anticipated? Did he get cold feet at the thought of giving up all that dough?'

Olivia swallowed. 'I don't know what you're talking about,' she said unsteadily. She stared at him, noticing how stark and drawn his face looked in the light. If she didn't know better, she'd have thought he'd suffered some kind of bereavement. 'I've told you, what Richard does is nothing to do with me.'

Joe's lips compressed. 'So what was he doing accompanying you to England?' he demanded. 'I notice you don't deny that that's where he went.'

'No. How could I?' Olivia shook her head. 'But I didn't know he was going to take that flight.'

'Really?' He sounded sceptical.

'Yes, really.' Olivia pressed the palms of her hands together and moved away from the door. 'I couldn't believe it when he came and sat beside me. But I should have known Diane would tell him which flight I intended to take.'

'Diane?'

'Yes, Diane,' said Olivia, a little uncomfortably. She licked her lips. 'I suppose she told you, too.'

'Diane told me nothing,' retorted Joe roughly. 'I haven't spoken to her for several days.'

'But—'

He frowned. 'Go on.'

'But—the night before I left—' She coloured. 'I was told Diane stayed with you at—at Malibu.'

'*We* were together the night before you left,' he reminded her harshly. 'How the hell was I supposed to be in two places at once?'

Olivia blinked. 'But Bonnie said—'

'Yes?' His eyes were cold. 'What did Bonnie say to convince you?'

'Well—that Diane was staying with you at—at Malibu.'

'She actually said that: that Diane and I were staying together?' he exclaimed savagely. 'Oh, come on, Olivia. You'll have to do better than that.'

'She did.' Olivia was desperate. 'I swear it.' She tried to remember the exact words. 'She said she was staying with Mr Castellano. What was I supposed to think?'

Joe's expression was remote. 'So that's why you invited Richard to go to England with you. You thought Diane was with me, so what the hell, you'd get your revenge?'

'No!' Olivia caught her breath. 'Oh, this is ridiculous! If you won't listen to reason, I might as well go.'

A sob rising in her throat, she turned towards the door, but before she could get it open Joe said, 'Wait!' With a muffled oath, he crossed the floor to halt in front of her. 'Just tell me why you came, hmm? I have to know.'

'Why?' Now it was Olivia's turn to be awkward. 'Why should I tell you anything? You're not going to believe me.'

'Perhaps I will,' he said harshly, his eyes dark and tormented. And, because she so badly wanted to reassure him, she gave in.

'I—I wanted to know if—if what happened between us meant anything to you,' she admitted jerkily. 'Richard—' She used her ex-husband's name reluctantly, but his part in her decision had to be explained. 'Richard said that he'd spoken to you after—after I went down to the Bistro. What he told you wasn't true; I have no desire to live with him again.'

Joe's eyes narrowed. 'But you told me you'd spoken to him.' He made an impatient gesture. 'That night, before I phoned, you said he'd been on the line.'

'He was.' Olivia was trembling. 'But I told him I didn't want to see him. I had no idea that later on he'd told you the opposite.'

Joe frowned. 'But you had left the suite, hadn't you?'

'Yes. Because you were asleep, and I wanted to get something to eat.' She sighed, tugging nervously at her braid. 'Oh, you might as well know all of it. I was frightened I was falling in love with you, and I told myself that if I had something to eat I wouldn't feel so hollow inside.'

Joe's eyes darkened. 'Are you serious?' He lifted one hand and tilted her chin up to his face.

'I wouldn't have flown over five thousand miles if I hadn't been serious,' she said honestly. 'Oh, Joe, I'm so sorry. But I had to tell you how I felt.'

Joe's fingers caressed the skin behind her ear. 'And how do you feel?' he asked huskily.

Olivia flushed now. 'I care about you,' she muttered with a downbent head.

'You care about me?' he echoed, using his other hand to force her to look up at him again. 'Like—does love came into that? I'd really like to know.'

Olivia groaned. 'You know it does,' she said hotly, half afraid he was playing with her. She took a breath that mingled his warmth and maleness with her surroundings. 'I know I'm nothing like Diane, but I can't help that.'

'Thank God,' he said in a curiously strangled voice, pulling her towards him. He buried his face in the hollow of her shoulder, and she felt his teeth against the skin of her neck. 'I guess it's my fault for letting you think that Diane meant something to me. I like her, sure; but she's really my brother's playmate, not mine.'

Olivia was shaking now at this admission. 'You—you mean you and she aren't—weren't—having an affair?'

Joe lifted his head and bestowed a warm kiss on her parted lips. 'No,' he said, when she was weak with languor. 'Mark introduced us, and I guess she saw me as a more lucrative source of cash.'

Olivia shook her head helplessly. 'I think you underestimate yourself,' she said, sliding her arms around his waist. 'Oh, Joe, are you really pleased to see me? You're not just being kind because I'm here?'

Joe's exhalation was fervent. 'Are you crazy?' he asked, sliding his hands down her spine to cup her bottom and bring her against him. His instinctive arousal pushed against her stomach, and she looked up at him tremulously. 'I didn't know what love was until I met you. Then, I wasn't sure that I wanted to know.'

'Because of what Richard said?'

'Partly. And because I was angry. I couldn't believe you'd walked out on me, and his call was just the final straw. Then, when I went down to the lobby and saw you, you were signing someone's copy of your book. I convinced myself you were more interested in selling books than pleasing me.'

'Joe—'

'I know, I know.' He pulled her over to the chair where he'd been sitting and drew her onto his knee. 'It was childish, but I couldn't help it. I was so jealous I'd have believed anything of you that night.'

Olivia cupped his face in her hands. 'You were jealous?' she exclaimed disbelievingly.

'You'd better believe it,' he told her roughly, sliding his hands beneath her shirt. 'I just wanted to get away, but I couldn't go to the house at Malibu because I'd said Mark could use it. So I chartered a flight and flew back here.'

'Oh, Joe...' She nuzzled her face into his neck as his hands explored her, finding the strap of her bra and releasing it with a satisfying little ping. 'I love you. I didn't know how I was going to live without you.' She hesitated. 'It's ironic but if it hadn't been for Richard I wouldn't be here.'

His hands stilled. 'Why not?' he asked, and although his expression was tense she knew she had to go on.

'Because I guessed—I *hoped*—it was because of what he'd told you that you didn't try to see me again. When I got on the plane, I had no hope of ever coming back.'

Joe's expression softened. 'In that case, I suppose I ought to thank him. Even if I wanted to kill him until a few minutes ago.' His hands gripped her waist and moved her until she was straddling his body. 'God, you can't know how good that feels.'

'I think I can,' she breathed, leaning in to him and ca-ressing his mouth with her tongue. She put her hand down between them and stroked the outline of his manhood. 'Does this mean you want me to stay?'

'Try and get away,' he told her hoarsely, his hands slip-ping beneath her skirt now to find the yielding waistband of her panties. 'Just—let me—' His breath quickened as he unfastened the button of his jeans, and she caught her breath as she realised what he planned to do.

'What about your mother?' she protested, even as she did what she could to assist him, and Joe offered a sound of anguish at her words.

'I don't think she'll disturb us,' he assured her huskily. 'She knows what an unmitigated bastard I've been since I got back.'

'Because of me?' asked Olivia faintly, hardly daring to believe what he was saying.

'Because of you,' he agreed with feeling, tearing the silk a little as he eased into her heat. 'God, it seems a lifetime since we were together.'

'For me, too,' she whispered against his ear. 'Um—your mother said you'd mentioned my name to her.'

'I did,' he agreed, biting the lobe of her ear. 'After we'd spent that afternoon together, I knew I wanted you. But as Diane was convinced you still cared about Richard I wasn't certain you weren't just using me to make him jealous.'

'Using you...' Olivia's breath escaped on a sob as he moved inside her. 'Oh, Joe, I'm so glad I came back.'

'So am I,' he told her achingly as his fingers found her, and her senses swam as her feelings soared away...

EPILOGUE

OLIVIA'S biography of Diane Haran was published to critical acclaim the following year. To her surprise, Diane had chosen not to change her biographer, even though by then she knew all about Olivia and Joe. But after meeting Mark Castellano, and discovering he was a younger, less intense version of his brother, Olivia decided she was hedging her bets. Diane was philosophical in some ways, and Mark was still a Castellano, after all.

But he was also a much less serious individual than his sibling, and although he was not averse to riding on Diane's coat-tails as an actor Olivia suspected he wouldn't want to settle down for some considerable time. It wasn't her concern, really, except insofar as Richard and Diane were separating. Richard never did produce the photograph, and Joe surmised Diane had paid him off.

Olivia wrote most of the biography after she and Joe returned from their honeymoon. They'd spent the weeks before the wedding arranging for Olivia's personal possessions to be transferred to the States. They'd also paid a flying visit to see her parents in Rotorua, and arranged for them to break their journey home in San Francisco, so that Olivia's father could be there to give her away.

It had been a whirlwind courtship but Olivia had loved every minute of it. She didn't really care what they did or where they went so long as they were together. Even Henry had settled down in his new surroundings, terrorising the neighbourhood's bird population from his favourite spot among the leaves of an old acacia.

Mrs Castellano—or Lucia, as she'd suggested Olivia should call her—had proved endlessly supportive, taking over the organisation of the wedding, which was to be in June, and welcoming the Pyatts into her home. There was no point, she'd said, in them returning to England before the wedding. She'd suggested an extension of their holiday, and offered her house as somewhere they might like to stay.

'It's just as well you've set the date,' she'd remarked to Olivia one afternoon, just a couple of weeks before the wedding. They had been studying catalogues of table decorations, making their final decisions over what flowers to choose. 'It's nicer to have the ceremony before you begin to show.'

Olivia, who had been studying a centrepiece of lilies and flame orchids, had looked at her future mother-in-law in surprise. 'Before what begins to show?' she asked uncomprehendingly. And then, as the realisation hit her, she said, 'You can't be serious!'

'Come on, Livvy.' Joe's mother had taken to calling her that, and she found it rather sweet. 'I thought of pretending I hadn't noticed, but I'm so excited, I can't keep it to myself. Doesn't Joseph know yet? Is that why you've kept it a secret for so long?'

Olivia didn't know what to say. She'd never dreamt that she might have conceived Joe's baby. Indeed, she'd lived for so long believing she'd never have a baby that any symptoms she'd noticed she'd attributed to something else.

'Nobody knows,' she said now dazedly. '*I* didn't know, until you mentioned it.' She swallowed, running a nervous hand across her abdomen. 'Do you think it's true?'

Lucia gave a knowing smile, dimples appearing in her cheeks. 'I'd say it was a definite possibility,' she murmured softly. 'Oh, my dear, when you turned pale at the sight of last night's oysters, I think I knew for certain then.'

Olivia shook her head. 'I had no idea,' she admitted honestly, and then explained why she'd been so unperceptive. She closed her eyes for a moment. 'Oh, God, I told Joe I couldn't have children. What is he going to think?'

'If I know my son, I'm fairly sure he'll be delighted,' Lucia assured her firmly. 'But thank you for the insight into my son's feelings for you. Knowing how much he's always said he wanted a family, he must love you very much.'

And Joe, when she told him, was delighted. 'But I thought you said—' he began, and she put a finger across his mouth.

'That was just another of Richard's lies,' she said, nestling closer to him. And then, changing the subject, she asked, 'Do you think we should tell my parents or not?'

The first draft of *Naked Instinct* was finished in October, and Diane, who was on location in Louisiana, had very few comments to make. Apart from approving the manuscript, and the title, she gave Olivia credit for writing it so quickly. And wished her luck in finding a publisher to take it on.

In fact, Olivia's own publisher was delighted to receive the manuscript from Kay Goldsmith, and the book itself was published just six months after Joe and Olivia's daughter was born.

'Two productions in one year,' murmured Joe one warm September evening, watching Olivia feed baby Virginia with possessive eyes. 'Can I make a request that next year you devote time to your husband? I love my daughter, but I'd also very much like some time with my wife—alone.'

SURRENDER TO SEDUCTION

ROBYN DONALD

CHAPTER ONE

GERRY DACRE realised that she'd actually heard the noise a couple of times before noticing it. Sitting on her bed to comb wet black hair off her face, she remembered that the same funny little bleat had teased her ears just before she showered, and again as she came back down the hall.

Frowning, she got to her feet and walked across to the window, pushing open the curtains. Although it was after seven the street-lamps were still struggling against a reluctant New Zealand dawn; peering through their wan light, she made out a parcel on the wet grass just inside the Cape Honeysuckle hedge.

The cry came again, and to her horror she saw movement in the parcel—a weak fluttering against the sombre green wall of the hedge.

'Kittens!' she exploded, long legs carrying her swiftly towards the front door.

Or a puppy. It didn't sound like kittens. How dared anyone abandon animals in her garden—anywhere! Anger tightened her soft mouth, blazed from her dark blue-green eyes as she ran across the verandah and down the wooden steps, across the sodden lawn to the parcel.

It wasn't kittens. Or a puppy. Wailing feebly from a shabby tartan rug was a baby. Little fists and arms had struggled free, and the crumpled face was marked with cold. Chilling moisture clung to its skin, to the knitted bonnet, to the tiny, aimlessly groping hands. So heartbreakingly frail, it had to be newborn.

'Oh, my God!' Gerry said, scooping up the baby, box and all, as it gave another weak wail. 'Don't do that, darling,' she soothed. 'Come on, let's get you inside.'

5

Carefully she carried it indoors, kicked the door closed behind her, and headed into the kitchen, at this time of day the warmest room in the old kauri villa. She set the box on the table and raced into the laundry to grab a towel and her best cashmere jersey from the hot water cupboard.

'I'll ring the police when I've got you warm,' she promised the baby, lifting it out and carrying it across to the bench. The baby let out another high-pitched wail.

Crooning meaningless words, Gerry stripped the clothes from the squirming body. It was, she discovered, a girl— and judging by the umbilical cord no older than a couple of days, if that.

'I'm going to have to find you some sort of nappy,' she said, cuddling the chilly baby against her breasts as she cocooned it first in cashmere and then the warm towel. 'I wonder how long you've been out there, poppet? Too long on a bitter winter morning. I hope your mother gave you some food before she abandoned you. No, don't cry, sweetheart, don't cry...'

But the baby did cry, face going alarmingly scarlet and her chest swelling as she shrieked her outrage.

Rocking and hushing, Gerry tried to lend the warmth of her body to the fragile infant and wondered whether she should bathe her, or whether that might make her colder. She pressed her cheek against the little head, relieved to find that it seemed marginally warmer.

The front door clicked open and the second member of the household demanded shrilly, 'What's on *earth's* going on?'

Two pairs of feet made their way down the hall, the busy clattering of Cara's high heels counterpointed by a long stride, barely audible on the mellow kauri boards.

It's not my business if she spends the night with a man— she's twenty, Gerry thought, propping the baby against her shoulder and patting the narrow back. The movement silenced the baby for a second, but almost immediately she began to cry again, a pathetic shriek that cut Cara's voice off with the speed of a sword through cheese.

She appeared in the doorway, red hair smoothed back from her face, huge eyes goggling. 'Gerry, what have you done?' she gasped.

'It's a baby,' Gerry said, deadpan, expertly supporting the miniature head with its soft dark fuzz of hair. 'Someone dumped her on the front lawn.'

'Have you rung the police?' Not Cara. The voice was deep and cool, with an equivocal note that made Gerry think of a river running smoothly, forcefully over hidden rocks.

Startled, she looked past Cara to the man who followed her into the room.

Not Cara's usual type, Gerry thought, her stomach suddenly contracting. Her housemate liked pretty television actors and media men, but this man was far from pretty. The stark framework of his face created an aura of steely power, and he looked as though he spent his life dealing with the worst humanity could produce. His voice rang with an authentic authority, warning everyone within earshot that he was in the habit of giving orders and seeing them obeyed.

'I was just about to,' Gerry said stiffly. Irritatingly, the words sounded odd—uneven and hesitant—and she lifted her chin to cover her unusual response.

Gerry had perfected her technique for dealing with men—a lazy, flirtatious approach robbed of any element of sexuality. Instinct warned her that it wasn't going to work with this man; flirting with him, she thought, struggling for balance, would be a hazardous occupation indeed.

A green gaze, clear and cold and glinting like emeralds under water, met hers. Set beneath heavy lids and bordered by thick black lashes, the stranger's eyes were startlingly beautiful in his harsh, compelling face. He took up far too much room in her civilised house, and when he moved towards the telephone it was with a swift, noiseless precision that reminded Gerry of the predatory grace of a hunting animal.

Lord, but he was big! Gerry fought back a gut-level appreciation of just how tall he was as he dialled, recounted the situation with concise precision, gave a sharp inclination of his tawny head, and hung up. 'They'll call a social worker and get here as soon as they can. Until then they suggest you keep it warm.'

'Her,' Gerry corrected, cuddling the baby closer. It snuffled into silence and turned its head up to her, one eye screwed shut, small three-cornered mouth seeking nourishment. 'No, sweetheart, there's nothing here for you,' she said softly, her heart aching for the helpless child, and for the mother desperate enough to abandon her.

'You look quite at home with a baby,' Cara teased, recovering from astonishment into her natural ebullience.

Gerry gave her a fleeting grin. 'You've lived here long enough to know that I've got cousins from here to glory, most of whom seem to have had babies in the past three years. I'm a godmother twice over, and reasonably hands-on.'

The baby began to wail again, and Cara said uncertainly, 'Couldn't we give it some milk off a spoon, or something?'

'You don't give newborn babies straight cows' milk. But if someone could go to the dairy—I know they sell babies' bottles there; I saw a woman buy one when I collected the bread the other day—we could boil some water and give it to her.'

'Will that be safe?' the strange man asked, his lashes drooping slightly.

Gerry realised that her face was completely bare of cosmetics; furthermore, she wore only her dressing gown—her summer dressing gown, a thin cotton affair that probably wasn't hiding the fact that she was naked beneath it. 'Safer than anything else, I think. Here,' she said, offering the baby to Cara, 'hold her for a moment, will you?'

The younger woman recoiled. 'No, I can't, I've never

held a baby in my life. She's so tiny! I might drop her, or break an arm or something.'

'I'll take her,' the green-eyed stranger said crisply, and did so, scooping the child from Gerry's arms with a sure deftness that reassured her. He looked at Cara. 'Put the kettle on first, then go to the dairy and buy a feeding bottle. My car keys are in my right pocket.'

She pouted, but gave him a flirtatious glance from beneath her lashes as she removed the keys. 'You trust me with your car? I'm honoured. Gerry, it's a stunning black Jag, one of the new ones.'

'And if you hit anything in it,' the man said, with a smile that managed to be both sexy and intimidating, 'I'll take it out of your hide.'

Cara giggled, swung the keys in a little circle and promised, 'I'll be careful. I'm quite a good driver, aren't I, Gerry?' She switched her glance to Gerry and stopped, eyes and mouth wide open. 'Gerry!'

'What?' she asked, halfway to the door.

Cara said incredulously, 'You haven't got any make-up on! I've never seen you without it before!'

'It happens,' Gerry said, and managed to slow her rush to a more dignified pace. At the door, however, she turned and said reluctantly, 'She hasn't got a napkin on.'

'It wouldn't be the first time a baby's wet me,' he said drily. 'I think I can cope.'

Oh, boy, Gerry thought, fleeing after an abrupt nod. I'll just bet you can cope with *anything* fate throws at you. Ruler of your destiny, that's you, whoever you are! No doubt he had another expensive dark suit at his office, just in case he had an accident!

In her bedroom she tried to concentrate on choosing clothes, but she kept recalling the impact of that hard-hewn face and those watchful, speculative eyes.

And that smile. As the owner of a notorious smile herself, Gerry knew that it gave her an undeserved edge in the battle of the sexes. This man's smile transformed his harsh features, honing the blatant male magnetism that came with broad shoulders and long legs and narrow hips and a height of close to six foot four.

It melted her backbone, and he hadn't even been smiling at her!

Where on earth had Cara found him?

Or, given his aura of masterful self-possession, where had *he* found *her*?

The younger woman's morals were no concern of hers, but for some reason Gerry wished that Cara hadn't spent the night with him.

Five minutes later she'd pulled on black trousers and ankle boots, and a neat pinstriped shirt in her favourite black and white, folded the cuffs back to above her wrist, and looped a gold chain around her throat. A small gold hoop hung from each ear. Rapidly she applied a thin coat of tinted moisturiser and lip-glaze.

Noises from outside had indicated Cara's careful departure, and slightly more reckless return. With a touch of defiance, Gerry delicately smoothed a faint smudge of eyeshadow above each dark blue-green eye. There, she told her reflection silently, the mask's back in place.

Once more her usual sensible, confident self, she walked down the hall to the living room. Previous owners had renovated the old villa, adding to the lean-to at the back so that what had been a jumble of small rooms was now a large kitchen, dining and living area.

The bookcases that lined one wall had been Gerry's contribution to the room, as were the books in them and the richly coloured curtains covering French windows. Outside, a deck overlooked a garden badly in need of renovation— Gerry's next project. It should have been finished by now, but she'd procrastinated, drawing endless plans, because once she got it done she might find herself restlessly looking around for something new to occupy herself.

Cara was sitting beside the man on one of the sofas, gazing into his face with a besotted expression.

Had Gerry been that open and easy to read at twenty?

Probably, she thought cynically.

As she walked in the stranger smiled down at the baby lost in his arms. Another transformation, Gerry thought, trying very hard to keep her balance. Only this one was pure tenderness. Whoever he was, the tawny-haired man was able to temper his great strength to the needs of the weak.

The man looked up. Even cuddling a baby, he radiated a compelling masculinity that provoked a flicker of visceral caution. It was the eyes—indolent yet perceptive—and the dangerous, uncompromising face.

After some worrying experiences with men in her youth, Gerry had carefully and deliberately developed a persona that was a mixture of open good humour, light flirtation, and warm charm. Men liked her, and although many found her attractive they soon accepted her tacit refusal to be anything other than a friend. Few cared to probe beneath the pleasant, laughing surface, or realised that her slow, lazy smile hid heavily guarded defences.

Now, with those defences under sudden, unsparing assault—all the more dangerous because she was fighting a hidden traitor in her own body and mind—she was forced to accept that she'd only been able to keep men at a distance because she'd never felt so much as a flicker of attraction.

'Flicker' didn't even begin to describe the white-hot flare of recognition that had seared through her when she first laid eyes on the stranger, a clamorous response that both appalled and embarrassed her.

Hiding her importunate reaction with a slightly strained version of her trademark smile, she asked, 'How's she been?'

'She's asleep,' he said, watching her with an unfaltering, level gaze that hid speculation and cool assessment in the green depths.

Something tightened in Gerry's stomach. Most men

preened under her smile, wrongly taking a purely natural movement of tiny muscles in her face as a tribute to their masculinity. Perhaps because he understood the power of his own smile, this man was immune to hers.

Or perhaps he was immune to her. She wouldn't like him for an enemy, she thought with an involuntary little shiver.

The baby should have looked incongruous in his arms, but she didn't. Blissfully unconscious, her eyes were dark lines in her rosy little face. From time to time she made sucking motions against the fist at her mouth.

'We haven't been introduced,' Gerry said. Relieved that his hands were occupied with the baby, she kept hers by her sides. 'I'm Gerry Dacre.'

'Oh, sorry,' Cara said, opening her eyes very wide. 'Gerry's my agent, Bryn, and she owns the house—her aunt's my mother's best friend, and for her sins she said she'd board me for a year.' She gave a swift urchin grin. 'Gerry, this is Bryn Falconer.'

Exquisitely beautiful, Cara was an up-and-coming star for the modelling agency Gerry part-owned. And she was far too young for Bryn Falconer, whose hard assurance indicated that his thirty-two or three years had been spent in tough places.

'How do you do, Bryn?' Gerry said, relying on formality. 'I'll sterilise the bottle—'

'Cara organised that as soon as she came in,' he said calmly.

'Mr Patel said that the solution he gave me was the best way to disinfect babies' bottles,' Cara told her. 'I followed the instructions exactly.'

Sure enough, the bottle was sitting in a special basin on the bench. Gerry gave a swift, glittering smile. 'Good. How long does it have to stay in the solution?'

'An hour,' Cara said knowledgeably. She glanced at the tiny bundle sleeping in Bryn's arms. 'Do you think she'll be all right until then?'

Gerry nodded. 'She should be. She's certainly not hungry now, or she wouldn't have stopped crying. I'll make a much-needed cup of coffee.' Her stomach lurched as she met the measuring scrutiny of Bryn Falconer's green eyes. 'Can I get you one, or some breakfast?' Cara didn't drink coffee, and vowed that breakfast made her feel ill.

The corners of his long, imperious mouth lifted slightly. 'No, thank you.' He transferred his glance to Cara's face and smiled. 'Don't you have to get ready for work?'

'Yes, but I can't leave you holding the baby!' Giggling, she flirted her lashes at him.

Disgusted, Gerry realised that she felt left out. Stiffly she reached for the coffee and began the pleasant routine of making it.

From behind her Bryn said, 'I don't run the risk of losing my job if I'm late.'

Cara cooed, 'It must be wonderful to be the boss.'

Trying very hard to make her voice steady, Gerry said, 'Cara, you can't be late for your go-see.'

'I know, I know.' Reluctance tinged her voice.

Gerry's mouth tightened. Cara really had it bad; last night she'd been over the moon at her luck. Now, as though a chance to audition for an international firm meant nothing to her, she said, 'I'd better change, I suppose.'

Gerry reached for a cup and saucer. Without looking at him, she said, 'You don't have to stay, Mr Falconer. I'll look after the baby until the police come.'

'I'm in no hurry,' he replied easily. 'Cara, if you're ready in twenty minutes I'll give you a lift into Queen Street.'

'Oh—that'd be wonderful!'

Swinging around, Gerry said grittily, 'This is a really important interview, Cara.'

'I know, I know.' Chastened, Cara sprang to her feet. 'I'll wear exactly what we decided on.'

She walked around Bryn's long legs and set out for the door, stopping just inside it when he asked Gerry, 'Don't you have to work too?'

Cara said, 'Oh, Gerry's on holiday, lucky thing. Although,' she added fairly, 'it's her first holiday since she started up the agency three years ago.'

'You're very young, surely, to be running a model agency?'

Although neither Bryn's words nor his tone gave anything away, Gerry suspected he considered her job lightweight and frivolous. Her eyes narrowed slightly, but she gave him her smile again and said, 'How kind of you. What do you do, Mr Falconer?'

Cara hovered, her lovely face bemused as she looked from one to the other.

'Call me Bryn,' he invited, hooded eyes gleaming behind those heavy lashes.

'Thank you, Bryn,' Gerry said politely, and didn't reciprocate. His smile widened into a swift shark's grin that flicked her on the raw. In her most indolent voice Gerry persisted, 'And what do you do?'

The grin faded as rapidly as it had arrived. 'I'm an importer,' he said.

Cara interrupted, 'I'll see you soon, Bryn.'

Bryn Falconer's gaze didn't follow her out of the room. Instead he looked down at the sleeping baby in his arms, and then up again, catching Gerry's frown as she picked up the package of sterilising preparation.

'Gerry doesn't suit you,' he said thoughtfully. 'Is it your real name?'

Gerry's brows shot up. 'Actually, no,' she drawled, emphasising each syllable a little too much. 'It's Geraldine, which doesn't suit me either.'

His smile had none of the sexy warmth that made it so alarmingly attractive. Instead there was a hint of ruthlessness in it as his gaze travelled with studied deliberation over her face. 'Oh, I don't know about that. "The fair Geraldine",' he quoted, astonishing her. 'I think it suits you very well. You're extremely beautiful.' His glance lingered on the flakes of colour across her high cheekbones. Softly he said, 'You have a charming response to compliments.'

'I'm not used to getting them first thing in the morning,' she said, angry at the struggle it took her to achieve her usual poised tone.

His lashes drooped. 'But those compliments are the sweetest,' he said smoothly.

Oh, he knew how to make a woman blush—and he'd made the sexual implication with no more than a rasp in the deep voice that sent a shivering thrill down her spine, heat and cold intermingled. Into her wayward mind flashed an image of him naked, the big limbs slack with satisfied desire, the hard, uncompromising mouth blurred by kisses.

No doubt he'd woken up like that this morning, but it had been Cara's kisses on his mouth, Cara's sleek young body in his arms.

Repressing a sudden, worrying flare of raw jealousy, Gerry parried, 'Well, thank you. I do make excellent breakfasts, but although I'm always pleased to receive compliments on my cooking—' her voice lingered a moment on the word before she resumed, '—I don't know that I consider them the *sweetest*. Most women prefer to be complimented on more important qualities.' Before he had a chance to answer she switched the subject. 'You know, the baby's sleeping so soundly—I'm sure she wouldn't wake if I took her.'

It was the coward's way out and he had to know it, but he said calmly, 'Of course. Here you are.'

Gerry realised immediately that she had made a mistake. Whereas they'd transferred the baby from her arms to his in one swift movement, now it had to be done with slow care to avoid waking her.

Bryn's faint scent—purely male, with a slight, distasteful flavouring of Cara's favourite tuberose—reached right into a hidden, vulnerable place inside Gerry. She discovered that the arms that held the baby were sheer muscle, and that the faint shadow of his beard beneath his skin affected her in ways she refused even to consider.

And she discovered that the accidental brush of his hand against her breasts sent a primitive, charged thrill storming through her with flagrant, shattering force.

'Poor little scrap!' she said in a voice too even to be natural, when the child was once more in her arms. Turning away, she fought for some composure. 'I wonder why her mother abandoned her. The usual reason, I suppose.'

'Is there a usual reason?' His voice was level and condemnatory. 'How would you know? The mothers in these cases aren't discovered very often.'

'I've always assumed it's because they come from homes where being an unmarried mother is considered wicked, and they're terrified of being found out.'

'Or perhaps because the child is a nuisance,' he said.

Gerry gave him a startled look. Hard green eyes met hers, limpid, emotionless. Looking down, she thought, He's far too old for Cara! before her usual common sense reasserted itself.

'This is a newborn baby,' she said crisply. 'Her mother won't be thinking too clearly, and could quite possibly be badly affected mentally by the birth. Even so, she left her where she was certain to be noticed and wrapped her warmly. She didn't intend her to die.'

'Really?' He waited a moment—making sure, she wondered with irritation, that she knew how to hold the baby?—before stepping back.

Cuddling the child, Gerry sat down on the opposite sofa, saying with brazen nerve, 'You seem very accustomed to children. Do you have any of your own?'

'No,' he said, his smile a thin line edged with mockery. 'Like you, I have friends with families, and I can claim a couple of godchildren too.'

Although he hadn't answered her unspoken question, he knew what she'd been asking. If she wanted to find out she was going to have to demand straight out, Are you married?

And she couldn't do that; Cara's love life was her own business. However, Gerry wondered whether it might be a good idea to drop a few comments to her about the messiness of relationships with married men.

Apart from anything else, it made for bad publicity, just the sort Cara couldn't afford at the beginning of her career.

She was glad when the sudden movement of the baby in her arms gave her an excuse to look away. 'All right, little love,' she soothed, rocking the child until she settled back into deep sleep.

He said, 'Your coffee's finished percolating. Can I pour it for you?'

'Thank you,' she said woodenly.

'My pleasure.' He got to his feet.

Lord, she thought wildly, he towers! From her perch on the sofa the powerful shoulders and long, lean legs made him a formidable, intimidating figure. Although a good height for a model, Cara had looked tiny beside him.

'Are you sure you don't want one?'

'Quite sure, thanks. Will you be able to drink it while you're holding the baby?'

What on earth had she been thinking of? 'I hadn't—no, I'd better not,' she said, wondering what was happening to her normally efficient brain.

'I'll pour it, anyway. If it's left too long on a hotplate it stews. I can take the baby back while you drink.' He spoke pleasantly.

Gerry tried not to watch as he moved easily around her kitchen, but it was impossible to ignore him because he had so much presence, dominating the room. Even when she looked out of the window at the grey and grumpy dawn doing its ineffectual best to banish the darkness, she was acutely aware of Bryn Falconer behind her, his presence overshadowing her thoughts.

'There.' He put the coffee mug down on the table before her, lean, strong hands almost a dramatic contrast to its blue and gold and white stripes. 'Do you take sugar or milk?'

'Milk, thank you.'

He straightened, looking down at her with gleaming, enigmatic eyes. 'I'm surprised,' he said, his voice deliberate yet disturbing. 'I thought you'd probably drink it black.'

She gave him the smile her cousins called 'Gerry's offensive weapon'. Slow, almost sleepy, it sizzled through men's defences, one of her more excitable friends had told her, like maple syrup melting into pancakes.

Bryn Falconer withstood it without blinking, although his eyes darkened as the pupils dilated. Savagely she thought, So you're not as unaffected as you pretend to be, and then realised that she was playing with fire—dangerous, frightening, peculiarly fascinating fire.

In a crisp, frosty voice, she said, 'Stereotyping people can get you into trouble.'

He looked amused and cynical. 'I must remember that.'

Gerry repressed a flare of anger and said in a languid social tone, 'I presume you were at the Hendersons' party last night?' And was appalled to hear herself; she sounded like a nosy busybody. He'd be quite within his rights to snub her.

He poured milk into her coffee. Gerry drew in a deep, silent breath. It was a cliché to wonder just how hands would feel on your skin, and yet it always happened when you were attracted to someone. How unfair, the advantage a graceful man had over a clumsy one.

And although graceful seemed an odd word to use for a man as big as Bryn Falconer she couldn't think of a better one. He moved with a precise, assured litheness that pleased the eye and satisfied some inner need for harmony.

'I met Cara there,' he said indifferently.

Feeling foolish, because it was none of her business and she knew it, Gerry ploughed on, 'Cara's very young.'

'You sound almost maternal,' he said, his expression inflexible, 'but you can't be more than a few years older than she is.'

'Nine, actually,' Gerry returned. 'And Cara has lived in

the country all her life; any sophistication comes from her years at boarding school. Not exactly a good preparation for real life.'

'She seems mature enough.'

For what? Gerry wondered waspishly. A flaming affair? Hardly; it would take a woman of considerable worldly experience to have an affair with Bryn Falconer and emerge unscathed.

He looked down at the baby, still sleeping peacefully, and asked, 'Do you want me to take her while you drink your coffee?'

The coffee could go cold and curdle for all she cared; Gerry had no intention of getting close to him again. It was ridiculous to be so strongly aware of a man who not only indulged in one-night stands, but liked women twelve or so years younger than he was. 'She'll be all right on the sofa,' she said, and laid her down, keeping a light hand on the child as she picked up the mug and held it carefully well away from her.

Sitting down opposite them, he leaned back and surveyed Gerry, his wide, hard mouth curled in a taunting little smile.

I don't like you at all, Bryn Falconer, Gerry thought, sipping her coffee with feigned composure. The bite of the caffeine gave her the impetus to ask sweetly, 'What sort of things do you import, Mr Falconer?'

'Anything I can earn a penny on, Ms Dacre,' he said, mockery shading his dark, equivocal voice. 'Clothing, machinery, computers.'

'How interesting.'

One brow went up. 'I suppose you have great difficulty understanding computers.'

'What's to understand?' she said in her most come-hither tone. 'I know how to use them, and that's all that matters.'

'You did warn me about the disadvantages of stereotyping,' he murmured, green gaze raking her face. 'Perhaps I should take more notice of what you say. The face of an angel and a mind like a steel trap. How odd to find you the owner of a model agency.'

'Part-owner. I have a partner,' she purred. 'I like pretty things, and I enjoy pretty people.' She didn't intend to tell him that she was already bored with running the agency. She'd enjoyed it enormously while she and Honor McKenzie were setting it up and working desperately to make it a success, but now that they'd made a good name for themselves, and an excellent income, the business had lost its appeal.

As, she admitted rigorously, had everything else she'd ever done.

A thunderous knock on the door woke the baby. Jerking almost off the sofa, she opened her triangular mouth and shrieked. 'That's probably the police,' Gerry said, setting her cup down and scooping the child up comfortingly. 'Let them in, will you?' Her voice softened as she rocked the tiny form against her breast. 'There, darling, don't cry, don't cry...'

Bryn got to his feet and walked out, his mouth disciplined into a straight line. Gazing down at the wrathful face of the baby, Gerry thought wistfully that although she didn't want to get married, it would be rather nice to have a child. She had no illusions—those cousins who'd embarked on marriage and motherhood had warned her that children invariably complicated lives—but she rather suspected that her biological clock was ticking. 'Shh, shh,' she murmured. 'Just wait a moment and I'll give you some water to drink.'

The baby settled down, reinforcing Gerry's suspicion that she'd been fed not too long before she'd been found.

Frowning, she listened as Bryn Falconer said firmly from the hall, 'No, I don't live here; I'm just passing through.'

Policemen were supposed to have seen it all, but the one who walked in through the kitchen door looked startled and, when his gaze fell on Gerry, thunderstruck.

'This,' Bryn said smoothly, green eyes snapping with

mockery, 'is Constable Richards. Constable, this is Geraldine Dacre, the owner of the house, who found the child outside on the lawn.'

'How do you do?' Gerry said, smiling. 'Would you like a cup of coffee?'

'I—ah, no, thank you, Ms Dacre.' His collar seemed to be too tight; tugging at it, he said, 'I was supposed to meet a social worker here.'

'She—or he—hasn't arrived yet.' Bryn Falconer was leaning against the doorpost.

For all the world as though this was his house! Smiling at the policeman again, Gerry said, 'If you have to wait, you might as well have something to drink—it's cold out there. Bryn, pour the constable some coffee, would you?'

'Of course,' he said, the green flick of his glance branding her skin as he strode behind the breakfast bar.

He hadn't liked being ordered around. Perhaps, she thought a trifle smugly, in the future he wouldn't be quite so ready to take over.

What the hell was she thinking? She had no intention of letting Bryn Falconer into her life.

CHAPTER TWO

HASTILY Gerry transferred her attention to the policeman. 'What do you want to know about the baby?' she asked. 'She's a little girl, and although I'm no expert I don't think she's any more than a day old, judging by the umbilical cord.'

He gave her a respectful look and rapidly became professional. 'Exactly what time did you first see her?' he said.

So, very aware of the opening and closing of cupboards in her kitchen, Gerry explained how she'd found the child, nodding at the box with its pathetic little pile of damp clothes. The policeman asked pertinent questions and took down her answers, thanking Bryn Falconer when he brought a mug of coffee.

The constable plodded through his cup of coffee and his questions until Cara appeared in the doorway, her sultry face alive with curiosity and interest.

'Hello,' she said, and watched with the eye of a connoisseur as the policeman leapt to his feet. 'I'm ready to go,' she told Bryn, her voice soft and caressing. 'Bye, Gerry. Have fun.'

Bryn smiled, the crease in his cheek sending an odd frisson straight through Gerry. Go now, she commanded mentally. Right now. And flushed as he looked at her, a hard glint in his eyes.

Fortunately the doorbell pealed again, this time heralding the social worker, a pleasant, middle-aged woman with tired eyes and a knack with babies. Cara and Bryn left as she came in, so Gerry could give all her attention to the newcomer.

'I'm rather sad to see her go,' Gerry said, watching as

Gone was the lingering miasma of ennui; the moment she'd seen him every nerve cell had jolted into acute, almost painful alertness.

Narelle and Cosmo were an Australian couple—sleek, well-tanned, wearing expensive resort clothes. Lacey, their adolescent daughter, should have been rounded and sturdy; instead her angular figure indicated a recent illness.

After the flurry of greetings Gerry sank into the chair Bryn held for her, aware that Lacey was eyeing her with the yearning intensity of a hungry lion confronted by a wildebeest. Uncomfortably, Gerry waited for surnames, but none were forthcoming.

'Isn't this a wonderful place for a holiday?' Narelle, a thin, tanned woman with superbly blonded hair and a lot of gold chains, spoke brightly, her skilfully shaded eyes flicking from Gerry to Bryn.

'Ideal,' Gerry answered, smiling, and was about to add that she wasn't exactly on holiday when Bryn distracted her by asking her what she'd have to drink.

'Fruit juice, thanks,' she said. After the fiasco with Troy she wasn't going to risk anything alcoholic in her empty stomach. She smiled at the waiter who'd padded across on bare feet, and added, 'Not too sweet, please.'

'Papaya, madam? With passionfruit and lime?'

'That sounds wonderful,' she said.

She was oddly uneasy when Lacey said loudly, 'I'll have one of those too, please.'

Her mother gave her a sharp look. 'How about a diet soft drink?' she asked.

'No, thanks.'

Narelle opened her mouth but was forestalled by Bryn, who said, 'Did you have a good flight up, Geraldine?'

Why the devil didn't he use her proper name? 'Geraldine' sounded quite different from her normal, everyday self. 'Yes, thank you,' she said, smiling limpidly.

If he thought that one compliment entitled him to a more intimate footing, he was wrong. All right, so her heart was the woman efficiently dressed the baby in well-worn but pretty clothes, then packed her into an official carrycot while the policeman took the box and its contents. 'For what it's worth, I think her mother fed her before she put her behind the hedge—she's not hungry. And she wasn't very cold when I picked her up, so she hadn't been there long.'

The social worker nodded. 'They usually make sure someone will find them soon.'

Gerry picked up her towel and the still dry cashmere jersey. 'What will happen to the baby?'

'Now? I'll get her checked over medically, and take her to a family who'll foster her until her mother is found.'

'And if her mother isn't found?'

The social worker smiled. 'We'll do our best for her.'

'I know,' Gerry said. 'I just feel a bit proprietary.'

'Oh, we all do that.' The woman gave a tired, cynical smile. 'When you think we're geared by evolution to respond to a baby's cry with extreme discomfort, it's no wonder. She'll be all right. It's the mother I'm worried about. I don't suppose you've seen a pregnant woman looking over the hedge this last couple of weeks, or anything like that?'

'No, not a glimpse.'

The policeman said, 'I'd say she's local, because she put the baby where she was certain she'd be found. She might even have been watching.'

Gerry frowned, trying to recall the scene. 'I don't think so. Apart from the traffic, I didn't see any movement.'

When they'd gone she lifted the cashmere jersey to her face. It smelt, she thought wryly, of newborn baby—that faint, elusive, swiftly fading scent that had probably once had high survival value for the human race. Now it was just another thing, along with the little girl's heart-shaking fragility and crumpled rose-petal face, to remind Gerry of her empty heart.

'Oh, do something sensible instead of moping,' she advised herself crisply, heading for the laundry.

After she'd dealt with the clothes she embarked on a brisk round of necessary housework that didn't ease her odd flatness. Clouds settled heavily just above the roof, and the house felt chilly. And empty.

Ruthlessly she banished the memory of wide shoulders, narrow masculine hips and a pair of gleaming green eyes, and set to doing the worst thing she could find—clearing out the fridge. When she'd finished she drank a cup of herbal tea before picking up the telephone.

'Jan?' she said when she'd got through. 'How are you?'

'I'm fine,' said her favourite cousin, mother of Gerry's goddaughter, 'and so are Kear and Gemma, but why aren't you at work?'

'How do you know I'm not?'

'No chaos in the background,' Jan said succinctly. 'The agency is mayhem.'

'Honor persuaded me to take a holiday—she said three years without one was too long. And she was right. I've been a bit blasé lately.'

'I wondered how long you'd last,' Jan said comfortably. 'I told Kear a month or so ago that it must be time for you to look around for something new.'

'Butterfly brain, that's me.'

'Don't be an idiot.' For a tiny woman Jan could be very robust. 'You bend your not inconsiderable mental energy to mastering something, and as soon as you've done it you find something else. Nothing butterfly about that. Anyway, if I remember correctly it was your soft heart that got you into the modelling business. You left the magazine because you didn't agree with the way it was going—and you were right; it's just appalling now, and I refuse to buy it—and Honor needed an anchor after she broke up with that awful man she was living with. Whatever happened to him?'

'He died of an overdose. He was a drug addict.'

'What a tragedy,' Jan sighed. 'If you're on the lookout for another job, will you stay in the fashion industry?'

'It's a very narrow field,' Gerry said, wondering why she now yearned for wider horizons. She'd been perfectly happy working in or on the fringes of that world since she'd left university.

'Well, if you're stuck you can take over from me.'

'In which capacity—babysitter, part-time image consultant, or den mother to a pack of wayward girls?'

Several years previously Jan had inherited land from her grandfather in one of Northland's most beautiful coastal areas, and had set up a camp for girls at risk. After marrying the extremely sexy man next door, she'd settled into her new life as though she'd been born for it.

Jan laughed. 'The camp is going well,' she said cheerfully, 'but I don't think it's you. I meant as image consultant. You'd be good at it—you know what style means because you've got it right to your bones, and you like people. I've had Maria Hastings working for me, but she, wretched woman, has fallen in love with a Frenchman and is going to live in Provence with him! And I'm pregnant again, which forces the issue. I sell, or I retire. I'd rather sell the business to you if you've got the money.'

'Well—congratulations!' It hurt. Stupid, but it hurt. Jan had everything—an adoring husband, an interesting career, a gorgeous child and now the prospect of another. Quickly, vivaciously, Gerry added, 'I'll think about it. If I decide to do it, my share of the agency should be enough to buy you out.'

'Have you spoken to Honor? Does she mind the thought of you leaving?'

'No. Apparently she's got a backer, and she'll buy my share at a negotiated price.'

'I don't want to over-persuade you,' Jan said quickly. 'I know you like to develop things for yourself, so don't feel obliged to think about it. Another woman wants it, and she'll do just as well. You're a bit inclined to let the people you like push you around, you know. Too soft-hearted.'

'You're not over-persuading.' Already the initial glow of enthusiasm was evaporating. What would happen when she got tired of being an image consultant? As she would. A shiver of panic threaded through her. Surely that wasn't to be her life? Her mother had spent her short life searching for something, and had failed spectacularly to find it. Gerry was determined not to do the same.

'Something wrong?' Jan asked.

'Nothing at all, apart from an upsetting start to my day.' She told her about the abandoned baby, and they discussed it for a while, until Gerry asked, 'When's your baby due?'

'In about seven months. What's the matter, Gerry?'

'Nothing. Just—oh, I suppose I do need this holiday. I'll let you know about the business,' Gerry said.

'Do you want to come up and stay with us? We'd love to see you.'

'It sounds lovely, but no, I think I want to wander a bit.'

Jan's tone altered. 'Feeling restless?'

'Yes,' she admitted.

'Don't worry,' Jan said in a bracing voice. 'Even if you don't buy my business a job will come hopping along saying, Take me, take me. I'm fascinating and fun and you'll love me. Why don't you go overseas for a couple of weeks—somewhere nice and warm? I don't blame you for being out of sorts; I can't remember when New Zealand's had such a wet winter.'

'My mother used to go overseas whenever life got into too tedious a routine,' Gerry said.

'You are *not* like your mother,' Jan said even more bracingly. 'She was a spoilt, pampered brat who never grew up. You are a darling.'

'Thank you for those kind words, but I must have ended up with some of her genes.'

'You got the face,' Jan said drily. 'And the smile—but you didn't get the belief that everyone owed you a life.

According to my mama, Aunt Fliss was spoilt stupid by her father, and she just expected the rest of the world to treat her the way he did. You aren't like that.'

'I hope not.'

'Not a bit. Gerry, I have to go—your goddaughter is yelling from her bedroom, and by the tone of her voice it's urgent. I'll ring you tonight and we can really gossip. As for a new job—well, why not think PR? You know everyone there is to know in New Zealand, and you'd be wonderful at it. One flash of that notorious smile and people would be falling over themselves to publicise whatever you want.'

'Oh, exaggerate away!' Gerry laughed, but after she'd hung up she stood looking down at the table, tracing the line of the grain with one long finger.

For the last year she'd been fighting a weariness of spirit; it had crept on her so gradually that for months she hadn't realised what it was. The curse of my life, she thought melodramatically, and rolled her eyes.

But it terrified her; boredom had driven her mother through three unsatisfactory marriages, leaving behind shattered lives and discarded children as she'd searched for the elusive happiness she'd craved. Gerry's father had never got over his wife's defection, and Gerry had two half-brothers she hardly ever saw, one in France, one in America—both abandoned, just as she'd been.

She sat down with the newspaper, but a sudden scatter of rain against the window sent her fleeing to bring in the clothes she'd hung on the line an hour before.

A quick glance at the sky told her they weren't going to get dry outside, so she sorted them into the drier and set it going. Staring at the tumble of clothes behind the glass door, she wondered if perhaps she *should* go overseas.

Somewhere warm and dry, she thought dourly, heading back to pick up the newspaper from the sofa. The model disporting herself beneath palm trees was one she had worked with several occasions in her time as fashion editor; Gerry was meanly pleased to see that her striking face was at last showing signs of the temper tantrums she habitually engaged in.

'Serves her right, the trollop,' she muttered, flicking the pages over before putting the newspaper down.

No, she wouldn't head overseas. She couldn't really afford it; she had a mortgage to pay. Perhaps she should try something totally different.

She read the Sits Vac with mounting gloom. Nothing there. Well, she could make a right-angle turn and do another degree. She rooted in a drawer for the catalogue of extension courses at the local university, and began reading it.

But after a short while she put it to one side. She felt tired and grey and over the hill, and she wondered what had happened to the baby. Had she been checked, and was she now in the arms of a foster-mother?

Gerry decided to clean the oven.

It was par for the course when halfway through this most despised of chores the telephone beeped imperatively.

An old friend demanded that Gerry come to lunch with her because she was going through a crisis and needed a clear head to give her advice. Heaving a silent sigh, Gerry said soothingly, 'Yes, of course I'll have lunch with you. Would you like to eat here?'

Her hopes were dashed. 'We'll go to The Blue Room,' Troy said militantly. 'I've booked. I'll pick you up in half an hour.'

'No, I'll meet you there,' Gerry said hastily. Troy was the worst driver she knew.

Coincidences, Gerry reflected gloomily, were scary; you had no defence against them because they sneaked up from behind and hit you over the head. Bryn Falconer was sitting at the next table.

'And then,' Troy said, her voice throbbing as it rose from an intense whisper to something ominously close to a

screech, 'he said I've let myself go and turned into a cab-
bage! *He* was the one who *insisted* on having kids and
insisted I stop work and stay at home with them.'

Fortunately the waiter had taken in the situation and was
already heading towards them with a carafe of iced water,
a coffee pot and a heaped basket of focaccia bread.

Very fervently Gerry wished that Bryn Falconer had not
decided to lunch at this particular restaurant. She was sure
she could feel his eyes on her. 'Troy, you idiot, you've
been drinking,' she said softly. 'And don't tell me you
didn't drink much—it only takes a mouthful in your case.'

'I had to, Gerry. Mrs Landless—my babysitter—had her
thirtieth wedding anniversary party last night. Damon
wouldn't go so she saved me a glass of champagne.'

'You could have told her that alcohol goes straight to
your head. Never mind—have some coffee and bread and
you'll soon be fine, and at least you had the sense to come
by taxi.'

Her friend's lovely face crumpled. 'Oh, Lord,' she said
bitterly, 'I'm making a total *idiot* of myself, and there's
bound to be sh-someone who'll go racing off to tell
Damon.'

Five years previously Gerry had mentally prophesied disaster when her friend, a model with at least six more years
of highly profitable work ahead of her, had thrown it all
away to marry her merchant banker. Now she said briskly,
'So, who cares? It's not the end of the world.'

'I *wish* I was like you,' Troy said earnestly and still too
loudly. 'You have men falling in love with you all the time,
and you just smile that *fabulous* smile and drift on by,
breaking hearts without a second thought.'

Acutely aware that Bryn Falconer was sitting close
enough to hear those shrill, heartfelt and entirely untrue
words, Gerry protested, 'You make me sound like some
sort of *femme fatale,* and I'm not.'

'Yes, you are,' Troy argued, fanning her flushed face
with her napkin. 'Everyone expects *femmes fatale* to be

evil, selfish women, but why should they be? You're so *nice* and you never poach, but *nobody* touches your heart, do they? You don't even *notice* when men fall at your feet. Damon calls you "the unassailable Gerry".'

Gerry glanced up. Bryn Falconer wasn't even pretending not to listen, and when he caught her eyes he lifted his brows in a cool, mockingly level regard that sent frustration boiling through her.

Hastily Gerry looked back at Troy's tragic face. Tamping down an unwise and critical assessment of Damon's character, she said firmly, 'He doesn't know me very well. Have some coffee.'

But although Troy obediently sipped, she couldn't leave the subject alone. 'Have you ever been in love, Gerry? I mean really in love, the sort of abject, dogged, I-love-you-just-because-you're-you sort of love?'

Gerry hoped that her shrug hid her burning skin. 'I don't believe in that sort of love,' she said calmly. 'I think you have to admire and respect someone before you can fall in love with them. Anything else is lust.'

It was the wrong thing to say, and she knew it as soon as the words left her mouth. Bryn Falconer's presence must have scrambled her brain, she decided disgustedly.

Troy dissolved into tears and groped in her bag for her handkerchief. 'I know,' she wept into it. 'Damon wanted me and now it's gone. He's breaking my heart.'

Gerry leaned over the table and took her friend's hand. 'Do you want to go?' she asked quietly.

'Yes.'

Avid, fascinated stares raked Gerry's back as they walked across to the desk. She'd have liked to ignore Bryn Falconer, but when they approached his table he looked up at her with sardonic green eyes. At least he didn't get to his feet, which would have made them even more conspicuous.

Handsome meant nothing, she thought irrelevantly, when a man had such presence!

'Geraldine,' he said, and for some reason her heart stopped, because that single word on his lips was like a claiming, a primitive incantation of ownership.

Keeping her eyes cool and guarded, she sent him a brief smile. 'Hello, Bryn,' she said, and walked on past.

Fortunately Gerry's custom was valuable, so she and the desk clerk came to an amicable arrangement about the bill for the uneaten food. After settling it, she said, 'I'll drive you home.'

'I don't want to go home.' Troy spoke in a flat, exhausted voice that meant reality was kicking in.

'How long's Mrs Landless able to stay with the children?'

'Until four.' Troy clutched Gerry's arm. 'Can I come with you? Gerry, I really need to talk.'

So sorry for Troy she could have happily dumped a chained and gagged Damon into the ocean and watched him gurgle out of sight, Gerry resigned herself to an exhausting afternoon. 'Of course you can.'

Once home, she filled them both up on toast and pea and ham soup from the fridge—comfort food, because she had the feeling they were going to need it.

And three exhausting hours later she morosely ate a persimmon as Troy—by then fully in command of herself—drove off in a taxi.

Not that exhausting was the right word; gruelling described the afternoon more accurately. Although Troy was bitterly unhappy she still clung to her marriage, trying to convince herself that because she loved her husband so desperately, he had to love her in return.

The old, old illusion, Gerry thought sadly and sardonically, and got to her feet, drawing some consolation from her surroundings. She adored her house, revelled in the garden, and enjoyed Cara's company as well as her contribution to the mortgage payments.

But restlessness stretched its claws inside her. Gloomily she surveyed the tropical rhododendrons through her window, their waxy coral flowers defying the grey sky and cold wind. A disastrous lunch, a shattered friend, and the prospect of heavier rain later in the evening didn't mean her holiday was doomed. She wasn't superstitious.

But she wished that Bryn Falconer had chosen to eat lunch anywhere else in New Zealand.

Uncomfortable, jumpy—the way she felt when the music in a horror film indicated that something particularly revolting was about to happen—Gerry set up the ironing board. Jittery nerves wouldn't stand up to the boring, prosaic monotony of ironing.

She was putting her clothes away in her room when she heard the front door open and Cara's voice, bright and lively with an undercurrent of excitement, ring around the hall. The masculine rumble that answered it belonged to Bryn Falconer.

All I need, Gerry thought with prickly resignation.

She decided to stay in her room, but a knock on her door demanded her attention.

'Gerry,' Cara said, flushed, her eyes gleaming, 'come and talk to Bryn. He wants to ask you something.'

Goaded, Gerry answered, 'I'll be out in a minute.'

Fate, she decided, snatching a look at the mirror and despising the colour heating her sweeping cheekbones, really had it in for her today.

However, her undetectable mask of cosmetics was firmly in place, and anyway, she wasn't going to primp for Bryn Falconer. No matter that her dark blue-green eyes were wild and slightly dilated, or that her hair had rioted frivolously out of its usual tamed waves. She didn't care what he thought.

The gas heater in the sitting room warmed the chilly air, but the real radiance came from Cara, who lit up the room like a torch. Should I tell her mother? Gerry thought, then dismissed the idea. Cara was old enough to understand what she was doing.

But that little homily on messing around with married men might be in order.

Not that Bryn looked married—he had the air of someone who didn't have to consider anyone else. Forcing a smile, Gerry said, 'Hello, Bryn. Did you have a good lunch?'

His eyes narrowed slightly. 'Very.'

Gerry maintained her hostess demeanour. 'I like the way they do lunch there—sustaining, and it doesn't make you sleepy in the afternoon.'

'A pity you weren't able to stay long enough to eat,' he said blandly.

Despising the heat in her skin, Gerry kept her voice steady. 'My friend wasn't well.' Before he could comment she continued, 'Cara tells me you want to ask me something?'

'I'd like to offer you a very short, one-off project,' he said, and without giving her time to refuse went on, 'It involves a trip to the islands, and some research into the saleability—or not—of hats.'

Whatever she'd expected it wasn't that. 'Hats,' she repeated blankly.

The green gaze rested a moment on her mouth before moving up to capture her eyes. 'One of the outlying islands near Fala'isi is famous for the hats the islanders weave from a native shrub. They used to bring in an excellent income, but sales are falling off. They don't know why, but I suspect it's because they aren't keeping up with fashion. Cara tells me you have a couple of weeks off. One week at Longopai in the small hotel there should be ample time to check whether I'm right.'

No, she wanted to say, so loudly and clearly that there could be no mistaking her meaning. No, I don't want to go to a tropical island and find out why they're no longer selling their hats. I don't want anything to do with you.

'I'd love to go,' Cara said eagerly, 'but I'm booked solid for a couple of months. You're a real expert, Gerry—you style a shoot better than anyone, and Honor says you've got an instinct about fashion that never lets you down. And you'd have a super time in the islands—it's just what you need.'

Gerry looked out of the window. Darkness had already fallen; the steady drumming of rain formed a background to the rising wail of wind. She said, 'I might not have any idea why they aren't selling. Marketing is—'

'Exactly what you're good at,' Bryn said smoothly, his deep voice sliding with the silky friction of velvet along her nerves. 'When you worked as fashion editor for that magazine you marketed a look, a style, a colour.' He looked around the room. 'You have great taste,' he said.

As Gerry wondered whether she should tell him the room was furnished with pieces from her great-grandmother's estate, he finished, 'I can get you there tomorrow.'

Gerry's brows shot up. It was tempting—oh, she longed to get away and forget everything for a few days, just sink herself into the hedonism of a tropical holiday. Lukewarm lagoons, she thought yearningly, and colour—vivid, primal, shocking colour—and the scent of salt, and the caress of the trade winds on her bare skin...

Aloud, very firmly, she said, 'If you got some photographs done I could probably give you an opinion without going all the way up there. Or you could get some samples.'

'They deal better with people,' he said evenly. 'They'll take one look at you and realise that you know what you're talking about. A written report—or even a suggestion from me—won't have the same impact.'

'Most people,' Cara burbled, 'are dying to get to the tropics at this time of the year. You sound like a wrinklie, Gerry, hating the thought of being prised out of your nice comfortable nest!'

And if I go, Gerry thought with a tiny flash of malice, you'll be alone here, and no one will realise that you're spending nights in Bryn's bed. Although that was unkind;

Cara knew that Gerry wouldn't carry tales to her parents. And she honestly thought she was doing Gerry a favour.

Hell, she probably was.

Green eyes half-closed, Bryn said, 'I'd rather you actually saw the hats. Photographs don't tell the whole story, as you're well aware. And of course the company will pay for your flights and accommodation.'

She was being stupid and she knew it; had any other man suggested it she'd have jumped at the idea. Striving for her usual equanimity, she said, 'Of course I'd like to go, but—'

Cara laughed. 'I told you she wouldn't be able to resist it,' she crowed.

'Where is this island?' Gerry asked shortly.

'Longopai's an atoll twenty minutes by air from Fala'isi.' All business, Bryn said, 'A taxi will pick you up at ten tomorrow morning. Collect your tickets from the Air New Zealand counter at the airport. Pack for a week, but keep in mind the weight restrictions.'

What did he think she was? One of those people who can't leave anything in their wardrobe when they go overseas?

Cara headed off an intemperate reply by breaking in, 'Gerry can pack all she needs for three weeks in an overnight bag,' she said on an awed note.

Bryn's brow lifted. 'Clever Gerry,' he said evenly, his voice expressionless.

So why did it sound like a taunt?

CHAPTER THREE

IT DIDN'T surprise her that Bryn Falconer's arrangements worked smoothly; he'd expect efficiency in his hirelings.

Everything—from the moment Gerry collected her first-class ticket at Auckland airport to the cab-ride through the hot, colourful streets of Fala'isi with the tall young man who'd met the plane—went without a hitch.

'Mr Falconer said you were very important, and that I wasn't to be late,' her escort said when she thanked him for meeting her.

A considerable exaggeration, she thought with a touch of cynicism. Bryn liked her as little as she liked him. 'Do you work for the hotel on Longopai?'

He shook his head. 'For the shipping company. Mr Falconer bought a trader to bring the dried coconut here from Longopai, so it is necessary to have an office here.'

Bryn had said he was an importer—clearly he dealt in Pacific trade goods.

At the waterfront Gerry's escort loaded her and her suitcase tenderly into a float plane. Within five minutes, in a maelstrom of spray and a shriek of engines, the plane taxied out, broke free of the water and rose over the lagoon to cross the white line of the reef and drone north above a tropical sea of such vivid blue-green that Gerry blinked and put on her sunglasses.

She'd forgotten how much she loved the heat and the brilliance, forgotten the blatant, overpowering assault on senses more accustomed to New Zealand's subtler colours and scents. Now, smiling at the large ginger dog of bewildering parentage strapped into the co-pilot's seat, she relaxed.

Between the high island of Fala'isi and the atoll of Longopai stretched a wide strait where shifting colours and surface textures denoted reefs and sandbanks. Gazing down at several green islets, each ringed by blinding coral sand, Gerry wondered how long it would take to go by sea through these treacherous waters.

'Landfall in distant seas,' the pilot intoned dramatically over the intercom fifteen minutes later.

A thin, irregular, plumy green circle surrounded by blinding sand, the atoll enclosed a huge lagoon of enchanting, opalescent blues and greens. To make it perfect, in the centre of the lagoon rested a boat, white and graceful. Not a yacht—too much to expect!—but a large cruiser, some rich man's toy.

Gerry sighed. Oh, she wouldn't want to live on a place like this—too cut off, and, being a New Zealander, she loved the sight of hills on the horizon—but for a holiday what could be better? Sun, sand, and enough of a mission to stop her from becoming inured to self-indulgence.

After a spray-flurried landing in the deeper part of the lagoon, Gerry unbelted as a canoe danced towards them.

'Your transport.' The pilot nodded at it.

Glad that she'd worn trousers and a T-shirt, she pulled on her hat. The canoe surged in against the plane, manned by two young men with dark eyes and the proud features of Polynesians, their grins open and frankly appreciative as they loaded her suitcase.

Amused and touched by the cushion that waited on her seat, Gerry stepped nimbly down, sat gracefully and waved to the pilot. The dog barked and wagged its tail; the pilot said, 'Have a great holiday.'

Yes, indeed, Gerry thought, smiling as the canoe backed away from the plane, swung around and forged across the glittering waters.

New Zealand seemed a long, long way away. For this week she'd forget about it, and the life that had become so terrifyingly flat, to wallow in the delights of doing practically nothing in one of the most perfect climates in the world.

And in one of the most perfect settings!

Following the hotel porter along a path of crushed white shell, Gerry breathed deeply, inhaling air so fresh and languorous it smelt like Eden, a wonderful mixture of the unmatched perfumes of gardenia and frangipani and ylangylang, salted by a faint and not unpleasing undernote of fish, she noted cheerfully. Her cabaña, its rustic appearance belying the luxury within, was one of only ten.

'*Very* civilised,' she said aloud when she was alone.

A huge bed draped in mosquito netting dominated one end of the room. Chairs and sofas—made of giant bamboo and covered in the soothing tans and creams of tapa cloth—faced wide windows which had shutters folded back to reveal a deck. Separated from a tiny kitchen by a bar, a wooden table and chairs stood at the other end of the room. Fruit and flowers burst from a huge pottery shell on the table.

Further exploration revealed a bathroom of such unashamed and unregenerate opulence—all marble in soft sunrise hues of cream and pale rose—that Gerry whistled.

Whoever had conceived and designed this hotel had had a very exclusive clientele in mind—the seriously rich who wanted to escape. Although, she thought, eyeing the toiletries laid out on the marble vanity, not too far.

The place was an odd but highly successful blend of sophisticated luxury and romantic, lazy, South Seas simplicity. Normally she'd never be able to afford such a place. She was, she thought happily, going to cost Bryn Falconer megabucks.

Half an hour later, showered and changed into fresh clothes, she strolled down the path, stopping to pick a hibiscus flower and tuck it behind her ear, where its rollicking orange petals and fiery scarlet throat would contrast splendidly with her black curls. Only flowers, she decided, could get away with a colour scheme like that! Or silk, perhaps...

According to the schedule her escort in Fala'isi had given her, she'd have the rest of the day to relax before the serious part of this holiday began. Tomorrow she'd be shown the hats. As the swift purple twilight of the tropics gathered on the horizon, she straightened her shoulders and walked across the coarse grass to the lounge area.

And there, getting up from one of the sinfully comfortable chairs and striding across to meet her, was Bryn Falconer, all power and smooth, co-ordinated litheness, green eyes gleaming with a metallic sheen, his autocratic features only hinting at the powerful personality within.

Gerry was eternally grateful that she didn't falter, didn't even hesitate. But the smile she summoned was pure willpower, and probably showed a few too many teeth, for he laughed, a deep, amused sound that hid any mockery from the three people behind him.

'Hello, Geraldine,' he said, and took her arm with a grip that looked easy. 'Somehow I knew just how you'd look.'

As she was wearing a gentle dress the dark blue-green of her eyes, with a long wrap skirt and flat-heeled sandals, she doubted that very much. Flattering it certainly was—the straight skirt and deep, scooped neckline emphasised her slender limbs and narrow waist—but fashionable it was not.

Arching her brows at him, she murmured, 'Oh? How *do* I look?'

His smile hardened. 'Rare and expensive and fascinating—perfect for a tropical sunset. A moonlit woman, as shadowy and mysterious as the pearls they dive for in one small atoll far to the north of here, pearls the colour of the sea and the sky at midnight.'

Something in his tone—a disturbing strand of intensity, of almost-hidden passion—sent her pulse skipping. Automatically, she deflected.

'What a charming compliment. Thank you,' she returned serenely, dragging her eyes away from the uncompromising authority of his face as he introduced his companions.

still recovering from that first sight of him, and for a moment she'd wondered what it would be like to hear that deep voice made raw by passion, but she was strong, she'd get over it.

'We've been here several times,' Narelle said, preening a little. 'Last year Logan Hawkhurst was here with the current girlfriend, Tania Somebody-or-other.'

Logan Hawkhurst was an actor, the latest sensation from London, a magnificently structured genius with a head of midnight hair, bedroom eyes, and a temper—so gossip had it—that verged on molten most of the time.

'And was he as overwhelming as they say?' Gerry asked lightly.

Narelle gave an artificial laugh. 'Oh, more so,' she said. 'Just gorgeous—like something swashbuckling out of history. Lacey had a real a crush on him.'

The girl's face flamed.

Gerry said cheerfully, 'She wasn't the only one. I had to restrain a friend of mine when he finally got married—she wept half a wet Sunday and said she was never going to see another film of his because he'd break her heart all over again.'

They dutifully laughed, and some of the colour faded from the girl's skin.

'Don't know what you women see in him,' Cosmo said, giving Bryn a man-to-man look.

His wife said curtly, 'He's very talented, and you saw quite a lot in his girlfriend, whose talent wasn't so obvious.' She laughed a little spitefully. 'He must like fat women.'

Fortunately the waiter returned with the drinks just then, pale gold and frosted, with moisture sliding down the softly rounded glasses.

Gerry had seen more than enough photographs of the woman Logan Hawkhurst had wooed all over the world and finally won; a tall, statuesque woman, with wide shoulders, glorious legs and substantial breasts, she'd looked as though she was more than capable of coping with a man of legendary temper.

Whatever, Gerry didn't want to deal with undercurrents and sly backbiting. Blast Bryn Falconer. This was not the way she'd envisioned spending her first evening on the atoll.

Even more irritating, Narelle set out to establish territory and pecking order. Possibly Bryn noted the glitter in Gerry's smile, for he steered the conversation in a different direction. Instead of determining who outranked whom, they talked of the latest comet, and the plays on Broadway, and whether cars would ever run on hydrogen. Lacey didn't offer much, but what she did say was sharply perceptive.

Gerry admired the way Bryn handled the girl; he respected her intelligence and treated her as an interesting woman with a lot to offer. Lacey bloomed.

Which was more than Gerry did. Infuriatingly, the confidence she took for granted seemed to be draining away faster than the liquid in her glass. Every time Bryn's hooded green gaze traversed her face her rapid pulse developed an uncomfortable skip, and she had to yank her mind ruthlessly off the question of just how that long, hard mouth would feel against hers...

How foolish of Narelle to try her silly tests of who outranked whom! Bryn was the dominant male, and not only because he was six inches taller than Cosmo; what marked him out was the innate authority blazing around him like a forceful aura, intimidating and omnipresent.

Dragging her attention back, she learned that Cosmo owned a chain of shops in Australia. Narelle turned out to be a demon shopper, detailing the best boutiques in London for clothes, and where to buy gold jewellery, and how wonderful Raffles Hotel in Singapore was now it had been refurbished.

Lacey relapsed into silence, turning her glass in her hand, drinking her fruit juice slowly, as Gerry drank hers, occasionally shooting sideways glances at Bryn. Another crush on the way, Gerry thought, feeling sorry for her.

Politeness insisted she listen to Narelle, nodding and putting in an odd comment, but the other woman was content to talk without too much input from anyone else. From the corner of her eye Gerry noted Bryn's lean, well-shaped hands pick up his beer glass. So acutely, physically aware of him was she that she fancied her skin on that side of her body was tighter, more stretched, than on the other.

'You've travelled quite a bit,' Lacey said abruptly, breaking into her mother's conversation.

'It's part of my job,' Gerry said.

'What do you do?'

She hesitated before saying, 'I work in fashion.'

Lacey looked smug. 'I thought you might be a model,' she said, 'but I *knew* you were something to do with fashion. You've got that look.' She leaned forward. 'Do models have to diet all the time to stay that slim?'

'Thin,' Gerry said calmly. 'They have to be incredibly thin because the camera adds ten pounds to everyone. Some starve themselves, but most don't. They're freaks.'

'F-freaks?' Lacey looked distinctly taken aback.

Bryn asked indolently, 'How many women do you see walking down the street who are six feet tall, skinny as rakes, with small bones and beautiful faces?'

Although the caustic note in his voice stung, Gerry nodded agreement.

'Well—not many, I suppose,' Lacey said defensively.

'It's not normal for women to look like that,' Bryn said with cold-blooded dispassion. 'Gerry's right—those who do are freaks.'

'Designers like women with no curves,' Gerry told her, 'because they show off clothes better.'

Narelle laughed a little shrilly. 'Oh, it's more than that,' she protested. 'Men are revolted by fat women.'

'Some men are,' Bryn said, leaning back in his chair as though he conducted conversations like this every day, 'but most men like women who are neither fat nor thin, just fit and pleasantly curvy.'

So she was not, Gerry realised, physically appealing to him. Although not model-thin, she was certainly on the lean side rather than voluptuous. His implied rejection bit uncomfortably deep; she had, she realised with a shock, taken it for granted that he found her as attractive as she found him.

Lacey asked, 'Are you in fashion too, Mr Falconer?'

'I have interests there,' he said, his tone casual.

Did he mean the hats?

With a bark of laughter Cosmo said, 'Amongst others.'

Bryn nodded. Smoothly, before anyone else could speak, he made some remark about a scandal in Melbourne, and Lacey listened to her parents discuss it eagerly.

Illness or anorexia? Gerry wondered, covertly taking in the stick-like arms and legs. Lacey had her father's build; she should have been rounded. Or just a kid in a growing spurt? Sixteen could be a dangerous age.

Had Bryn discerned that? Why else would he have bothered to warn her off dieting? Because that was what he'd done, in the nicest possible way.

Gerry drained her glass and settled back in her chair, watching the night drift across the sea, sweep tenderly through the palms and envelop everything in a soft, scented darkness. The sound of waves caressing the reef acted as a backdrop; while they'd been talking several other people had come in and sat down, and now a porter was going around lighting flares.

If she were alone, Gerry thought, she'd be having a wonderful time, instead of sitting there with every cell alert and tense, waiting for something to happen.

What happened was that a waiter came across and bent over Bryn, saying cheerfully, 'Your table is ready, sir.'

'Then we'd better eat,' he said, and got to his feet, towering over them. 'Geraldine,' he said, holding out his hand.

Irritated, but unable to reject him without making it too

obvious, Gerry put hers in his and let him help her up, smiling at the others. He kept his grip until they were half-way across the room, when she tugged her fingers free and demanded, 'What on earth is going on?'

'I'd have thought you'd know the signs,' he said caustically. 'If she hasn't got anorexia, she's on the brink.'

'I didn't mean Lacey,' she snapped. 'What are you doing here?'

'I discovered I had a few days, so I decided it would be easier for you if I came up and acted as intermediary.'

Impossible to tell from his expression or his voice whether he was lying, but he certainly wasn't telling the whole story.

'Just like that?' she said, not trying to hide her disbelief. 'You didn't have this time yesterday.'

'Things change,' he told her blandly, pulling out a chair.

He was laughing at her and she resented it, but she wasn't going to make a fool of herself by protesting. So when she'd sat down she seized on the comment he'd made. 'What do you mean, you thought I'd have been able to recognise anorexia?'

'You deal with it all the time, surely?' he said.

She replied bluntly, 'Tragically, anorexic young women who don't get help die. They don't have the stamina to be models.'

'I know they die,' he said, his face a mask of granite, cold and inflexible in the warm, flickering light of the torches. 'How many do you think you've sent down that road?'

His grim question hurt more than a blow to the face.

Before she could defend herself he continued, 'Your in-dustry promotes an image of physical perfection that's com-pletely unattainable for most women. From there it's only a short step to eating disorders.'

'No one knows what causes eating disorders,' she said, uncomfortable because she had worried about this. 'You make it sound as though it's a new thing, but women have always died of eating disorders—they used to call it green sickness or a decline before they understood it. Some psychologists believe it's psychological, to do with personality types, while others think it's caused by lack of control and power. If you men would give up your arrogant assumption of authority over us and appreciate us for what we are— not as trophies to impress your friends and associates—then perhaps we could learn to appreciate ourselves in all our varied and manifold shapes and sizes and looks.'

'That's a cop-out,' he said relentlessly.

She lifted her brows. 'I'm always surprised how responsibility for this has been dumped onto women—magazine editors, writers, models.'

'Are you a feminist, Geraldine?'

The surprise in his voice made her seethe. 'Of course I am,' she said dulcetly. 'Any woman who wants a better life for the next generation of girls is a feminist.'

'Don't you like men?'

'Of *course* I do,' she retorted even more sweetly. 'Some of my best friends are men.'

His smile turned savage. 'Are you trying to be provocative, or does it come naturally to you?'

The taunting question hit her in a vulnerable place. Her father's voice, ghostly, earnest, echoed in her ear. 'Don't tease, Gerry, darling. It's not fair—men don't know how to deal with a woman who teases.'

Banishing it, she counter-attacked. 'Do you think you're the only person who's ever accused me of forcing women into a strait-jacket? Sorry, it happens all the time. Interestingly, no one ever accuses me of forcing the male models into one, or the character models. Just the women.'

He didn't like that; his eyes narrowed to slivers of frigid green.

Strangely stimulated, she went on, 'And with interests in clothing, as well as computers and coconut, don't you think you're being just the tiniest bit hypocritical? After all, some of the money that pays for this fantasy of the South

Pacific—' her swift, disparaging glance scorched around the area '—comes from the women you're so concerned about…those so-called brainwashed followers of fashion.'

As a muscle flicked in the arrogant jaw she thought resignedly, Well, at least I've had half a day in the sun!

But it was something stronger than self-preservation that compelled her to lean forward and say, 'Let's make a bargain, Bryn. You work to stop all the actors and politicians and big businessmen from arming themselves with pretty, slaves-to-fashion trophy women, and I can guarantee that the magazines and fashion industry will fall neatly into line behind you.'

'Are women so driven by what men want?' he asked idly, as though he wasn't furious with her.

A hit. She laughed softly. 'Give us a hundred years of freedom and things will probably be different, but yes, men are important to us and always will be—just as men are affected by women. After all, nature set us up to attract each other.'

'So the desire to find a male with money and prestige is entirely natural, whereas a man's search for a mate who will enhance his prestige is wrong?'

Amusement sparkled in her voice. 'A woman's desire for wealth and prestige is linked, surely, to her instinctive knowledge that her children will have a better chance of surviving if their father is rich and has power in the community? Whereas a man just likes to look good in the eyes of other men!'

Since her university days, Gerry realised, she'd forgotten the sheer pleasure of debating, the swift interchange of ideas intended to provoke, to make people think, not necessarily meant to be taken seriously. Then she made the mistake of looking across the table, and wondered uneasily if for him this was personal. Behind the watchful face she sensed leashed emotions held in check by a formidable will.

'Women want a man who looks good in the eyes of other men,' he retorted. 'You've just said they see losers as bad bets for fatherhood. Besides,' he added silkily, 'surely the reason some men seek younger mates is *their* instinctive understanding that to perpetuate as many of their genes as possible—which is what evolution is all about—they need to mate with as many women as possible? And that young women are more fertile?'

'So men are naturally promiscuous and women naturally look for security?' she challenged. 'Do you believe that, Bryn?'

'As much as you do,' he said ironically, looking past Gerry to the waitress.

Gerry chose fish and a salad; she expected Bryn to be a red meat and potatoes man, but he too decided on fish. She must have looked a little startled because he explained, 'The fish here is one of the natural wonders of the world. And they cook it superbly.'

Those green eyes didn't miss a trick.

From now on she'd be more cautious; no more invigorating arguments or discussions. Even if he was one of the few men who made her blood run faster, she'd be strictly businesslike. She certainly wasn't interested in a man who'd slept with Cara. And who'd then, she realised far too late, had the nerve to trash the modelling industry.

Unless he'd been being as provocative as he'd accused her of being? She shot him an uneasy look, and wondered whether that strong-framed face hid a devious mind.

Possibly. So over a magnificent meal she firmly steered the conversation into dinner-party channels, touching on art, books, public events—nothing personal. Bryn followed suit, yet Gerry found herself absorbed by that intriguing voice with its undercurrent of—what?

It made her think of secrets, his voice—of violent emotions held under such brutal control that the prospect of releasing them assumed the prohibited glamour of the forbidden. It made her think all sorts of tantalising, exciting things.

Fortunately, before she got too carried away, a glance at

his harsh face with its uncompromising aura of power banished those nonsensical thoughts.

This man had no time for subtlety. He probably hadn't been deliberately winding her up with his contempt for models; he'd slept with Cara because he wanted her, and he wouldn't see any contradiction between his words and his behaviour.

Her appetite suddenly leaving her, Gerry looked down at her food.

Bryn Falconer fascinated her, but she knew herself too well—had dreaded for too long the genes that held the seeds of her destruction—to allow herself to act on that excitement.

'Did you see the baby in the newspaper?' he asked.

'Yes, poor wee love, while I was in the first-class lounge waiting for the plane.' And had slipped into sentimentality at the photograph of the crinkled little face, absorbed in sleep. Turning her half-empty glass, she kept her eyes fixed on the shimmering play of light in the crystal. 'The social worker said they'll do their best to find her mother and help her make a home for the child, but if that isn't possible the baby will be adopted. In the meantime she'll be with a foster family.'

'Clock ticking, Geraldine?' he asked. His eyes mocked her.

Repressing the swift, raw antagonism detonated by his lazy percipience, she parried lightly, 'Babies are special. I just hope she has a happy life, and that her mother is able to deal with whatever made her abandon her.'

'You have a kind heart.' An enigmatic note in his dark voice robbed the words of any compliment.

'I am noted for my kindness,' she said evenly. Putting the glass down, she pretended to hide a yawn. 'I'm sorry, I'm tired. Do you mind if I go now?'

'Am I so dull?' he asked with a disconcerting directness.

Startled, she looked up, to be pierced by glinting, sardonic green eyes. 'Not at all,' she said abruptly, antipathy prickling through her veins. Any other man would have accepted her face-saving explanation instead of challenging it.

'It's only nine o'clock. Cara tells me you've been known to stay out all night.'

'Staying out doesn't mean staying up,' she returned tartly, so irritated that Cara should gossip about her that she only realised what she'd implied when his mouth tightened. Almost immediately those firm lips relaxed into a smile that sent complex sensations snaking down her spine.

'Of course not,' he said, drawling the words slightly.

Oh, great, now he thought she was promiscuous. Well, she wasn't going to explain that because she disliked driving at night she tended to borrow a bed when the party looked like running late—and she certainly wasn't going to tell him that she spent the night in those beds alone!

This was a man who'd slept with a woman at least ten years younger than he was. He had no right to look at her like that, with lazy speculation narrowing his eyes.

Getting to her feet, she donned her most serene expression. 'Thank you very much for a lovely meal.'

He rose with her. 'I'll walk you to your room.'

'You don't need to,' she said steadily. 'I'm sure I'm perfectly safe here.'

'Absolutely, unless you consider the flying foxes. They tend to swoop low over the paths and some people find them scary.'

'I don't,' she said, but he came with her anyway.

After a silent walk along the sweet-smelling paths, lit by flares and the moon, he stopped at the door of her chalet while she unlocked it, and said, 'Goodnight, Geraldine.'

'Gerry,' she said before she could stop herself. 'Nobody calls me Geraldine.'

In the soft, treacherous moonlight his face was all angles and planes, an abstract study of strength emphasised by his eyes, their colour bleached to silver, hooded and dangerous. 'Who named you Geraldine?'

Startled, she gave him a direct answer. 'My mother.'

'Did she die young?'

'Oh, yes,' she said flippantly. 'But she'd left me long before she died. She was a bolter, my mother—she got bored easily. She died in a car crash, running away from her third husband to the man who was going to be her fourth.'

'How old were you when she left?'

Past pain, Geraldine had learnt, was best left to the past, but by telling him she'd opened the way for his question. 'Four. That was pretty good, actually. She left my half-brothers before they were able to recognise her.'

'Yet you can find sympathy for the woman who abandoned the baby?'

She shrugged. 'It's always easier to forgive when it's not personal. Besides, my mother made a habit of it, and she left chaos behind her. She had a talent for wrecking lives.'

'Did she wreck yours?' His voice was reflective.

Gerry lifted her head. 'No. I couldn't have asked for a happier childhood—my father devoted himself to me. But he never married again.'

'Then she only wrecked one life,' he pointed out objectively. 'If you don't include hers, of course.'

Reining in a most unusual aggression, Gerry retorted, 'She didn't do much for my half-brothers or their fathers.'

'She sounds more disturbed than malicious.' He stopped abruptly, as though he'd said more than he'd wanted to.

Looking up, Gerry caught the sudden clamping of his features. 'You're right,' she said lightly, mockingly. 'There are always two sides to every question, and we will never know what drove my mother headlong to destruction.'

He said brusquely, 'Thank you for your company at dinner. I'll see you at breakfast.'

'I always have breakfast in my room,' she said calmly. 'I'm not at my best in the mornings.'

'You coped very well with a totally unexpected incident

yesterday morning. I'm sure you'll manage a working breakfast.'

'In that case, of course,' she said in her briskest, most professional tone. 'What time would you like me to be there?' She didn't say sir, but the intimation of the word hung in the air.

'Eight o'clock,' he drawled.

'Then I'll say goodnight.' Gerry tossed him a practised smile and went inside, closing the door behind her with a sharp, savage little push.

But once inside she didn't turn the light on. From a shuttered window, she watched as Bryn Falconer strode along the path between hibiscuses and the elegant bunches of frangipani. Light fell through the slender trunks of the coconuts in lethal silver and black stripes.

He looked so completely at home in these exotic, alien surroundings. It would be easy to imagine him as a sandalwood trader or a pearl entrepreneur two hundred years ago, fighting his way through a region noted for its transcendent beauty and its dangers, taking his pleasures as seriously as he took its perils.

And because that sort of fantasy was altogether too inviting she made herself note the unconscious authority in his face and air and walk. Lord of all he surveyed she thought with an ironic smile.

An intriguing man—and one who was sleeping with Cara.

She shouldn't forget that just because she hated the thought of it. And while she was about it, why not remind herself that although she found him fascinating now, it wouldn't last.

There had been other men. She'd had two serious relationships, and although she'd honestly believed she loved both men, too soon the attraction had died like a flash of tinder without kindling, leaving her with no self-respect.

Because she hated hurting anyone she'd eventually given up on this man-woman thing.

This fiery, dramatic attraction would pass. She just had to keep her head while she waited it out.

CHAPTER FOUR

MORNING in the tropics was always a time of ravishingly fresh beauty. It would have been perfect if Gerry had been able to eat her breakfast alone on the small balcony with its view of the sea.

Nevertheless, she smiled as she showered and dressed. One of the exasperating things about winter was the extra clothes needed to keep warm, so she revelled in the freedom of a sundress and light sandals.

Not that she'd skimp on her make-up; painting up like a warrior going to battle, she thought with a narrow smile as she opened her cosmetics kit. She'd learned from experts how to apply that necessary mask so skilfully that even in the penetrating light of the sun she looked as though she wore only lip colouring.

And she'd be especially careful now, for reasons she wasn't prepared to go into. Frowning a little, she smoothed on tinted moisturiser with sunscreen; and the merest hint of blusher to give lift and sparkle to her olive skin.

Bryn had made it obvious that this was business, so he'd get the works—subtle, understated eyeshadow to deepen the intensity of her dark blue-green eyes, and two shades of lipstick, carefully applied with a brush and blended, blotted, then applied again.

Grateful that, as well as a tendency to restlessness, her mother had bequeathed her such excellent skin, Gerry slid into a gauzy shirt the exact blue of her sundress. She did not want her shoulders exposed to Bryn Falconer's unsettling green gaze.

Sunlight danced through the whispering fronds of the palms, and close by a dove cooed, a sound that always lifted her heart. Cynically amused at the anticipation that seethed through her, she picked a frangipani blossom and tucked it into the black curls behind her ear.

In the dining area Bryn rose from a chair as the waitress showed her to his table. Gerry recognised excellent tailoring and the finest cloth in both his trousers and the short-sleeved shirt. Clearly his business paid him very well.

And she'd better stop admiring those wide shoulders and heavily-muscled legs, and collect her wits.

'Good morning,' he said, eyeing her with a definite gleam of appreciation.

'It's a magnificent morning,' she said, squelching the forbidden leap of response as she allowed herself to be seated. 'What happens today?'

'Eat your breakfast first.' He waited a second, then added, 'If you have breakfast.'

She concealed gritted teeth with a false, radiant smile. 'Always,' she returned.

She chose fruit and yoghurt and toast, watching with interest as he ordered a breakfast that would have satisfied a lumberjack.

He looked up, and something in her face must have given her away, because that gleam appeared in his eyes again. 'There's a lot of me to keep going,' he said smoothly.

Unwillingly she laughed. 'How tall are you?'

'Six feet three and a half,' he said, deadpan.

'I thought so. Are your family all as big as you?'

Not a muscle moved in the confident, striking face, but she got the distinct impression of barriers clanging down. 'My mother was medium height. My father was tall,' he said, 'and so was my sister. Tall and big.'

All dead, by the way he spoke.

'You,' he resumed calmly, 'are tall, but very feminine. It's those long, elegant bones.' He paused, his eyes sliding over her startled face. 'And you walk like a breeze across the ocean, like the wind in the palms, graceful and unselfconscious. You don't look as though you know how to make a clumsy movement. Feminine to the core.'

He put his hand beside hers on the table. Emphasised by crisp white linen, the corded muscles of his forearm exuded an aura of efficient forcefulness. In the dappled light of the sun the glowing vermilion and ruby hibiscus flowers in the centre of the table seemed to almost vibrate against his golden-brown skin.

Beside his, her slender fingers, winter-pale, looked both sallow and ineffectual. And out of place.

Gerry gave herself a mental shake. Stop it, she commanded; you're competent enough.

Lean, blunt fingers rested a fraction of a moment on the shadowed veins at her wrist; his touch went through her like fire, like ice, speeding up the pulse that carried its effects in micro-seconds to the furthest part of her body. Dry-mouthed, a sudden thunder in her ears blocking out the mournful calling of the doves, she quelled an instinctive jerk. Even though he lifted his hand immediately, the skin burnt beneath his touch.

If his plan had been to show her how fragile she was against his strength he'd succeeded, but she saw no reason to let him know.

'Thank you,' she said. Thank heavens her voice didn't betray her. It sounded the same as it always did—cool, a little amused. 'But all women are feminine, you know, just as men are masculine. It goes with the sex.'

And could have bitten her tongue. Why did everything she said to him, everything he said to her, seem imbued with an undercurrent of innuendo, an earthy sensuality that neither of them would acknowledge?

'Some women seem to epitomise it,' he said drily, and glanced up with a smile for the waitress arriving with coffee.

Feeling as though she'd been released from some kind of hypnotic spell, Gerry filled her lungs with fresh, salt-tinged air, and studiously applied herself to getting as much caffeine inside her as she could.

Not that she needed any further stimulus. Her nerves were jumping beneath her skin, and thoughts skittered feverishly through her mind.

Nothing like this, she thought distractedly, had ever happened to her before. Still, although it would be foolish to pretend she was immune to Bryn's dark magnetism, she had enough self-discipline to wait it out. If she deprived this firestorm of fuel, it would devour itself until it collapsed into ashes, freeing her from his spell.

All she had to do was behave with decorum and confidence until it happened. And whenever she felt herself weakening, she'd just recall that he'd slept with Cara.

Yes, that worked; every time Gerry's too-pictorial brain produced images of them in bed together, she felt as though someone had just flung a large bucketful of cold water across her face.

Uncomfortable, but exactly what she needed.

'So what are your plans for this morning?' she asked when her leaping pulses had steadied and she was once more sure of her voice.

'We go for a walk,' he told her.

Gerry allowed her brows to lift slightly. 'A walk?'

'Yes. You do walk, I assume?'

She refused to acknowledge the taunt. 'Naturally,' she said graciously.

'Good. There are only three vehicles on the island.' He smiled. 'Nobody knows who you are, and nobody will expect anything more than a hotel guest's interest in the handicrafts.'

'We're keeping this a secret now?' she asked directly.

'I'd prefer no one to know what you're here for.' He met her gaze with a bland smile that set her teeth on edge.

Shrugging, she looked away. 'You're the boss.'

He was partly right—nobody knew who Gerry was. However, the people they met certainly knew who he was, and they did not view her as a casual hotel guest. They thought she was Bryn Falconer's woman.

He added fuel to their speculation by his attitude, a cool attentiveness that had something possessive about it.

She should have been profoundly irritated. Instead, her body tingled with life, with awareness, with a charged, vital attention, so that even when he was out of her direct sight she knew where he stood, felt him with a sixth sense she'd never experienced before.

Before long she realised the islanders' smiles and open interest meant they approved. The women who sat in groups plaiting the fine fibre greeted Bryn with pleasure and a familiarity that surprised her. Perhaps he was related to them; that would explain his concern.

On the floor of one of a cluster of thatched houses, incongruous beneath corrugated iron roofs, one old woman grinned at Bryn and made a sly comment in the local tongue, a little more guttural than the Maori spoken in New Zealand. He laughed and said something that set her rolling her eyes, but she retorted immediately, her dark eyes flicking from Gerry's set face to Bryn's.

Bryn shot back an answer that had everyone doubling over with mirth. Night school, Gerry decided with a flash of anger; as soon as she got back home she'd register in a Maori conversation class. For years she'd intended to, and now she was definitely going to do it.

'Sorry,' Bryn said, making no attempt to translate.

'That's all right,' she said too sweetly, her smile as polished and deadly as a stiletto. 'I'm a humble employee—it's not for me to show any offence.'

Mockery glinted in his eyes. 'I like a woman who knows her place. Let's go and see how they make the hats.'

As she watched the skilled, infinitely patient fingers weaving fine strands of fibre, Gerry said, 'They do need updating. Are you serious about increasing exports?'

'This is all the islanders have got,' he said. 'They use

the income from the industry to pay for secondary and ter-
tiary education for their children and for health care.
Fala'isi provides primary education and a nurse and clinic,
but anything else they have to work for themselves. And
this is the only export they have.'

'I thought you said they had pearls.'

He shook his head. 'Not here. We're negotiating to set
up a pearl industry, but that's a long-term project. The hats
are an assured market—if we can keep and expand it.'

'If I sent some photographs, could they copy them?'

Bryn asked the old woman, who was working with two
small, almost naked children playing around her feet.
Clearly the leader of the group, she frowned and answered
at length.

'Yes,' Bryn said, 'they could do that.'

After a round of farewells they left the village behind
and walked on beneath the feathery, rustling crowns of coconut palms. The heat collected there, intensifying, thick.
Eventually Gerry gave in and eased her shirt off.

Bryn didn't even look at her.

So much, she thought acidly, for not wanting to expose
myself. Aloud she said, 'I can find photographs of hats that
will sell much better than these. Luckily everyone in the
world wants to keep the sun off their face now. But to make
it work properly, they need an agent to keep them in contact
with what's going on in fashion. There'll always be a small
market for the classic styles, but if they want to expand
they need someone with a good knowledge of trends.'

Bryn nudged a thin black and white dog out of his way.
Fragments of white shell clattered as the dog scrambled up
and slouched towards a large-leafed bush. Once in the
shade, it gave itself a couple of languid scratches and
yawned fastidiously before settling to sleep. Three hens and
a rooster clucked amiably by, ignoring the dog, which
pricked its ears although it didn't lift its head from its paws.

Gerry laughed softly. 'I'll bet he'd give one of his teeth
to chase them.'

'Not if he wants to live. All food is precious here.'

Something oblique in his voice caught her attention. She gave him a sharp sideways glance. 'I suppose it is,' she said, because the silence demanded a response.

'Are you thirsty?' he asked abruptly.

His words suddenly made her aware that her throat was dry. 'Yes, actually I am.'

'Why didn't you say?'

She reacted to the irritation in his voice with a snap. 'There's no shop close by, so what's the use?'

'Dehydrating in this climate can be dangerous. And drinks are all around us. If—' with an intolerable trace of amusement in the words '—you like coconut milk.'

'I do, but I certainly don't want you going up there,' she answered, tipping back her head to eye the bunches of nuts, high above them at the top of the thin, curved trunks.

'It's not dangerous.'

A boy with brilliant dark eyes and a ready smile came swinging through the palms, armed, as many of the children were, with a machete half as tall as he was. After he and Bryn had conducted a cheerful conversation, the boy used a loop of rope to climb the palm with verve and flair. Trying to tell herself he'd probably done it a hundred times before, Gerry watched with anxiety.

'He's an expert,' Bryn reassured her with a smile. 'All the boys here can climb a coconut palm—it's a rite of passage, like learning to kick a football.'

'No doubt, but at least when you play rugby you're on the ground, not a hundred feet above it,' she said, breathing more easily when she saw the boy cut a green nut from the bunch at the crown of the palm and begin swinging down.

Back on the ground, he smiled bashfully at Gerry's thanks, sliced the top off the green nut with a practised flick of the machete, and presented it to her with a gamin grin, before disappearing through the palms towards the beach.

'Mmm, lovely,' Gerry said when she'd drunk half of the clear, refreshing liquid. 'Do you want some?'

She didn't expect Bryn to say yes, but he did, and drank the rest of the liquid down. Strangely embarrassed, she looked away. It seemed such an intimate thing, his mouth where hers had been, the coconut milk going from her lips to his.

You're being stupid, her common sense scolded. Just because he makes your skin prickle, because he has this weird effect on you, you're concocting links. Stop it this minute. Right now. And don't start it again.

'We'd better go back,' Bryn said. 'We've come quite a way and it's starting to get hot.'

On the way back she asked casually, 'When did you learn to speak Maori?'

'I grew up speaking it,' he said drily.

Not exactly a mine of information. Perversely, because it was clear he had no intention of satisfying her curiosity, she pursued, 'You're very fluent.'

'I should be. I lived here until I was ten.'

The depth of her need to know more startled her. It was this which silenced her rather than his brusque answer. Staring through the sinuous grey trunks of the coconut palms to the dazzle of sea beyond, she thought, I'm not going to try to satisfy such a highly suspect curiosity.

'My father,' he said coolly, 'was a beachcomber. It's not a word used much nowadays; I think he felt it had a romantic ring to it.'

Surprised at her sympathy, Gerry said, 'I don't suppose they were particularly good specimens of humanity, but there's a tang of romance to the term.'

'Not for me,' he said. 'He and my mother eloped from New Zealand and eventually made their way to Longopai. They sponged off the islanders until she died having my sister when I was five. After a few months my father drifted on without us, leaving us with a family here. He never came back.'

'That,' she said in a voice few of her friends had heard, 'was unforgivable.'

'Yes.' He looked down at her, eyes as transparent as green glass, but she had the feeling that he wasn't actually seeing her. 'You know what it's like.'

'At least I had a father who loved me,' she said fiercely. 'You were alone.'

'I had my sister. We weren't unhappy; in fact, we probably led a more idyllic life than most children. Our foster family accepted us completely, and we went to school and played and worked with the other kids until I was ten. My mother's parents discovered that we existed, so they sent someone up to collect us and take us back to New Zealand.'

'That would have been a difficult adjustment.'

He was silent for a moment, then said, 'We weren't the easiest of children to deal with, but our grandparents did their best to civilise us.'

'They succeeded,' she said promptly.

His laugh sent a shiver down her spine. 'In all outer respects,' he said. 'But for the first ten years of my life I ran wild. It's not an easy heritage to outgrow.'

It sounded like a warning, yet why should he warn her—and of what?

She asked, 'Was it difficult to adapt to life in New Zealand?'

'I loathed it.' He spoke reflectively, but beneath the smooth surface of his voice Gerry heard raw anger.

'It must have been terrible,' she said quietly.

'They sent me to a prep school to be beaten into shape. Fortunately I have a good brain, and I played rugby well enough to be in the first fifteen.'

A picture of the young boy, dragged away from the only home he'd ever had, pitched into a situation he had no knowledge of or understanding for, transmuted her sympathy into something more primitive—outrage. 'Your sister?'

'Didn't fare so well,' he said roughly. 'As I said, she was

a big girl, nothing dainty about her. She liked to play rugby too, but our grandparents didn't approve of that. In fact, they didn't approve of her at all, especially when she reached adolescence and shot up until she hit six feet.' He surveyed her with hard, unsparing calculation. 'She wasn't like you—she had no inborn style. She was plain, and because she wasn't valued she became clumsy. By the time she was fifteen she was utterly convinced that she was ugly and uncouth and worth nothing.'

Gerry dragged in a deep breath, fighting back the primal fury that coursed through her. 'Your grandparents have a lot to be ashamed of,' she said, thinking of her cousin Anet, another big, tall woman.

But Anet had been born into a family that loved her, and urged her to make the most of her natural athletic ability. After winning a gold medal in the javelin at the Olympics, she'd settled down to married life with a magnificent man who adored her.

Even after three children, the way Lucas Tremaine looked at his wife sent shivers down Gerry's spine. 'Children should be cherished,' she finished curtly.

A car came chugging down the narrow track towards them, if car it could be called. It might have originally been covered in, but consisted now of four wheels, a bonnet and the seats. When the elderly grey-haired driver saw them he slowed down and stopped.

'Message for you, Bryn,' he shouted above the sound of the engine, 'back at the hotel. They want you now.'

Bryn nodded. 'Hop up,' he said to Gerry.

Gerry was sorry the apology for a car had arrived just then. She hadn't satisfied that ravenous curiosity to know more about Bryn, but she understood now why he despised fashion magazines. No doubt his sister had yearned to look like the models in their pages.

What had happened to her? She cast a glance up at Bryn's implacable profile and as swiftly looked away again.

He'd put her so far out of his mind that she might as well not be there.

Trying not to resent his withdrawal, she leapt down when the car halted in front of the high, intricately thatched building that housed the office and the manager's quarters.

'I'll see you at lunchtime,' Bryn said curtly, and strode into the office.

As Gerry walked to her chalet, sticky and slightly salt-glazed, the taste of green coconut milk still faint on her tongue, she decided it didn't take much intuition to guess that he probably owned the hotel. He certainly organised the sale of the hats, and from what he'd said he was the person who was negotiating the pearling project. It was clear that he felt a profound obligation to the islanders who had given his sister her happy, early years.

Gerry admired that.

'Did you get your message?' she asked during lunch, looking up from her salad.

'Yes, thank you.'

She hesitated, then decided to go ahead with the decision she'd made while showering before the meal. 'Now that I've worked out what the problem is with the hats, there's no need for me to stay. It must be costing you a packet for my accommodation.'

'A week,' he said calmly, his eyes very keen as he studied her face. 'You can stay for the week you were hired for. Besides, you haven't seen much of the hat-making industry.'

Made uncomfortable by his concentrated scrutiny, she shrugged. 'Very well,' she said lightly. 'I'll do that tomorrow.'

His smile was narrow and cutting. 'Bored, Geraldine?'

'Not in the least,' she said truthfully. This seething, elemental attraction was about as far removed from boredom as anything could be. And it didn't help that she was terrified he'd notice its uncomfortable physical manifestations—the increased pulse-rate beating in her throat, the heat in her skin, the darkening of her eyes.

If he had noticed, he didn't remark on it. Irony charged his voice as he said, 'After that you can lie in the sun and gild those glorious legs until the week is up.'

'Tanning is no longer fashionable, I'm afraid.' Her smile was syrupy sweet.

Although he didn't rise to the bait, the hooded, predatory gleam of green beneath his lashes sent a sizzle of sensation down the length of her backbone.

She'd leave the day after tomorrow, but because she liked to keep things as smooth and amicable as possible she wasn't going to make a point of it. Bryn was a man accustomed to getting his own way, and she'd always found it simpler not to oppose such people head-on. She just ignored them and did what she wanted to. As a strategy, it usually worked very well.

He insisted she rest in the heat of the day, and because she was surprisingly tired she lay on the chaise longue in her suite and watched the tasselled shadows of the coconut palms on the floor. She did try to read one of the books she'd brought with her, but when her eyelids drifted down she allowed her fantasies to break through the bounds her conscious mind had set on them.

Later, under another cool and reviving shower, she tried to persuade herself that she must have been asleep, because her thoughts had run together and blurred, just like dreams. But they were all of the same man: Bryn Falconer, with his ice-green eyes and hard, strong face, its only softening feature lashes that were long and thick, and curled at the tips.

Gerry's mother had taught her too well that when you fell in love you created mayhem; you left shattered souls behind. Her father had taught her that falling in love meant unhappiness for the rest of your life. He'd taken one look at her mother and wanted her, and when she left him he'd been broken on the wheel of his own passion.

As his daughter grew into a mirror image of the beautiful, flighty, selfish woman who had abandoned them both, he'd warned her about the impact of her beauty. Gerry had seen it herself; men liked her and wanted her without even knowing her, because she had a lovely face and a way of flirting that made them feel wonderful.

So she'd grown up distrusting instant attraction.

Had some cynical fate made sure it had happened to her—a clap of thunder across the sunlit uplands of her life, dark, menacing and too powerful to be ignored?

For a lazy hour she'd lain in the soothing coolness of the trade winds and listened to the waves purring onto the reef, and slipped the leash on her imagination. She'd drowned in the sensuous impact of images of Bryn smiling, talking, of Bryn holding the baby…

Sheer, moony self-indulgence, she thought crossly.

All right, so she was physically attracted to the man— he was sexy enough to be a definite challenge, and that aura of steely power set her nerves jumping and her pulses throbbing—but she wasn't going to get carried away on a tide of imagination and wish herself into disillusion.

Armed with resolution, she went down to the lagoon and swam for twenty minutes in a sea as warm as her bath. She was wringing out her hair as she walked up the beach— swiftly, because the sand burned the soles of her feet— when her skin tightened in a reaction as primitive as it was involuntary.

Tiger-striped by shadow, Bryn stood beneath the palms. His eyes were hidden by sunglasses, and for a moment her heart juddered at his patient, watchful stance. Face bare of cosmetics, she felt like some small animal caught in the sights of a hunter, vulnerable, naked. Her legs suddenly seemed far too long, far too bare, and her bathing suit, sedate and sleek though it was, revealed too much of her body.

He didn't smile, and when he said, 'Hello,' an oblique

note in his voice sent something dark and primitive scudding through her.

'Hello,' she replied, keeping her eyes fixed on her small cache of belongings on the sand only a couple of feet away from him. He looked like some golden god from the days when the world was young, imperious and incredibly, compellingly formidable.

Furious with herself, she forced her shaking legs to walk up to her bag. She grabbed the towel from beneath it, and ran it over her shoulders, then dropped it to pick up a pareu. One swift shake wrapped it around her sarong-fashion. She secured it above her breasts with a knot, and anchored back the wet strands of her hair with two combs.

'Good swim?' His voice was gravelly, as though he'd been asleep.

At least he still wore his shirt. 'Glorious. The water's like silk,' she murmured, banishing images of him sprawled across a bed from her treacherous mind.

'That has to be the most interesting way to wear a length of cotton,' he observed gravely.

'Take your sunglasses off when you say that,' she growled in her best Hollywood cowboy manner.

He removed the sunglasses and stuffed them into his pocket. 'Sorry,' he said, a slow smile lingering as he surveyed her with open appreciation. 'I hope you put sunscreen on.'

She could feel his gaze travel across her shoulders, dip to the delicate skin of her cleavage, the smooth length of her arms. Pinned by that too-intimate survey, she thought confusedly that one of the reasons tanning had been so popular was that, like her cosmetics, it gave the illusion of a second skin; exposed under Bryn's questing scrutiny, she felt vulnerable.

With stiff reserve Gerry said, 'Naturally I take care of my skin.'

He seemed fascinated by the pearls of sea water on her shoulders, each cool bubble falling from her wet hair. One lean finger skimmed the slick surface. Such a light touch, and so swiftly removed, yet she felt it right to the pit of her stomach. Her body shouted *yes,* and melted, collapsed in a wave of heat, of painfully acute recognition.

'Oh, you do that,' he said, his voice a little thicker. 'And very well, too. Your skin's flawless—shimmering and seductive, with a glow like ripe peaches. What Mediterranean ancestor gave you that colouring?'

'My mother left before I had a chance to ask her about her ancestors, but one of them was French,' she said harshly, hearing the uneven crack in her voice with horror.

And she forced herself to step away from the tantalising lure of his closeness, from the primal incitement of his touch. Dry-mouthed, her brain cells too jittery to frame a coherent thought, she blundered on, 'However, that's a nice line. I'm sure Cara liked it.'

Something colder than Saturn's frozen seas flickered within the enigmatic depths of his eyes. 'She'd giggle if I said that to her.'

No doubt, but Cara clearly wasn't too young or unsophisticated to sleep with. Gerry shrugged and turned towards the path to the hotel.

Bryn said coolly, 'She spent the night at my place. Not, however, in my bed.'

Gerry made the mistake of glancing back. 'It's none of my business what Cara—or you—do,' she said, struggling to hold her voice steady in the face of the level, inimical challenge of his gaze and tone.

'Do you believe me?' he asked.

'Is it important that I do?'

He smiled, and his gaze lingered on her mouth. 'Yes,' he said levelly. 'Unfortunately it is.'

CHAPTER FIVE

GERRY hesitated, aware that she was about to step into the unknown, take the first, terrifying stumble over a threshold she'd always evaded before. Every instinct shouted a warning, but even a faint, cautionary memory of her mother, and the damage she'd caused in her pursuit of love, couldn't dampen down the fever-beat of anticipation.

'I do believe you,' she said slowly, her fingers tightening on the knotted cotton at her breast. 'I hope you don't hurt her. Although she thinks she's very sophisticated, she's a baby.'

'She knows she's in no danger from me.'

'That's not the point. She's very attracted to you.'

Frowning, he said abruptly, 'I can't do anything about that.'

If she had any intelligence she'd shut up, but something drove her to say, 'You *are* doing something about it. You're encouraging it.'

Broad shoulders moved in a slight shrug. Coldly, incisively, his eyes as hard as splintered diamonds, he said, 'I met her at a dinner party, saw that she was a little out of her depth, and watched her drink too much. I didn't trust the man hovering around, so I offered her a bed for the night.' He repeated with a dark undertone of aggression, of warning, '*A* bed, not *my* bed.'

Gerry's humiliating resentment wasn't appeased. 'I know I shouldn't worry about her,' she said, trying to sound as though she were discussing a purely maternal instinct instead of a fierce, female possessiveness unrecognised in her until she'd met Bryn. 'It's just that she's such a kid in some ways.'

One brow lifted slightly as he said, 'You're also her role model, her idea of everything that's sophisticated and successful.'

'I know,' she said, wishing they could talk about someone other than Cara. 'She'll grow out of it.'

'Oh, I'm sure she will. Hero-worship is an adolescent emotion.' Voices from behind made him say with a caustic flick, 'And here is someone else all ready to worship at the shrine of high fashion.'

It was the Australian family—slightly overweight father, artificial wife and the too-thin daughter with the seeking eyes and vulnerable mouth. Although they were all smiling as they came up, their body language gave them away; they'd been quarrelling.

Gerry tamped down her guilty exasperation at their intrusion.

'Had a good day?' Cosmo asked heartily.

'Lovely, thank you.' Gerry smiled at him and saw his eyelids droop. By now thoroughly irritated, she transferred the smile to his wife and daughter. 'What have you been doing?'

'Swimming,' Narelle said with a little snap.

Lacey eyed Gerry. 'I've been diving,' she offered. 'Did you know that when you go down a bit everything turns blue? Even the fish and the coral? It's nothing like the wildlife documentaries.'

Gerry nodded sympathetically. 'They're specially lighted in the documentaries. Still, the ones close to the surface where the sunlight reaches are gorgeous.'

'It's not the same, though,' Lacey said with glum precision.

'It just shows how careful lighting can glamorise things,' Bryn observed.

Gerry kept her countenance with an effort. 'Exactly,' she said drily.

The younger woman shrugged. 'Oh, well, there's a lot

to look at down there, even if it is all blue. I saw a moray eel.'

Narelle pulled a face. 'Ugh.'

Without looking at her, Gerry said, 'In some places they tame them by feeding them.'

'I wouldn't want to get too close to one.' Lacey shuddered, an involuntary movement that turned into a sudden stumble. She flung out a thin arm and clung for a moment to Gerry, fingers bruising her arm. After a moment she straightened and stepped back, face pasty, her angular body held upright, Gerry guessed, by sheer will-power.

Narelle had been laughing at something Bryn said. She turned now, gave her daughter a swift, irritated glance and said, 'Let's go up and shower. All that lying on the beach is exhausting.'

Lacey's eyes wrung Gerry's heart. Adolescence could be the cruellest time; she herself would have suffered much more if she hadn't had a father who loved her, good friends, aunts who'd listened to her and taught her what to wear, and a plethora of cousins to act as sisters and brothers.

This girl seemed acutely alone, and beneath the prickly outer shell Gerry discerned a kind of numb, stubborn fear. She walked up to the cabañas beside her, talking quietly about nothing much, and slowly a little colour returned to Lacey's face.

An hour later, when they met again in the open-air bar, Gerry was glad to see that Bryn was with the younger woman, and that she was laughing. She had, Gerry realised, the most beautiful eyes—large and grey, and when she was amused they shone beneath thick lashes.

Did she remind Bryn of his sister, who'd been awkward and unhappy? What had happened to her?

Gerry chose a long, soothing glass of lime juice to drink, oddly touched to have Lacey follow suit. Bryn's gaze moved from Lacey's face to Gerry's; she almost flinched at the nameless emotion chilling the crystalline depths.

'So what did you two do today?' Narelle asked flirtatiously.

'Checked out hats,' Bryn said.

'Oh, did you? I saw some in the shop here, but they're hopelessly old-fashioned. Quite resolutely unchic.' She dismissed the subject with a wave of her ringed hand. 'We bought pearls. They're good quality.'

And sure enough, around her throat was a string of golden-black pearls, the clasp highlighted with diamonds.

'They're very pretty,' said Gerry politely, and listened as Narelle told her how much they were worth and how to look after them.

A little later, when Narelle suggested that they eat together, Gerry smiled but said nothing. For a moment it seemed that Bryn might refuse, but after a keen glance at Lacey, silent in loose jeans and a white linen shirt, he agreed.

Gerry enjoyed her usual substantial meal, and wondered as Lacey demolished a much bigger one. In spite of Narelle's protests she even ate dessert.

As they drank coffee in the scented, flower-filled night, Lacey made an excuse and left them. A few moments later Gerry followed her to the restroom, slipping quietly in to the sound of retching.

'Lacey, are you all right?' she asked.

Silence, and then a shocked voice. 'I—ah—think I must have a bug,' Lacey muttered from behind the door.

'I'll get your mother.'

'No!' Water flushed. Loudly Lacey said, 'She's not my mother; she's my stepmother. My mother lives in Perth with her new husband.'

Gerry said, 'You shouldn't have to suffer through a stomach bug; I'm sure the hotel will have medication.'

'I'm all right,' Lacey said sullenly.

But Gerry waited until eventually Lacey opened the door and glowered at her. Then she asked, 'How long have you been throwing up after each meal? Your teeth are still all right, so it can't have been going on for long.'

'What do you mean?' the younger girl demanded belligerently, turning her back to wash out her mouth.

Remorselessly Gerry asked, 'Didn't you know that your teeth will rot? Stomach acid strips the enamel off them.'

Colour burned along the girl's cheekbones. Her hands moved rhythmically against each other in a lather of foam.

Gerry pressed on. 'Does your stepmother know?'

'No,' Lacey blurted. 'And she wouldn't care. All she's ever done is pick at me for being fat and greedy and clumsy.'

'Your father will certainly care.'

Doggedly, Lacey said, 'I should have been like my mother instead of like him.' She eyed Gerry. 'She's tall too.'

I hope to heaven this is the right way to tackle this, Gerry thought. Her hands were damp and tense, but she took a short breath and ploughed on. 'You're never going to be tall. Even if you kill yourself dieting—and that's entirely possible—you'll never look like your mother. She's a racehorse; you're a sturdy pony. Each is beautiful.'

Lacey glared in the mirror at her with open dislike. A stream of water ran across her writhing hands, flooding away the bubbles. 'It's not fair,' she burst out.

Leaning over to turn off the tap, Gerry said, 'Life's not fair, but you're stacking the odds against yourself. If you don't get help, all your potential—all the essential part of you that's been put on earth to make a difference—will be wasted trying to be something you're not.'

'That's easy for you to say!' Lacey flashed. 'You eat like a horse and I'll bet you don't put on a bit of weight.'

Gerry said calmly, 'That's right. But when I was fourteen I was already this tall, and so thin one of my uncles told me I could pass through a wedding ring. I hated it. I towered over everyone in my class, and I was teased unmercifully.'

'I wouldn't mind,' Lacey muttered.

'Do you like being teased?'

The younger woman bit her lip.

Hoping desperately she wasn't making things worse, Gerry went on, 'You have to find some sort of defence against it, but trying to turn yourself into the sort of person an aggressor thinks you should be is knuckling under, giving up your own personality, becoming the slave of their prejudices.'

Lacey frowned. 'It's fashionable to be thin,' she objected.

'In ten years' time the fashion will have changed. It wouldn't surprise me if it swung back to women like you, women with breasts and thighs and hips. Don't you want to get married?'

'Who'd have me?' she snapped, drying her hands without looking at Gerry.

'A man like the actor who was here last time, whose girlfriend caught your father's eye. I'll bet she wasn't skinny and smelling of vomit all the time.'

Lacey's shoulders hunched. 'She had big boobs and too much backside,' she mumbled, 'but she had long legs.'

'Are you sliding into bulimia because you want to attract boys? Because if you are I can tell you now they don't like women who throw up after every meal, whose skin goes pasty and coarse, whose teeth rot, who smell foul and who look like death.'

'Someone said I was fat,' Lacey muttered, a difficult blush blotching her face and neck. 'A boy I like.'

'So you're putting yourself into death row because someone with no manners—an adolescent dork—makes a nasty, untrue remark?' Brutal frankness might work if the girl wasn't too far down the track. Whatever, she couldn't just stand by and do nothing. 'You're letting someone else force you into his mould.'

'I—no. It's not like that.' But Lacey's voice lacked conviction.

'Is that how you'll go through life? Not as an intelligent person, which you are—you showed that the other night— with valuable talents and ideas and gifts, but a tadpole in a flooded creek, tossed every which way by other people's opinions?'

Open-mouthed, Lacey swung around to stare at her. 'A t-tadpole?' She started to laugh. 'A *tadpole*? No, I d-don't want to be a tadpole!'

'Well, that's where you're heading.' Gerry grinned. 'Instead of being a very self-possessed woman, with confidence and control over your own life. If you give up on yourself you risk losing everything that makes you the individual, unique person you are.'

'I wish it was that simple!' But a thoughtful note in Lacey's voice gave Gerry some hope.

'Nothing's ever simple,' she said, thinking of her reluctant, heated attraction to Bryn Falconer.

'I suppose you think I'm stupid,' Lacey said defensively.

'I told you what I think you are—intelligent, aware, with a sly wit that is going to stand you in good stead one day.'

'And fat,' Lacey finished cynically.

Gerry frowned. 'Promise me something.'

'What?'

Gerry chose her words with care. 'Promise me that when you go home you'll see a counsellor or a woman doctor you trust.' *Or I'll tell your parents.* The unspoken words hung in the scented air.

Lacey bit her lip, then blurted, 'If I do, will you write to me?'

'Yes, of course I will.' Gerry said, 'Are you on e-mail? I'll give you my address.' She hooked a tissue from her small bag and scribbled her address and telephone number on it. 'There. Ring me if you need to talk to someone. And, Lacey, you've got the most beautiful eyes.'

Scarlet-faced, the younger girl ducked her head and stammered her thanks.

'Right, let's go,' Gerry said, still worried, but hoping that somehow she'd managed to get through to the girl.

Apart from Bryn, who gave them both a swift, keen glance, no one seemed to have noticed that they'd been gone quite a while; Narelle was trying covertly to place someone on the other side of the room, and Cosmo was looking at his empty glass with the frown of a man who wonders if it would be sensible to have another.

As Gerry picked up her coffee cup Bryn's dark brows drew together into a formidable line and he looked over her head. From behind came a cheerful voice, 'A telephone call for Ms Dacre.'

'Thank you,' she said, taking the portable telephone from the tray and getting back to her feet. She walked across to the edge of the dining area and said, 'Yes.'

'Gerry, oh, thank God you're there, it's Cara.'

'What's happened?'

'M-Maddie—Maddie Hopkinson—is in hospital.'

Maddie, an extremely popular model who'd come back to New Zealand after three years based in New York, was to have left for Thailand for a shoot the day after next. An important shoot—the start of a huge, Pacific-wide campaign. She'd been through a difficult period, getting over the American boyfriend who'd dumped her when she insisted on coming home, but over the past month or so she seemed to have recovered her old fire and sparkle.

Icy tendrils unfolded through Gerry's stomach. 'In *hospital*? What's the matter with her?'

'She OD'd.' Cara sounded scared.

'*What?*'

'Drugs—her flatmate thinks it might have been heroin.'

Gerry had worried about Maddie, talked to her, suggested counselling, but had never suspected the model was taking drugs. Glancing automatically at her watch—silly, because Langopai was in the same time zone as New Zealand, so it was eight o'clock there too—she asked, 'When was this?'

'Last night.' Cara hesitated, then said in a voice that had horror and avidity nicely blended, 'Sally—the girl she shares a flat with—rang me this morning. Gerry, I went to see her this afternoon—there were police at her door and they wouldn't let me in.'

Shock stopped Gerry's brain. She drew in a deep breath and forced the cogs to engage again, logic to take over from panic. 'Why hasn't Honor contacted me?'

'Because she doesn't know anything about it,' Cara said. 'I've been ringing and ringing her flat, but all I get is the answer-machine. And it's Queen's Birthday weekend, so she won't be back until Tuesday.'

Blast Honor and her habit of taking off for weekends without letting anyone know where she was! Striving very hard to sound calm and in control, Gerry said, 'All right, I'll get a plane out of here as soon as I can. In the meantime, look in my work diary and get me the phone number of—' Her mind went blank. 'Maddie's booker.' The bookers at the agency organised each model's professional appointments.

'Jill,' Cara said. 'All right, I'll be back in a moment.'

While Cara raced off to get her diary from her bedroom Gerry gnawed on her lip and tried to work out what to do next. From the eight or nine guests enjoying the ambience of the communal area came a low, subdued hum of conversation punctuated with laughter. Lights glowed, dim enough to give the soft flattery of candles; she noted with an expert's eye the line and drape of extremely expensive resort wear, the glimmer of pearls, the sheen of pampered skin, the white flash of teeth.

Hurry up, Cara! And hang in there, Maddie, she mentally adjured, thinking of the exquisite, fragile girl lying in her hospital bed with a police guard at the door. Lately there had been a lot of publicity about heroin being chic amongst models and photographers. Oh, why hadn't she noticed something was wrong?

And how would this affect the agency? Her head

throbbed, and she had to take another deep breath. Swinging away to look out over the lush foliage beyond the public area, she scrabbled in her evening bag and found a ballpoint pen.

'I've got it.' Cara's voice wobbled, then firmed. 'Here's Jill's number.' She read it off.

Gerry wrote it on another tissue. 'OK.' She gave Cara the name of the advertising agency in charge of Maddie's shoot. 'Get me the art director's number—it's there.'

'She won't be at work now,' Cara said. 'It's Friday night.'

'She might be. Her home number's there as well, so get it too.'

'Gosh, you're so organised.' Sounds of scrabbling came through the static, until Cara said in a relieved voice, 'Yes, here they are.'

'Let's hope to heaven she either works late or stays home on a Friday night.' Gerry spread out the tissue and began to copy the numbers down as Cara read them out.

When the younger woman had finished she said, 'Gerry, it took me ages to get through to you so you might have trouble ringing New Zealand. Do you want me to ring Jill and tell her what's happened?'

Gerry hesitated. 'Good thinking. And if I haven't got hold of her, ask her to track down the art director and tell her that I suggest Belinda Hargreaves to take Maddie's place. I know she was second choice, and if I remember right she hasn't got anything on at the moment. Jill's her booker too, so she'll know.'

'What if the ad agency or the client doesn't want Belinda?'

Gerry said, 'I'll deal with it when I get back. Don't worry. Many thanks for ringing me. Cara, how is Maddie?'

'She's alive, but that's all I've been able to find out. The hospital won't tell me anything because I'm not a relation, and apparently her brother is still on his way back from Turkestan or somewhere.'

Gerry twisted a curl tight around one finger. Pushing guilt to the back of her mind, she said, 'Send her flowers from us all. And get me the number of the hospital, will you?'

Where the *hell* was Honor? Probably spending the weekend with a man; she had a cheerful, openly predatory attitude where the other sex were concerned, swanning unscathed through situations that would have scared Gerry white-haired.

Why couldn't she have waited until Gerry got back before going off like this? And why, when she knew Gerry would be away, hadn't she left a contact number?

But of course she hadn't known that Gerry was coming up to Longopai. Clearly she'd believed that if anything needed attending to, Gerry would do so, even though she was on holiday.

After soothing Cara some more, Gerry said goodbye, dropped the telephone at the main desk and organised to pay for all phone bills with her credit card, then went back to the table, composing her expression into blandness.

'Problems?' Bryn said, getting to his feet. The ice-green gaze rested on her face, expressionless, measuring.

Damn, how did he know? 'I have to make a few calls,' she said lightly, avoiding a direct answer.

It was none of his business, and she refused to give him a chance to make more comments about her agency exploiting young women. She was feeling bad enough about Lacey and Maddie. Summoning her best smile, she said to the table at large, 'If you'll excuse me, I'll leave you now.'

'That's all right,' Cosmo said breezily. 'See you tomorrow, then.'

She smiled and said goodnight, startled when Bryn said, 'I'll walk you up to your cabaña.'

After a moment's silence she said, 'Thank you.'

He took her arm in a grip that had something both predatory and possessive about it. Back erect, head held high, she smiled at the Australian family and went with him.

When they were out of earshot he said, 'What problem?'

Steadily she said into the sleepy heat of the night, 'I'm sorry, I can't tell you. It's important and urgent—I need to get back to New Zealand as soon as possible.'

'Someone ill?' His voice was cool.

She dithered. 'I—no, I don't think so. I'm needed back at the agency—there's an emergency. I'm sorry about the hats—but I do know now what the problem is, and I'll send you recommendations. If that's not enough, I will, of course, repay the money you've spent—'

'Don't be an idiot.' Although his voice was crisp and scornful, he continued, 'If you have to go, you have to go.'

Surprised that he didn't try to hold her to their agreement, she asked, 'Is there any chance of leaving the island tonight?'

'No,' he said abruptly. 'The seaplane's not authorised for night flights.'

Stopping, she said, 'I'll see if the desk clerk can organise a seat for me on the first flight tomorrow.'

'I'll do it,' he said, urging her on. 'And get you onto a flight out of Fala'isi tomorrow.'

He was being kind, but something drove her to say, 'I can't put you to all that trouble.'

'I have more pull here than you,' he said coolly.

There was no sensible reason why she shouldn't accept his help. Struggling with an inconvenient wariness, she said, 'Thanks. I'd be very grateful.'

'What's happened?'

Gerry resisted the temptation to tell him everything and let him take over. So this, she thought, trying for her usual pragmatism, is the effect a pair of broad shoulders and an air of competence have on susceptible women. Odd that she, who prided herself on being capable and practical and the exact opposite of susceptible, should want to succumb like a wilting Victorian miss.

'Just some trouble at the agency. It's nothing you can help with,' she said woodenly, 'but thank you for offering.'

'You don't know what I can help with.'

Beneath the smooth, amused surface of his voice a note of determination alerted her senses. 'I do know you can't do anything about this,' she said.

He left it at that, although she thought she could sense irritation simmering in him. 'I'll organise your flights to New Zealand and be back in half an hour,' he said.

'Thank you very much.' She made the mistake of glancing upwards. In the soft starlit darkness his face was a harsh sculpture, all tough, forceful power. Sensation slithered the length of her spine, melting a hitherto inviolate impregnability.

It would be easy to want this man rather desperately— so easy, and so incredibly perilous. He was no ordinary man; her cousin Anet's husband had something of the same sort of hard, contained intensity.

No, that was silly. Lucas had fought in a vicious and bloody guerrilla war; he wrote books about conspiracies and events that shook the world. Bryn was an importer. A successful businessman could have nothing in common with a man like Lucas.

After she'd closed the door behind her she exhaled soundlessly. It had been surprisingly difficult to turn down Bryn's offer of a listening ear. He hadn't liked it—no doubt he was accustomed to being the person everyone relied on.

Gerry had never relied on a man in her life, and she wasn't going to start now.

With a swift shake of her head she dialled the hospital, who would only tell her that Maddie was as well as could be expected. After thanking the impersonal voice, Gerry hung up and began damage control.

Jill, the booker who managed Maddie's professional life, already knew of Maddie's illness—although not, Gerry deduced, its nature—and was doing her best to tidy up the situation; she agreed that Belinda was the best replacement they could offer, and had already got in touch with her. Belinda was ready to go.

'Oh, that's great,' Gerry said, breathing a little more easily. 'Now I have to convince the art director at the ad agency that Belinda can do it.'

'I could do that,' Jill said.

'I'm going to have to crawl a bit—it should be me. Still, if you don't hear from me within the hour, start ringing her.'

'Will do. What are her numbers?'

'Bless you,' Gerry said, and told her. Hanging up, she breathed a harassed sigh.

It wasn't going to be easy.

After a frustrating and infuriating twenty minutes she gave up trying to contact the art director, who didn't even have an answering machine. It was useless to keep trying; she needed a good night's sleep, so she'd try again the next morning. And if she still couldn't get her, Jill would.

Swiftly, efficiently, she began to pack.

Half an hour to the minute later there was a knock on the door. Bracing herself, she opened it.

Bryn said, 'I've booked you on a flight from Fala'isi at six o'clock tomorrow morning.'

'But the seaplane—'

'I'll take the cabin cruiser and get you to Fala'isi before then.' His gaze took in her suitcase. 'Good, you're ready. Let's go.'

Taken aback, she protested, 'But—'

He interrupted crisply, 'I thought you wanted to get back to New Zealand in a hurry?'

'Yes! I—well, yes, of course I do.' Yet still she hesitated. 'I presume you know how to get from here to Fala'isi in a strange cabin cruiser?'

His mouth curved. 'The cruiser's mine. And with radar and all the modern aids, navigation's like falling off a log. Besides, I do know these waters—I come up here quite often.'

Feeling stupid, she said, 'Well—thank you very much.'

He lifted her case and she went with him through the

palms, past the public area, out onto the clinging, coarse white coral sand of the beach, where the hotel's outrigger canoe was ready. The two men who'd picked her up from the plane were there; they said something in the local Maori to Bryn, who answered with a laugh, and before long they were heading across the lagoon, the only sound a soft hissing as the hulls sliced through the black water.

Gerry had a moment of disassociation, a stretched fragment of time when she wondered what she was doing there beneath stars so big and trembling and close she felt she could pick them like flowers. The scents of sea and land mingled, the fresh fecundity of tropical vegetation balanced by the cool, salty perfume of the lagoon.

Thoughts spun around her brain, jostling for their moment in the light, then sliding away into oblivion. She should be trying to work out how to help Maddie. Bryn would be disgusted if he knew; poor Maddie's condition would be another nail in Gerry's coffin, another thing to despise her for.

Was he right? Was her career one that drove young women down Lacey's path? Would Maddie have begun using heroin if she hadn't been a model? Would Lacey be bulimic if she hadn't longed to be thin?

Stricken, she pushed the thoughts to the back of her brain and looked around.

The starlit silence, the swift flight of the canoe, the noiseless islanders and the awe-inspiring beauty of the night played tricks on her mind. She wondered if this was what it would be like to embark on a quest into the unknown, a quest from which she'd return irrevocably transformed. Her eyes clung to Bryn's profile, arrogant against the luminous sky. Something tightened into an ache inside her; swallowing, she looked hastily away.

You've been reading too much mythology, she told herself caustically. What you're doing is catching a plane home to Maddie's personal tragedy, and there's nothing remotely magical about that!

Paddles flashed, slowing the canoe's headlong flight; carefully, precisely, they eased up to the white hull of the cruiser. Bryn stood up, and in one lithe movement hauled himself up and over the railing. Within two minutes he'd unzipped the awning and lowered steps from the cockpit. Gerry climbed up and waited while Bryn stooped to take her case from the hands of one of the men.

'Thank you,' she said.

They smiled and waved and sped off into the darkness.

CHAPTER SIX

FEELING oddly bereft, Gerry said, 'What happens now?'

Bryn gestured at a ladder and said, 'I'm going up to the flybridge because I can see better from up there. You might find it interesting to watch as we go out.'

'Can I do something?'

'No.'

The surprisingly large flybridge was roofed in and furnished with comfortable built-in sofas. One faced a bank of intimidating gauges and switches and dials beneath what would have been the windscreen in a car. There was even, Gerry noted, what appeared to be a small television screen. The other sofa was back to back with the first, so that it faced the rear of the boat where awnings blocked out the night. There was enough seating for half a dozen people.

Without looking at her, Bryn sat down in front of the console and began to do things. The engine roared into life and small lights sprang into action.

Wishing that she knew more about boats, Gerry perched a little distance from him and wrinkled her nose at the hot, musty air. Presumably the awnings at the back were usually raised—lowered? removed?—while the boat was in use.

As though she'd spoken, Bryn pressed a button and two of the side awnings slid to one side, letting in a rush of fresh air.

Desperately worried though she was about Maddie, Gerry couldn't entirely squelch a humiliating anticipation. A lazy inner voice that came from nowhere, all purring seductiveness, murmured, Oh, why worry? A few moments of fantasy can't do any harm.

Turning his head, Bryn asked, 'Will you hold her steady

while I haul up the anchor? Keep her bow pointed at the clump of palms on the very tip of the outer passage. You won't have to do anything more than that, and it's so calm you won't have any trouble.'

Her stomach lurched slightly, but he made the request so casually that she said, 'Fine,' and got to her feet, gripping the wheel tightly while he disappeared. She stared at the graceful curves of the palms until her eyes started to blur. She rested them by watching Bryn down on the deck in front.

He began to haul on the anchor chain, bending into the task with a strength that sent an odd little flutter through her. Broad shoulders moving in a rhythm as old as time, he pulled with smooth precision, power and litheness combining in a purely masculine grace.

He'd be a magnificent lover, prompted that sly inner voice.

A sudden rattle, combined with the stirring wheel in her hands, persuaded her to shut off the tempting images conjured by that reckless inner voice. Guiltily she looked back at the palm trees, breathing her relief that the bow still pointed in the right direction

'Good work,' Bryn said, coming up noiselessly beside her and taking over. 'Are you tired?'

'A bit.' She moved aside to gaze out across the water, smooth and dark as obsidian, polished by the soft sheen of the tropical stars. Heat gathered in her veins, seeping through her like warmed honey. She felt like a woman from the dawn of time, aware yet unknowing, standing on the edge of the first great leap into knowledge. 'It's a wonderful night.'

'Tropical nights are known for their seductive qualities,' Bryn agreed, his voice pleasant and detached.

It sounded like a warning. Gerry kept her gaze fixed on the lagoon. 'I'm sure they are,' she said drily.

'But you don't find them so.'

She shrugged. 'They're very beautiful. So is a summer's night at home—or a winter's one, for that matter.'

'A dyed-in-the-wool New Zealander,' he jibed.

'Afraid so. I think if you've been happy in a place you'll always love it.'

'And in spite of growing up motherless you were a happy child?'

'I was lucky,' she said. 'I had innumerable relations who treated me like their own child. And my father was very devoted.'

'His death must have hit you hard,' he said, looking down at the instruments behind the wheel.

'Yes.' Four years previously her father's heart had finally given up the struggle against the punishing workload he'd been forced to take on in his retirement years.

'I liked him,' Bryn said.

Gerry nodded, not surprised that they had met. New Zealand was small, and most people in a particular field knew everyone in it. Her father had earned his position as one of New Zealand's most far-sighted businessmen, building up his small publishing business into a Pacific Rim success.

She'd mourned her father and was over his death—or as over it as she'd ever be—but because the memory still hurt she asked, 'Did you ever try to find out what happened to *your* father?'

If he snubbed her, she wouldn't blame him.

But he answered readily enough, although a stony undernote hardened his words. 'He'd been hired as crew on a yacht headed for Easter Island. He died there in an accident.'

'A lonely place,' she said, thinking of the tiny, isolated island, the last outpost of Polynesia, so far across the vast Pacific that it was ruled from South America.

'Perhaps that's what he wanted. Loneliness, oblivion.' His voice was coolly objective. 'He didn't even have a headstone.'

For some reason the calm statement wrung Gerry's heart. 'Have you been there?'

'A year ago.'

She stared at the white bow wave chuckling past. 'Did you find anyone who knew him?'

'Several remembered what had happened. Apparently he got drunk and set out to swim ashore. He was washed up on the beach the following day. I tried to trace the yacht, but to all intents and purposes it sailed over the edge of the world. It certainly didn't turn up in any of the registers after that.'

At least she had been loved and valued! Tentatively she asked, 'He must have been shattered by your mother's death. Do you remember him?'

'Only that he was a big man with a quick, eager laugh. The islanders called him a starchaser, because you can never catch a star.'

'Like my mother,' she said softly, warmed by a sense of kinship. 'I don't know whether she ever knew what she wanted, but she certainly never got it.'

'Damaged people, perhaps. Both of them unable to accept responsibility for themselves or their children.'

Gerry nodded, watching as the bow swung, steadied, headed towards the black gap in the reef that was the channel. 'That passage looked very narrow from the air. Is it difficult to take a boat through?'

'Not this one. Longopai's trading vessel has to stand off and load and unload via smaller boats, but a craft this size has no trouble.' She looked up and saw a corner of his mouth lift, then compress. He went on, 'I know the channel as well as I know the way I shave. Besides, with the equipment on the *Starchaser* it would take an act of God or sheer stupidity to get us into any sort of trouble. Relax.'

Why had he called his boat after his father? Some sort of link to the man who'd abandoned him and his sister— or a warning? A glance at his profile, all hard authority in the greenish light of the dials and screens, destroyed that idea. No hint of sentiment or whimsy in those harsh male angles and lines. A warning, then.

Aloud, Gerry said lightly, 'I trust you and the *Starchaser*'s instruments entirely.'

He sent her a sharp glance before saying equivocally, 'Good.'

Nevertheless she didn't distract him with conversation while he took the cruiser through the gap, admiring the efficient skill with which he managed the craft in a very narrow passage. Once through, the boat settled into a regular, rocking motion against the waves.

'I forgot to ask,' Bryn said. 'Do you get seasick?'

'I haven't ever done so before.'

'There's medication down in the head if you need it.'

'The head?' she asked, smiling.

He turned the wheel slightly. In an amused voice he said, 'The bathroom. There are three on board, one off each of the staterooms and another for the other cabins.'

'Such opulence,' she said lightly.

'Never been on a luxury cruiser before?' he asked, the words underlined with a taunt.

'Quite often,' she said, then added, 'But always as a mere day passenger. And for some reason I assumed that luxury didn't mean much to you.'

He shrugged. 'I like comfort as much as the next man,' he said. 'But I can do without it. The boat is used mostly by guests from the hotel, and as they're brought here by the promise of luxury—and pay highly for it—the boat has to follow suit. There's no luxury at all on Longopai's trading vessel.'

'Does the vessel belong to the islanders?'

'Yes. They had no regular contact with the rest of the world. The trader has made quite a difference for them.'

Had he bought it for them?

Somewhere to the south lay Fala'isi, lost for now in the darkness. With a throb of dismay Gerry thought that she could stand like this for the rest of her life, watching the stars wheel slowly overhead in a sky of blue-black immensity, and listening to Bryn.

As soon as she realised where it was leading, she banished the delusion.

She was not, she told herself sternly, falling even the tiniest bit in love with Bryn Falconer. 'Do you know Lacey's address?' she asked, filling in a silence that was beginning to stretch too long.

'I could find out. Why?'

'I want to send her a photograph of my cousin and her husband,' she said. 'Anet threw the javelin for an Olympic gold; she's as tall as me and about three sizes bigger—a splendid Amazon of a woman.'

'Anet Carruthers? I saw her win. She threw brilliantly.'

'Didn't she just! One of my most exciting experiences was watching her get the gold. Her husband is gorgeous, and I think it might cheer Lacey up if she could see them together.'

'You continually surprise me,' he said after a moment.

'People who make incorrect assumptions based solely on physical appearance must live in a state of perpetual astonishment,' she returned evenly.

He laughed quietly. 'How right you are. I'm sorry.'

'You judged me without knowing anything about me,' she said, the words a crisp reprimand.

'Admitted. First appearances can be deceiving.'

When he strode into her house Gerry had thought him a hard man, exciting and different and far too old for Cara. Certainly she'd not suspected him to be capable of tenderness for a baby, or such kindness as this trip to Fala'isi. A little ashamed, she said, 'Well, anyone can make a mistake.'

She fought back a bewildering need to ask him more about his life, find out who his friends were and whether they shared any. Pressing her lips firmly together, she forced herself to think of other, far more urgent matters.

How was Maddie? And why—*why*—did someone with her advantages throw everything away in servitude to a drug?

When she recovered—Gerry refused to think she might not—they'd do their best for her, see that she got whatever help she needed to pull her life together. Honor would know what to do; she'd spent four years with a heroin-addicted lover. In the end she'd escaped with nothing but her dream of opening a modelling agency.

Frowning, Gerry wondered again whether Bryn was right. Did the constant pressure of unrealistic expectations lead young women into eating disorders and drug abuse?

She hugged her arms around her, turning slightly so that she could see the face of the man silhouetted against the soft glow of the instrument panels; as well as the powerful contours, the faint light picked out the surprisingly beautiful, sensuous curve of his mouth.

Something clutched at her nerves, dissolved the shield of her control, twisted her emotions ever tighter on the rack of hunger. For the first time in her life she felt the keen ache of unfulfilled desire, a needle of hunger and frustration that stripped her composure from her and forced her to accept her capacity for passion and surrender.

Hair lifted on the back of her neck. This was terrifying; she had changed overnight, altered at some deep cellular level, and she'd never be the same again.

'Why don't you go on down and sleep?'

Bryn's voice startled her. Had he noticed? No, how could he? 'I think I will,' she returned.

'The bed in the starboard cabin won't be made up, but the sheets are in the locker beside the door.'

'Is starboard left or right? I can never remember.'

'Right,' he said. Amused, he continued, 'Starboard and right are the longer words of each pair—port and left the shorter.'

'Thanks. Goodnight, Bryn. And thank you. This is wonderfully kind of you.'

'It's nothing.' He sounded detached.

Rebuffed, she made her way down to the cockpit, and then down three more steps to the main cabin. At the end a narrow door opened into an extremely comfortable little cabin, with a large double bed taking up most of the floor space. Close by, her suitcase rested on a built-in bench beneath a curtained band of windows.

After making the bed and discovering the secrets of the tiny *en suite*—only here it was a head, she reminded herself—Gerry slipped off her shoes and lay down. Soon this would be over. She'd fly back to New Zealand, and after that she'd make sure she didn't see much of Bryn. He was too dangerous to her peace, too much of a threat. And banishing the treacherous little thought that he'd never bore her, she courted sleep.

She woke to the gentle rocking of the boat, a bar of sunlight dazzling her closed eyes. For several moments she lay smiling, still mesmerised by dreams she no longer remembered, and then as her eyes opened and she stared through the gap in the curtains she gasped and shot upright.

Daylight here was just after six, so by now she should be high on a jet, heading back to New Zealand. A startled glance at her watch revealed that it was nine minutes past eight. No, she should be landing in the cold grey winter of Auckland. Jolted, she leapt off the bed and ran from the cabin.

Bryn was stretched out on a sofa, but his eyes were open, densely green and shadowed in his grim face. As Gerry skidded to a halt and demanded breathlessly, 'What's going on? Why are we stopped?' he got up, all six feet three and a half of him.

Tawny hair flopped over his forehead; raking it back, he said, 'The bloody electronics died, so I can't get the boat to go—or contact anyone.'

Her stomach dropped. Taking a short, involuntary step backwards she asked, 'Where are we?'

'I used the outboard from the inflatable to get us inside

a lagoon, so we're safe enough, but it won't take us to Fala'isi.'

A swift glance revealed that they were anchored off a low, picture-postcard atoll. Blinking at a half-moon of incandescent white sand, Gerry concentrated on calming her voice to its usual tone and speed. 'Can the islanders get us to Fala'isi? It's really important that I get back as soon as I can.'

'There are no islanders.' At her blank stare he elaborated. 'It's an uninhabited atoll about a hectare in extent.'

'Flares,' she urged. 'Distress flares—haven't you got any?'

'Five. I plan to fire them if we hear a plane or see a boat. It's our best chance of being found.'

'You don't sound very hopeful,' she said tautly.

Wide shoulders moved in the slightest of shrugs. 'The plane to Longopai flies the shortest route, and we're well off his track, but if he's looking in the right place at the right time he'll see a flare. The same goes for boats.'

While she stood there, scrabbling futilely for a solution, he asked without emphasis, 'Why is it so important for you to get back?'

'There's a problem with the agency,' she evaded woodenly.

'Surely you have someone in charge while you're away?'

'Honor McKenzie—my partner—but they can't get hold of her.'

He frowned. 'Why?'

'She's gone away without leaving a contact number,' Gerry snapped.

'Is that usual?'

She moved edgily across to the window, staring out. The boat rocked in the small waves; somewhere out there a fringing reef tamed the huge Pacific rollers. On the atoll, three coconut palms displayed themselves like a poster for a travel agency, and several birds flashed silver in the sun as they wheeled above the vivid waters of the lagoon. The sky glowed with the rich, heated promise of a tropical day.

It's not the end of the world, she told herself, taking three deep breaths. Even if I don't get back today or tomorrow it's not the end of the world. Jill will contact that wretched art director at the ad agency, and organise Maddie's replacement—the bookers know their stuff so well they can function without Honor.

Even if the art director or the client throws a tantrum and refuses to use Belinda, *it's still not the end of the world*.

But her body knew better. The last—the very last!—thing she wanted to do was spend any time shut up in a boat—however luxurious—with Bryn Falconer. An hour was too much.

Stomach churning, she said, 'Every so often Honor likes to get away from everything.'

'When you're not there?'

The dark voice sounded barely interested, yet a whisper of caution chilled her skin.

'She'll probably be back on Tuesday, but I need to get back *now*.' Her voice quavered. Gamely, she snatched back control and, because anything seemed better than letting him know that she was acutely attracted to him and terrified of it, she added, 'One of our models is ill, and there are things to be organised. I told Cara I'd be back today. She'll worry.' Quickly, before he had a chance to probe further, she asked, 'How on earth could everything fail on the boat? Surely the engine isn't run by electronics?'

'I'm afraid that it is,' he said. 'Just like your car—if the computer dies, it won't go.'

'Why can't you fix it? You're supposed to be an expert on computers, aren't you?' Shocked outrage shimmered through her voice, putting her at a complete disadvantage.

'Geraldine, I import them,' he said, as though explaining something to a child. 'I don't make them, and when my computers go down I call in professionals to fix them. I'm sorry, but I can't find out what the problem is.'

'So that means we have no facilities—we're not able to cook—'

'Calm down,' he said easily. 'The kitchen and heads are powered by gas. There's a small auxiliary engine that I can use to charge the generator with, so we'll have light. You're not going to be living in squalor, Geraldine.'

The taunting undernote irked her, but she ignored it. 'Can't you use that other engine to fix the electronic system? No, that wouldn't work.'

'Electronic systems don't run on fossil fuels,' he agreed tolerantly. 'Besides, the fault is in the electronics themselves, not the power.'

She cast a glance at his face with its shadow of beard. Although he didn't look tired, he might have been up all night getting them to safety. Dragging in another breath, she asked more moderately, 'How long do you think we'll have to wait here?'

His eyes were hooded and unreadable. 'I have no idea. Until someone comes looking for us.'

'When will they miss you?'

'They won't,' he told her. 'The islanders are accustomed to me taking off whenever I feel like it. But if you told Cara you'd be back today I'd say it will be tonight or tomorrow.'

Relief flooded her. 'Yes,' she said slowly. 'Yes, of course.'

'As soon as you don't turn up she'll alert people, and we'll be found.'

Gerry sank down onto the leather sofa. 'I'm sorry,' she said after a moment. 'I don't usually fly off the handle like that.'

'Everyone involved in a shipwreck is entitled to a qualm or two.'

Damn him, his mouth quirked. She bared her teeth in what she hoped looked like a smile. 'I suppose it is a shipwreck,' she said. 'On a desert island, of all places. How fortunate there are no pirates nowadays.'

'The world is full of pirates,' he said. His tone was not exactly reassuring, and neither were his words.

Gerry stared at him. 'What do you mean?' she asked uncertainly.

'Just that there are people around who would steal from you,' he said. 'If for any reason I'm not on board, be careful who you let in. Not that you're likely to have to face such a situation, but Fala'isi—and Longopai too—have their share of unpleasant opportunists.'

If that was meant to be reassuring, he should take lessons. A stress headache began to niggle behind one eye. Straining for her usual calm pragmatism, she said, 'Then I hope we get away before the local variety turns up. I have to tell you that although it sounds really romantic, being stranded has never appealed to me. And a steady diet of fish and coconuts will soon get boring.'

'There are staples on board,' he said casually. 'Plenty of water and tinned stuff. With fish and coconuts we have enough for a couple of weeks.'

'A couple of weeks!' she repeated numbly.

'Cheer up, we won't be here for that long. Would you like some breakfast?'

Gerry suddenly realised that she was still wearing the crumpled clothes she'd slept in. Worse, she hadn't combed her hair or cleaned her teeth.

Or put any make-up on.

Abruptly turning back to her cabin, she said, 'Thanks— just toast, if we've got bread. And coffee. I'll go and tidy up first.'

In the luxurious little bathroom Gerry peered at herself in the mirror, hissing when she saw a riot of black hair around her face, and eyes that were three times too big, the pupils dilated enough to make her look wild and feverish. Hastily she washed and got into clean clothes before reducing her mop to order and putting on her cosmetics.

When at last she emerged Bryn was making toast in the neat kitchen. A golden papaya lay quartered on the bench, its jetty seeds scooped from the melting flesh. Beside a hand of tiny, green-flecked bananas stood a bowl of oranges and the huge green oval of a soursop.

'Where did you get all this?' she asked.

'No sensible person travels by sea without loading some food,' he said evenly. 'It's a huge ocean, and every year people die in it, some from starvation. How many pieces of toast do you want?'

'Only a couple, thanks. I'm not very hungry.'

'You have a good appetite for someone so elegant.'

Sternly repressing a forbidden thrill of pleasure at the off-hand compliment, Gerry said, 'Thank you. Perhaps.'

He gave her a narrow glance, then smiled, reducing her to mindlessness with swift, intensely sexual charm. 'You're right,' he said blandly. 'Commenting on someone's appetite is crass. And you must know that you're not just elegant; you have the sort of beauty that takes the breath away.'

Shaken by her clamouring, unhindered response, Gerry said unevenly, 'From one extreme to the other. You're exaggerating—but thank you.'

'There should be a tablecloth in the narrow locker by the table,' Bryn told her. 'Plates and cutlery in the drawers beside it.'

Still quivering inside, she set the table, using the familiar process to regain some equilibrium.

By the time she sat down to fruit and toast she'd managed to impose an overlay of composure onto her riotous emotions. To her surprise she was hungry—and that bubble in her stomach, that golden haze suffusing her emotions was expectation.

Worried by this insight, she looked down at the table. In the morning sunlight the stainless steel knives and forks gleamed, and she'd never noticed before how pristine china looked against crisp blue and white checks, or how clean and satisfying the scents of food and coffee were.

Bryn was wearing a pale green knit polo shirt that emphasised the colour of his eyes and his tanned skin. He looked big and dangerous and powerfully attractive. Fire ran through her veins; resisting it, she forced herself to butter her toast, to spread marmalade and to drink coffee.

'I'll clean up in the kitchen if you want to go and fiddle with the electronics,' she offered when the meal was over.

'Sea-going vessels don't have kitchens.' He sounded amused. 'You come from the country with the biggest number of boats per person in the world, and you don't know that a boat's kitchen is called a galley?'

She shrugged. 'Why should I? My family ski and play golf in the winter, and play polo and tennis and croquet in the summer.'

'I'm not surprised,' he said, and although there was almost no inflection in his voice she knew it wasn't a compliment.

Smiling, each word sharpened with the hint of a taunt, she returned, 'All the yuppie pastimes.'

'But your family aren't yuppies,' he drawled. 'They're the genuine twenty-four-carat gold article, born into the purple.'

'Hardly. Emperors of Byzantium we're not!'

'No, just rich and aristocratic for generations.'

She lifted her brows, met gleaming eyes and a mouth that was hard and straight and controlled. Some risky impulse persuaded her to say, 'Do I detect the faint hint of an inferiority complex? But why? If your grandparents sent you to a private school they had money and social aspirations.'

The moment the words left her mouth she wished she'd kept silent. Instinct, stark and peremptory, warned her that this man didn't take lightly to being taunted.

'My maternal ones did. The other two lived in a state house with no fence and no garden, and a couple of old cars almost buried in grass on the lawn.' His voice betrayed nothing but a cool, slightly contemptuous amusement. 'Don't worry, Geraldine, I won't tell your family and friends that you've been slumming it.'

Damn, she'd hit a nerve with her clever remark. Beneath the surface of his words she sensed jagged, painful rocks...

Stacking her coffee mug onto her bread-and-butter plate, she said, 'I'm not a snob. Like most New Zealanders with any intelligence, I take people as I find them.'

'And how do you find me?'

Something about the way he spoke sent slow shivers along her spine, summoned that suffocating, terrifying intensity. Prosaically she said, 'A pleasant, interesting man.'

'Liar,' he said uncompromisingly. 'You find me a damned nuisance, just as much a nuisance as I find you. And you're every bit as aware of me as I am of you. The moment I walked into that pretty, comfortable, affluent house and saw you, tall and exquisite and profoundly, completely disturbing, I knew I wasn't going to find it easy to forget you.'

The startled breath stopped in her lungs; she sat very still, because he'd dragged her reluctant, inconvenient response to him from behind the barriers of her will and her self-discipline, and mercilessly displayed it in all its sullen power.

After swallowing to ease her dry throat, she said huskily, 'Of course I found you attractive. I'm sure most women do.'

'I'm not interested in most women.'

Gerry's heart lifted, soared, expanded. Ruthlessly she quelled the shafting pleasure, the slow, exquisitely keen delight at his admission that he wanted her with something like the basic, undiluted hunger that prowled through her veins.

But she couldn't allow it to mean anything. She said, 'I don't think now is a good time to be discussing this.'

'Look at me.' The words were growled as though compelled, as though they'd escaped the cage of his self-control.

Caught unawares, Gerry lifted her lashes. A muscle flicked in his autocratic jaw, and the beautiful sculpture of his mouth was compressed. But it was his eyes that held her captive, the pure green flames so bright her heart jumped in involuntary, automatic response. For a tense, stretched moment they rested with harsh hunger on her mouth.

And then he broke contact and said roughly, 'I agree. It's the wrong time. But it's not going to go away, Geraldine, and one day we're going to have to deal with it.'

Struggling to regain command of her emotions, she said in her most composed, most off-putting voice, 'Possibly. In the meantime, forgive me if I point out that while I tidy up here, you could employ your time better by trying to find out exactly what has gone wrong with your boat.'

He laughed and got to his feet, towering over her. 'Of course,' he said, and left the cabin.

Half an hour later she pulled the bed straight and stood up, frowning through the window. The dishes were washed and stacked away in their incredibly well-organised storage. She'd firmly resisted the urge to explore more of the kitchen. Her cabin was tidy. The bathroom had been cleaned. She didn't know what was behind the door into the other stateroom, and she wasn't looking.

So what could she do now? Apart from fret, of course.

Consciously, with considerable effort, she relaxed her facial muscles, drew in a couple of long, reviving breaths, and coaxed every tense muscle in her body to loosen.

Only when she was sure she had her face under control did she walk through the luxurious main cabin and up the short flight of stairs.

Bryn had pulled off a panel and was staring at a bewildering series of switches and wires. Although he didn't show any signs of knowing she was there, she wasn't surprised when he said shortly, 'Sometimes I think the old-fashioned ways were the best. I could probably do something about a simple engine failure.'

His tone made it obvious that it galled him to have to

admit to ignorance. In spite of her frustration, Gerry hid a smile. 'Complexity—the curse of the modern world,' she said.

Clearly he wasn't going to allude to that tense exchange over the breakfast table; it hurt that he could dismiss it so lightly and easily.

'Don't humour me,' he said abruptly, and pushed the panel back into place, screwing it on with swift, deft movements. When it was done he looked up, green eyes speculative. 'Well, Geraldine, what would you like to do? You'll get bored just sitting on the boat.'

'It depends how long we stay here,' she said coolly, not responding to the overt challenge. She looked across at a life preserver; written in red on it was the name *Starchaser*, and under it 'Auckland New Zealand', for its port of registration. 'It's a lovely boat,' she said kindly.

Bryn laughed at her. 'Thank you. Do you want to go ashore?'

The sun was too high in the sky, beating down with an intensity that warned of greater heat to come. 'Not just yet,' she said politely. 'There doesn't look to be much shelter there. I'd sooner stay on board until it cools down.'

'Then I'll show you the library.'

The books, kept in a locker in the main cabin, were an eclectic collection, ranging through biographies to solid tomes about politics and economic theory. Not a lot of fiction, she noted, and—apart from a couple of intimidating paperbacks probably left behind by guests—nothing that could be termed light. Or even medium weight.

'It doesn't look as though you read for entertainment,' she observed.

He gave her a shark's grin. 'I don't have time. I'm sorry there's nothing frothy there.'

'That,' she returned sweetly, 'sounds almost patronising, although I'm sure you didn't mean it to.'

'Sorry.'

She didn't think he was, but at least she hoped he

wouldn't make any more cracks like that. 'Readers of froth
are not invariably dumb. People who like to read—real
readers—usually enjoy variety in their books, and froth has
its place,' she said acidly. Just to show that she wasn't
impressed by his outmoded attitude, she added, 'Stereotyping is the refuge of the unreasonable.'

A swift flare of emotion in the clear green eyes startled
her. 'You're the first person to ever accuse me of being
unreasonable,' he said, the latent hardness in his voice very
close to the surface.

'Power can isolate people.' Rather proud of the crisp
mockery that ran beneath her statement, she picked up a
book and pretended to read the blurb.

The written words made no sense, because Bryn was
deliberately surveying her face, the enigmatic gaze scanning from her delicately pointed chin to the black lashes
hiding her eyes before returning to—and lingering on—her
mouth. Something untamed and fierce flamed through every
cell in Gerry's body, but she bore his scrutiny without
flinching. Yet that forbidden joy, that eager excitement,
burst through the confines of her common sense once more.

'So can outrageous beauty,' he said.

Gerry knew that men found her desirable, and other
women envied her the accident of heritage that gave her a
face fitting the standards of her age. She had turned enough
compliments, refused enough propositions, ignored enough
gallantries, to respond with some sophistication.

Now, however, imprisoned in the glittering intensity of
Bryn's gaze, her breath shortened and her heart picked up
speed, and—more treasonable than either of those—heat
poured through her, swift and sweet and passionate, setting
her alight.

He recognised it. Harshly he said, 'I'm no more immune
than any other man to the promise of a soft mouth and eyes
the blue-green of a Pacific pearl, skin like sleek satin and
a body that would set hormones surging through stone. If
you want a quick affair, Geraldine, over as soon as we leave

here, I'll be more than happy to oblige you, but don't go getting ideas that it's going to last, because it won't.'

Unable to hide her flinch, or the evidence of fading colour and flickering lashes, she kept her head high. 'No, that's not what I want, and you know it,' she said. 'I don't do one-night stands.'

CHAPTER SEVEN

BRYN'S eyes darkened and held hers for a fraught, charged moment before he said in a voice that betrayed no emotions, 'Good. It makes things much cleaner.'

He turned, and as though released from a perilous enchantment Gerry picked up a book and walked across to the stairs, hoping her erect back and straight shoulders minimised the visible effects of that excoriating exchange.

Anger swelled slow and sullen; Gerry, who hadn't lost her temper for years, had to exert her utmost will to rein it in. Because although Bryn had been unnecessarily brutal, he'd seen a danger and scotched it, and one day she'd be relieved by his cold pragmatism.

The last thing she wanted was to fall in love—or even in lust—with this man. Bryn Falconer wasn't the sort of lover a woman would get-over quickly; indeed, Gerry suspected that if she let down her guard he'd take up residence in her heart, and she'd never be able to cut herself free from the turbulent alchemy of his masculinity.

And that would be ironic indeed, because by her twenty-fourth birthday she'd given up hope of finding a lasting love, one that would echo down the years.

Retreating to the shade of the canvas shelter he'd rigged over the cockpit, she sat down—back stiff, shoulders held in severe restraint, knees straight, ankles crossed—and pretended to read. The words danced dizzily, and eventually she allowed her thoughts free rein.

How many times had she thought herself in love, only to endure the death of that lovely excitement, the golden glow, with bitter resignation? At twenty-three, after breaking her engagement to a man who was perfect for her, she'd realised she was tainted by her mother's curse. After that she'd kept men at a distance. Her mother's endless search, the pain she'd caused her husbands and her children, had been a grim example, one Gerry had no intention of following.

In spite of the intensity of her infatuation for Bryn, it would die.

And she was happy with her life, apart from her dissatisfaction with her career. She loved her friends and cousins, loved their children, was loved and valued by them.

Movement from the main cabin, and the sharp click of a closing door, indicated that Bryn had gone into his stateroom; Gerry wondered why he'd slept on the sofa the previous night. Had he wanted to know when she woke so that he could tell her of their situation? A treacherous warmth invaded her heart.

He emerged almost immediately and came into the cockpit. Gerry pretended to be deep in the pages of her book, but beneath her lowered lashes her eyes followed him as he went up the stairs to the flybridge.

She could hear him moving about up there, and to block out the graphic images that invaded her mind she concentrated on reading. At first her eyes merely skipped across the pages, but eventually the written word worked its magic on her and she became lost in the book, an account of a worldwide scam that had ruined thousands of lives.

'Interesting?' Some time later Bryn's voice dragged her away from the machinations of the principal characters.

Frowning, she put the book down. 'Fascinating,' she said levelly. 'One wonders how on earth criminals can ignore the agonies of the people whose lives they're shattering.'

'One does indeed,' he said, his voice almost indifferent. 'One also gathers that you hate being interrupted when you're reading.'

Colour heated her skin. Irritated with herself for being rude enough to reveal her annoyance, and with him for being astute enough to pick it up, she said wryly, 'I do, but there's no excuse for snarling. I'm sorry.'

'I like your honesty,' he surprised her by saying, 'and you didn't snarl—you have beautiful manners which you use like a shield. When you're angry you hide behind them, and then you retreat.'

Shocked, she stared at him and felt heat flame across her cheekbones. 'Well, that's put me well and truly in my place,' she said uncertainly.

He gave her that narrow-eyed, sexy smile. 'I didn't intend to do that,' he said. 'Just a clumsy attempt to analyse what it is about you I find so intriguing. If you need anything in the next half hour or so, call out. I'm going to have a look at the engine to see if there's anything I can do.'

And he turned and went below.

Determinedly Gerry returned to her book; determinedly she followed the twists and turns of the scam, the links with drug lords, the whole filthy odyssey from genteel white-collar crime to dealing in sex and slavery and obsession. Yet as she read she was acutely aware of Bryn's movements, of the gentle swaying of the deck beneath her as he walked around below. When, some time later, he arrived in the doorway, every sense sprang into full alert.

'You'd better have something to drink,' he said. 'It's easy to dehydrate in this heat.'

Reluctantly she uncurled from the chair and followed him into the cabin. 'I'll make a pot of tea. How are we off for water?'

'There's enough if you don't spend hours in the shower.'

'No more than three minutes at a time, I promise.'

'Good.' His unsmiling look lifted the hairs on the back of her neck. 'Are you enjoying the book?'

'Not exactly *enjoying*. It's absolutely appalling, but riveting.'

He began to discuss it as though he assumed she had the intelligence to understand the complicated financial manoeuvring. So he didn't entirely think she was a flippant, flighty halfwit. And she shouldn't be comforted by this thought.

After they'd drunk the tea Bryn disappeared once more into the bowels of the boat, presumably to see whether he could find anything there that had failed. Freed from the driving necessity to appear calm, Gerry fretted about Maddie, hoping to heaven the girl was recovering, wishing that she'd seen what the problem was.

Maddie had come back from New York saying that she needed to take time to reconsider her life. Perhaps she had been trying to kick a drug habit; if only she'd said something about it, they could have helped.

It was utterly wicked that all that youth and intelligence and promise could be wiped out in the sick desire for a drug! Gerry didn't normally worry about things she couldn't change; over the years she'd learned to cultivate a practical, serene outlook. Now, however, she sat stewing until Bryn reappeared.

Her attempt to reimpose some sort of control over her features failed, for after one swift, hard glance he demanded abruptly, 'What's the matter?'

Trust him to notice. 'You mean apart from being stranded?' She relaxed her brows into their normal unconcerned arch.

'Don't worry, someone will find us soon.'

'But first they have to miss us.'

'I assume that will happen as soon as you don't arrive back in New Zealand.' He spoke patiently, as though they hadn't already had this conversation.

Gerry bit her lip. 'Of course it will. I'm sorry, I'm not helping the situation.'

Cara would begin to worry by evening. No doubt she'd ring the airline; they'd have noticed that Gerry hadn't arrived for the flight Bryn had booked for her, and as soon as they contacted the hotel on Longopai they'd realise what had happened. They'd have search parties out by tomorrow morning at the latest.

Which wouldn't be too late, if Jill, Maddie's booker, had managed to contact the ad agency…

Bryn said, 'Of course you're concerned, but you're in no danger.'

Taking refuge behind her sunglasses, Gerry gave him a collected smile. 'I know,' she said obligingly.

He'd noticed the hint of satire in her tone because his mouth tightened fractionally, but he didn't comment.

They ate lunch—a light meal of salad and fruit, and crusty bread he must have swiped from the hotel kitchen— and then Gerry tried to ease the tension that had gathered in a knot in her chest by retiring to her cabin to rest through the heat of the afternoon.

To her astonishment she slept, not waking until the sun had dipped down towards the horizon. After washing her face she combed her hair into order, pinning it back behind her ears to give her a more severe, untouchable look, then reapplied her make-up.

The main cabin was empty, but a glance up the stairs revealed Bryn standing beside the railings. Something about his stance made her skin prickle; he looked aggressive, all angles and bigness and strength.

She thought she moved as silently as he did, but his head whipped around before she'd come through the door. He surveyed her with eyes half-hidden by thick lashes.

'Good sleep?' he asked.

'Great.' She walked across to the side of the craft, stopping a few feet away from him to peer down through the crystal water. A battalion of tiny fish cast wavering shadows on the white sand beneath them. 'No signs of any rescuers?'

'No.'

Still staring at the pellucid depths, she said casually, 'So we sit and wait.'

'Basically, yes.' He sounded aloof, almost dismissive. 'I'm taking the dinghy onto the island. Want to come?'

'I'd love to. I'll just go and get my hat.'

After anchoring it to her head with a scarf around the brim she rejoined him, sunglasses hiding her eyes, her armour in place. Although he didn't look at her long, bare legs as she got into the dinghy, as she sat down on the seat she wondered uneasily whether she should have put on a pair of trousers.

Awareness was an odd thing; both of them kept it under iron control, but no doubt he could sense the response that crackled through her, just as she knew that he was acutely conscious of her, that those green eyes had noticed her feeble attempts at protection.

He moved a vicious machete well away from her feet, and began to row the inflatable across the warm blue waters of the lagoon.

'Don't tell me there's anything dangerous on the island,' she commented brightly, trying to ignore the steady, rhythmic bunching of muscles, the smooth, sure strokes, the purposeful male power that sent the small craft surging through the water.

'Not a thing. This is a foraging expedition. Note the bag to put coconuts into.'

'I thought you had an outboard motor for this dinghy?' she asked, more to keep her thoughts away from his virile energy than because she wanted to know.

'I'd rather not use it. It's unlikely, but we might need it.'

If they weren't rescued. Chilled, she nodded.

The inflatable scraped along the sand as they reached the beach. Hiding her sharp spurt of alarm with a frown, Gerry waited until the craft had come to a halt, then stepped out into water the texture of warm silk and helped Bryn haul the dinghy out of the reach of the waves. He didn't need her strength, but it gave her a highly suspect pleasure to do this with him.

Looking around, she asked, 'Do we really need coconuts?'

'Not now.' His voice was cool and judicial. 'But we

might if we don't get rescued straight away. I believe in minimising risks, so we'll drink as much coconut milk as we can bear and save the water.'

Gerry believed in minimising risks too, but at the moment all she could think of was the possibility of him falling. 'Do you know how to get up there?'

'Yes.' He gave her a brief, blinding smile. 'Don't worry, I spent a lot of time climbing coconut palms when I was a kid.'

'I didn't spend any time splinting broken limbs—as a kid or when I grew up—so you be careful,' she told him briskly.

He laughed. 'It's amazing what you can do if you have to. I could probably splint my own if it comes to that, but it won't. Don't watch.'

She should go for a walk around the island—she knew that he wouldn't do anything unless he was convinced he could. But she said, 'And miss something? Never!'

'You'd better get into the shade then.'

Retreating into the welcome coolness of the sparse undergrowth, she watched as he looped a rope around a palm bole. He certainly seemed to know what he was doing. With an economy of movement that didn't surprise her, he used the loop of rope to support him while he made his way rapidly to the tufted crown of the palm.

He was back on the ground in a very short time, nuts in a bag he'd tied around his shoulders, not even breathing heavily.

Gerry strolled across and eyed them as he dumped them in the shade. 'Now all we have to do is catch some fish and we'll really be living naturally.'

His brow lifted. 'We?'

She grinned. 'Normally I'd be squeamish,' she admitted, 'but when it comes to a matter of life and death I'm prepared to do my bit. And it's all right to kill something if you actually use it.'

'Well, that makes living on a desert island much easier,'

he said, not trying to hide the slightly caustic note in his voice. 'But we won't catch much at this time of the day. Wait until the evening. Do you want to walk around the island?'

'Yes, I'd like that.'

He smiled at her, his eyes translucent in their dark frame of lashes. 'Let's go,' he said.

The island was tiny, a dot of sand in a maze of reefs and other islets, all with their crown of palms, all too small and lacking in food and water to have permanent settlers. 'But the people from Longopai come down in the season to fish and collect coconuts,' Bryn told her. 'I've been here often. That's how I knew how to get in last night.'

Gerry looked respectfully at the reef. 'We were lucky,' she said. 'Are coconuts native to the Pacific?'

'No one knows, although most authorities believe they came from Asia. The palm's certainly colonised the tropics; in fact, if it hadn't, these islands of the Pacific could never have been settled. The Polynesians and Micronesians would have died of starvation before they reached any of the high islands where they could grow other foods. Coconuts and fish; that's what the Pacific was founded on. And that's what many live on still.'

'But it's no longer enough,' she said, thinking of the islanders who needed the money from the hats they exported to provide for their children's education.

'It never was—why do you think the Polynesians became the world's greatest explorers? But the islanders certainly want more than any atoll can provide now.'

Gerry looked around at the huge immensity of sea and sky. 'And that's unfortunate?'

He shrugged. 'No, it's merely a fact of life. The world is going to change whether I agree with it or not. Anyway, I'm glad I live now. We have great challenges, but great advantages as well.'

They walked across the thick, blinding sand, talking of the scattered island nations of the Pacific and their problems: the threat of a rising sea level, desperate attempts to balance the disruptive effects of tourism, the almost empty exchequers of many of the little countries.

It took less than twenty minutes to circle the islet. As Bryn hefted the coconuts onto his shoulder, Gerry eyed the cruiser, so big and graceful in the lagoon, and smiled ironically at its impotence.

'"How are the mighty fallen",' she quoted. 'If *Star-chaser* had been a yacht we could have sailed it to Fala'isi. As it is, until it's fixed it's just a splendid piece of junk.'

'It provides us with shelter, and gas for cooking,' he said.

'True, but I'm sure you'd have been able to make some sort of shelter here on the atoll. And build a fire for cooking.'

One brow shot up. 'Yearning for the romance of a desert island?' he asked derisively. 'You wouldn't like it, Geraldine. There's no water, and you'd hate getting dirty and sweaty and hot.'

'I could do what the islanders do, and swim,' she pointed out crisply. 'You're not a romantic.'

'Not in the least.'

When he stooped to pull the little craft into the water she grabbed a loop of rope and yanked too.

'I can do it,' he said.

Strangely hurt, she stood aside until the dinghy bobbed on the surface.

'In you get,' Bryn told her. He waited until she was seated before heaving the inflatable further out into the water. Without fuss he got in himself, picked up the oars and sent the dinghy shooting through the calm, warm lagoon. 'I've lived on atolls like this and it's a lot of hard work. At least on the boat I can pump water up from the tanks manually, and we don't have to find timber for a fire every day.'

Gerry nodded. She should, she thought, looking back at the palms bending towards their reflections, be still worried sick, struggling to get back to New Zealand. But although one part of her remained anxious and alarmed, the other, seditious and unsuspecting, was more than content to be stranded in the sultry, lazy ambience of the tropics, safe with Bryn.

And that should be setting off sirens all through her, because Bryn Falconer was far from safe. Oh, he'd look after her all right, but his very competence was a threat.

In spite of that secret yearning for a soul-mate, common sense warned that loving a man as naturally dominant as Bryn would not be a peaceful experience, however seductive the lure. Her glance flashed back to Bryn's harsh-featured face and lingered for several heart-shaking moments on the subtle moulding of his mouth before returning to the shimmering, glinting, scalloped waves.

The lure, she admitted reluctantly, was *very* seductive. A forbidden hunger rose in her; she had to spurn the impulse to lean across and wipe the trickle of sweat from his temple, let her fingers tarry against the fine-grained golden skin and smooth through the tawny hair...

In other words, and let's be frank here, she told herself grimly as she swallowed to ease her parched mouth and throat, you want him.

So powerfully she could taste the need and the desire with every breath she took. This was something she couldn't control, a primeval gut-response, lust on a cellular level.

She'd fallen in love before, only to have time prove how false her emotions had been. It would happen again.

And yet—and yet there *was* a difference between the way she'd felt with other men, and the way Bryn affected her. This couldn't be curbed by will or determination; it had its own momentum, and, although she could leash any expression of it, she couldn't stifle the essential wildness of passion.

It would have been easier to deal with if he'd been Cara's lover. Oh, she'd still want him like this—no holds barred, a violent, simple matter of like calling to like—but she'd have an excellent reason for not acting on that hunger.

A gentle bump dragged her mind back from its racing thoughts to the fact that they'd reached the cruiser again. The long, corded muscles in Bryn's arms flexed as he held the dinghy in place while Gerry got shakily to her feet and climbed the steps into the cockpit.

'Catch,' he said, throwing her the rope before coming up after her, lean and big enough to block the sun.

'Give me the painter,' he commanded.

Handing the rope over, she drawled, 'Painter? Why not call it a rope, for heaven's sake?'

'Because that's not its name.'

She watched carefully as he wound the rope around the cleat. 'It doesn't look very safe,' she said, her voice sharp-edged because she hated the way he made her feel—like a snail suddenly dragged from its shell, naked and exposed. 'Shouldn't you do an interesting knot—a sheepshank, or a Turk's Head, or something Boy Scouts do?'

'Trust me,' he said on a hard note, 'it'll keep the dinghy tied on.'

'I trust you.' She turned towards the steps down to the cabin and asked over her shoulder, 'Do you want anything to drink? Tea? Coffee?'

'Something cold,' he said. 'Check out the fridge.'

His retreat into detachment was a good thing—on the boat there was little hope of avoiding each other.

Yet it stung.

Telling herself not to be a fool, Gerry extracted glasses from their cupboard—as cleverly constructed as everything else on the boat, so that even in the worst seas nothing would break—and poured lime juice over ice before carrying them up to the cockpit. Bryn was staring at the horizon, watchful green eyes unreadable beneath the dark brows.

'Here,' she said, offering the glass.

He turned abruptly and took it, careful not to let his fingers touch hers, and drank it down. 'Thanks,' he said, hand-ing over the glass without looking at her.

Rebuffed, Gerry went back to the kitchen and drank her juice there.

Let someone find them soon, she prayed, before she did something stupid like letting Bryn see just how much she wanted him.

CHAPTER EIGHT

To HER relief they spent the rest of the day at a polite distance. While Bryn poked about the internal regions of the boat, Gerry wondered about washing her clothes, finally deciding against it. She didn't know how much water the tanks held, and she had enough clean underwear for three days. They certainly wouldn't take long to dry in the minuscule bathroom.

The afternoon sun poured relentlessly in through the cabin windows. Although she opened them, in the hope of fresh air, eventually the heat drove her into the cockpit where, still hot under the awning, she read, keeping her attention pinned very firmly to the printed page.

Towards sunset Bryn got out fishing lines from lockers in the cockpit.

Looking up, Gerry asked, 'Can I help?'

'No, I'll take the dinghy out into the centre of the lagoon.'

He didn't ask her to go with him, and she didn't offer. In the rapidly fading light Gerry kept her eyes on the western sky, watching the sun silkscreen it into a glory of gold and red and orange, until with a suddenness that startled her the great smoky ball hurtled beneath the horizon. As the last sliver disappeared a ray of green light—the colour of Bryn's eyes—stabbed the air, a vivid, astonishing flash that lasted only a second before dusk swept across the huge immensity of sky, obliterating all colour, cloaking everything in heated velvet darkness.

Gerry stared into the dense nothingness until her eyes adjusted to the lack of light. A few hundred metres away she could see the outline of the dinghy with Bryn in it—

patient, predatory, still—and was amazed by her sudden atavistic fear at the contrast between that stillness and his usual vital energy. A moment later she detected a swift movement, and shortly afterwards the dinghy headed back towards the cruiser.

Determined not to spend the rest of the evening in the same silence as the afternoon, Gerry met him with a smile. 'And what, oh mighty hunter, did you catch?'

He laughed shortly. 'A careless fish.'

She'd expected a whole fish, but he'd already filleted and scaled it. 'Will it be all right fried?' she asked.

'Unless you have more exotic ways of dealing with it.'

'I'm your basic cook—and that's probably overstating the case—so I'll stick to the tried and true,' she said, adding with a hint of mischief, 'Of course, you could cook it.'

His eyes gleamed in the starlight. 'I think the traditional division of duties is that I catch and kill, you cook.'

'You Tarzan, me Jane,' she said, laughing. 'That went out with the fifties.'

'Not entirely.'

'In any civilised country,' she retorted, heading down the companionway and thence into the kitchen. Perhaps she should try to think of it as the galley. You're getting used to this lazy life out of life, she warned herself severely. Be careful, Gerry.

'We're not in a civilised country here,' he said, following her.

'So it's lucky that I'm quite happy to cook,' she parried, aware of something else running through the conversation, a hidden current of provocation, of advance and retreat, of unspoken challenge.

Too dangerous.

She made the mistake of looking up at him. He was smiling, a mirthless, fierce smile that didn't soften his face at all.

Gerry's heart gave a wild thump; without volition she took a step backwards, and although she held her head high and kept her gaze steady she knew he'd seen and noted that moment of weakness.

'*Can* you cook it?' he asked, lounging against the bar that separated the galley from the main cabin.

She took the fish and slid it onto a plate and into the fridge. 'I'll manage,' she said evenly.

'Then I'll leave you to get on with it.'

Gerry's breath came soundlessly through her lips as he straightened up and walked towards his cabin. 'Damned arrogant man,' she muttered as she pulled out a tin of coconut cream. She didn't like arrogance; both the men she'd thought she'd loved had been kind and pleasant and intelligent and tolerant.

Nothing like Bryn Falconer.

Banishing him from her mind, she wondered whether perhaps she should use the coconut he'd got that day. Except that she didn't know how you turned the milk in it into the cream you bought in tins—suitable for delicious oriental-style sauces that were especially suitable for fish.

'Give me modern conveniences every time,' she muttered as she found the tin opener in its special slot in a drawer.

Bryn emerged as she was lowering the floured fish fillets into the big frying pan. Through the delicate sizzle she heard him close the door; she didn't look over her shoulder, but as he went past she thought she smelt his clean, just-washed fragrance.

'Would you like some wine?' he asked.

Then she did look up, and once more her heart lurched. He'd changed into a short-sleeved shirt and fine cotton trousers. Lean-hipped, long-legged, he moved with a smooth grace that pulled at her senses.

'Yes, thank you,' she said simply. Keep it light, her common sense warned her. Pretend that this is just another man, just another occasion.

He reached into what she'd assumed to be another cupboard. It was a bar fridge, from which he pulled out a bottle of wine. Once more everything was stored so carefully that it was safe whatever the height of the waves.

'All mod cons on this boat,' she teased as he removed the cork in one deft movement and poured the subtly coloured, gold-green vintage into two elegant glasses. 'It's more luxurious than my house.'

He picked up a glass, set it down close to her. 'Even you,' he said calmly, 'must know that boats are referred to as women, so she's she, not it.'

'All these funny traditions! Why?'

'Perhaps because they're inherently beautiful,' he said, his voice a blend of whisky and cream, of honey and dark, potent magic. 'And dangerous. And therefore profoundly attractive to men.'

Gerry turned the fillets of fish with great care before she could trust herself to answer. Picking up the glass of wine, she lifted it to her lips and took a small, desperate sip. Then she set it down and allowed herself a smile, although it felt cold and stiff on her lips. 'An interesting theory,' she said lightly, dismissively, 'but I think it's just part of the desire to confuse the uninitiated—which is why the kitchen is a galley and a rope is a painter. It's jargon, and it connects people with the same interests so that they can feel part of a common brotherhood, shutting others out.'

'Feeling lost and alone, Geraldine?'

Ashamed at the snap in her words, she shrugged. 'I suppose I am.'

'Don't you trust me to look after you?' A steely thread of mockery ran beneath the words.

She bit her lip. 'Of course I do,' she said, keeping her voice steady.

'Then it must be the situation back in Auckland.'

Shocked by the strength of her temptation to tell him all about it, she poked gingerly at the fish fillets. Bryn was a hard man, and sometimes she could kick him, but he would know how to deal with almost anything that came his way. However, the problem wasn't hers to tell. Maddie had a future—Gerry refused to believe otherwise—and the fewer people who knew about her addiction the better.

Even though Cara would probably tell Bryn once they got back to Auckland.

No, not if she was asked not to. Cara was young, and she could be foolish, but she was trustworthy.

'Partly,' Gerry said coolly, 'but there's nothing I can do about that so I'm trying not to worry. Besides, Honor McKenzie, my partner, is probably back by now and dealing with it.'

'A very pragmatic attitude.'

'My father was big on being sensible.'

'If I had a daughter who looked like you I'd do my best to bring her up to be sensible,' Bryn agreed lazily.

Yet James Dacre had worked himself into the grave saving a business that had been run into the ground by a greedy manager, who'd then decamped into the unknown with everything James had spent his lifetime building. He hadn't been sensible, but he'd been honourable.

Tight-lipped, Gerry said, 'He was a man who believed in responsibility.'

'I know.'

Gerry pulled the frying pan from the gas ring and lifted each perfect, golden piece onto a plate, warm from the oven. Picking up the plates and heading towards the table, which she'd set while Bryn was showering, she said, 'He paid back every last dollar the firm owed before he died.'

He carried a bowl of pasta salad across to the table. 'Leaving you with nothing.'

If he'd sounded curious, or even sympathetic, she'd have been short with him, but his voice revealed nothing more than a cool impersonality. 'That wasn't important,' she said crisply as she set the plates down. 'I can make my own way. But it'll be a cold day in hell before I forgive the man who sent my father to an early grave. I just wish I knew where he is now.'

Bryn's enigmatic glance lingered on her angry face. 'Do you have a taste for vengeance?'

She sat down. After a moment she said flatly, 'No. I'd like to, because nothing would give me greater pleasure than to see the man who killed my father in exactly the same situation—sick, tired, so exhausted that in the end nothing mattered any more. Dad used to say that eventually you reap what you sow. He didn't, but it gives me some comfort to believe that of the man who drove him to his death.'

'Eat up,' Bryn said, his voice unexpectedly gentle.

Obeying, Gerry was eventually able to taste the food she'd prepared. She finished her glass of wine a little more quickly than was wise, so refused another, and was oddly pleased when Bryn only drank one too.

Over the meal they spoke of impersonal things; Bryn's attitude reminded her of the day they'd met. He'd been gentle then too, holding the baby with strength and security and comfort. He'd be a good father.

What would he be like as a husband?

'That's an odd smile,' he said idly.

'I was hoping that the baby is all right.'

'Unfortunately that's all you can do—hope.' He'd helped her clean up and wash the dishes, then banished her while he made coffee. Now he came from behind the bar and handed her a cup and saucer. 'What made you think of her?'

'I don't know.' She put the coffee down on the table in front of her and frowned. 'Bryn, why on earth should everything die on the boat? Surely the communications and the engine don't work off the same systems?'

'No.'

He sat down beside her, alarming her. She could cope when he was opposite her—she was fine with the table between them, or a metre or so of space. But the sofa seemed very small suddenly, and his closeness stifled every ounce of common sense. Swallowing unobtrusively, she sat up straighter, trying to keep her eyes on the steam that swirled up from her coffee.

'Occasionally kids from Longopai get into the *Starchaser*,' he said. 'I can't say it was definitely them, but someone removed most of the diesel; that same someone left the communications system on so that the batteries are completely drained.'

'I'm surprised you're not furious,' she said, ironing out the husky note in her tone into a somewhat clipped curtness.

His crystalline gaze flicked across her face and his smile sizzled right through her. It was, she thought, as elemental as a force of nature. Did he know its effect on susceptible women?

Almost certainly. He was too intelligent not to.

'I can remember what I was like at ten,' he said, wry laughter in his words. 'All devilry and flash, keen to see how things worked; I'd have examined *Starchaser* from bow to stern, from propeller to aerial, and I'd probably have drained the battery as well.'

'And stolen the diesel?' she asked.

He shrugged. 'You know as well as I do that to Polynesians what belongs to a brother belongs to you, and on Longopai I'm everyone's brother. Someone needed it. They'll replace it. If we hadn't had to get away so quickly I'd have been told there wasn't enough fuel to get me to Fala'isi.' Unsmiling, he added, 'In fact, they're probably out looking for us now.'

God, Gerry thought, drinking her coffee too fast, I hope they find us first thing tomorrow.

He asked suddenly, 'What have you done to your finger?'

'Cut it while I was chopping the onions. It's nothing.'

He held out an imperative hand. 'Let me see.'

While she hesitated he took her hand and turned it over, examining the small cut with frowning eyes. 'It looks deep.'

'It's fine,' she said quickly, tugging away.

To no avail. Bryn ran the tip of a finger across the cut and then, without pausing, down and across her palm. The touch that had been comforting changed in a few short centimetres to wildly sensuous.

He must have heard the sharp, indrawn breath she couldn't control, but he lifted her hand to his mouth and kissed the small cut, and the palm of her hand before saying harshly, 'I'll get some antiseptic. Cuts can become badly infected in the tropics.'

Numbly, fingers curling, she watched him head towards a drawer. The place he'd kissed burned, echoing the fire that swept through her blood.

He took a tube from the drawer and tossed it to her with the curt command, 'Rub it well in, and put it on several times a day.'

Eagerly Gerry bent her head and unscrewed the cap, and smoothed the pale ointment onto her finger.

It stung a little, but she ignored the pain to babble into the tense silence, 'It's nice that you're still so close to the islanders you grew up with. I have a vast number of cousins, but I always wanted real brothers and sisters.'

'Don't you have two brothers?'

'Half-brothers,' she said. 'From different fathers—one in America, one in France. I've met them occasionally, and we have nothing in common. My father did his best to turn me into a lady, but I'd have liked brothers to be mischievous with.'

'You have enough of an advantage now,' he said harshly.

Startled, she looked up, into eyes as unfathomable as the wide ocean. Her breath came quickly. 'I don't know what you mean,' she said stupidly.

'I think you do,' he said, irony underscoring each word. 'You know how you affect men. The first time I saw you I thought you were a dark-eyed witch—half-devil, half-angel, all woman—with a smile that promised the delights of paradise. And then I realised that your eyes are a fascinating, smoky mixture of blue's innocence and green's provocation, and I was lost...'

Spellbound by the gathering passion that roughened his voice, she let him pull her up and into his arms. She had known he was strong—now she felt that strength, the virile force and power, and her immediate, ardent response sang through her like a love song as Bryn's mouth found her lashes and kissed them down, traced the high sweep of each cheekbone, the square chin. Bryn's scent—fresh, fiercely male—filled her nostrils, and his mouth on her skin was heaven, gentle and powerful and agonising. Dazed, she heard her own wordless murmur as she lifted her face in supplication.

Yet he didn't take the gift so freely offered. Instead his lips found the pulse-point beneath her ears, the soft, vulnerable throbbing in her throat, and each time he touched her fire licked through her veins.

It stunned her with its heat, with its intensity. The only point of contact was his mouth, a slow, potent pledge of rapture against her waiting, welcoming skin. It was insulting, this deliberate display of control when Gerry was rapidly losing the ragged threads of hers. Harried by desperation, she wanted to feel his hands on her—had been wanting that ever since she'd met him, even though she'd believed he was Cara's lover.

For a moment she held back, remembering that she should be worrying about Maddie, and then he kissed the corner of her mouth, tormenting her with a promise of passion, a compulsion of desire such as she'd never experienced before.

She didn't hear his laugh; she felt it, a quick brush of air against her skin, a recognition that he knew what he was doing to her. Splintered by a sudden, dangerous fury, she forced her heavy lids upwards and clenched her hands on his arms.

'Wait,' she commanded.

'Why?' he asked, narrowed eyes green diamonds set in thick black lashes. A smile curled the ruthless mouth.

Swift shock ran the length of Gerry's spine, but she tried again. 'Stop teasing me,' she said, hearing the helpless, hopeless note of need in her voice.

'How am I teasing you?'

Still angry, she reached up and kissed him boldly on his taunting, beautiful mouth.

She wanted to pull back immediately, to show him that she wasn't completely mesmerised, but it was too late. When her lips met his he laughed again and crushed her to him, strong hands moulding her against his body, his mouth ravishing every thought from her brain.

It was like being taken over, she thought just before she succumbed to the hunger that had been building in her ever since she'd looked over a baby's downy head and met his eyes.

He no longer kept up the farce of gentleness, of tenderness. He kissed her with the driving determination of a man who had finally slipped the leash of his will-power and allowed his desire free rein. Gerry's curbed hunger exploded, overwhelming every warning, every ounce of common sense her father had tried to drum into her.

With molten urgency she returned Bryn's kiss. Her pulses galloped as he lifted her and sat down on the sofa with her in his arms, and without taking his mouth from hers pulled her across his knees and slid his hand beneath the wrap-around front of her blouse, fingers cupping her breast.

Sensation rocketed through her. Her mouth opened and he took swift advantage, thrusting deep in a blatant simulation of the embrace both of them knew was coming. Gerry twisted under the remorseless lash of desire; every sense was overloaded. Bryn's experienced caress was transformed into an unbearably stimulating friction that smashed through the remaining fragile barriers of her will.

His taste was pure male, exotic, stimulating, his arms a

welcome, longed-for prison, the surface texture of his chest exquisitely erotic to the tips of her fingers as she unsteadily pulled the buttons of his shirt free and ran her hand across the heated skin below.

Gerry felt his shudder like a benediction.

'Yes, you like that,' he said, lifting his head so that the words touched her lips, to be drunk in without too much attention to meaning. 'You like the power your beauty gives you, the way men respond to the primitive allure beneath that sophisticated, glossy outer appearance. I'm just like all the rest, Geraldine—I want you. But what do you want? Because if this keeps on for much longer I'm not going to be able to stop.'

She lifted weighted eyelids, met the blazing green of his eyes with a slow smile. 'You,' she said, and because her voice shook, she tried again. 'I want you.'

Something perilously close to satisfaction flared in his eyes. 'Good.'

Her lashes drifted down, but instead of kissing her eager mouth he shocked her by pushing back the lapel of her shirt and kissing the soft skin his hand so possessively caressed.

Fire seared away everything but the hunger that shattered her last vestige of composure. Her legs straightened, and she stiffened, blind to everything but the savage need to take and be taken.

When his mouth closed around the tip of her breast a hoarse, low sound was torn from her throat, to be lost in the conflagration of her senses. He began to suckle and she gasped again, splaying her hands over his chest, blindly seeking satisfaction. The delicate friction of his body hair against her hot skin shivered from her fingers to the pit of her stomach.

On impulse she turned her head and sought the small male nipple and copied his actions, an intimacy she'd never offered before, never known. Under her cheek his chest wall lifted, and she heard the beat of his heart, heavy, demanding.

'Geraldine,' he muttered, his voice reverberating through her.

And when he got to his feet and carried her into her cabin she made no protest.

Stranded in the dazzling, shape-shifting haze he'd conjured around her, she lay back against the pillows and watched with unsated eyes while he tore off his shirt and the trousers she'd admired earlier. No hesitation spoiled the moment, no fear—nothing but a glowing anticipation that wrapped her in silken fur, clawed at her with primal, eager hunger.

With the light from the main cabin reflecting lovingly on Bryn's golden skin, he came down beside her and said with an odd thickness in his voice, 'I seem to have thought of nothing but this since I first saw you—lovely, elusive Geraldine, lying in my bed, waiting for me...'

Deft hands slipped her shirt from her, smoothed her shorts down. She shivered at the skill with which he undressed her, shivered again—and for a different reason—when the long fingers stroked down her legs, lingering across the smooth skin on the inside of her thighs before moving to her calves.

'Fine-boned and elegant,' he said, and found her ankles and her feet.

She had to clear her throat to say, 'I've never thought of my calves and feet as erotic zones.'

'Haven't you?' He sounded amused, and bent and kissed the high arch. As her foot curled in involuntary reaction he said in a deeper voice, 'Every part of a responsive woman is an erotic zone. If you don't know that it's high time you learned.'

She learned. Where Bryn wanted to go was where she wanted to be, and he wreaked such dark havoc with his mouth and his enormously skilled, knowledgeable hands that in a few minutes he'd proved his statement and she was begging for mercy, her body craving the consummation only he could give her.

'Not yet,' he said huskily. 'Not yet, little witch.'

In self-defence she tried to turn the tables by caressing him, but perhaps she lacked the experience, for when she had completely unravelled he was still master of himself—and of her body's responses.

By then, wild-eyed and panting, she didn't care.

'Now,' she gasped, almost sobbing as she finally pulled at his broad shoulders.

Later she would remember that they were slick with sweat, and that his eyes were hooded slivers of glittering emerald, so focused that she thought they burned wherever they rested. But at that moment she was completely at the mercy of her body's need for completion, torn by this unfamiliar passion.

In answer he came over her and entered her violent, supplicating body in one strong thrust.

Gerry gasped. He froze, the big, lithe body held in stasis. 'You should have warned me that it's been a long time for you,' he said, his voice raw with barely maintained control.

He was going to leave her. He thought he'd hurt her so he was going to abandon her to this savage, unfulfilled need.

'It's all right—it doesn't matter,' she said, her voice thready in the quiet cabin.

He said something so crude she flinched. 'It matters,' he growled. Beneath her importuning hands she felt the swift coil and bunching of muscles as he prepared to get up.

She looked up into a face stripped of everything but anger. Driven by a merciless compulsion, she fastened her arms across his broad back and offered herself to him, arching beneath him, flexing muscles she hadn't known she had, moving slowly, sensuously against him.

'No!' he commanded.

Gerry thought she'd lost, but within seconds she saw her triumph in his eyes as the anger prowling in the metallic opacity was joined by a consuming hunger, basic, white-hot.

Her heart jerked within her chest. Bryn withdrew, but only to bury himself again to the hilt in her, and as she enclosed him in her heated flesh, tightening her arms around his back to pull him down against her, he said, 'This is what you want, isn't it?'

She couldn't answer, and he demanded, 'Gerry?'

'Yes, damn you!' she shouted, twisting her hips against him.

He curled his fingers in her hair, holding her face back so that he could see it. This was not satisfaction—that was far too weak a term to use. On his face was exultation, pure and simple, and she couldn't deny him it because it was her victory too.

With deliberation, with authority and steady male power, he began to move in her. Holding his gaze, she locked her feet around his calves and returned movement for movement, passion for passion, until the knot of pleasure inside her began to unravel, sending her soaring, hurtling over some distant edge and into a world where nothing existed but she and Bryn, and the boat moving slightly, peacefully beneath them in the embrace of the Pacific.

A starburst of rapture tore a cry from her and she imploded into ecstasy, stiffening into rigidity, and then, when the exquisite savagery began to fade, responding anew to Bryn's desire.

And soon, even as the fresh nova ripped through her, she saw his head go back and a fierce, mirthless grin pull his lips into a line as he too found that place where nothing else mattered.

Like that, they lay until their breaths slowed and their hearts eased and sleep claimed them.

Much later, after she'd slept in his arms and they'd woken and made love again—love that had started slow and lazy, without the edge of unsated desire, and then exploded into incandescent passion, desperate and all-consuming—Gerry yawned, a satisfying gape that almost cracked her face in two, and eased herself free.

'Where are you going?' he asked, his voice husky.

'Bathroom,' she muttered.

'Head,' he said lazily. 'On a boat it's called the head.'

He was laughing at her, and she laughed too, and kissed the curved line of his mouth and said, 'Whatever, I need to shower. I'm sticky.' A thought struck her. 'Have we enough water and power for frivolous showers?'

'Plenty, if we shower together.'

'It's too small,' she protested.

'We'll fit.'

They did—just. Bryn laughed at her shocked face.

'It's not decent,' she said demurely, 'and it's too hot.'

'The water will cool us down.'

Green eyes gleamed as he soaped her, became heavy-lidded and purposeful when she insisted on doing the same for him.

'You're as sleek as a panther,' she said from behind him, sliding wet hands across his back.

'Panthers have fur.'

Gerry linked her hands across his chest and pressed her cheek against his shoulderblade. 'Mmm,' she said slowly, 'I'd like that.'

Beneath her palms she felt his chest lift as he laughed.

The water sputtered and she let him go so that he could turn around and rinse the soap off. A lean hand turned the shower off, then he looped an arm around her and kissed her, hard and fast, before picking her up. As he edged by the rack he grabbed a towel and tossed it onto the bed, and her in the middle of it, and came down and made love to her with a ferocity that blew her mind.

Gerry woke to a voice, a low murmur that teased the edge of her hearing. Almost as soon as her tired brain registered what was happening, the sound died into silence, and before she had a chance to get up Bryn came in through the door. Opening her eyes, she saw that it was dawn, a still, soft light that held the promise of delight.

But not as much as Bryn's slow, possessive survey.

'Who were you talking to?' she asked, smothering a yawn with the back of her hand.

His brows rose. 'Talking? No—oh, I did express my opinion of his thieving habits to a gull that tried to snatch the bait from my line.'

'Did you catch any fish?'

'I lost the urge,' he said gravely, sitting down on the bed.

Colour leaped again through her skin. He was wearing a terrible old pair of shorts, but he at least had some clothes on whereas she had nothing.

'You blush from your heart upwards,' he said, a dark finger tracing the uppermost curves of her breasts.

Drugged with satiation, she said languidly, 'I suppose everyone does.'

'I don't blush,' he said.

'Neither do I, normally.'

'And we established very effectively last night that this isn't normal behaviour for you,' he said without much expression.

'I wasn't a virgin,' she said, 'but I don't make a habit of—' her skin warmed again when he moved a curl back from her cheek and tucked it behind her ear '—of sleeping with men I barely know.'

'At first I thought you were—a virgin, I mean.'

'It had been a long time.'

'We didn't get much sleep,' he said absently. 'You must be tired.'

Raising her head, she bit his shoulder, quite hard, then licked the salty skin. She could hear the sudden harshness of his breathing.

'I'm hungry,' she said demurely.

He laughed deep in his throat and turned her towards him, his eyes fierce and primal. 'So am I,' he said, taking her with him as he slid down onto the tumbled sheets. 'Let's see what we can do about it, shall we?'

Later—an hour or so later—Gerry yawned prodigiously and muttered, 'You're insatiable.' Each word slurred off her tongue.

Bryn kissed her. 'Apparently,' he said lazily.

Something in his tone alerted her, but her eyes were heavy and she could feel waves of exhaustion creeping up from her toes, dragging her further and further into unconsciousness. Although she tried for clearer pronunciation, her words ran together again. 'What bothers me is that I seem to be too…'

He said something, but she couldn't fathom it out, didn't even want to. The rumble of his voice was the last sound she heard before sleep, voracious and draining, claimed her.

CHAPTER NINE

GERRY woke to find the sun high in the sky. Dry-mouthed, filmed with sweat, she stretched, aware of the change in Bryn's breathing as he too woke. Her body ached pleasantly, and when she moved she felt a slight tenderness between her legs.

And although she'd spent the night in his arms, now, more than ever, she craved the protection of her cosmetics.

She croaked, 'I need another shower and a large glass of water. I think I'm dehydrated.'

He laughed. 'I've got a better idea.'

Naked and entirely confident, he got to his feet and stooped over her, eyes glittering, dark face intent. Gerry's heart leapt in her breast, but he picked her up and carried her through the cabin and out into the cockpit. She smiled as she realised what he planned to do. No man had ever carried her around before, no man had ever made her so sure of herself, so positive in her sexuality.

He jumped with her still in his arms. Supple and languid from the night, Gerry welcomed the cool embrace of the sea, an embrace that soon turned warm. They sank down through the water; opening her eyes, Gerry squinted at the sun-dazzle above, and the harsh lines of Bryn's face, arrogant, tough, exultant.

As his legs propelled them towards the surface she wondered how such a man could be as tender as he was fiery, both gentle and ruthless, a dominant male who refused to take his own satisfaction until his lover had reached the peak of her ecstasy. Her previous lover had been considerate, but nothing she'd experienced came anywhere near the transcendent sensuality of Bryn's lovemaking.

Chilled, she realised that he'd set a benchmark; when this idyll was over she might never find another man who could love her as he had. Was this aching sense of loneliness and incompletion the goad that had spurred her mother on her futile search?

In an explosion of crystals they burst through the surface into the kiss of the sun, and she broke away from him, striking out for the island.

It was further than she thought. Although a good swimmer, she was tired when she got there. Not so Bryn, who kept pace easily with her. As they walked through the shallows and side by side across the white unsullied sand, Gerry thought they were like Adam and Eve, and wished futilely that they didn't have to return to their responsibilities.

He waited until they'd reached the shelter of the palms before asking, 'Do you want to eat breakfast here?'

It would be a perfect way to end this time out of time. Today someone would come looking for them and they would go their separate ways. Oh, in spite of his specific denial, they might resume their affair in Auckland, but it would never again be like this. The mundane world had a habit of tarnishing romance.

And that belief too she'd probably inherited from her mother.

Gerry pushed her hair back from her face. 'I'd love to.'

'OK, stay here in the shade. I'll swim back to the boat and load up the dinghy.'

'What if you get a cramp?' Stupid, she thought despairingly. Oh, that was stupid. Why fuss over a man so obviously able to look after himself?

'I know how to deal with it,' he told her calmly, his eyes transparent as the water, cool and limpid and unreadable. 'And if a shark comes by I'd be much happier knowing you weren't in the water with me.'

She cast a startled glance around. 'Are there sharks here?'

'It's not likely.' He set off towards the water.

Gerry watched while his strong tanned arms clove the water, only relaxing when he hauled himself up into the cruiser and waved.

Swimming had cleared some of the sensuous miasma from her brain, but she needed to think about the fact that during the night she had surrendered much more than her body to Bryn—she had handed over a part of her heart.

It terrified her.

Biting her lip, she stared down at the strappy leaves of a small plant, tough and dry on this waterless island, a far cry from the usually lush tropical growth. Idly she began to plait the leaves together.

Long ago she'd become reconciled to the fact that she was like her mother. Oh, she fell in love—no problem there. Only then, inevitably, she fell out of love. Sooner or later her dreaded boredom crept in, draining each relationship of joy and interest.

This time it might be different; Bryn was nothing like the other men she'd loved.

'No,' she muttered. She'd gone through this exercise before—tried to convince her sensible inner self that what she felt was real and true, an emotion enduring enough to transcend time and familiarity.

A stray breeze creaked through the fronds of the coconut palms above. Frowning, she rubbed her eyes. Last night Bryn had kissed her lashes down; her breath came quickly as she recalled things he'd said, the raw, rough sound of his voice, the sinfully skilled hands...

Impossible to believe that she'd ever grow tired of him!

But that was just sex, and Bryn was a magnificent lover. Gerry might not be experienced—her second love affair, six years ago, had been her only other physical relationship—but she recognised experience and, she thought grimly, a great natural talent. Bryn knew women.

Surely she'd never be able to look at him without responding to his heart-jolting impact!

And it wasn't just sex. He was sharp and tough and intelligent, he made her laugh, he refused to let her get away with using her charm instead of logic—oh, he fascinated her.

Would that last? Perhaps. She knew couples who still preferred each other's company after years of marriage.

Emotionally, however, he was uncharted territory.

Appropriate, she thought, her fingers stilling as she looked around the tiny islet. Bryn was a desert island—she understood nothing of his emotions, his feelings. And so, she thought painfully, was she. She had never known the particular power of transformation that accompanied such unselfconscious selflessness.

Even if he was the one man who could fix her wayward emotions—he'd shown no signs of loving her. Oh, he'd enjoyed taking her, and he'd met and matched her gasping, frenzied response with his own dynamic male power—but he didn't know her, so how could he love her? And in spite of the dark sexual enchantment that bedazzled them both, she suspected that he didn't like her much.

Even if he hadn't stated that it wouldn't last, they had no future.

It hurt even to think it, but Gerry fought back an icy pang of desolation to face facts squarely. And once she'd forced herself to accept them, her way was clear.

She'd enjoy this passionate interlude and then she'd end it before it had a chance to fizzle into damp embers. That way they'd both keep their dignity.

Some unregenerate part of her wondered just how Bryn would take a dignified dismissal. That bone-deep assurance indicated a man unused to rejection. Perhaps he'd pursue her, she thought with a flash of heat.

Why should he? cold logic demanded mockingly. He'd understand. What they shared was sex, and Bryn could get that from almost any woman he wanted. Why should he care if she turned him down? Beyond a momentary blow to his ego it wouldn't mean a thing.

She gazed at the pattern she'd made with the long leaves

of the plant. An ironic smile hurt her mouth. Somehow she'd managed to weave them together into a lopsided heart. Swiftly, deftly, she separated them, straightened out a couple she'd twisted, and turned back to the beach.

Bryn was almost there, the sun gilding his skin as he rowed the dinghy in. Until then Gerry hadn't bothered about her nakedness, but now she felt conspicuous and stupidly shy.

'Stay in the shade,' he called as the dinghy grounded on the glaring sand. 'I'll bring the stuff up.'

She waited in the shade, absently scratching a runnel of salt on her forearm. Naked, moving easily and lithely around the small craft, Bryn's sheer male energy blazed forth with compelling forcefulness. Incredibly, desire clutched her stomach, ran like electricity through her nerves, sparked synapses through her entire body. All that strength, she thought dizzily, all that power, and for a short time—for a few racing hours—it had been hers.

A hamper under one arm, something that turned out to be a rolled up rug under the other, he strode across the sand like a god worshipped by the sun, muscles moving with unstudied litheness beneath the mantle of golden skin.

Erotic need turned into a ripple, a current, a torrent of hunger. Gerry drew in a deep, ragged breath. Damn it, she'd never been at the mercy of her urges, and she wasn't going to start now!

She'd thought she'd succeeded in controlling her reaction, but Bryn took one look at her set face and asked, 'What's the matter?'

'Nothing.'

Although he wasn't satisfied, he didn't pursue it. Handing her the rug, he said, 'Spread this out, will you?'

She found a spot between bushes, shaded and secluded, yet with enough breeze for comfort. Bryn set the hamper down and helped her with the rug, then tossed her a length of cotton coloured in startling greens and blues and an intense muted colour halfway between them both.

'I thought you might want a pareu,' he said drily as he wound another length, in tans and ochres and blacks, around his lean hips.

With shaking fingers Gerry wrapped herself in the cotton, tucking two corners in just above her breasts to make a strapless sundress. Keeping her face turned away from him, she knelt on the rug to examine the contents of the hamper.

'My grandfather used to say,' Bryn told her as she took the lid off the hamper, 'that only a fool allowed himself to be manoeuvred into an untenable situation. If someone finds us while we're eating breakfast, I'd rather be clothed.'

'Me too,' she said fervently, looking up.

He smiled, and it was like being hit in the heart with a cannonball of devilish, sexually-charged charm. No man, she thought, setting out delicious slices of pawpaw and melon, should be able to do that. It gave him a totally unfair advantage.

'Here,' he said, offering her a tube of sunscreen. 'I didn't bring your make-up, but this will give you some protection.'

'Thank you,' she said stiltedly, wishing that he wasn't so astute. Of all her acquaintanceship only Bryn seemed to have realised that cosmetics were the shield she donned against a prying world.

Hastily she spread the lotion onto her face and arms and legs, on the soft swell of her breast above the cotton pareu, and as far down her back as she could reach.

When she'd finished, he said, 'Turn around, I'll do the rest.'

Even slick with sunscreen, the power and strength of his hands set her nerve-ends oscillating, sending tiny shocks through her body.

'You have such an elegant back,' he said evenly. 'But then, you're elegant all over, from the way you walk, the way you hold your head on that slim, poised neck, to the graceful, spare lines of your face and throat and body, the narrow wrists and fragile ankles—and that air of fine, steely strength and courage.' His hands swept up across her shoulders and fastened loosely around her throat, his fingertips resting against the turbulent pulse at its base. 'A true thoroughbred,' he said, the latent harshness in his voice almost reaching the surface.

She had to swallow, and his fingers would have felt her tense muscles. 'A fortunate genetic heritage,' she said. 'Like yours.'

He laughed and withdrew his hands. 'From a beach bum and a spoilt, frail little rich girl?' he asked sardonically.

Reaching for the tube, she said, 'Turn around and I'll put sunscreen on you.' She was playing with fire, but she didn't care. Some note in his voice had made her wince, and she needed to try and make things better for him.

For a moment she thought he'd refuse, but almost immediately he presented his back to her, the smooth golden skin taut and warm over the muscles beneath—the shape of a man, she thought fancifully, cupping her palm to receive the sunscreen. Her hands tingled as she spread the liquid.

'Even if your father wasn't the most responsible man in the world,' she said, 'he had the guts to actually do what many men only dream of. And so did your mother. Has it ever occurred to you that your father knew you'd be well looked after when he left Longopai? Or that he probably intended to come back?'

'An optimist as well,' he jeered. 'No, it hasn't.'

Aware that she'd trespassed onto forbidden ground, she massaged the lotion into his skin. 'Then at least you should take credit for overcoming your heredity.'

His shoulders lifted as he laughed, deep and low and humourless. 'Perhaps I should thank heaven that I had such a brilliant example of what not to do, how not to be. At least I accept responsibility for my actions. And for my mistakes. Have you finished there?'

'Yes.' She recapped the tube and gave it to him to pack, then poured them both coffee.

With little further conversation they ate breakfast, a feast of fruit, plus rolls he'd taken from the freezer and heated in the oven. Passionfruit jelly oozed across the moist white bread, tangy and sweet, and the coffee he'd carried in a Thermos scented the salt-laden air.

'A truly magnificent repast,' Gerry sighed, sucking a spot of jelly from the tip of one finger. Looking up, she caught Bryn's green gaze on her mouth, and grinned. 'And don't tell me your grandfather used to insist on table napkins at all times. So did my father, but I still lick the occasional finger.'

'You shouldn't be allowed to,' he said.

Eyes widening, she stared at him.

'It's all right,' he said roughly. 'I do have some self-control. We'd better get back on board.'

It was an excuse to move, and she leapt to her feet with alacrity. Although desire pulsed through her with swift, merciless power, making love again would stretch already over-strung muscles and tissues.

Working swiftly, they repacked the hamper and folded the rug. Swiftly they walked across the scorching sand, and swiftly made their way across the peacock water to the sleek white cruiser.

Once she was aboard, Bryn handed up the hamper. 'Leave it there, I'll carry it below,' he said. 'Here, take the painter and cleat it.'

Gerry took the rope—the painter, she corrected herself—and wound it around a horizontal bar of metal bolted to the deck as Bryn stepped aboard. The boat lurched a second under the transfer of weight, and she mis-stepped and tripped. Lightning-fast, he reached for her, but in her efforts to save herself from hitting the deck she slammed her arm across the instrument console. As she staggered, some of the levers moved.

To her astonishment an engine roared into life.

'What—?' Stunned, she stared at the lever she'd clutched, and then at Bryn as he got there in two swift strides and turned the engine off. Silence echoed around them, broken only by the drumming of her pulse in her ears.

'Why didn't you tell me you'd got the engine going?' she asked, racked by an enormous, unwanted sadness. It had come so quickly, the end of a fragile, beautiful dream.

Had he too not wanted this to end?

One glance at him put paid to that wistful hope. The bone structure of his face had never been so prominent, never seemed so ruthless.

'I didn't,' he said.

Chilled, she shook her head, every uneasy instinct springing into agitated life. 'Then why did it start just then and not when you tried it yesterday?' she asked, watching the play of reflection from the water move across the brutal framework of his face.

He surveyed her with hard eyes that gave nothing away, opaque and green and empty. In a level voice he said, 'Because you turned it on.'

'What?' She blinked, unable to believe that she'd heard correctly.

Bryn looked like something carved out of granite, the only warmth the red gleam summoned by the sun from his tawny hair. Calmly, without inflection, he said, 'I brought us here deliberately. We're staying until I decide to take you back to Fala'isi.'

She spluttered, 'What the hell do you mean?'

'Just that.'

'Are you saying you've *kidnapped* me?'

'No,' he said, eyes steady as they rested on her face. 'You came with me of your own free will so I think the technical term is probably imprisonment.'

By now a whole series of minor questions and queries had jelled. Anger bested fear as adrenalin accelerated her heart, iced her brain. 'You lured me away from New Zealand,' she said, never taking her eyes from his face. 'You made up some specious reason to get me to the hotel, and then you deliberately marooned us here. I gather the boat isn't disabled?'

'No.'

'And the communications system works too?'

'Yes.'

Her knees gave way. Collapsing into one of the chairs, she fought back rage and a bitter, seething disillusionment. When she could trust her voice again she asked, 'Why?'

'If you don't know, you're better off not knowing,' he said with deadly detachment. 'As for luring—no, you came to Longopai on a legitimate mission.'

'A photograph would have been enough to solve that,' she said with bared teeth. She'd been so stupid, allowing herself to be tempted by a week in the islands! Drawing in a ragged breath, she promised, 'But it won't solve your problems when I go to the police once I'm back in New Zealand.'

His smile sent a shudder through her. 'I don't think you will,' he said calmly. 'Who'd believe you? They'd assume that you came to Longopai of your own free will to join me. In fact, they'd know it—why do you think I asked you in front of Cara?'

Gerry said shakily, 'If you don't let me go—today—I'll see you in every court in New Zealand.'

'And if you do that,' he said ruthlessly, 'I'll tell them that you wanted to come, that you wanted to stay, and that your charge is a malicious fabrication because I refused to marry you. It will be my word against yours, because you'll have nobody to back you up.'

'If you think that you can—that you can get away with raping me—'

'Raping you?' His voice roughened, became thick and furious.

Shocked, she realised that she'd almost pushed him into losing control. Gerry wouldn't have believed it to be possible, but his face hardened even further.

However, he pulled back from the brink. 'That wasn't

rape,' he said with calculated indifference. 'I took ⌐ you weren't willing—eager—to give. I must admit ⌐ flattered to realise that you hadn't slept with anyone some time. I should have remembered that your friend ⌐ Auckland called you unassailable.'

Troy and her drunken ravings, Gerry thought explosively, so angry she could barely articulate the thought.

Gritting her teeth, she said, 'I'd have thought you were sophisticated enough to understand that you can't trust anyone in their cups.'

'Oh, you have a reputation extending well past old friends who ingest mind-altering substances,' he said. 'Didn't you know that, Geraldine? She only said what everyone else says behind your back. The unassailable Gerry! When you smile you make the sun come out, you dazzle with your warmth and your beauty and your laughter, you promise all delight but it's a promise you never keep.'

To the sound of her heart breaking, she asked, 'So what was last night, then?'

His contempt had sliced through the thin shield of her composure, but it was nothing to the wound his smile inflicted. In a deceptively indolent voice he said, 'Oh, you make love like Aphrodite, but it didn't really mean much, did it? You're not grieving now—you're furious.'

Thank God he couldn't read her heart; she'd get out of this with her pride reasonably intact. And because it was so appalling that she should be thinking of pride when every instinct was mourning, she remained silent, lashes lowered as she stared stubbornly at the deck. On her deathbed, she thought, she'd remember the pattern of the boards.

Casually, dismissively, Bryn went on, 'Don't worry, Geraldine, you're quite safe as long as you behave nicely and don't try to run away.' He paused, and then finished, 'I won't sleep with you again.'

'Why did you sleep with me last night?' She tried to speak as easily as he had.

were beginning to ask questions,' he said. 'It
_d a good idea to cause a diversion.'

_he frail edifice of the night's happiness shattered around
_er. She ground out, 'What the hell is going on?'

'If you're as innocent as you seem to be, nothing that
need concern you,' he said dismissively.

Her hands clenched. Not now, she thought, fighting back
the red tide of fury and pain to force her brain into action.
After a rapid, painful moment of thought, she said, 'Cara.'

'What about her?'

Think, she commanded. Damn it, you have to think, because he's not going to tell you anything. Perhaps if you
make him angry...

Steadying her voice, she said scornfully, 'She's in love
with you and you used her to get to me.'

His expression didn't change at all, and when he spoke
his voice was amused, almost negligent. 'Cara's dazzled,
but her heart won't be dented.'

'God, you're a cold-hearted sod!' The words exploded
from her, filled with the fear she refused to accept. 'Why
are you keeping me here? What is going on?'

'I can't answer that,' he said, and turned away.

Rage gripped her. 'You mean you won't answer.'

'It doesn't make any difference.'

Finally overwhelmed by anger and pain, she hurled herself forward and hit him, using the variation of street fighting she'd been taught in self-defence lessons years ago.

He was like steel, like rock, but she got in one kidney
punch that should have laid him low. He staggered, then
rounded on her. Although big men were usually slow, she'd
known Bryn was not. However she hadn't been prepared
for the lethal speed of his response.

Oddly enough, it gave her some satisfaction. She struck
out again, fingers clawing for his eyes, and he parried the
blow with his forearm, face blazing with an anger that
matched hers.

What followed was an exhausting few minutes of vicious

struggle. Eventually she realised that he wasn't trying
hurt her; he was content to block her every move. Sh
slipped several blows past his guard, but he kept them away
from every vulnerable part, until at last, sobbing with frustration, she gave up. Then he locked her wrists together in
a grip as tight as it was painful.

'Feel better?' he asked silkily.

As the adrenalin faded into its bitter aftermath, she
gained some consolation from the fact of his sweating.
Meeting his narrowed, glittering eyes defiantly, she gasped.
'I wish I could kill you.'

'You had a bloody good try. Where did you learn to fight
like that?'

'I took lessons years ago.' Her heart threatened to burst
through her skin, and the corners of her pareu had loosened,
so that she was almost exposed to him. Panting, she said,
'Let me go. I won't try it again.'

'You'd better not '

He meant it. Shivering, she pulled away, and this time
he let her go, watching her while he wiped his hands on
the cloth around his hips as though she had contaminated
him.

Yanking the ends of her pareu together, she breathed in
deeply until she was confident enough of her voice to say,
'For an importer you know how to handle yourself.'

'For a woman who works in high fashion you know
some remarkably lethal moves.'

In spite of the heat she felt deathly cold. Swallowing,
she said, 'I'd like to go to my room, thank you.'

He went with her—standing guard, she thought with a
flash of anger. At her door he said, 'Give me a call when
you want to come out and I'll unlock the door.'

In the flat tone of exhaustion she said, 'Let's hope the
boat doesn't sink.'

'You should have thought of that before you at-
tacked me.'

Without looking at him, Gerry went inside and listened the key turn in the lock.

Numbly she walked across to the windows and pushed the glass back. For a moment she wondered whether she should try to get out of a window, but the ones that opened were far too small to take her. Pulling the curtains would stop some of the fresh air, but she couldn't bear the possibility of Bryn checking on her through the window, so she dragged them across.

Then, refusing to think, refusing to feel, she lay down on the big bed and by some kind miracle of sympathetic fate went almost immediately to sleep.

The curtains shimmered gold when she woke, telling her it was late afternoon. She lay for long minutes on the bed, lethargic and aching, trying to work out why Bryn had kidnapped her and was intent on keeping her here.

It had to be something in New Zealand. What? Had Cara's telephone call given him an excuse, or had it been the trigger? Perhaps he'd have suggested a trip in the boat anyway, hiding his purpose with a fake affair.

The thought ached physically through her. But it could wait; she'd deal with it when she knew what was going on.

Cara was the only link, and Gerry's decision to go back to New Zealand had precipitated this abduction, if abduction it could be called when the abductee had co-operated so eagerly.

No, she wouldn't think of that. Please God, Honor would soon arrive back from wherever she'd been to look after the agency, and Maddie—

Maddie.

Gerry's heart stopped. Maddie had overdosed on heroin. Was that—could that be—the link? Had Cara rung Bryn to tell him about it?

No. Why would she? And what would it mean to him?

She could have, Gerry's rational brain said relentlessly.

Or Bryn could have monitored the calls Gerry her cabaña after she'd left him.

An importer with a legal business and impeccable dentials as a businessman—a man like Bryn Falconer would find it quite easy to set up an illicit organisation to ship in drugs.

Nausea made Gerry gag, but she rinsed out her mouth and washed her face and sat down again. If that unscrupulous importer could persuade a credulous young girl like Cara, who had contacts with people going overseas, that he needed to bring stuff in without Customs knowing—then perhaps the agency could be used as a distributing point.

An island like Longopai would be very useful too, she thought, remembering the trading vessel he had bought for the islanders so that they wouldn't be dependent on the schedules of others.

Such a man could probably persuade Cara to store the stuff in her house; grim logic reminded Gerry he'd wanted Cara's landlady away from Auckland.

No, it was impossible. She'd been watching too many late-night television shows.

Yet here she was, caged in a boat on the Pacific, an almost-willing prisoner who'd swallowed everything Bryn told her because she was attracted to him. Oh, she'd been a fool!

Common sense should have told her that it was highly unlikely—to say the least!—that every system on a boat like *Starchaser* would fail together. Yet she'd been so mesmerised by Bryn's physical magnetism that she'd swallowed his sketchy explanation hook, line and sinker.

A blast of fury surged through her, was suppressed; it clouded the brain. What she needed was clear-headed logic. Unclenching her teeth, she wooed calmness.

From now on she wasn't going to take anything for granted. 'Think,' she muttered. 'Stop wailing and think!'

Could Cara be so criminally naive as to fall in with a scheme like that? Probably not, but she was easily daz-

..d Gerry had first-hand experience of just how ..le Bryn could be.

..o, it was utterly ridiculous! Gerry got to her feet and ..ced through the stateroom, shaking her head. She was spinning tales out of shadows.

She had absolutely no proof, nothing but the wildest speculations.

Yet Bryn had lied about the boat, and kept her prisoner. And he'd made love to her because she'd asked questions— what questions? Was it when she asked who he'd been talking to? He must have been using the radio. Humiliation stung through her but she ignored it.

Also, he certainly hadn't been fooling when he'd locked the door behind her.

Unless he was a psychopath he must have good reasons for his actions.

Psychopath or drug importer—both seemed so unlikely she couldn't deal with them. Yet she would have to accept that she might well be in danger—in such danger that her only hope of saving herself lay in pretending she was the stupid piece of fluff he clearly thought her to be.

Adrenalin brought her upright, but before it had time to develop into full-blown terror a flash of memory made her sink back down again. The first time they'd met, Bryn had held a baby in his arms, and smiled at it with tenderness and awe and a fierce protectiveness.

That had been when she fell in love with him, Gerry thought now. Could a man who'd looked at a child like that cold-bloodedly sleep with a woman and then murder her?

Her heart said no, but she'd already found out she couldn't trust that unwary organ. She'd have to work on the assumption that Bryn Falconer was exactly that sort of man.

She rubbed a shaking hand across her forehead. Why did he need to keep her out of the way now?

Because Maddie had overdosed?

No, it was too far-fetched, too much like some thriller. She was overwrought, and so stressed by his betrayal that her mind was running riot.

But why else would he be keeping her here incommunicado? Obviously he hadn't booked her plane seat to New Zealand, so no one except Cara and Jill were expecting her. With bitter irony, Gerry realised that he'd probably rung Cara and reassured her, giving her some excellent reason why Gerry wasn't coming home. A tropical fever perhaps, she thought wearily. Not dangerous, but debilitating. And perhaps he'd asked Cara to tell Jill that everything was all right.

Gerry tried to remember whether she'd told him about her conversation with the booker. No, she wouldn't have, but if he'd monitored her calls from Longopai he'd know Jill wouldn't be sending off search parties.

He really didn't have anything to worry about. The islanders were his—if he asked them not to speak they wouldn't.

And if he wanted to kill her then he'd probably find a way to get rid of Cara too.

Panic clawed at her gut. She rested her hands on her diaphragm and concentrated on breathing, slow and easy, in and out, in and out, until her racing brain slowed and the terror had subsided.

Ridiculous; it was all ridiculous. This was Bryn who made love like a dark angel, Bryn who'd been gentle when she needed gentleness, fierce when she needed ferocity, Bryn who had made her laugh and talked to her with intelligence and a rare, understated compassion.

Unfortunately history was full of women who had been betrayed by the men they'd loved, men they'd given up everything for.

So she was going to take any chance she could to get away. She'd never forgive herself if she didn't do something to protect Cara.

First, she'd try to use the communications system and send out an SOS.

If she got out of this unscathed, she promised herself grimly, she'd not only take those Maori classes, she'd do a course in maritime navigation and communications.

Or perhaps it would be simpler never to set foot off dry land again.

Gone was the lingering miasma of ennui; the moment she'd seen him every nerve cell had jolted into acute, almost painful alertness.

Narelle and Cosmo were an Australian couple—sleek, well-tanned, wearing expensive resort clothes. Lacey, their adolescent daughter, should have been rounded and sturdy; instead her angular figure indicated a recent illness.

After the flurry of greetings Gerry sank into the chair Bryn held for her, aware that Lacey was eyeing her with the yearning intensity of a hungry lion confronted by a wildebeest. Uncomfortably, Gerry waited for surnames, but none were forthcoming.

'Isn't this a wonderful place for a holiday?' Narelle, a thin, tanned woman with superbly blonded hair and a lot of gold chains, spoke brightly, her skilfully shaded eyes flicking from Gerry to Bryn.

'Ideal,' Gerry answered, smiling, and was about to add that she wasn't exactly on holiday when Bryn distracted her by asking her what she'd have to drink.

'Fruit juice, thanks,' she said. After the fiasco with Troy she wasn't going to risk anything alcoholic in her empty stomach. She smiled at the waiter who'd padded across on bare feet, and added, 'Not too sweet, please.'

'Papaya, madam? With passionfruit and lime?'

'That sounds wonderful,' she said.

She was oddly uneasy when Lacey said loudly, 'I'll have one of those too, please.'

Her mother gave her a sharp look. 'How about a diet soft drink?' she asked.

Narelle opened her mouth but was forestalled by Bryn, who said, 'Did you have a good flight up, Geraldine?'

Why the devil didn't he use her proper name? 'Geraldine' sounded quite different from her normal, everyday self. 'Yes, thank you,' she said, smiling limpidly.

If he thought that one compliment entitled him to a more intimate footing, he was wrong. All right, so her heart was

CHAPTER TEN

WHEN Bryn opened the door some hours later Gerry was sitting on her bed, hands folded in her lap, face carefully blank, while the flicker of fear burnt brightly in her mind.

'You look like a good little girl,' he said, a smile just touching the corners of his mouth.

Gerry's heart leapt frantically. No, she thought gratefully, she couldn't believe he had any connection to the wild concoction of ideas she'd dreamed up.

'I always try to please kidnappers,' she said with a slight snap.

His mouth tightened. 'Come out and have a drink.'

He looked dangerous, but not murderous. Still buoyed by that spurt of relief, she knew that of course he wasn't a murderer! He had, however, lied to her and abducted her, and he wouldn't tell her why.

So she had to work on the assumption that he was up to something that was not for her good.

Getting to her feet, she picked up the letter she'd written to keep her mind from tearing off into ever wilder shores of conjecture, then preceded him into the main cabin.

Once there, she said, 'I've written to Lacey. I'd like to send it to her if you have her address.'

'Send it to the hotel and ask them to forward it,' he said coolly.

'It's not sealed. Do you want to read it?' She held it out to him.

His brows drew together. 'Stop pushing,' he commanded softly.

But she couldn't. 'I haven't written anything that might lead her to think I'm in dire danger.'

'Keep on like that, and you might be. If you send it to the hotel they'll make sure Lacey gets it.'

Gerry said chattily, 'I made her promise to contact a doctor when she gets back home. I thought I'd better remind her of it just in case I go missing.'

'You won't go missing,' he said between his teeth. 'How did you extract a promise like that from her?'

'I threatened to tell her parents. Oh, I didn't say so, but she knew I would. She wants to stop; the bulimia terrifies her but she's also determined not to put any weight on. She needs professional help, and I more or less blackmailed her into seeing someone she trusts when she gets home.'

He said nothing, and she went on abruptly, 'I'm beginning to wonder whether there might not be some truth in what you said about magazines sending all the wrong messages.'

'Guilty conscience, Geraldine?'

She shrugged moodily, trying to sound and look normal, trying to reassure herself that a man who worried about the messages high fashion was sending to young women couldn't possibly be a drug peddler. 'No. The magazine I worked for concentrated on style rather than fashion, and we did a lot with models who weren't size eights. As for the agency, we represent all sorts—character as well as fashion—and I can assure you that none of our models are anorexic or bulimic.'

But one was a drug addict. Just how much did she know about the models?

Swiftly she went on, 'Lacey worries me. She's big-boned, the sort of build with no middle ground between gaunt and voluptuous. She's also bitterly unhappy with her stepmother, and I gathered that her mother doesn't want her living with her and her new husband. I don't entirely believe that the fashion business is to blame for the increase in eating disorders. There are millions of women throughout the world who read fashion magazines, and although they're nothing like the models they're happy with their lot.'

Bryn walked across to the drinks fridge. 'I know.'

He caught her surprised glance. A cynical lift of his mouth made him look suddenly older. 'Wine?' he asked.

'No, thank you. Something with fruit in it.'

He poured her pineapple juice, and lime and soda for himself. If he'd chosen beer she might have had a chance to try and get him drunk.

Hardly. Bryn Falconer was a very controlled man; it was difficult to imagine him drinking to excess.

Silence stretched between them. Refusing to show how intimidated she was, Gerry sipped her drink. Outside the sun had set; as the darkness thickened a bird flying overhead gave a strange, wild cry, and she only just prevented herself from jumping.

'Relax,' he said, something like irritation flicking through his voice. 'I told you before, you're in no danger. Stop looking at me as though you expect me to leap on you.'

'I'm not accustomed to being held prisoner,' she returned crisply. 'It makes me angry.'

'You're not just angry,' he said. 'You're scared.'

Damn. She made her muscles respond in a smile, packed though it was with irony. 'You must forgive me, but in spite of all your protestations about not wanting to harm me, you are holding me here for reasons I'm not allowed to know. I think a certain amount of wariness is normal in such situations. Of course I *believe* you when you say I'm safe,' she finished, her voice dripping polite sarcasm. 'How long will I be forced to stay here?'

'Until I'm told it's safe to let you go.'

So he wasn't doing this on his own. Well, she'd realised that there had to be other people in it with him, whatever *it* was!

Feeling her way, she said, 'A week? A month? A year?'

But of course he wasn't goaded into revealing anything. 'Until I let you go,' he repeated levelly, his face impassive, as though they'd never looked at each other with naked lust, never made love, never slept a long night in each other's arms.

'What excuse did you give Cara for my not coming back?'

'I told her you had a very mild case of dengue fever. She said that you weren't to worry, she and Jill would cope,' he told her, and before she had a chance to say anything more went on, 'I'll get dinner.'

He'd cooked steak, and served it with potatoes and taro leaves cooked in coconut milk. Gerry had no appetite, but she forced as much as she could down because she wasn't going to weaken herself by starving.

After the meal she said, 'I'd like to go back to the cabin now.'

Hot anger glittered in Bryn's gaze, was immediately extinguished. 'Of course,' he said courteously.

So Gerry sat in the small room, nerves taut, and listened to the sound of the waves on the reef. Towards ten o'clock she heard his voice drift in through the open windows. It was impossible to make out individual words, but from his tone—crisp, businesslike, resolute—it was clear that he was using the radio.

She was never going to trust any other man, no matter how attractive she found him and how tenderly he looked at babies.

Thoughts prowled through her mind, rattling the bars and poking hideous faces as the slow tropical night wheeled through its cycle, splendid, indifferent, majestically beautiful. Lying tense and fully-clothed on the bed, Gerry spent hours trying to convince herself that the man who had made love to her with such fiery tenderness couldn't possibly want to harm her.

Dawn came as a surprise. Yawning, she rubbed her eyes and realised that somehow she'd managed to fall asleep.

A glance in the mirror revealed dark circles under her eyes, and sallow, colourless skin. Hastily she showered before making up with every ounce of skill and care she could call on, not satisfied until her face gazed back at her—smooth and unmarked by betrayal, the sleepy eyes and full mouth delicately enhanced so that no one could guess how

much time it had taken to manufacture that discreet, inconspicuous mask.

She dressed in white linen trousers and a muted silk shirt in her favourite shades of blue and green, slid her narrow feet into blue sandals, and straightened her shoulders and lifted her chin. With her best model gait she walked across to the door.

It was unlocked. Hardly daring to breathe, she slipped through it.

Bryn looked up from the galley. 'Good morning,' he said, scanning her with half-closed eyes that sent a shiver from the top of her head to the base of her spine, so masculine and appreciative was that swift, hot glance. It disappeared in the length of a blink; he lifted his brows and said easily, 'Ah, the exquisite, sophisticated, aloof Ms Dacre once more! It's almost a pity; I've grown to like the slightly tousled Geraldine who lurks beneath the cosmetics.'

Smiling, showing her teeth, she murmured, 'How sweet.'

He laughed. 'Come and have some breakfast.'

No, she thought hopefully, whatever the reason he kept her here, it couldn't possibly be because he was smuggling drugs. That had been a fevered figment of her imagination; he couldn't look at her like that, or tease like that couldn't *laugh* like that—and wish her any harm.

With a cautiously lifting heart, she sat down at the table and began to eat.

He didn't lock her into her cabin again; as though they'd silently negotiated a truce they tidied the boat and repaired to the cockpit, sitting out of the sun. Bryn read what looked like business papers from a locked briefcase, and Gerry tried to concentrate on a book.

With very little success. A volatile cocktail of emotions—raw fury and desolation and pride mixed with a persistent, stubborn hope—washed through her like rollers pounding the shore. Ignore the hope, she told herself, it will weaken you. Polish up that pride.

And look for an opportunity to get to the instrument console and radio for help, even though you have no idea how to use it.

However, he'd placed himself between her and the console, and during the long morning he made sure she didn't have a chance to get near it.

The sun was high in the sky when something beeped from the panel. Bryn looked up. 'Would you mind going below?' he asked pleasantly.

'Not at all,' Gerry replied with steely composure, gathering up the unread book as she got to her feet.

Of course she couldn't settle; clutching the book, she stood in the main cabin and stared blindly through the windows while Bryn's voice echoed in her ears.

Should she be frightened?

No.

However hard she tried to see him as a criminal, she couldn't. Oh, she could imagine Bryn killing a man in self-defence, but even in her most paranoid fears she hadn't been able to be afraid of him. A deep-seated instinct told her he was a man with his own strict code of honour.

Her lips stretched in a painful, wry smile. In spite of everything her foolish heart trusted him. Nevertheless that same organ gave an enormous jump when he appeared in the doorway, brows drawn together, face grim.

'Well?' she demanded.

He came down the last step. 'Tell me about your partner in the agency,' he commanded.

'Honor?' Totally bewildered, Gerry stared at him. 'What's happened? Is she all right?'

'As far as I know she's fine,' he said. 'How long have you known her? Where did you meet her?'

She asked, 'Do you know whether a model called Maddie Ingram is all right? She was in hospital.'

It was a test. If he knew about Maddie, he knew too much.

He paused a second before saying, 'She's recovering.'

A clutch of terror diluted Gerry's relief. Yet her voice

stayed steady when she asked, 'Why do you want to know about Honor?'

'Because it's important.' The relentless note in his voice warned her that she wasn't going to be able to stall.

Feeling oddly disconnected, she said slowly, 'She used to be a model—I've known her for years.'

'Is she a friend?'

She gave him a startled look but could read nothing from the harsh face or hooded eyes.

'Not exactly a friend,' she answered slowly. 'We get on well together, and she's an excellent partner.'

'What made you decide to go in with her?'

He sounded like a policeman—polite, determined, relentless. The hairs on the back of her neck stood up. 'After my father died I was restless, and when the magazine I worked for was taken over, and the new owners put in an editor who took it down a path I despise, I started looking around for another job. Honor had just broken up with the man she'd been living with.'

Drugs, she recalled sickly. He'd been a heroin addict. She cast a swift glance at Bryn's stone-featured face and continued, 'He'd run through all her money and she was desperate. The only thing she knew was modelling, so she suggested we open an agency. At the time it seemed a good way of getting over my grief. A model agency is the next best thing to chaos that you've ever come across—you don't have time to think.'

'How was the agency set up?'

'On a shoestring. Neither of us had any money what we did have were contacts. And I have a reputation for seeing promise in unlikely people.'

'Who actually runs the agency?'

Gerry said crisply, 'In an agency as small as ours we can all do everything. We've got bookers, of course—they organise the models' bookings—but Honor and I do almost everything else, and we take the responsibility for planning careers.'

'All right,' he cut in. 'Who deals with the finances?'

Frowning, Gerry said, 'We have an accountant.'

'Who is sleeping with Honor McKenzie.'

She looked up sharply. There had been no inflection in his tone, but something warned her that she wasn't going to like what was coming. 'I hope not,' she said just as brusquely. 'He's married to a very nice woman.'

'He's been your partner's lover since before the agency opened.'

Gerry said quietly, 'I didn't know that.'

'Do you know where Honor was when Cara rang you in a panic about Maddie Ingram?'

Who the *hell* was he? Or rather, *what* was he? He certainly didn't sound like your average rich importer. And where was this all heading? Chilled by nameless fear, Gerry shook her head. 'Cara said she couldn't contact her, but that's not unusual. She takes the occasional long weekend off.'

In an expressionless voice he told her, 'She was in Tahiti.'

Tahiti? Six hours away from New Zealand by air? Her expression must have revealed Gerry's astonishment, but she said evenly, 'I don't understand why this is important.'

'She was meeting an emissary from a Colombian co-caine-trafficking cartel.'

Gerry's jaw dropped.

Calmly, mercilessly, Bryn went on, 'Colombians made the big time with cocaine but now they're moving into her-oin—it's easier to transport and yields far higher profits. In New Zealand, what heroin comes in—and that's not been much until recently—has been sourced in Asia.'

'From the Golden Triangle,' Gerry said dully. She'd read about the wild region on the border of Thailand and Myanmar where drug lords ruled an empire based on mis-ery.

Although she knew now what he was going to tell her, she was gripped by an overwhelming relief, a giddy sense of being reprieved from something too dreadful to contemplate because her suspicions of Bryn were baseless.

'Yes. The Colombians want this traffic; using New Zealand as a staging post, they can move into Australia and Asia.' Sources say they have over forty thousand acres of opium poppy under cultivation, and they're planting more. They're also aggressive marketers. Their product is cheaper and purer than the Asian stuff, and they're "double-breasting"—offering a free sample of heroin to each buyer of cocaine.'

She said, 'You think there's a connection between Maddie's overdose and Honor.'

He frowned. 'There's certainly a link with the agency.'

'How do you know?'

'There have been whispers about the agency for a year or so, but nothing tangible, nothing the police could put a finger on. However, Maddie told a friend she had a contact there, and the friend, thank God, told Maddie's brother. He went to the police, and your agency has been under investigation since then.'

'How do I know that you're not lying, that this isn't some elaborate scam?' Gerry couldn't believe it. She knew Honor much better than she knew him, and she'd never suspected her partner of any connection with drug-dealing. 'And why did you stop me from going back to New Zealand?'

'The police asked me to keep you away from the agency for as long as possible.'

'Why?'

'They were still not entirely convinced that you weren't part of the drug ring.' He spoke unemotionally, but she realised he was watching her with an intense, unnerving concentration, dispassionate and intimidating. 'Although they had a search warrant they needed time to get into your computers and drag everything out. They've been there since half an hour after Cara rang you.'

'I see,' she said in a stifled monotone. Thoughts barged around her head, colliding, melding in turmoil. She drew a deep breath and said harshly, 'Why do the police think Honor had something to do with Maddie's OD? And how—how do you know who she met in Tahiti? You can prove that, I assume?'

'She's been under surveillance, and, yes, it can be proved.'

Sweat sprang out across her skin in great beads as she closed her eyes, but blocking him out didn't help. 'Who are you? Apart from being an importer?'

Eyes as cold as quartz, he told her, 'I'm not—I lied to you. I own a construction company. We do projects all around the Pacific Rim, and the company was used in a smuggling racket some years ago. I worked closely with Customs and the police to get to the bottom of that, so I have contacts within each department.'

Frowning, Gerry asked, 'And how did you get mixed up with this?'

After an infinitesimal pause he answered, 'I'm a good friend of Peter Ingram, Maddie's brother. He contacted me a couple of months ago, after he'd found out she was back on heroin. He had to leave for Turkestan and I promised I'd keep an eye on her. I also went to the police. They contacted me a few weeks ago to see if I could get you out of the way for a few days.'

'So you set out to find some dimwitted person with a connection to the agency and picked up Cara, who led you to me.' Her voice was brittle, as brittle as her heart.

His mouth tightened but he said evenly, 'Yes. You were the most likely suspect.'

'Why?' Her emotions were lost in a hollow emptiness.

'A tip-off.'

She stared at him. 'A tip-off?' she said numbly. 'Who from?'

He was still watching her with cool, unsparing assessment. 'A long-time drug user. The police suspect that he mistook you for Honor. Or she might have used your name occasionally.'

Sinking down onto the sofa, she looked down at her feet.

Nausea made her swallow. Bryn had believed this; he'd been sure that she was a prime mover in this trade, and he'd slept with her, made love to her...

It was only marginally less shattering than if he'd been the dealer of death. Her throat ached with tears, tears she'd never be able to shed. She said, 'And on that basis, a tip from a known drug user, you assumed that I ran a drug ring.'

'There were other factors. When the police began investigating, a trail led them to a Swiss bank account, supposedly set up by you.'

With a sense of complete unreality, Gerry noticed that her hands were trembling. Sweat collected across her shoulders, ran the length of her back. Her arid throat prevented her from speaking until she'd swallowed again, and even then her voice emerged thin and shaken. She could discern nothing in Bryn's hard face, nothing in his tone, to tell her whether he believed this or not.

'No,' she said.

'It certainly gave credence to the tip-off,' he said neutrally.

Had Honor done this? Gerry had always been reasonably confident about her judgement of character until then; now she realised that the woman she'd worked with and trusted could have plotted to send her to prison, to ruin her life. She shook her head.

'It made sense,' Bryn went on with grim persistence. 'Although your father had indulged you all your life, his insistence on paying back his creditors left you penniless.'

'I had a salary,' she flared.

'Peanuts to what you'd been accustomed to. Before he divested himself to pay off his creditors your father was a rich man.'

Gerry said tautly, 'My father stopped supporting me when I left university, and since then I've lived off my income. I agreed wholly with him when he decided to pay back the money his manager had taken.'

'It seemed likely that you might look for a way to up

your income to that level again. Also, you'd done a lot of travelling when you were with the magazine, especially in Asia and the Pacific. Plenty of chances to make contacts there. And then there was the friend I saw you eating lunch with the day I met you. She'd taken something.'

'She'd had less than a glass of wine. Troy's very susceptible to alcohol—it makes her drunk so quickly she can't even eat a sherry trifle.' With an effort that took all of her nervous energy, she steadied her voice. 'So when we made love you really thought that I was running a smuggling ring. Not only that, but that I was introducing my models to heroin.'

'By then I was almost convinced that you were innocent.'

His impersonal, judicial tone fired her anger to fury—a fury mixed with weary disillusion.

'Almost.' She straightened her spine. 'Go on,' she said tonelessly. 'Tell me how you decided that it was Honor.'

'You don't seem surprised,' he observed shrewdly.

Slowly Gerry said, 'I am—but not shocked. In some ways she's surprisingly amoral, so perhaps I should have wondered if that extended into other areas of her life. But she didn't try to fiddle the books—I learned from my father's experience, and I go over the records regularly.'

'You went over the records she wanted you to see. There were others, but she kept her illegal activities totally separate from the agency.'

'Except for Maddie,' she said bitterly.

He shrugged. 'Except for Maddie. Nevertheless, the police realised that, in spite of the tip-off, Honor McKenzie had just as many chances as you to travel, she had as little money as you, and she'd also lived with a man who was deep in the drug culture.'

'She isn't a user,' Gerry said, adding wearily, 'at least, I don't think she is.'

'She isn't, and neither is her lover, who actually set this whole thing up. The people who sell rarely are. They know what damage their wares cause.'

'If there was a bank account in my name, how did the police decide that it was Honor who organised the trade, not me?' Her cool voice hid, she hoped, the intense desolation that racked her.

'It all seemed just a little too pat—especially when it was discovered that the accountant and Honor were lovers. He was a suspect in a fraud case five years ago—they couldn't pin anything on him, but the Fraud Squad were convinced that he was not only guilty but the organiser of the scam. A month ago your accounting department hired a clerk, an undercover agent who's a computer expert. If you know what you're doing you can find anything that's ever been on a computer, even if it's been dumped in the trash. She was surprised to find security so tight in your accounting department, but she dug away discreetly, only to be even more surprised to find a not too difficult trail leading to a Swiss bank account—in your name.'

Gerry licked dry lips. 'I see,' she said quietly. 'You mean the agency has been used to launder money?'

'No, but the agency's computers had been used to organise it all. Apparently by you. And that increased the police suspicions, because the trail was a little too clear, a little too obvious. So they began looking into Honor's affairs, and they found that she'd gone to Thailand earlier this year, and while she was there she'd met a couple of extremely unsavoury characters. The New Zealand police liaise very closely with the Thai drug squad, and they'd been watching these men.'

Thank heavens for suspicious police. Gerry's shoulders ached with the effort it took to keep them straight.

To her astonishment Bryn asked, 'Do you want a drink—a cup of tea, something?'

Her stomach roiled at the prospect. 'No thanks. Go on.'

'Honor has been living just above her income; she seems to be taking great care not to exceed it by enough to cause suspicion. But even then you weren't entirely in the clear. They were certain Honor was guilty, but your status was problematical. She and her lover might well have intended to use you as a scapegoat, hence the nice clear trail to the Swiss account.'

'So the police decided that you should sniff around much more closely,' she said, not even trying to inject some emotion into the words. 'What a pity I'm not good at pillow talk.'

Although green fire smouldered in the depths of his eyes, his voice remained level. 'In the end they decided to apply a little pressure.'

'How?'

'You were got out of the way and put in a situation where any calls could be monitored.' His voice was hard. 'Honor was contacted by someone who told her he could sell heroin at a cut rate—much better heroin than she was getting from Asia. He sent her a sample which had been tagged.'

'Tagged?'

'Treated so that it is easily identifiable. She didn't even try to contact you; instead, she and the accountant took off for Tahiti after they'd sold the heroin on. It was traced through several people, including the person who'd named you. He's been taken into custody, and he talked enough to convince the police he'd never met the woman he called Gerry. The accountant and Honor were arrested half an hour ago as they landed from Tahiti.'

Gerry couldn't bear to look at him, couldn't bear to think of Honor, peddling beauty and death. Reining herself in, she asked, 'It still isn't conclusive proof that I'm in the clear?'

He frowned. 'The police have been through your affairs with a fine-tooth comb, and nothing but the tip-off connects you to the smuggling. You live within your income, you have no secret assets, and the hidden bank account has been examined by the Swiss—although it was set up under your name, the beneficiaries turned out to be Honor and the accountant. That's proof enough, Geraldine.'

'Why?' Gerry asked harshly. She should be relieved, but

she was too shattered to feel anything. 'What made her do it?'

'She's in it for the money.' Contempt seared the words. 'She met the accountant, and the two of them set it up; you were the perfect scapegoat.'

'So you did your duty as a good citizen and got me out of the way while they investigated Honor. I admire your dedication to the cause.'

He shrugged. 'By then I was as certain as anyone could be without proof that you were in the clear.'

'But you needed that proof,' she said, her quiet comment hiding, she hoped, the pain behind it. 'And you made love to me to stop me from making any connections. You must think I'm a total fool. I must *be* a total fool.'

'I made love to you because I couldn't help myself,' he said roughly.

Why did he lie? Did it matter? Driven by the need to escape, to lick her wounds in private, she said, 'It seems you make a habit of using women. First Cara, then me—'

He said ferociously, 'Will you stop saying that? I haven't even kissed Cara, and as for you—doesn't it tell you something that when I should have kept you at arm's length I couldn't wait to get into bed with you?'

'It tells me that—' She stopped, twisting her head. 'What's that? It sounds like a plane.'

Bryn swore under his breath, but didn't try to stop her when she brushed past him and ran up the steps. The seaplane headed towards them and came in slowly, settling into the lagoon in twin feathers of spray.

Bryn said, 'I called him up half an hour ago, but he said he'd be at least an hour.'

'You can't trust anyone nowadays, can you?' Gerry said bitterly.

'I'll get your luggage,' he said tightly, disappearing down the steps.

Biting her lip, Gerry walked across to the railing, watching through a mist of tears as the plane taxied to a stop. What had she expected? Making love to her had been hardly honourable, but then, he had done it for the good of the country, she thought tiredly.

And she was not in love with him.

Not even one tiny bit.

It was a silent trip in the dinghy to the plane. All Gerry had to rely on now was her dignity. She forced a smile for the pilot and his hairy, enthusiastic co-pilot, who barked a greeting and had to be restrained from hurtling into the lagoon. Without hearing the pleasantries Bryn and the pilot exchanged, she clambered in.

Bryn looked up, green eyes burning in the emphatic framework of his dark, autocratic face. 'Goodbye, Geraldine,' he said, and expertly backed the dinghy away, rowing steadily towards the *Starchaser*.

She couldn't summon a reply; instead she nodded and settled back into her seat.

'Put your seatbelt on,' the pilot yelled.

She did up the clasp and turned her head resolutely away, watching the island skim past until the engine noise altered and they lifted above the vivid lagoon. As soon as they were in the air she allowed herself to wipe her eyes and blow her nose, and watched steadfastly as the water fell away beneath them and the bright, feathery crowns of the coconut palms dwindled into a fringe within the protective white line of the reef, and then were left behind.

CHAPTER ELEVEN

'ALL right,' Gerry said with a sigh, 'let's call it a day.'

Troy covered a yawn. 'It's been a long one,' she said with a grimace, looking at the cluttered circular table with its central rack of files.

Gerry got to her feet and stretched. 'Oh, well, it's over now.'

The past six months had been horrendous, with Honor in prison awaiting trial, and then the trial itself, culminating in long sentences for both her and her lover. Gerry had been appalled to discover how cleverly the whole operation had been managed. Honor had targeted the rich and the famous—people who'd wanted to avoid any sleaze or violence or danger.

The agency had been thoroughly compromised, but although they had lost models, many had stuck by Gerry. Which was surprising, as Honor's defence had suggested with infinite delicacy that Gerry had been the prime mover in the heroin ring and that Honor had been framed.

Gerry thought drearily that her models' loyalty had been virtually the only good thing about these last six months.

No, that was untrue. She'd learned enough basic Maori at night classes to make herself understood, and Lacey hadn't vomited for three months. She and the Australian girl kept in close touch with e-mail, and it certainly sounded as though Lacey was getting her life together.

Abruptly Gerry said, 'I'm going to sell the agency.'

Troy stared. 'Why? You've worked like a slave to control all the damage, and now that things are going smoothly again you want to leave. It doesn't make sense. What will you do?'

It was impossible to tell her the real reason—that Gerry was heartsick for a man who hadn't been near her since, grim-faced and impervious, he'd watched her leave him. Bryn hadn't appeared in any of the court proceedings; for all she knew, he could have disappeared off the face of the earth.

She said, 'I'm going to have a holiday. And I think I might learn to cook. Properly.'

Troy's mouth opened, then closed on her unspoken comment. After a moment, she nodded. 'Good idea. And after you've learned to cook properly—what then?'

'I'm going to write a column for one of the magazines—personal style, to thine own self be true, where to shop for good, elegant, stylish clothes that suit and don't break the budget—that sort of thing. Under a pseudonym, of course. The editors think—and I agree—that it would be better to lie low for a while until the stink from this has died down, if it ever does. Mud sticks.'

Troy said briskly, 'Don't be an idiot. Anyone who knows you knows you had nothing to do with Honor and her rotten get-rich-quick scheme.' She paused before asking, 'Are you going to be able to earn enough to live on?'

'I should get a decent sum for the agency. It's worth quite a bit, so I'll pay off the mortgage on the house, repay the bank loan that I took out to buy Honor's share of the agency, and invest any money left over. I won't be able to live on that, but as well as the magazine column, I've been thinking about going back to journalism—freelancing.' She gave a wry smile. 'There'll be enough variety in that to stop me getting bored. I used to enjoy writing articles, and I was good at it.'

'You were brilliant at it,' Troy said, eyeing her thoughtfully. 'I think it's a wonderful idea. Have you got a buyer for the agency?'

'The first person with the money,' Gerry answered cynically. 'No, it'll have to be someone I trust. I haven't got it back into running order to sell it to anyone I don't like. I probably haven't thanked you for coming in as assistant and general dogsbody, either. Honestly, Troy, it's made all the difference.'

'I've loved doing it.'

'How does Damon feel about it?'

Her friend set two pens carefully down on the table. 'At first he hated it, and whined about how bad a wife and mother I am, even though the new nanny is working out brilliantly—the kids love her, and she's so good with them.' She picked up a pen and fiddled with it. 'Anyway, it doesn't matter what he thinks. I've left him.'

Gerry landed limply in the chair beside her. 'Oh,' she said inadequately.

Troy flushed, but held her head high. 'And it's not because he's having an affair with one of his executives, either. I'd decided before I knew about that. I just looked at him and thought, Would anyone who really loved me treat me the way he does? And I thought, No, if you love someone you want them to be happy, instead of making them miserable as sin. So I got my lawyer to draw up a separation agreement. Damon's flounced off to live with his dark-haired, clever girlfriend, and the kids and I are in the house with the nanny.'

'I'm sorry,' Gerry said. Sorry, she meant, for shattered illusions and broken dreams, not sorry that Damon had gone. 'Why didn't you tell me?'

Troy looked self-conscious. 'Well, you've been so busy with the agency, and so worried about the court case, I didn't want to add to your woes. And I needed to do this on my own. I've always turned to you and cried all over you and generally leaned on you; I thought it was about time I grew up and made some decisions for myself, and carried through on them.'

'You've certainly done that,' Gerry said, feeling oddly abandoned.

Troy shook her head. 'Yes, well, it hasn't been easy,' she admitted, 'but really I've known ever since we got married that I'd been a fool—I just didn't want to admit it. You know me, stubborn as hell. This job has been a lifesaver, and I've loved it.' She looked around the office with its posters of models on the walls, its air of being in a continual state of chaos, and said, 'And I'd have to talk it over with my financial advisers, but I'd like to buy the agency very much. I know you bought Honor out—she hasn't any other claim on it, has she?'

'No,' Gerry said shortly. She'd gone to the finance company expecting to be turned down, but it had been no problem, and Honor, needing the cash for lawyers, had been eager to be rid of her share.

'Good.' Troy put the pen down. She looked eager and excited, more like the woman who'd been a very successful model than the overwrought wife who'd wept in the restaurant six months ago. 'Do you remember Sunny Josephs, who used to be booker for me in the days when I was setting the catwalks on fire? She went off to Chicago just after I married, and did really well there, but she wants to come home. She wrote to me a couple of months ago and asked if there was something she could buy into here. There wasn't at the time, but if she's interested in coming in as my partner, it would be perfect. She knows more about the industry than anyone else, and having her here would give me more time with the kids.'

'It sounds ideal,' Gerry said.

'It does, doesn't it?' Her friend smiled. 'OK, then, I'll get my financial person to talk to yours.'

Troy had worked hard, earning trust and respect from the models. Her background had helped, but it was her driving desire to succeed that would make her a success. If she wanted to put the small fortune she'd earned from her days as a model into the agency, she'd do well.

Gerry drove home through a late summer dusk, enjoying the incandescent colours of sunset staining the western sky. Auckland had wound down for the day, but there were still too many cars on the roads and plenty of people on the streets. Through her windows floated that indescribable mixture of flowers and car fumes and salt and barbecues—the scents of Auckland in summer.

But in her heart it was always winter, and even as she scoffed at herself for being melodramatic she accepted that the interlude with Bryn had altered her life, changed something basic in her soul.

She couldn't have fallen in love so quickly, so what she felt for him had to be sheer, teeth-clenching frustration, an intense, unsatisfied desire. If they'd had a torrid affair she'd be restless by now, seeking ways to be free of him without hurting him.

Turning into her gate, she hit the button for the garage and watched the door fold upwards. As she nudged into place beside the empty space where Cara's sporty little model usually sat, she smiled. After a couple of edgy months pining for Bryn, Cara had found herself a boyfriend. Simon played professional rugby and had been picked for the All Blacks, New Zealand's national team.

It had to be true love, Gerry had decided, because although he was a dear, and very intelligent, with a degree in history, he was a far cry from the handsome models and television stars Cara had preferred before him. In spite of this, Cara seemed totally besotted, and although Simon viewed his love with a slightly sardonic gaze, he clearly loved her deeply. Gerry hoped it would last, especially as Cara was talking about moving in with him.

Her new housemate wasn't home either. Improbably named Alfred, he was six feet two of impossibly gorgeous male with shoulders as wide as barn doors. He drove a beat-up Falcon with rusty doors and a hood that rattled, in which he'd been living until Gerry offered him a room and bed, and was headed for super-stardom as a model. So far he'd stuck close to home because his father was ill, but it wouldn't be long before he was snapped up by the overseas market.

She'd miss him. Not only was he funny and a good cook, but he'd provided eager muscle when she'd remodelled the garden that spring.

The prospect of finding another housemate was depressing. But then, she thought, walking between banks of cosmos to the door, everything depressed her this golden summer. Since she'd flown away from an unnamed atoll and left Bryn Falconer behind, life had seemed too much trouble.

She'd hoped that when she sent a carefully selected folder of photographs of hats for the Longopai islanders to copy he might contact her, but he hadn't, unless you counted a formal, perfectly phrased letter written by his secretary to thank her for her efforts on the islanders' behalf.

Even now that Gerry had secured the future of her models and cleared her name as far as it could be cleared, and was confident the agency would be in good hands, she couldn't summon much enthusiasm for either a holiday or her latest venture into journalism.

She stooped to smell a heavy peach and yellow Abraham Derby rose, losing herself in its intense, heady fragrance. As she stood up and walked towards the front verandah a blackbird, deciding she was an imminent threat to avian life, flew screaming across the lawn towards the hedge.

'Oh, grow up!' Gerry told it crisply, and bent to examine the round, glossy leaves of her Chatham Island forget-me-nots. It was a gamble, growing them this close to the equator, but given the right place they could thrive even in Auckland's warm, humid, maritime climate. These ones looked all right so far, but getting them through the summer would be tricky.

As a car stopped outside the hedge a latent, atavistic intuition pulled her skin taut. Every sense on full alert, she straightened, staring at the house, unable to swivel around.

'Geraldine.'

How had she known? She hadn't seen him, certainly hadn't heard him, and yet from the moment the car drew to a halt she'd known it was Bryn.

Gathering her inner resources, she slowly turned. As he came towards her, her heart contracted fiercely, squeezing her emotions into one solid, unreachable ball. 'Hello, Bryn,' she said quietly. 'How are you?'

'I'm well, thank you. And you?'

He looked good. Green eyes gleaming, golden skin glow-

ing in the apricot light of dusk, white shirt open at the neck
and with the sleeves rolled back to reveal his muscular forearms, dark trousers cut with the spare, unforgiving elegance
of English tailoring—oh, yes, he looked more than good.

Gerry felt tired and grubby.

'I'm well too,' she said courteously. She most emphati-
cally did not want him inside her house again, and yet she
could see that he wasn't going to go until he'd got whatever
it was that had brought him there.

Sure enough, he said quietly, implacably, 'Invite me in,
Geraldine.'

'Come inside, Bryn.' Her voice was flat, composed.

'Thank you.'

She led him to the kitchen and asked, 'Would you like
a beer?'

'If you're having one.'

'I'll have juice.' Stooping, she picked up a bottle of
Alfred's ice beer and a jug of grapefruit juice before closing
the fridge door.

'Can I get down some glasses?' Bryn said.

'Unless you drink it from the bottle?' She winced as the
glass bottom of the bottle rang against the stainless steel
bench.

Black brows lifting, he shook his head. 'Do you?'

'No. My father had very strong ideas on how a young
lady should behave—feminism passed him by completely.'
She indicated a cupboard door, and as Bryn reached for
two heavy-based glasses she opened the drawer and took
out a bottle-opener. 'Drinking anything from the bottle was
about as low as you could go and still call yourself human.'

'Let me do that,' Bryn said.

Gerry set her jaw. He certainly could; then he might not
notice her shaking hands.

His were perfectly steady, as steady as his voice. 'Your
father was a gentleman of the old school.'

Her heart thudded with erratic impatience; deliberately,
carefully, she armoured herself against the pulsing, driving
need he'd brought with him.

'Yes,' she said.

He gave her a glass and lifted his own. 'So here's to the future,' he said pleasantly, and drank.

Gerry looked away. The future. Yes, she could drink to that. 'The future,' she echoed, and took a tiny mouthful of juice. 'Come and sit down,' she urged in her most gracious, hostessy voice.

His mouth twisted slightly, but he stood back to let her lead the way to the sitting area. Once there, however, he stayed standing and surveyed the room with a long, considering gaze. 'When I walked in here the day we met,' he said, 'I thought how warm and welcoming, how serene and elegant and mischievous this room was.'

'Mischievous?' she echoed warily.

He smiled. 'It's decorated with an impeccable eye for colour and proportion but a closer look reveals the quirky things that save it from stultifying good taste. Like the glass frog on the table, and the clock.'

'It's an American acorn clock,' she said, trying to stifle the warm glow caused by his appreciation, 'about a hundred and fifty years old. I fell in love with its shape and the lovely little picture on glass, and the dealer let me pay it off by instalments, bless her.' She couldn't stop babbling. 'It was a bargain too—I got it for about half what it's worth.'

He looked at her with an enigmatic smile. 'You're nervous,' he said. 'Why?'

Gerry fought for self-possession, and managed to produce a fairly good approximation. With a faint snap in her tone she said, 'I didn't expect to see you again.'

He drank half the beer and set it down. 'I stayed away,' he said calmly, 'because I was warned that it might compromise the case if I saw you while it was in progress. And because I had a couple of things I wanted to do, and something I had to come to terms with.'

Her breath stayed locked in her chest. 'Such as?' she asked, almost dizzy with expectation too long denied.

'I had to track down the man who duped your father.'

He spoke equably, as though this was just another task ticked off.

'How did you know who he was?'

'Everyone in New Zealand knew who he was. We're too small a country for that sort of thing not to get around.'

Gerry's mouth dried. 'And did you find him?'

'In Australia, living a comfortable life in Perth.' His voice was considered, but when she stole a look at him she drew in a jagged breath at the cold glitter in his eyes.

She said, 'What happened?'

'I confronted him. He did a lot of wriggling, but in the end we came to an understanding. He agreed that you should be reimbursed, and what's left of the money is now waiting in a holding account. I know that nothing can repay you for your father's pain and death, but at least you have what is rightfully yours and the cause of it has been punished.'

'I don't believe it,' Gerry said numbly. 'How did you do it?'

His smile was sardonic. 'You don't want to know. It was legal, if a trifle unethical.'

'And will he find someone else to steal from?'

His face hardened. 'Not for some years, anyway. He's now in prison.'

She drank some of the juice, welcoming the sharp, tangy taste. 'Did you put him there?' she asked.

'I gave him a choice,' he said calmly. 'He chose what he felt was the lesser of two evils.'

She stole a careful look. 'What was the alternative?'

'Extradition to New Zealand.'

Gerry met his eyes. They were flat and deadly and opaque; he looked a very formidable man indeed. Her stomach performed a few acrobatics and she said mutedly, 'I'm very grateful.'

'You're not, you're worried, but it will be all right.' He smiled ironically. 'He didn't deserve to get away with it.'

'No, he didn't, but I don't want you doing my dirty work for me. And revenge is never a good basis for action.'

'This wasn't revenge,' he said coolly. 'It was justice.'

Still troubled, she moved to look out of the window at the new garden. Angular rust-red flowers of kangaroo paw lifted towards the sky, the spiky leaves reflected in the still, smooth water of the pool. Nosing its way slowly from beneath a waterlily leaf, the biggest and reddest of the gold-fish headed across towards the other side, then gave a flick of its long white tail and disappeared into the depths.

Gerry's galloping heartbeat had eased into something like its normal speed, but she could taste the awareness on her tongue, feel Bryn's presence on her skin. Was informing her of the incarceration of her father's manager all he'd come back for? Caution clogged her tongue as she said, 'Thank you.'

'If you don't mind,' he said, 'I'd like to tell you about my sister.'

She almost held her breath. 'No, I don't mind at all.'

He looked down at his empty glass and said austerely, 'I told you that she was tall.'

'And unhappy.'

He nodded. 'Yes. It was all right while we both went to primary school, but when I was sent away to boarding school she lived for the times I came home. After I'd finished school I took an engineering degree at Christchurch, and when I came home the last time she was so thin and ill I was horrified. I took her to the doctor; he diagnosed anorexia. Apparently she'd been tormented at school about her height and her size. My grandmother was also ill, so I can't entirely blame her for not noticing what was going on.'

Gerry had guessed—of course she'd guessed—but she was horrified just the same. 'I'm so sorry,' she said, feeling wretchedly inadequate.

'I stayed with her, but it was too late. She died of heart failure.' His voice thickened. 'She was seventeen.'

She went across and wrapped his hands in both of hers. 'Oh, Bryn,' she said.

His fingers tightened on hers. 'I should have noticed.'

'How could you? You weren't there. And ten years ago people didn't know much about eating disorders.'

He let her hands go. Rebuffed, she stepped back, watching him reimpose control over his features. 'I blamed everyone—my grandparents, popular culture, the fashion magazines Anna used to pore over—but I've realised it was to hide my own guilt.'

Gerry said quietly, 'It's a normal reaction. And perhaps you were right. Our preoccupation with thinness is unhealthy.'

'I blamed you too,' he said.

'I know.'

He paused, then said deliberately, 'When I saw you with that baby in your arms I thought, Damn it all to bloody hell, there she is. My woman. It was as simple and inevitable as that, a sudden, soul-deep recognition. You were everything I thought I despised—fashionable, elegant, well-bred, beautiful, working in a career I loathed. And possibly an importer of heroin. I had to manufacture reasons for disliking you, for stopping you from affecting me, but you cut straight through into my heart and took up residence there.'

Her stomach dropped. He waited, but when she couldn't speak he said coolly, 'I soon found out that you weren't superficial and foolish; you had a natural kindness that made you take poor Lacey under your wing, and you tolerated being stranded with grace and fortitude.'

'It had to be one of the most luxurious strandings anyone's ever had,' she said huskily.

'I should have kept my distance. I'd never been at the mercy of my hormones before, but every time I saw you my gut clenched and I wanted you. I had no intention of making love to you,' he said curtly. 'I couldn't believe that you could be connected with the heroin ring, but it was a measure of how far I'd fallen in love with you that I let my passion override my common sense.' When she remained silent he added harshly, 'That had never happened to me before.'

Head bent so that he couldn't see her face, she asked, 'If you loved me, why didn't you tell me? We might not have been able to meet during the trial, but I'd have known.'

He waited so long to answer that she looked up swiftly, and saw the autocratic features set in lines of self-derision and irony. 'I was afraid to put it to the test. You gave me no indication that you wanted me for anything other than a lover.'

Gerry had lived with the knowledge of her love for so long that she couldn't believe her ears. While impetuous words clogged her tongue, he went on.

'You can't know how it felt to put you on the plane and let you go when every instinct was hammering at me to keep you with me by whatever means I had to use.'

She drew in a deep, impeded breath. The first wild delight at seeing him, at hearing him tell her what she'd only ever imagined in fantasy, was fading, leaving her fearful and tense. She asked, 'What were the other things you wanted to do?'

'I needed to see Lacey. I was determined that she wasn't going down the same road as Anna.'

'She didn't tell me,' she said in surprise.

'I asked her not to. I had to persuade her father to let her see a counsellor. She's helped, but it was your letters and your encouragement that pulled her back from the brink. She's going to be all right.'

'And the thing you had to come to terms with?'

He walked across to the French windows and stood looking out over her newly revamped garden. It had been a good summer and the plants were growing apace, lush and vigorous. On the edge of the wide deck a large pot held a tumble of petunias in soft lilacs and white and pinks.

Bryn turned away and said quietly, 'I've fought against loving anyone ever since my mother died and my father abandoned us. It hurt too much. I didn't rationalise like that, of course, when I was a kid, but I made sure I only loved Anna. And then she died. When I met you I resented what I felt for you and I was scared. Loving you—needing you—

gave you power that I was intensely reluctant to yield. It took me some time to accept that when you love someone as much as I love you, there is no capitulation. Or, if there is, it's surrender to all that's good, to a happiness I've never expected, never hoped for because I didn't think it existed. Even though I suspected you, I learned to love you. I need you, Geraldine, and I think you need me too.'

A volatile mixture of joy and dread filled her. Almost whispering, she said, 'Bryn—I must—'

Two strides brought him back to stand in front of her. For the first time, she could read what lay in the clear, glimmering depths of his eyes. Her heart turned over and agony gripped her, froze the words on her tongue, speared through her in an unrelenting torment.

With the rough note in his voice more pronounced than she'd ever heard it, he said, 'So, Geraldine, now that you're in the clear and your life's back on track, will you marry me?'

She allowed herself one radiant moment of pure, keen happiness, sharp and penetrating as a knife-blade, and then, because she didn't dare hope for more, she said, 'I'm not in the clear—I probably never will be. After the defence's insinuations plenty of people think I was in it up to my neck and managed to frame Honor. Or, if not that, that I knew what she was doing and condoned it.'

'That's stupid—'

She gave him a tight smile. 'I've been asked if I can get the stuff,' she said without bitterness.

'By whom?' There was no mistaking the lethal intentness in the quiet voice.

'It doesn't matter.'

'It matters,' he said, that menacing silky note back in his words. 'I want to know so that I can tell whoever did that they'd better back off or they'll have me to deal with.'

Gerry managed to say on a half-sob, 'It wouldn't help, Bryn. And having a wife who's been mixed up in a very unsavoury case isn't going to help your reputation.'

'If you don't want to marry me, just say so,' he said. 'Don't make excuses.'

'I don't want to marry you,' she said, listening to the sound of her heart shattering.

To her astonishment he laughed. 'Good,' he said outrageously. 'I'm going to have a wonderful time changing your mind.'

She looked at him—indomitable, tall and strong and tough—and knew that she wouldn't win. While she searched for ways to handle this—and to fight the insistent whispering from her treacherous heart that this time it might be the true, the real thing—he took her glass and raised her shaking hands to his mouth and kissed her fingertips.

In a dark, smoky voice he said, 'Marry me, Geraldine, and I'll do my utmost to make you happy, I swear it.'

'No,' she said, unshed tears burning behind her eyes. 'You don't understand, Bryn. I can't promise you that—or anything. I fall in love, but it never lasts. Eventually I get bored, or irritated, or desperate—or all three. My self-esteem takes a beating every time it happens, and you'll end up hating me. Even if you're willing to take the chance, I'm not.'

'How long does it usually last?' he demanded, not giving an inch.

She shook her head, but he lifted her chin with a hand that wouldn't be denied, and stared into her eyes as though trying to force her surrender. 'How long, damn you?'

'It's useless. I won't do this to you.'

'I won't let you go. I've been looking for you all my life and I'm not going to give up now.'

She read the truth in his eyes. Concentrated purpose blazed there, masterful, unsparing. Joy battled with terror in her heart. Summoning her utmost strength of will, she said, 'I'll be your mistress—live with you—but I won't marry you. I won't ask anything of you at all except that when I want to go you let me.' Her eyes were as hard as his; she should be sending him away, but she was racked by love, by her need for what he alone could give her.

She expected him to refuse. Bryn wasn't a man who surrendered to another's will; he'd said he was possessive, and she believed him, and the only thing she could offer him would be sheer torture for both of them.

As well as an insult.

But after staring at her for several heart-racking moments he demanded, 'What's the longest you've ever stayed in love?'

'A year,' she said, closing her eyes. 'Not more than a year.'

Silence, taut and terrifying, crackled between them. She couldn't look at him, couldn't bear the sound of her heart thudding unsteadily, painfully, in her ears.

At last he said heavily, 'All right. If that's what it takes. Only I'm setting a condition too. Two, in fact.'

'What?'

'That we don't refer to this again, and that if we're still together after two years you marry me.'

Tears roughened her voice as she said, 'All right. We'll do that.'

Gerry walked towards the front door. Yes, there he was, smiling, the green eyes lit with the secret flame that was for her and her alone, the autocratic face intent only on her.

'Good day?' he asked, shrugging off his jacket.

She smiled and reached up to kiss him briefly. 'Great. At ten o'clock this morning—just as I was driving over the Harbour Bridge—I finally got a handle on the article about computers, and I've just about finished it.'

'Of course you have,' he said.

'You must have begun to wonder, especially when you found me fretting at the laptop at three o'clock this morning,' she teased against his mouth.

'I can think of much more interesting things to do at three in the morning than obsess over an article.' His arms tightened around her and he kissed her again, his mouth demanding, seeking, a potent, heated promise.

Gerry's heart sped up. 'Mmm,' she breathed when his head lifted, 'you did. Much more interesting...'

She'd never get used to seeing him like this, eyes gleaming, all tension gone from his face.

After dropping a hard, swift kiss on her mouth, he straightened, saying, 'What are we doing tonight?'

'Nothing.' She said the word casually. Not that he'd be fooled; during the past two years he'd learned to read her most guarded tone and expression. Yet in many ways he was still an enigma to her. Oh, she understood the imperatives that drove him, and she had come to appreciate his standards and values, but although he was a tender, fierce, sensual lover, and a man she could rely on utterly, she had no idea whether he wanted to change things now that the two-year period was over.

'What are we eating?' he asked cautiously.

Laughing, she hugged him. 'I ordered in,' she said promptly. 'It'll be here in three-quarters of an hour.'

He didn't open champagne, but as she sat on the bed and talked to him while he changed from dark suit to trousers and shirt that showed off his broad shoulders and long legs so well, she told herself that she didn't care. What they had was precious enough for her; in fact, if she was any happier she might well explode with it.

The meal—prepared by one of Auckland's best restaurants—was superb, and the wine Bryn chose magnificent, a wonderful New Zealand white. At last, when they were both replete, Bryn asked, 'Brandy?'

'No, thank you.' She was curled up on the huge sofa, watching him with heavy eyes, anticipation licking feverishly through her veins. Light shimmered in a tawny aura around his head, played across the authoritative features, the arrogant nose, the strong line of jaw, the beautiful sculpture of his mouth.

He looked up and his mouth hardened. 'When you look at me like that, I want you,' he said deliberately. 'In fact, when I'm with you I'm in a constant state of arousal, but all it takes is one sleepy glance from those blue-green eyes and my body springs into violent life.'

Although his deep voice was slow and tranquil and composed, sensation sky-rocketed through her.

She smiled, and he laughed under his breath. 'Sheer magic. That smile's enough to charm the birds from heaven. I think I must be addicted to you.'

'It works both ways,' she said, aware of a faint disappointment, knowing that she had no right to be disappointed; she had set the parameters of their relationship. If he didn't want to change them she'd accept his decision, because she knew now that she loved him with a love that would last all her life.

'Addiction?' He walked across to the sofa, smiling with a set, savage movement of his mouth as she made room for him and held out her arms. Softly he said, 'Let's see if we can appease this addiction a little, shall we?'

During their time together he had introduced her to ways of making love that had thrilled and shocked her, but this time he took it very tenderly, very gently, as though she were still a virgin and this was their first time.

'It has to be addiction,' he said much later, when they were lying together, heart pressed to heart, 'because I can never get enough of you, never satisfy this need to take you. You walk ahead of me, just out of reach, too much your own woman to ever become wholly mine.'

Muscles flexed beneath skin sheened slightly with sweat as he sat up and reached for his trousers on the floor. Gerry ran an indolent finger down his spine, smiling when she felt the skin tighten beneath her fingertip. 'I am yours,' she said lazily. 'You know that.'

He smiled grimly and turned back to her. 'I know you like what you can do to me.'

From his hand dropped a shower of pearls, darkly peacock blue as a tropical lagoon at twilight, rounded and gleaming and luminous, landing on her sensitised skin with gentle impact, sliding coolly across her breasts and stomach and waist.

'Oh, darling,' she said, her voice velvet and replete, 'what on earth are these for?'

Casually pushing them aside, Bryn dropped a kiss on the slight curve of her stomach. 'It's our anniversary,' he said.

Although the vow he'd extracted from her two years ago had been uppermost in her mind for the past couple of weeks, she was filled with a quite ridiculous apprehension.

'And so?' she asked.

He scooped up a handful of pearls and spread them across her skin. 'Satin against satin. You haven't left me,' he said, not looking at her.

'No.'

'Do you want to?' His voice was level and detached, almost indifferent.

'No,' she said again, her heart pounding so heavily she thought he must be deafened by it. And because she owed him this surrender, she added jaggedly, 'Not ever.'

'In that case, I suppose the only decision we have to make is where we get married.'

Vast, consuming relief—and a strange, superstitious pang—shot through her. 'If you think,' she said forcefully, 'that that is any sort of proposal, you'd better think again.'

'Do you want me to go down on my knees?' His mouth was taut, and still he wouldn't look at her. 'I will if you want me to. You know that I'd do anything to keep you, anything at all.'

She wound her arms around him, pulling his lean, naked body down to her. 'All you need to do is say that you forgive me for thinking that what I feel for you was anything like the way I felt for any other man,' she said unevenly. 'These past two years have been the happiest in my life. I don't ever want to leave you—sometimes I wake up in the middle of the night terrified that it's all been a dream, that you don't love me, that I drove you away because I was stupid enough to think that I was like my mother. And I stare into an empty world, dark and hopeless.'

His mouth touched her trembling one, stifling the feverish words.

'Hush,' he murmured, 'there's nothing to forgive. Nothing. I love you, and I'd follow you to the ends of the earth, give you anything you ever asked for, even if it was a life together with no formal ties.'

'I was frightened when I made that stipulation,' she admitted.

'I know. But I was almost convinced that you loved me. I have no idea what drove your mother, but you're not like her. Along with the passion and the fire and that keen, astute brain, you're sane and kind and loving—all I'll ever want. And I knew it the moment I walked into the kitchen in the villa and saw you cuddling that baby—even though I still thought you were mixed up with the drug ring.'

'The sight of me holding a baby convinced you I wasn't?' she asked, running her fingertips over the smooth swell of his shoulder.

'Yes. Even though I knew of that trail to Switzerland, neatly labelled with your name. You were so concerned about the child. It didn't jell with Geraldine the smart, sophisticated woman of the world, or Geraldine the drug smuggler. But it wasn't faked. After that, although I struggled hard to keep an unbiased mind, in my heart I knew you couldn't have done it, because you valued life too much to be caught up in a filthy trade like that.'

She kissed the side of his throat and said, 'Maddie's all right now. I had lunch with her today.'

'Good.' But he spoke absently. His mouth touched a certain spot below her ear and she shivered. 'Speaking of babies,' he said huskily, 'how do you think I'd be as a father?'

She smiled dreamily. 'You'll be a wonderful father,' she whispered. 'But we'd better get married first because children need stability. They need to know that their parents are going to be there for them. They need to know that their parents care enough about each other to get married.'

Although they'd decided on a small wedding, somehow it turned into a huge one, a riotous affair with cousins and

children and friends mingling in a day-long summer cele-
bration. Afterwards they went to Longopai, their honeymoon interrupted only by a visit to the atoll where they'd
first made love, and first known that they loved.

It was there, lying in the shade of the palms, that Bryn
said, 'By the way, I've found the baby.'

'What?'

He opened a sleepy eye and smiled into her puzzled face.
'The abandoned baby. The one you found outside your
house.'

Against his chest she asked, 'How did you find her? The
social welfare wouldn't tell you.'

'I sent someone to dig deep. She's been adopted. Would
you like to see her?'

'Could I?'

'We wouldn't be able to tell them who we are. And I
think it should only be the once.'

She nodded. 'Yes, they have their lives,' she said slowly,
reluctantly. Then she smiled. They hadn't used any precau-
tions at all since the wedding. With any luck she might be
pregnant herself.

A month later she walked across the crisp green grass of
the Domain in Auckland towards a hillside seething with
excited children and parents. A cool wind blew, but the
children in their vivid clothes lit up the glowing green hillside as vividly as the array of kites.

'Over there,' Bryn said, nodding at a couple. The
woman, young and slightly overweight, bent to tie up the
laces of a child, while a thin young man looked up from a
kite laid out on the ground and said something that made
both mother and daughter laugh.

Gerry looked at the child. Chubby, rosy in the crisp air,
she had candy-floss hair and big blue eyes. Her mother
straightened the hood of her anorak, and picked her up. The
child snuggled against her mother's shoulder, and both
watched as her father lifted the kite and began to run with

it. The gusting wind caught it, snatched it and tossed it high into the sky on the end of its string.

The child laughed and clapped her hands, and her mother smiled at her. Another facet of love, Gerry thought.

Quietly she said, 'Goodbye,' and added as mother and daughter followed the man and the kite, 'I didn't even realise that I needed to see her—just to make sure.' She raised a radiant face and said, 'You know me better than I do myself.'

Bryn hugged her and turned her around, walking her back to the car. 'Underneath that elegant mask you're as soft as butter,' he teased.

'So are you.'

He laughed. 'Where you're concerned, yes. But then, why wouldn't I be? You make my life complete.'

'Not just me,' she said demurely. 'I hope not, anyway, because in eight months' time there's going to be another of us.'

His arm tightened around her. When she looked up she saw the sudden intense glitter of tears in his eyes, and then he said, 'Geraldine.'

In that word, said with such raw need, such tenderness, she heard everything she'd ever want to hear. Hand in hand, they walked down the hill and into their future.

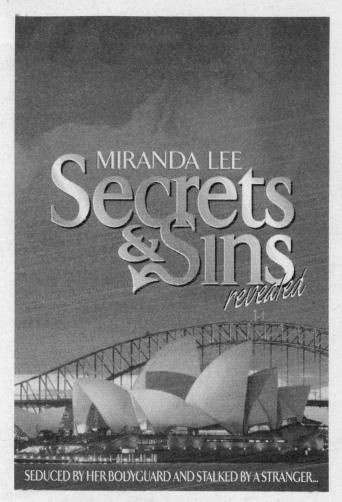

Available from 15th March 2002